THE SUMMERHILL
MANOR BLOOD CURSE

THE SUMMERHILL MANOR BLOOD CURSE

The year was 1820 and the location was North Carolina

WYATT ALLEN

iUniverse

THE SUMMERHILL MANOR BLOOD CURSE

Copyright © 2017 Rick Miller.

All rights reserved. No part of this book may be used or reproduced by any means, graphic, electronic, or mechanical, including photocopying, recording, taping or by any information storage retrieval system without the written permission of the author except in the case of brief quotations embodied in critical articles and reviews.

This is a work of fiction. All of the characters, names, incidents, organizations, and dialogue in this novel are either the products of the author's imagination or are used fictitiously.

iUniverse books may be ordered through booksellers or by contacting:

iUniverse
1663 Liberty Drive
Bloomington, IN 47403
www.iuniverse.com
1-800-Authors (1-800-288-4677)

Because of the dynamic nature of the Internet, any web addresses or links contained in this book may have changed since publication and may no longer be valid. The views expressed in this work are solely those of the author and do not necessarily reflect the views of the publisher, and the publisher hereby disclaims any responsibility for them.

Any people depicted in stock imagery provided by Thinkstock are models, and such images are being used for illustrative purposes only.
Certain stock imagery © Thinkstock.

ISBN: 978-1-5320-2336-1 (sc)
ISBN: 978-1-5320-2337-8 (e)

Library of Congress Control Number: 2017906801

Print information available on the last page.

iUniverse rev. date: 05/02/2017

CONTENTS

Chapter 1 1
Chapter 2 17
Chapter 3 36
Chapter 4 43
Chapter 5 56
Chapter 6 64
Chapter 7 67
Chapter 8 76
Chapter 9 82
Chapter 10 85
Chapter 11 112
Chapter 12 120
Chapter 13 125
Chapter 14 133
Chapter 15 140
Chapter 16 155
Chapter 17 166
Chapter 18 188
Chapter 19 219
Chapter 20 235
Chapter 21 238
Chapter 22 248
Chapter 23 253
Chapter 24 270
Chapter 25 275

CHAPTER 1

Margaret exhausted from her trip and tired of telling the woman a few feet behind her to keep it down, called for the conductor. The conductor appeared through the doorway asking "What is it Ma'am?"

Margaret yelled "Stop this train right now."

"Ma'am we cannot do that." Said the conductor.

"I'm not asking you, I'm telling you. Do you know who I am? I am Margaret Summerhill, my husband, is Colonel George Summerhill, my father is Thomas Piermont the third. He owns this railroad. Now I am only going to tell you one more time, if you want to keep your job?

"***STOP! THIS, TRAIN!!!***" Screamed Margaret stomping her foot.

The conductor looked at her saying, "Yes ma'am."

Disappearing back through the doorway obviously heading to the engine car. In a few minutes, she could feel the train coming to a stop on the tracks.

The conductor long with engineer, returned to the car with Margaret.

The engineer asked "Yes ma'am, what is it?"

Margaret pointed to the mouthy woman and screamed "Get that bitch!!! Out of my car now, I have told her repeatedly to shut her mouth and now I will no longer stand for it, clear out this car," demanded Margaret.

"But ma'am, we're full up in the back." Said the conductor hoping that she would reconsider.

"I don't give a **damn!** Clear them out, or put them off the train now," commanded Margaret. "That is," if you want to keep your job?"

The conductor and the engineers, started herding people through the door going to the back cars. Margaret saw people outside walking alongside the train cursing at her from the windows, a few minutes later the engineer and the conductor came back into the car with her.

"Will there be anything else ma'am?" Asked the conductor.

"No, now you can resume your duties, take me home," commanded Margaret sitting down in her seat and crossing her arms like a spoiled child.

Both the conductor and engineer disappeared through the doorway. Margaret felt the motion of the train, as it began moving forward, continuing - on their way, settling back down she fell fast asleep, now that the car was finally quiet.

The next time Margaret was awoken it was by the engineer, telling her, "Ma'am, we're at the station."

Margaret got up, saying, "It's about time, never have I had such a terrible trip home."

"Yes, ma'am we do apologize, and hope that you will not say anything to your father," pleaded the engineer.

"Oh" you can count on the fact that I will, you'll be lucky if you get to keep your job." Said Margaret, pointing her finger at him,

Stomping off the train heading inside the station, to the desk clerk and demanded that someone, take her home.

A man that was in the station, walked up to her saying, "Mrs. Summerhill, I could not help but overhear that you need a ride home, well ma'am, it just so happens I've got a delivery to make a few miles away from your mansion and I would be glad to give you a ride." Said the man, eager to help her.

"What! I am not writing on some freight wagon," screeched Margaret.

"I'm sorry ma'am, I was only being courteous," explain the man.

"Will go away, go about your business." Said Margaret, in utter disgust.

"No! you, are going to take me home, right now," commanded Margaret, pointing at the clerk.

"Yes ma'am, let me close my office." Said the clerk as he rushed out from behind the counter and started closing the doors. Margaret followed him out as he locked the door behind them. She climbed into his buckboard with his assistance saying, "This thing isn't much better than a freight wagon."

•••

Loading her luggage on the back of his buckboard he said. "I'm sorry Mrs. Summerhill, if I would've known you were coming home today, I would have...!"

"Silence!! Just take me home," demanded Margaret.

The clerk climbed onto the buckboard, beside Margaret and headed out of town, toward her estate.

On the road, the clerk just trying to spark up idle conversation said. "I hope you had a good trip?"

Margaret said with anger in her voice, "I did not! My ride home on the train was hideous, there was a woman a few feet back behind me, that would not shut her mouth."

"Oh" I'm sorry ma'am, did you say something to the conductor about her?" Asked the clerk.

"I did better than that, I put her **damn** ass out!" Said Margaret.

"Off the train?" Asked the clerk.

"Yes, I saw the fat bitch, walking down alongside the train cursing at me, through the windows. "All she had a do was shut her mouth, so that I could get some rest, but anyway, that's enough idle conversation, with the likes of you, just shut up and take me home," demanded Margaret.

As they rode up to the estate, one of Margaret's slave boys, about 10 years old, was coming across the yard headed to the slave quarters. Margaret hollered over at him saying, "Hey boy, come here."

The little boy came running over to her, saying, "Yes ma'am."

"Take my bags inside," demanded Margaret, as she climbed down off the buckboard with the clerk's assistance. Margaret went straight into her mansion, without so much as thanking the clerk, for anything. He got back on his buckboard and rode away. Margaret stopped the boy just inside the foyer saying,

"That's far enough, place them against the wall and go about your duties," barked Margaret.

The little slave boy said. "Yes ma'am." And ran out of the house, heading back down to the slave quarters.

• • •

Margaret walked in and sat down in a chair removing her hat and feeling thankful to be home. The whole house was silent except, Margaret thought she heard voices coming from inside her mansion. She stood to her feet and quietly listened. Then in a few minutes she heard the voices again thinking, *"There is definitely someone in the mansion."*

She began following the voices although they were muffled and sounded like a couple of people talking. After investigating further, she determined that the voices were indeed coming from somewhere upstairs. she climbed the stairwell toward where she taught the voices were coming from. As she drew closer to the voices she soon realized they were coming from her bedroom. Margaret stopped just outside the door to listen, she could hear heavy breathing and moaning, it sounded like someone having sex.

She burst into the room and there was a slave girl on top of her husband. Margaret rushed into the room cussing them both. "Her husband was an unbelievable son of a bitch and the slave girl was a little slut."

Margaret, reached up grabbing a handful of the slave girls' hair and pulled her off her husband. As she tightened her grip in the girls' hair. She began dragging her across the floor and out of the bedroom. The slave girl was kicking and screaming and with both of her hands-on Margaret's still gripping her hair, attempting to keep her from pulling it out. As she kept on dragging the naked girl down the stairs to the front door. Still holding the slave girl by the hair of the head. She called down to the slave quarters as loud as she could be saying, "I want all of you up here right now."

Several men and even a few women come running up to the mansion to find out what their mistress wanted. When they arrived to their surprise she was standing in the doorway of the mansion still holding the naked girl by her head. The men ran up to their mistress saying, "Yes ma'am."

Margaret said angrily, "Take this slut to the barn and tie her up, I will be right there."

Two of the men grabbed the naked girl one by each arm and dragging her still kicking and screaming all the way to the barn, pleading with them to let her go. Margaret turned around to see her husband coming down the stairs with just his trousers on asking her,

"What are you going to do?"

She looked at him with anger in her eyes and yelled,

"I will deal with you later," slamming the door to the mansion behind her, heading down to the barn. As she entered the barn the two men were still holding the slave girl.

"Stretch the little slut, out from post to post," screamed Margaret.

"Yes ma'am." Said the men as they tied the girls' hands each one to a different piece of rope and stretch her from one post to the other. Margaret walked over to a wooden box next to one of the horse stalls, getting a riding crop and walking over to the naked girl. She began whipping her, all over her legs and back and arms. Then she came around to the front of her and begin whipping her stomach, breast and even hit the girl in the face, not missing an inch of the girl's naked body.

She continued to beat the girl over and repeatedly, the whip was cutting into her flesh as she screamed and begged for her to stop.

But this only further angered Margaret so she continued whipping the girl, even harder and faster. Blood was slinging all over the walls and the other slaves that were standing there watching it.

She relentlessly continued to whip the girl until she could not swing her arms anymore. When Margaret stopped to catch her breath, the slave girl went limp. The only thing holding her up was the blood covered ropes, dripping from all that cuts across her naked body. Margaret walked over and looked down at the naked, bloody half dead girl and dropped the blood covered riding crop on the ground beside her. Turned around and started to walk out the barn.

One of the slave men asked, "Forgive me mistress, what do we do with the girl now?"

Margaret turned around and looked at the girl saying, "Let her hang there until she dies, I don't give a damn."

• • •

Margaret started to leave the barn, when an older slave woman ran up dropping to her knees, begging her saying, "Please mistress I'm the girl's mother, please I'm begging you have mercy."

Margaret, looked down at the woman saying, "Fine, release her and give her to her mother."

Then Margaret continued out of the barn, heading back up to the mansion to deal with her husband.

When she returned up at the house, her husband was sitting in a chair watching her as she walked in like a little boy waiting to be punished by his mother.

She walked over looked down at him saying,

"I have only two things to say to you, one!! No one and I mean no one, better not find out about this George, for If they do, I will tell my father and he will destroy you, then when you've lost everything, no friends or family and down in the gutter, I will then in fact kill you." Said Margaret with anger in her voice and looking at him with pure hatred in her eyes.

George started to say, "Margaret. I..."

She interrupted him saying, "I don't want to hear a word, not one word." Said Margaret hurt fully.

Then she turned around and started upstairs. She got halfway up the stairway turned back around, looking at her husband, replaying in her mind the slave girl going up and down on him in her bed saying, "Oh yes" and another thing. **You!!** will never, touch me again, with those filthy hands, do you understand me?" Asked Margaret through her teeth, greeting them as she dropped her eyebrows, looking at him with pure utter disgust.

George without saying, a word he watching his wife, as she turned around continuing, up the stairs, going into the adjoining bedroom. Margaret going into the room, sat down in front of a dressing table with a large mirror, just staring at herself, wondering,

"How her husband could want a slave girl with such a beautiful wife? Well, that's his loss."

She said to herself out loud.

You see Margaret so loved herself. She would sit for hours, sometimes all day long in front of that mirror brushing her long hair, admiring her beauty.

Things went on like that for a while, days turned into weeks, Weeks turned into months. Margaret true to her word, never let her husband touch her again. In the public eye, she put on the front of a happy loving wife and amongst her friends. But at home, it was a different story.

She grew to hate George even more. The very sight of him began to turn her stomach, because she saw him sneaking out of the house at night going down to the slave quarters, she knew what he was doing. But if no one else did, she had no feeling regarding his encounters.

•••

Till one day while Margaret, was entertaining the Mayor and his wife, out under the gazebo, in the garden. Some of the slave women were coming across the yard. The Mayor's wife, watched as they walked toward them. heading down to the slave quarters.

She turned, looked at Margaret saying, "Oh I wasn't aware that you let them interbreed."

Margaret looked at her saying, "Excuse me."

"Oh!!!! Yes, my dear, that one is obviously with child, how quaint." Said the Mayor's wife, as she giggled?

"Oh yes" I think that's quite smart of George, to let them breed, it only increases the workforce, after all if you grow them, you don't have to buy them." Said the Mayor as he and his wife both were giggling.

Margaret for the first time noticed that the slave girl, that her husband had been frequently visiting late at night, was in fact with child. she began to wonder, "Could that be his, little bastard?"

From that day forward Margaret really kept a close eye on that slave girl.

Till one day Margaret noticed the girl's mother, walking down to the slave quarters and call to her.

"Woman, come here!!" yelled Margaret.

The slave woman walked over to her mistress asking "Yes ma'am."

"I was looking out across my garden the other day and you know what I saw?" Asked Margaret with a condescending voice.

"No ma'am." Said the slave woman, dropping her head careful not to look at Margaret's face.

"I'll tell you what I saw, that little slut daughter of yours, is with child, you wouldn't happen to know whose it is now would you? Ask Margaret gritting her teeth and pointing at the old woman as she continued to say and don't lie to me, or I will whip you to an inch of your life."

"No ma'am, I can't be sure." Said the old slave woman with fear in her voice that her answer would not please her mistress and she would in fact whip her.

"All right fine, act like you don't know. But I'm only going to tell you this one time, so you better hear me. The night that little bastard!! Is being born, before it sees the light of day, I better be standing there, do you understand me?" Asked Margaret pointing her finger at the old slave woman once again.
"Yes ma'am." Said the old woman afraid of what her mistress was going to do with the baby.
"When she goes into labor someone better come and get me, or I will sell the whole damn bunch of you! Do I make myself perfectly clear?"
"Yes ma'am," answered the slave woman.
"Good, I'm glad we understand each other. Now go about your duties." Said Margaret satisfied that her threat had made some - kind - of - impact on the woman.

Margaret kept a close eye on the slave girl as she made her way around the estate going back and forth, getting bigger and bigger.

Until one day Margaret decided it was time to confront George. upon searching the mansion, she found George in his study sitting at his desk going over some papers, telling him in a somewhat hurtful, but stern voice.
"I see that little slut! You been visiting late at night, is carrying a child. Is that your little bastard?" Asked Margaret with pure hatred in her voice.

George looking up at her with a guilty look on his face asking, "What the hell are you talking about?"
"Don't play games with me you son of a bitch, you know damn well what I'm talking about, that little slut of yours is pregnant and I'm asking you are you the father?" Said Margaret with utter disgust in her voice.

"No, it's not mine, if she's pregnant I don't know anything about it." Said George, lowering his head.

"Of, course you don't, you bastard!!" said Margaret underneath her breath as she walked out of the room slamming the two pocket doors shut going up to her room.

Then in a few minutes George come bursting into Margaret's room, grabbing her by both arms next to her shoulders saying, "I have had enough of this, you're my wife and year damn sure going to start acting like it."

Then George started trying to kiss her. Margaret turned her head away fighting him, but to no prevail. She was a small woman and he easily overpowered her, picking her up off the floor, carrying her over, throwing her down on the bed, tearing some of her clothes off. Margaret frantically tried to fight him off, but realizing there was no use, she just let her body go limp, laying there motionless staring off into space.

As George mauled her like an animal. Not feeling any more resistance from her. George stepped back looking down at her half-naked body lying on the bed not moving.

He reached forward grabbing her and pulling her up face to face to him, considering her dark, cold eyes. Margaret said. with a very cold feeling voice, "I hate you!"

George looking at her, finally realizing that the love they once shared was gone forever. It was as though she was no longer even human. he released her letting her fall back onto the bed, standing to his feet. He looked down at her not saying, a word. Then he turned around and walked out of her room (**never to return**)

• • •

A couple weeks passed and George announced that He was going away. Margaret could care less. What she did care about was that he was taking Robert their son. This hurt Margaret's heart, to watch her son leave not knowing if she would ever see him again. As the weeks turned into months, Margaret waited for some word that her son was all right.

Not receiving any day after day, hardened her heart even more. Then one late-night Margaret was readying herself for bed.

When she heard one of her little slave boys, come running up from the Quarters saying, "The baby's coming! the baby is coming!"

Margaret emerging from the mansion, followed him back down to the slave quarters. Although it was poorly lit by candlelight Margaret could still see the girl stretched out on a rickety old wooden table. Two of the older slave women one of each side of the girl tending her, helping her to deliver her child. Margaret stood quietly in the corner watching and waiting to see the baby born.

It was a hard labor, almost more than the girl could stand, she lost consciousness a couple times from the pain, until finally the child was born. Margaret watched attentively from a dark corner in the room as they cleaned the child up.

One of the women turned, looked at it saying, "congratulations it's a little girl, but she's...,"

The woman paused for a moment, lowering her head in fear, because the baby was white.

The slave girl, seeing her baby started screaming in tears,

"No dear God, no."

Margaret walked toward them, looking down at the child saying,

"Give it to me now."

One of the slave women turned around and reluctantly handed the baby to Margaret. She held it up in the light, looking at the slave girl saying,

"I cannot have this."

Then she turned around and started to walk out of the slave quarters with the baby.

The slave girl cried and pleaded with Margaret saying,

"No!! Please dear God, mistress please give me my baby."

As the girl tried to get up she fell to the floor, weakened from the delivery, she could not follow Margaret as she closed the door behind her. Walking back up to the house with the baby in her arms,

Margaret went to the barn and got a feed sack, she then put the baby in it, twisting the top of the sack around and tying it off tight with a piece of string.

As Margaret was making her way through the garden, behind the main house and over to the well. It began raining and lightning, it was striking all around her, as though God knew what she was going to do.

Margaret slipped in the mud several times falling to the ground, with the baby in the feed sack. She finally made her way up to the Well and stood there for a couple minutes. The baby crying in the feed sack with lightning striking all around her, Margaret while raising the baby up in the air over the well. She heard a woman's voice crying and pleading coming from behind her. It was the slave girl finally gathering up enough strength to follow after her.

She pleaded with Margaret,

"Please don't kill my baby girl, I'm begging you mistress, for the love of God! Have mercy."

Margaret turned and looked at her and said "You can have somebody else's little bastard." While dropping the baby in the well.

The slave girl grabbed the side of the well, looking down into the deep dark hole screaming

"Oh, my God! Fell to the ground crying uncontrollably. Margaret turned around and walked toward the main house. The slave girl screamed at her, saying,

"You are an evil woman with a heart of stone."

By that time the girl's mother, along with the other two slave women that had been tending her had made it to the well. Helping the slave girl up off the ground trying to console her. They urged her to return to the slave quarters so that she did not anger Margaret further.

Margaret went back into the house and up to her room, sitting down in front of her mirror, humming to herself. She began brushing her long hair and a marring her beauty, with no remorse or feeling, about what she had done.

When the slave women got the girl back to their quarters, she looked at her mom asking her,

"How could she be so cold hearted? She threw my baby down the well." Said the girl falling to the ground, weakened from the delivery and she had in fact lost a lot of blood.

Her mother sat down on the floor, holding her head in her lap, watching her. As she was dying. Her mother looked down at her saying,

"As God is my witness, she will pay for this."

She watched her daughter close her eyes for the last time. The old woman overwhelmed by grief. Not only by the loss of her granddaughter in such a horrific way. But to lose her daughter as well, was almost more than the old woman could bear. She sat there on the floor rocking her daughter's lifeless body in her arms, vowing that Margaret would pay.

Then she along with a couple of other slave women cleaned the girl's body and wrapped her in linen, preparing it for burial.

The next day two of the men, picked the girl's body up caring it out of the slave quarters, along with the mother, and all the other slaves on the estate. They carried the girl's body up the hill, heading back into the woods to an old slave cemetery, to place her beneath the ground.

Margaret watched from the balcony of the mansion. As they pass by, she hollered down to the crowd, asking,

"Where are all of you going?"

"To bury the young girl mistress, she died last night." Said one of the slave women.

"It doesn't take all of you to put one girl in the ground." Said Margaret and demanded that they get back to work.

The girl's mother and the two men carrying the body continued to the burial site. All the other slaves turned around and went about their duties. Margaret quite pleased with herself, that she could show the authority, walked back into the house and into her room.

Margaret sat for hours in front of the mirror wondering about her son, wishing that she would hear something, anything to put her mind at ease. The day seem to drag out. Until finely night, did approach. Margaret readied herself for bed. All along she climbed into her big bed and cried herself to sleep feeling afraid for her son and the fact that she would probably never see him again alive

• • •

One late night, Margaret was awakened by a sound downstairs, calling to George in fear, but realizing that he was gone away and could not answer her, she collected herself and went downstairs to investigate the noise.

Margaret now more aggravated then scared, because someone or something had woken her up, started downstairs, as she enters the main part of the house, there sitting in the middle of the floor with candles lit all around her in a circle, with a large wooden bowl with several small items in it. Some of them belonging to Margaret, in front of her was the old slave woman, chanting some type of language to herself.

Margaret upon seeing her and feeling frightened, but angry as well yelled at her saying,

"What are you doing in my house? How dare you come in here, in the middle of the night?" Yelled Margaret.

She walked toward the old woman, Margaret entered the circle of candles freezing in one spot, not being able to move her legs, or feel them. As she attempted to move the infliction grew even higher, up to her waist and into her chest, then into both arms freezing them in place. Margaret looked down at the slave woman, she was facing her with her eyes rolled back in her head, all Margaret could see was the yellow of them. As the old woman was still chanting, Margaret realized, that she was doing this to her, screamed asking in total fear and anger.

"What the hell have you done to me?"

But the old woman kept on chanting. Margaret yelled one last time

"Answer me, damn you."

The old slave woman stood to her feet, walked up to Margaret staring deep into her eyes and said

"You had a heart of stone, now all of you will be."

Then she started chanting even louder sealing Margaret's fate. Margaret could not move her neck, she tried to scream, one last time as she tried to take a breath, but the pressure on her chest was immense, till her eyes clouded over and darkness filled them. Finally, the old woman stopped chanting, and looked at the image of Margaret.

She gathered up all her incantation items and left the manor, letting the door close and lock behind her, all that remained in the room was, a statue with the image of what once was, Margaret.

Several people came to the mansion, inquiring on the whereabouts of Margaret, but it remained an unanswered question and soon she was forgotten about. Days turned into weeks, weeks turned into months and then years. Until finally, Robert returned home, only to find a shell of what was once the Summerhill manor. Most of the slaves were gone, all but a few, that simply had nowhere else to go, but now they were in fact freemen. Upon Roberts arrival and discovering his mother had been missing, conducted - an - investigation of his own, in the end not finding any cause or reason for her disappearance, finally gave up on it.

All that remained of his mother was a life like statue of her. That she undoubtedly had commissioned for. Robert knew how vain his mother was, so it came to no surprise that she would have an image, of herself created to look at. Although the image was just made of stone, it still seemed to somehow comfort him, to be close to it, as though it was his mother. He would talk to it from time to time and polish it, making sure that it was well taken care of. After all, it's all he had left. George, his father had recently been killed by unknown assailants, over a few dollars and now to return home only to find his mother was missing. Robert was left all alone in.

Present time

CHAPTER 2

James was awoken startled by his wife shaking him and saying, with concern in her voice

"Honey, somebody's banging on the door."

Raising up on his elbows he looked over at the time and feeling confused, he said.

"It is 7 o'clock in the morning, who would be here, at 7 o'clock on Saturday, banging on the door?"

Cindy said. with a puzzled look on her face,

"I don't know honey."

Then James got up and reluctantly pulled on his pants, walked over and looked out the window. It was Mr. Carmichael the landlord. James said.

"Oh hell, honey" it's Mr. Carmichael."

"What are you going to tell him?" Cindy asked.

"The truth." Said James as he walked over to the door and unlocked it, going out on the front porch saying,

"Good morning Mr. Carmichael."

"James, your late again." Said Mr. Carmichael

"Yes Sir, I know." Said James lowering his head.

Then Mr. Carmichael said. "You can't keep doing this."

"Yes Sir, I know it's just that work is slow right now." Said James making an excuse.

"I understand that, but I have got bills too you know." Said Mr. Carmichael.

"Yes Sir, I'm doing a big job right now and I should be done with it, by the end of this week, if you could be a little bit more patient with me, I know you have been and I do appreciate it."

"Well, James I..."

Mr. Carmichael paused, because Michael, James youngest son, came walking out the house and wrapped his arms around one of his dad's legs.

Mr. Carmichael looked down at the boy saying,

"Okay, I'll tell you what James, I'll give you a couple more weeks, but if you can't come up with the money by then, I am sorry, but you're going to have to go."

"Thank you, Mr. Carmichael I will have the money for you, Sir, I promise you I will."

"Okay James, I'll see you then." Said Mr. Carmichael.

Then he turned around and got in his SUV and drove away.

James walked back in the house. Cindy met him in the kitchen and asked

"What did he say?"

"He said. we can have a couple more weeks, but if we didn't have the money, we have got to move on."

"James I wish you'd let me get a job to help out," pleaded Cindy.

"No, I'm not doing that, I wasn't raised that way, a man, if he is a man, is supposed to take care of his wife and kids." Said James angrily.

"But honey, you are doing the best you can." Said Cindy as she was trying to calm her husband.

• • •

"I'm trying to." Said James while fumbling through the mail, looking at all their bills. He came across a letter to Cindy, from some lawyer. James heart sunk in his chest, as he looked to her with confusion and asked,

"What is this, divorce papers?"

"No honey," of course not! Let me see it." Said Cindy. Reaching for her mail. James handed her the letter and watched as she opened it.

He was hanging on her every word, as she began to explain it to him. Saying,

"I get these things all the time, it's from some lawyer saying, I've got a great uncle that died, leaving me a lot of money and he will send me all my information by courier, If I give him a credit card number." Said Cindy.

James looked at her with confusion and disbelief on his face.

Cindy said. "It's a scam honey, here look for yourself, "and handed him the letter.

James took the letter and looking it over. He began reading it to his self. The letter was from an estate lawyer in North Carolina. For the Summerhill manor, he glanced through it saying,

"Cindy honey, you need to read this sounds legit."

"No I told Tracy about it, she said that it's a scam there are people out there. Just sitting around looking for ways to get your money."

"I don't know Cindy this sound pretty straight forward to me. The man even has a number here you can call him 555 -265 - 6389 extension 9374." Said James handing her back the letter. She looked through it and asked,

"You really think there might be something to this?"

"I don't know honey, but it can't hurt to call the number, to find out what the guy has to say."

"James, would you call him. You know I don't talk very well to people on the phone."

"Give it here." Said James. Taking the phone and dialing the number on the letter. It rang a few times. Then finally a man's voice came on it saying,

"This is Marcus Wilcox, I'm either with a client, or in court, please leave your name, number and a brief message, stating the reason you are calling and I will return your call as soon as possible, thank you."

"Mr. Wilcox, my name is James Parker, my wife's name is Cindy Parker, if you are a legitimate lawyer and this is not a scam, please if you would call us back. Our number is 555 -784 -3945, this is in regards to a letter that my wife keeps receiving from you, thank you."

Cindy said. "I don't know honey, I think it's a scam. So, does Tracy,"

"Well, has Tracy ever seen this letter or have you just told her about it?"

"I told her about it, but she has seen that kind of thing on the computer and in the mail a lot and she says that's what it sounds like to her," explained Cindy.

James looked at her, saying,

"Well, I've heard about this kind of thing too honey, but I don't think that's what this is."

Cindy said. with excitement in her voice.

"You do think this is real, I have a great uncle that has left me a bunch of money? Wouldn't that be wonderful?" Said Cindy now really getting excited.

James, not wanting to get her hopes up said.

"I don't know baby, I'm just saying, we need to check it out,"

At the same time, James's cell phone began ringing. he answered it saying,

"Hello."

"James this is Mr. Gilmore,"

"Yes Sir Mr. Gilmore, what can I do for you Sir?"

"Well James," I talked to my wife this morning, you're just about done, here aren't you?"

"Yes Sir, I am, a little touch up here in there and I'll need you to, to go over everything."

"If you would please, my wife has decided, that she would love for you to go ahead and run the trim around the fireplace and paint the family room. We have already got the paint."

James answered him, saying,

"No problem,"

"About how much longer do you think, it will take with this additional room added on James?" inquired Mr. Gilmore.

"Well Sir," if I come today, I should be done around 3 o'clock."

"All right, we will have you some money by then."

"Thank you, sir, very much."

"No!! Thank you, James, you are doing a wonderful job, both my wife and I are quite pleased with your work."

James said. "Thank you, sir, we'll see you in a little bit, goodbye." And hung up the phone, turned to his wife saying,

"Honey that was Mr. Gilmore. They did decide to go ahead and paint the family room and run trim around the fireplace, I'm going to go take care of that today and try to get this job done. I was going to wait until Monday, but now I am going to knock it out so I can give Mr. Carmichael our rent."

James walked into the bathroom to grab a quick shower and put on his work clothes. A few minutes later, he came back into the living room saying,

"I shouldn't be too long, they are meeting me with some money about 3 o'clock. I should be back home around 4 o'clock, or so."

Cindy ask, "But honey, what if that lawyer calls, what do I say to him?"

"Talk to him Cindy, take your time, answer his questions and talk to the man, find out what he truly wants." James leaned over to kiss his wife, went out the door and got in his truck heading to the job.

• • •

Cindy went into the kitchen, started washing dishes then cleaned the counter. Little Michael was sitting at the table eating his breakfast, playing with one of his hot wheels, running it all around the table while eating. Billy was on the couch playing video games. When suddenly, the phone rang. Cindy looked at the clock it was a little bit after 10 o'clock. She walked over, picked it up saying,

"Hello."

A man's voice said. "Hello, I am attorney Marcus Wilcox, is this the Parker residents?"

"Yes Sir, it is," answered Cindy.

"Can I speak to a James or Cindy Parker?"

"My husband is not here now, but can I help you?"

"Mrs. Parker, you're the one I really need to speak to ma'am, you're a hard lady to find, I have been trying for several weeks now to get a hold of you."

Cindy asked, "This isn't a scam?"

"No ma'am," I assure you it is not, I am an attorney at law handling your uncle's estate, "explained Mr. Wilcox.

Cindy walked over to the table set down in the chair, because she felt lightheaded. And weak kneed

"You sure you got the right woman? "Asked Cindy in disbelief.

"Yes ma'am."

"How can this be?" Asked Cindy once again, not understanding.

"Well, you are Cindy Collins Parker, your father was Larry Collins, your mother was Stephanie Collins, is that correct?"

"Yes Sir," answered Cindy, feeling even more confused thinking, *"How could he know my parents?"*

"Then I got the right lady."

Cindy said. "I still don't understand."

"Well Miss Parker, it's a lot to explain, I'd rather not do it over the phone, if that would be all right with you?"

"Please don't try, I would rather my husband be here too. He understands a lot more about these things then I do,"

"I understand, what I need is for you and your husband to come to my office. I'm located in the professional center at 1311 Walnut Ave. In Asheville, North Carolina.

"NORTH CAROLINA!" yelled Cindy.

"Yes ma'am." Said Mr. Wilcox.

"We can't come to North Carolina, we can't afford something like that. I'm sorry Mr. Wilcox, but that's impossible." Said Cindy frantically interrupting him.

"Ma'am, everything's going to be taking care of for you and your family, you will come to the Asheville regional Airport, I will have a car pick you all up and take you to your hotel, The Asheville Marriott, your airfare and hotel accommodations, everything will be provided for you." Said Mr. Wilcox, trying to reassure her.

"Please hold on a minute this is a lot for me to take in. I wish my husband was here." Said Cindy with fear and confusion in her voice.

"Ma'am, it's okay, relax I'm here to help you, everything is going to be taken care of, I need you to come and sign some legal documents and I will go over your inheritance and your estate, upon your arrival."

"My inheritance and estate?" Repeating Cindy, once again interrupting him, still feeling confused and somewhat frightened.

"Yes ma'am," we will go over everything together here. Now what I need from you, is to come into my office at 9 o'clock on Monday morning, you and your husband, and like I said. we will go over everything. It's nothing to be frightened of, I assure you."

"Mr. Wilcox pleases Sir, can I have my husband call you later?"

"Of course, Mrs. Parker, it's going to be all right relax, Like I said I'm here to help you," explain Mr. Wilcox, trying not to overwhelm her with too much information.

"Thank you, Sir, it is a lot for me to take in."

"I understand, have your husband call me back later and I will go over the details with him."

"Thank you, Sir." Said Cindy with relief in her voice.

"You're quite welcome and ma'am, congratulations, have a good day."

• • •

Cindy sat there at the table, holding the phone in her hand, trying to go over in her mind, everything that the lawyer had said to her, thinking to herself in disbelief and a little bit of excitement. She thought,

"Could this be true, have I really inherited a lot of money?"

She was overwhelmed with emotions as the thought of it kept running through her head.

She kept thinking,

"If it is true, I could help James. He wouldn't have to work so hard."

Cindy got a little bit more excited of the thought of it. She kept watching the clock, hoping any minute to hear his truck, drive up, bubbling over with so much excitement that she could not stand it any longer.

"I have got to tell someone," she said out loud. She thought, as she picked up the phone. *"I'll call Tracy."*

It rang a couple times, finally she answered saying,

"Hello."

"Hey Tracy, it's me, what are you doing?"

"Hey girl what's going on?" Asked Tracy.

"James got that letter, I've been telling you about. The one from that lawyer telling me I have an uncle that died and has left me an inheritance."

Tracy asked "Did you tell him that it's a scam?"

"Well he called the number on the letter and he did get a lawyer's office, He left a message for him to call us back."

"Cindy honey, I hope you guys don't fall for that. Honey, there are people out there that are thinking of hundreds of ways to take advantage of you. What did this guy's say his name is?"

Cindy answered her saying, "Marcus Wilcox,"

"Hold on a minute." Said Tracy. While searching through her computer, looking for the name of Marcus Wilcox.

Then she asked,

"Where did he say, his office was?"

Cindy answered her saying,

"North Carolina,

"What is the address, sweetie?" Inquired Tracy.

"1311 Walnut Ave, in the professional center and the phone number to his office is, 555 – 265 – 6389, extension 9374." Answered Cindy.

Then Tracy was silent on the phone, although Cindy could hear her typing, while waiting and anticipating the answer from her friend, on whether the guy was truly real. Finally, after a few minutes Tracy said. with surprise in her voice,

"Well honey, there is a Marcus Wilcox in the Professional center in North Carolina, at 1311 Walnut Ave." "Okay!" "Looks like the guy is real."

"He is?" Asked Cindy with excitement.

"It appears so sweetie. What all did he tell you?" Inquired Tracy with confusion in her voice.

"While he wants us to fly, out there and meet with him, in his office Monday morning. He also said everything will be provided for us."

"He didn't want any money?" Asked Tracy, with disbelief in her voice.

"No that's the thing, he said everything. The plane tickets, hotel accommodations, everything will be taken care of for us, "answered Cindy with even more excitement.

Once again there was just silence on the phone, until Tracy said. with a little bit, exciting and jealousy in her voice, "My God, Cindy this is real!"

"Do you really think so?" Asked Cindy, feeling overwhelmed with joy.

"Yes, I do Cindy." Said Tracy. Feeling even more jealous.

Cindy's hands begin to tremble. Her heart raced in her chest as the excitement overwhelmed her, to hear her friend confirm that it was in fact true, by saying,

"No more living paycheck, by paycheck, for you sweetie."

"Well you know I'm not going to forget about you Tracy, I hope you know how much I love you." Said Cindy including her.

"What else did he say honey? "Inquired Tracy.

"He wants us to come into his office Monday morning at 9 o'clock and he would go over my inheritance and the estate, with me and James."

"WOW! Sweetie, I'm so happy for you guys, if anybody ever needed a break in life, it was you and your husband. He works so hard, to take care of you and the boys, speaking of which, what are you going to do with the boys? Are you going to try and take them with you?" Asked Tracy.

"I don't know, I guess we'll have to. I don't know what else we can do with them?" said Cindy.

"Well it's just a suggestion mind you, but I can keep the boys for you guys. I mean it's only going to be for a couple days, right?" Inquired Tracy.

"You really want to do that for us?" Asked Cindy.

"Of course, sweetie, you know how much I love those boys and it's not like I haven't kept them before." Said Tracy with love in her voice.

"Thank you, Tracy, I will talk to James about it okay." Said Cindy.

"Well listen sweetie, I need to get back to work, but call me later and let me know what you guys are wanting to do."

"I will Tracy and thank you." Said Cindy.

"Anytime sweetie, I will talk to you later." Said Tracy ending the conversation.

When Cindy hung up the phone, she sat there going over everything Tracy has said. in her mind. Until the excitement, so overwhelmed her that she felt like dancing. She couldn't believe it was real. Cindy started smiling and couldn't stop. Thinking about, *"How she could really help James raise his boys, with all the nice things that life has to offer them."* It would be like a dream come true for all of them.

Then she thought.

"This kind of thing doesn't happen to people like us."

Cindy looked up at the clock, realizing it was only 1:18. In the afternoon. Bubbling over with excitement. She could hardly wait to tell him what she had found out. But it would be quite some time before he would be home, so she thought,

"I know, I'll vacuum the living room to help pass the time, until James gets here."

She got the vacuum and started cleaning the floor, while hundreds of thoughts ran through her mind. About what they could do together. They never had money and she wondered *"How much, it would be and what the lawyer meant when he said. the estate?"*

The only time she had heard something mentioned like that, is when someone was talking about a big house on the lot of land. she wondered to herself *"If that's what he meant."*

She finished vacuuming the floor anticipating James arrival. Cindy realizing, she was once again watching the clock. Remembered that old saying,

"A watched pot will never boil."

she tried to find other things to occupy her mind.

Michael and Billy were fighting on the couch over the controller for a video game. Upon hearing this Cindy said

"Why don't you two boys cut that out and go outside and play? But don't go far."

The boys, while still fighting went to their rooms to get dressed so they can go out. A few minutes later, they came back in the living room set down and put on their shoes and ran outside, letting the door slam behind them.

Once again, she was sitting all alone at the table in the kitchen.

Overwhelmed by information and emotions, she thought about calling James, to inquire on how much longer he would be. But she decided not to, because it would only prolong his being done and coming home. Arriving at that conclusion she walked outside and set down on the steps of the deck.

It was a beautiful day, the birds were singing and there wasn't a cloud in the sky, the sun was shining, flowers were blooming all around her and everything seem to have a brightness about it that made them look brand-new. That she hadn't noticed before. The boys were bickering over something, next to the garage. Noticing this she hollered at them asking,

"Now what are you two fighting about?"

Michael, came running over to her showing her a hot wheel, saying, "This is mine, I found it."

"No, it's not, that's mine." Said Billy, grabbing for the toy.

Cindy said. "Michael, you have plenty of hot wheels. If that's your brothers, then give it back to him."

"Yes ma'am, Here, take your dumb all hot wheels, I didn't want it anyway." Said Michael angrily.

"I don't know why you boys can't get along, you fight over everything." Said Cindy with disappointment in her voice.

Then finely Cindy, saw her husband's truck coming down the road. Once again, the excitement began to build up inside her from head to toe. She couldn't wait to tell him what she had found out. She watched him as he pulled into the yard and sat there in his truck. He looked up and motioned for her to come over to him. Cindy walked around to the driver side. She could tell that he was disturbed about something by the look on his face.

James said. "Climb in."

Cindy walked around and climbed into the truck. The boys came running up to the truck saying,

"Hey dad, what's going on?"

James said. "You boys go play, I need to talk to your mom."

Cindy asked, "What is it honey?"

"I Paid Mr. Carmichael, our rent, I had to pay some late charges. It took almost all our money. We only have a couple hundred dollars, until my next job. I'm so tired of struggling, seems like I work all the time and we aren't getting anywhere. I don't even have time to spend with you and the boys, because I work so much." Said James lowering his head.

"Well don't worry honey, we will get through somehow, we always do, let me tell you what I found out, it might cheer you up. I told Tracy about that lawyer Marcus Wilcox, she looked him up honey, He's real." Said Cindy bubbling over with excitement.

"What did he call you back?" Asked James with surprise in his voice.

Cindy answered him, saying,

"Yes, he did."

"Well what did he say?" Inquired James.

"He told me a lot of things, some of which I didn't understand. But I told him, when you got home, I would have you call him and you could go over all the details with him. Answered Cindy.

"Details! What details?"

"That's some of what I don't understand James, you need to call him honey,"

"Okay I'll call him back. But first I'm hungry, would you make me a sandwich with something?" Asked James.

"Sure honey, come on inside,"

James got out of his truck and followed her in. Cindy walked to the refrigerator, while looking inside saying, honey there is some rotisserie chicken in here. Would that be alright along with maybe a piece of provolone cheese, some lettuce, vine ripened tomato and mayonnaise on sourdough bread?" How about a bag of kettle chips and a warm, homemade brownie to go with it?" Asked Cindy eager to please her husband.

"Yes, honey that sounds great!" said James. Walking over and sitting down at the kitchen table. Cindy poured him a glass of sweet tea and made his sandwich and lovingly waiting with him until he was finished.

• • •

The excitement was almost more than Cindy could stand, for him to call that lawyer back. It seemed as if it took him forever to eat that sandwich. Finally, he was done, and not being able to stand it any longer, Cindy asked,

"James, you want me to get the phone for you?"

James looked at her saying,

"Okay, hand it to me along with the letter with the guy's number."

Cindy jumped to her feet and grabbed the phone. She was trembling from so much excitement that he was finally going to call the man. as she was handing the phone to him, she dropped it in his plate where his sandwich had been on the table.

James looked at her and ask, "What has gotten into you?" "Calm down Cindy."

"I'm just so excited, James, aren't you?" Asked Cindy trying to contain herself.

James dialed the number on the letter. It rang a couple times and finally a man answered it, saying,

"This is Marcus Wilcox; how can I help you?"

"Yes Mr. Wilcox, I am James Parker."

"Yes Mr. Parker, I've been waiting for your call, I talked to your wife earlier today and told her that I need, you and her to come to my office, Monday morning at 9 o'clock, so that I can go over her inheritance and estate with you both. And she indicated to me, that she would have you call me back later and we can go over the details."

"Hold on a minute. Her estate and inheritance?" said James with confusion and disbelief in his voice.

"Yes Sir," answered Mr. Wilcox.

"You mean this is real?" Asked James with confusion.

"Yes Sir, I assure you this is very real. Your wife has inherited a large sum of money. Plus, she is the sole heir to the Summerhill family, therefore, she inherits all their wealth and the Summerhill Mansion."

James sat there in silence, not saying, a word.

"Mr. Park are you still there?"

"Yes, give me a minute please, I am taking it all in." "Okay! What do you need from us?" Asked, James starting to realize that it was in fact real.

"Like I told your wife earlier, everything will be provided for you. The plane tickets, hotel accommodations and there will be a car, at the airport to pick you up. Now I need you all to come to my office, here in North Carolina at the professional center. Because she needs, to sign some legal documents transferring the estate over to her and her inheritance.

"Okay, she said we needed to go over some details, you and I." Said Jane still feeling a little confused, but trying to make sense out of all of it.

"Yes Sir, you two will be leaving your airport there in Detroit at a time of your choosing, arriving at Asheville regional Airport here, in North Carolina. I will have a car waiting for you, it will take you to the Asheville Marriott Hotel, where your room has already been provided for upon your arrival. Just go to the front desk and tell them who you are.

Then Monday morning I'll have a car come to pick you up at the hotel and bring you to my office, so that your wife can sign the necessary documents. I will then go over the estate and her inheritance, with the both of you at that time. Then we will travel to the estate, so that you can see the Summerhill Manor. I just need to know what time you are departing from the Detroit airport so I can have the car waiting when you arrive."

"Mr. Wilcox please try to understand, sir, this is a lot for us to take in, but I assure you, I will have her there to take care of it."
"Okay then Mr. Parker, I look forward to meeting you and your wife,"
"Yes Sir, we're looking forward to meeting you too, I have got some arrangements to make before we can leave. But will be there Monday morning." Said James assuring him.
"Thank you, Mr. Parker, have a nice day Goodbye." Said Mr. Wilcox.
James hung up the phone, turned around and looked at his wife.
She could hardly sit still. Her bottom lip was trembling, her legs and hands were shaking and she was smiling from ear to hear anticipating on what her husband had to say next. But he just sat there staring at her.

Cindy not being able to stand it any longer ask him,
"Is it real honey? Oh God, please tell me it's real," pleaded Cindy.
"Yes honey, I think it's real. I think you have inherited a lot of money," explained James.
Cindy jumped to her feet and screamed
"Oh, my God!" over and over as she was jumping up and down.
She was screaming so loudly the boys come running in the house. Concern for their stepmother, they asked,
"What is it?"
James said. "It's alright boys your mom his not lost her mind. She just found out she inherited a lot of money."

• • •

"Does that mean we're rich?" Asked Billy with excitement in his voice, as he began to think of all the things, that he could buy if it was true.
"It appears " said James, confirming the boy's hopes.

"When does, mom get her money?" Asked Billy already making a list in his mind.

"Well, me and your dad, have got to go away for a couple days and take care of everything. You and Michael are going to stay with aunt Tracy," answered Cindy.

Michael said. "I want to go with you mommy."

"I'm sorry baby, you can't go this time we've got a lot of things we need to take care of." Said Cindy trying to make him understand.

"Don't worry, you'll come soon enough." Said James confirming his wife's wishes to leave the boys behind.

"Oh, honey all our money troubles are over." Said Cindy, looking at her husband with joy, overwhelming her.

James just sat there, looking down at the table, Cindy concern for him asked, "What is it honey, why aren't you happy?"

James didn't answer her. He just sat there letting everything wandered through his mind.

Cindy walked over to him now with even more concern saying, "James talk to me," "What's wrong?"

"Well, this is going to be really hard for me to take. I wasn't raised that way Cindy."

"What way James I don't understand." Said Cindy?

"I was raised that, I would take care of you and the boys. Not the other way around. I feel like my whole world has just been swept away." Said James lowering his head.

"Oh honey, you're my husband, everything that is mine is yours, I didn't just inherit a lot of money we did."

"Now we can have whatever we want, you can even get you a new truck, if you want one. We will have all the money to do anything you want and you know what the biggest thing is, now I can really help you raise your boys! Well, our boys, with all the wonderful things that this life has to offer them." Said Cindy trying to make him understand.

"It would be nice to get out of the city before our boys, end up in some gang and destroy their lives." Said James trying to have some degree of comfort about all of them.

"Yes, it would and all our dreams can come true." Said Cindy with tears in her eyes.

"I don't know how all of this is possible, I knew your mother and father. They weren't rich people." Said James trying to make some sense of it all.

"I don't know honey, the lawyers said he would explain all of that, oh yes, you don't mind Tracy, keeping the boys, do you? I didn't have time to ask you."

"Of course, not, it might be best not to take them with us, until we know what's going on," answered James. Putting her mind at ease.

"That's my thought exactly. Oh, honey isn't it going to be wonderful!!" Said Cindy absolutely bubbling over with excitement.

"Okay, when do you want to go?" Asked James.

"Well we can get everything ready and then take the boys over the Tracy's she should be home in about another hour, and we can drop them off, on our way to the airport said Cindy.

"I guess we can do that." Said James as he walked out the door.

Returned a few minutes later with a couple overnight bags and saying,

"They won't let you bring a lot on airplanes anymore, not sure exactly what you can take." Said James confused about what to do.

"Tracy travels a lot for the newspaper, she can tell us." Said Cindy taking one of the overnight bags from him.

"Okay go ahead, call her and make sure it is okay, that she keeps the boys and asked her what we can take with us on the plane." Said James.

Cindy walked over and got the phone to call Tracy. She dialed her number. Then in a couple minutes. Tracy answered it, saying,

"Hello, this is Tracy, how can I help you?"

"Hey Tracy, we are going to go and meet with this lawyer this weekend and find out about my inheritance, you said it would be okay to leave the boys with you. It will only be a couple days."

"Of course, honey, anything I can do to help," answered Tracy excitably!

"We have got to fly and we don't, know what we can take on the plane." Said Cindy.

"That's easy enough nothing! Take a bag with some close in it, don't try to take anything else. They won't allow it. Your best bet would be to take an overnight bag as a carry-on, keep it over your head in the storage compartment close to you. That way they won't lose your luggage and no one can steal it." Said Tracy helping her to understand.

"Okay Tracy, we'll bring the boys over in about another hour or so is that okay?" Asked Cindy waiting for confirmation.

"Yes, that will be fine. I'll be home by then." Said Tracy reassuring her.

"Thank you, Tracy, we we'll see you then

"No problem, I'll see you then. Sweetie bye." Said Tracy, hanging up the phone.

Cindy hung up the phone and turned around, looked at James sating,

"She said take an overnight bag, as a carry-on with some clothes in it, don't try to take anything else and keep it in the storage compartment above our heads. That way, no one can steal our stuff and the airport won't lose it."

"What did she say about keeping the boys?" Asked James.

"She said that would be fine. She will be home in about another hour or " answered Cindy.

"Okay honey, I guess we can start getting ready." Said James.

James grabbed one of the overnight bags heading into their room. He put four pairs of jeans and four different pairs of socks along with some T-shirts, in the bag. Cindy got a couple short outfits, tank tops and some blue jeans and placed them in her overnight bag. Then she went into the boys' room and gathered up them some clothes for a couple days placing them in the additional overnight bag to take too Tracy.

She called the boys and told Michael to get his hot wheels, color book and crayons a few other toys that he can play with, while they're over there at Tracy's.

Then she told Billy to do the same thing.

Billy, gathering up things to go, grabbed a handful of games looked at them and asked,

"Mom, you know, if aunt Tracy still has her video player?"

"I don't know, honey, she probably does"

"I'm going to take some games anyway." Said Billy, stuffing them in his overnight bag.

"That sounds like a good idea. You and your brother both can play them. I want you to, to promise me you won't fight and give aunt Tracy any trouble. I am counting on the both of you." Said Cindy. Looking at both boys waiting for a reply.

Billy said. "Yes ma'am,"

"Michael, you hear me?" Asked Cindy with authority in her voice.

"Yes ma'am, why can't I go?" Asked Michael while pouting.

"We have been through this, you can't, not this time." Said Cindy.

Michael started to say something else...

When James came walking in, to get Cindy's overnight bag, having already placed his in the truck. He asked

"Is everyone already?"

That's when he noticed Michael was pouting. he asked him

"What's wrong with you?"

Cindy while packing some things for Michael looked at him and then James saying,

"He wants to go. I told him he can't go this time, so he's pouting about it."

"Michael get your stuff together and get in the truck right now." Said James. With authority in his voice.

"Yes Sir." Said Michael fumbling through his things still pouting.

James walked through the house, making sure everything was turned off and all the windows were locked.

He stood there for a minute, looking around, satisfied that everything was took care of. He turned around and walked out, closing and locking the door behind him.

The boys were already fighting about who is going to sit where in the truck. James walked out to the truck saying,

"I don't care where you are sitting just get in the truck now."

The boys climbed in, the back seat and was sitting there very quietly.

James puts Cindy in the truck and close the door, walked around to the other side of his truck and climbed in. Sitting there for a minute, staring out into space. Cindy concern asked "What is it honey?"

"I am just checking over everything in my mind, so that I don't forget something."

Then he reached down and cranked his truck, backed out of the driveway and headed over to Tracy's house.

When they arrived, Tracy met them in the driveway to get the boys. She asked. James

"What he really thought about all this?"

He looked over at her and said

"I don't know what to think about it all. I guess I'll know more after I talk to this lawyer."

Then James told the boys to be good and don't give Tracy any trouble."

Cindy hugged Tracy's neck and she said. "Don't worry, I'll take care of the Rug rats."

"We know you will." Said Cindy.

"You guys call me. Let me know when you get there." Said Tracy.

"We will." Said James, thanking her once again.

Then they waved at Tracy and the boys as they drove away, heading to the airport.

● ● ●

CHAPTER 3

James pulled into the parking area where you can leave your vehicle while you travel.

He pulled a ticket from the box raising the gate up, as it did. James pulled in and parked his truck. As they were getting their bags out, an airport shuttle came by to get and take them to the airport terminal. They put their bags on the shuttle and climbed aboard, with several other individuals, when the shuttle pulled up in front of the terminal, they all climbed out and when inside. James walked up to the ticket counter saying, "My name is James Parker, this is my wife Cindy Parker, were supposed to have tickets waiting here for us."

The woman said. "I'll need a picture identification for both of you."

James and Cindy both showed the woman their driver's license, she looked at them carefully and said "One moment please," as she looked to her computer.

"Yes Sir. Sign right here Please."

James signed his and his wife's name and the woman handed them their tickets. They were four seats, C and D in first class. Cindy looked at the tickets saying,

"WOW!!, first class and everything."

"Now if you will run your bags through the scanner, you can be on your way." Said the woman.

James placed their bags one behind the other, on the conveyor belt and ran them through the scanner. The woman on the other side. Picked them up, she tagged them and handed them back to James saying,

"Enjoy your flight Sir."

James looked over at Cindy saying, "Don't Look Like, our flight leaves for about another 45 minutes and it looks like it's about a two-hour flight. I'm going to call Mr. Wilcox and let him know where departing."

He walked over to a phone booth picking it up the phone and dialed the lawyer's number. It rang a couple of times. Then his secretary answered it, saying, Mr. Wilcox office, can I help you?"

"Yes ma'am, this is James Parker would be possible for me to speak to Mr. Wilcox?"

"Hello, Mr. Parker. Yes Sir, hold on a minute please."

"Hello, this is Marcus Wilcox."

"Mr. Wilcox. This is James Parker were getting on the plane now, Sir. We got about a two-hour flight, so we could be there. I would say no later than 9:30, 10 o'clock."

"All right, Mr. Parker all have a car waiting for you. Enjoy your flight,"

"Thank you, Sir. Bye." Said James.

Then he turned to his wife saying, "Let's go ahead over to the gate, they might be letting the passengers aboard."

He took his wife's hand and they walked over to gate 11, as they walked toward the gate. James noticed that they were in fact. Letting the passengers on board. He walked up to the flight attendant over by the door, handed her their tickets she tore a piece off it and handed them back saying,

"We hope you enjoy your flight Sir."

James and Cindy walked down a long corridor door, at the other end. There was another flight attendant and an airport security officer holding a hand scanner, the officer scanned both James and Cindy very carefully. Then the flight attendant told them to watch their head and duck down to go through the door of the plane. Inside a stewardess, met them, as they came through the door, she looked at their tickets saying, "Please follow me."

they followed her down, through the plane, to their seats. Then the stewardess said.

"Let me take your bags for you," and she placed them in the storage compartment above their heads. Then she said.

"I'll be back to see if you need anything after we get underway. Enjoy your flight."

Cindy asked "How long before we depart?"

"We probably got about another 30 minutes and will get underway. Please have a seat and buckle yourselves in."

Then two men that were undoubtedly the pilot and copilot, came walking past James and Cindy headed to the cockpit, to stewardesses came together in the hall, James overheard one say,

"He said button it up,"

Then one of them disappeared down the row of seats. Both James and Cindy, felt their ears pop, as they closed and latched the door to the plane. The other stewardess stood in the hallway, instructing the passengers, where the exits were and all the routine safety instructions. Everything from the proper way to use your oxygen mask, if it is deployed. To the fact that this seats have flotation devices in them, in case the plane were to come down in the water. Then the stewardess said. "If there is such an emergency and the plane suddenly loses altitude be sure and place your head down between your knees."

Then after she finished the safety instructions and literally scaring the hell out of the passengers. A man's voice, came through the intercom, saying,

"Good evening ladies and gentlemen, this is your Captain, we want to thank you for flying Air America and it looks like clear skies all away to Asheville North Carolina, should be a smooth flight. Now please if you would fasten your seatbelt, pleasure tables in your upright position put up all your loose belongings, were about to get underway and enjoy, your flight."

James looked over at Cindy. She's grinning from ear - to - ear hanging on one of his arms. She could hardly contain herself. James asked, "Could you be any more excited?"

"I don't think so. Aren't you excited?"

"I don't know, honey, I'm still trying to take it all in. So many things are happening all at once," answered James.

Then they felt the plane's forward motion as it began taxiing out to the runway. They could hear the engines powering up.

James said. "Here we go baby."

Cindy gritted her teeth and grabbed his arm, holding it tight. As the plane began to move forward faster and faster, till they felt the nose lift off the ground, then the pressure pushed them back in their seats from the speed of the plane lifting, they felt it in their stomachs. Cindy said. "Oh, my stomach."

"I know, me too." Said James.

They could fill the plane climbing higher and higher for several minutes and finally it leveled out.

"What an experience that was." Said James.

Then once again the Captain's voice came on the intercom saying,

"This is you captain; the seatbelt signs are off. if you need to get up and go to the restroom you can. We will be cruising at 15,000 feet, you may experience a little turbulence, nothing to worry about, the stewardess will see to your needs, enjoy your flight."

The stewardess came walking down the aisle, one of them stopped and asked James and Cindy,

"Can I get you anything?"

"Cindy said. "I would like something cold to drink please."

"Yes ma'am, what would you like? Asked the stewardess"

"What do you all have?" Asked Cindy.

"Just a minute, I'll be right back." Said the stewardess, as she turned around and walked back to the galley, then in a few minutes she returned with a menu and handed it to them. Cindy said. "Ho honey, look at all of this."

Cindy said to the stewardess,

"I think I'll have a cola."

"Yes, make that too please said. James and a couple bags of peanuts thank you."

The stewardess turned around and went back to the galley, A few minutes later, she returned with two cola's and four bags of peanuts and handed them to the couple.

"Thank you, ma'am." Said Cindy.

Then the stewardess asked

"Would either of you, like to listen to some music?"

Cindy said "Yes I would please."

The stewardess handed her a set of headphones and showed her where to plug them in. Feeling quite comfortable because their seats would recline back. James said to his self,

"I might take me a little nap."

He looked over at Cindy, she was bouncing her head to the music, having the time of her life. he reclined back, in his chair and slipped off into a deep sleep.

"In what felt like just a few minutes. James was waking up from the Captain's voice coming over the intercom once again, saying,

"This is your captain will be landing in a few minutes the seatbelt signs are on, please if you would put your seats and fold-down table's in the upright position and fasten your seatbelts once again will be landing shortly."

James said "Well that didn't take very long."

Cindy looked at him and smiled saying,

"Oh honey, I am so excited I am about to pee my pants."

Then, once again, the Captain's voice came over the intercom, saying,

"We are on final approach. We've made good time for all of you that are catching another flight."

James and Cindy could fill the plane turning and slowing down. They could almost feel it dropping from the sky and finally the planes jerked back as the wheels touch down and begin to taxi, on the runway to the terminal. The Captain's voice came on the intercom again saying,

"We want to thank you for flying Air America. Please remain seated until the plane comes to a full stop at the terminal, look around your seats and gather up all your belongings and once again thank you for flying Air America."

James and Cindy could fill the plane slowing and finally it came to a stop. Once again, their ears Popped, as a stewardess unlatched and open the door to the plane. They noticed, all the passengers getting up and walking out. James stood up and grabbed their bags from the overhead storage compartment. They followed the other passengers out of the plane going down the long corridor, until they came to another flight attendant who once again said.

"Thank you for flying air America. We hope you have enjoyed your flight."

• • •

James and Cindy walked through the airport terminal, out to the front entrance, there was a man standing out there, holding a sign with their names on it.

They walked up to him and James said. "I'm James Parker, this is my wife Cindy Parker."

"Yes Sir, I'm here to take you to your hotel,"

"Thank you." Said James as they followed the man and to their amazement, he took them to a long black luxurious limousine. He opened the back door for them. As they climbed into the elegant surroundings, the unbelievable magnificence of it, overwhelmed the couple.

Cindy said. "OH, my God! They are treating us like royalty."

"Yes, I know, it's almost too good to be true," commented James.

Cindy said "I know, honey, I still can't believe it."

Then the man got into the limousine and drove them through the town, to their hotel, The Asheville Marriott. When they arrived, the driver got out and walked to the back of the limousine opening the door for them. People were staring and whispering, as they walked into the hotel. Obviously, wondering who they were. The limousine driver told James

"I'll be back to get your Monday morning about 8:30, to take you to Mr. Wilcox office, have a good night sir."

James said "Wait a minute, what is your name?"

The limousine driver looked to him, with puzzlement on his face and asked,

"Sir, is something wrong?" With fear in his voice that he may have done something.

James smiling at the man said. "Not at all, I just would like to know your name."

The limo driver. Looked at James and paused for a minute, then he said. "it's William... William Bedford Sir."

"Nice to meet you Willy that is if I can call you that, I'm James Parker, this is my wife Cindy we want to Thank you for driving us around." Said James handing the man a tip.

William smiling from ear - to - ear took James hand and shook it, saying,

"Forgive me, Sir, it's just that people don't usually ask me my name and yes Sir, you can call me Willy if you like and it's very nice to meet both of you. I hope you have a wonderful stay here with us and I'll see you both Monday morning at 8:30,"

CHAPTER 4

James and Cindy, with their bags in hand turned around and walked into the hotel up to the front desk to the hotel clerk saying,

"My name is James parker, this is my wife Cindy Parker, were supposed to have a room reserved here for us."

The hotel clerk looked at his computer and asked,

"Do you have some identification?"

James showed him his driver's license.

"Yes sir, please sign here." Said the hotel clerk.

James sign their names. Then the hotel clerk handed them their key card saying,

"You're in room 807, enjoy your stay."

Then James and Cindy went to the elevator, got in and went up to the eighth floor, they walked down the long corridor, until they came to room 807.

James stuck the key card in the door, pushing down on the handle, the door opened. The room was magnificent, had a huge king-sized bed, big flat screen TV on the wall, with all the necessities of home. French doors that opened out onto a balcony, from which he could see the whole area around the hotel. It also had a huge bathroom with a giant tiled shower, with glass doors. The stool was in a separate little room, off to the side for privacy.

They were both overwhelmed, because they had never seen anything so nice.

I think I'm going to take a shower, you want to join me?" Asked Cindy.

"No honey, you go ahead, I think I'm going to unpack and unwind a little bit."

Cindy started pulling off all her close. James Stood there watching her. He leaned back against the wall, staring at his beautiful little wife.

She stood in front of the mirror took her hair down and climbed into the shower. She turned on the water, standing back, holding out her hand. Letting the water hit it until it got warm enough for her. Then she stepped under it. She turned around and let the warm water hit her, starting on the back of her head, running down her long beautiful hair. She looked around inside the shower, till she found a bar of hotel soap, pulled it out of the wrapper and said to James,

"Honey, throw this away for me," opening the glass door and handing him the empty paper.

• • •

He took it from her, looking at her body under the water. He noticed how beautiful she was. He watched her to the glass doors as she soaked up her body thinking,

"What a beautiful body she has."

As his eyes followed her every curve and shape. Then she said. "Honey, wash my back please," Cindy soaked up a rag, open the glass door, handing it to him. He walked over to the shower taking a rag from her as she turned around, pulled her hair over her shoulder. James took the rag and began rubbing his wife's back across her shoulders and down each of her sides, then he ran the rag down the crease of her back to her beautiful little heart-shaped butt.

Cindy said. "Oh God, honey that feels so good, thank you."

Then she turned around and took the rag from his hand and stepped back in the shower, closing the door.

James returned to his previous spot, against the wall and resumed watching his wife shower.

Cindy reached up and turned the shower off, standing there, dripping on the shower floor, took her hands and pulled them the links of her hair, pushing the water to the tips and wrung it out.

She rolled it around to the top of her head and asked,

"Would you hand me a towel honey?" As she opened the shower door, James handed her a towel. She wrapped it around the top of her head encasing her hair twisted it and tucked it behind her head. Cindy stepped out other shower, grabbed another towel and begin drying her body off. Saying,

"Honey, you've got to try that I feel so much better."

"I will later."

"Okay, I'm going to order some room service." Said Cindy.

"That's a good idea, what are you going to get?" He asked.

"Let's have a stake and potato, macaroni and cheese and a chef salad."

"That's sounds good and see if they have sweet tea." Said James.

Cindy picked up the phone saying, "This is room 807, we would like to order some room service.

"Yes, ma'am what would you like?" Asked the man at the front desk.

"Two steaks rare to medium, more on the rare side, two baked potatoes with everything, macaroni and cheese, and two chef salads with ranch dressing."

"Oh yes, do you have sweet tea?"

"Yes ma'am." Said the man.

"Okay, four large sweet teas."

"How long will it be?" Asked Cindy.

"About 45, minutes." Said the man.

"Okay Thank you." Said Cindy hanging up the phone, she said. "It will be about 45 minute's honey."

"Okay want to sit on the balcony with me?" Asked James.

"Sure, let me get my night clothes on and I'm going to call Tracy and check on the boys first. If you don't mind." Said Cindy digging for her cell phone in her bag.

• • •

"Please don't get on there and talk all night. I like to spend some time with you." Said James.

"Don't worry honey, I'll only be a few minutes. You should take a quick shower, you'll feel so much better. You've got time before our dinner gets here."

"You know I think I will. Maybe it will relax me more." Said James as he got up and went into the bathroom. He pulled off all his clothes and climbed into the shower, turned on the hot water.

James likes the water hotter than Cindy does, he stood there letting the hot water hit, his neck and run down his back, feeling bewildered and somewhat confused and a little bit frightened, he thought,

"I wasn't raised that way, she is going to have all the money that, she could ever possibly need. what does she need me for and what if one day, she decides she don't need me anymore, shall have everything she needs and wants, with all that money?"

Then James thought of something, he didn't before.

"Maybe it's not that much money. Maybe it's a small inheritance and estate might be something that we could sell. I could build her a better home and she was still need me to take care of her."

Feeling a little bit more optimistic about the situation, he hurried up and washed his hair and his body, eager to get back out there to her.

James got out of the shower and dried his self-off and put on his night clothes, as quickly as he could.

When he came out of the bathroom. Cindy was sitting on the balcony watching the sunset, she looked at him and smiled asking. "Doesn't that feel better?"

"Actually, you're right. I do feel better," answered James.

"Well the boys are fine and Tracy sends her love...,"

Just then there was a knock at the door, interrupting her.

"That will be our dinner." Said Cindy. Jumping to her feet.

Then she said. "Honey, I need some money for a tip."

"Look in my pants pocket, get my money clip."

"What do you think? Two or three dollars? "Asked Cindy.

"Whatever you think will be fine honey," answered, James leaving the choice of how much to be made by her.

Cindy grabbed his pants, got his money clip and pulled out a couple of dollars, walking over to the door, opening it. A tall, thin man with a hotel uniform on, came walking in, pushing a little cart with a dinner tray on it.

Cindy said. "I'll take it, thank you," handing him a tip.

"Thank you, ma'am, enjoy your meal." Said the man, as he turned around and left the room.

Cindy pushed the tray out onto the balcony in between her chair and his. Then she took the covers off their dinner saying,

"Wow! This all looks wonderful!"

"Yes, and look at the sunset." Said James pointing to the horizon.

"I know honey isn't it beautiful, when's the last time you and I sat to watch the sunset?" Asked Cindy wanting to know if he remembered.

"I don't know baby, I can't remember." Said James with a confused look on his face

Cindy looked at him, shaking her head saying,

"We were in the back of your truck, up on top of that hill by that old Bicentennial Cemetery."

James in amazement, asked her, "You remember when it was?"

Cindy, winking at him." Said. "Of course, I do, women remember these things. I mean we have to, because men don't remember anything that they don't want to." Said Cindy looking sideways at James shaking her head once again.

James trying to defend himself said to her, "I don't know what you're talking about, I remember all kinds of things.

"Yeah! Like what?" Asked Cindy, waiting for his reply.

"Well I..., Honey, you look cold, let me get you a jacket." Said James attempting to avoid the question and figuring she wasn't ready to go in yet.

"Yeah! I thought so yes, it is a little chilly out here so would you please?" Asked Cindy, rubbing her arms.

"Of course, I will sweetheart, you need anything else, while I am, in there?" Asked James play in the obedient husband.

Cindy answered him saying, "No just the jacket thanks you anyway, trying to show her appreciation.

In a few minutes, James returned with a jacket and a blanket. That he got down off a shelf in one of the closets.

Cindy look at him and asked "What is that for?"

James smiling at her said. "Oh, I got an idea,"

Cindy looked at him and smiled, saying, "I bet you do."

"No seriously, I've got an idea." Said James as he pushed the table to one side and the tray back into the room and spread the blanket out on the floor of the balcony, then he went back inside returned once more with a couple of pillows and dropped them side-by-side on the blanket,

Cindy afraid he might want to make love on the balcony for the whole world to see, ask him, "Honey no really, what are you doing?"

"I thought you might want to lay beside me and look at the stars," he answered her, looking up at the heavens.

Cindy looked up and noticed, it seemed like there were millions of them. She stood there in awe and began thinking.

"I haven't done anything like that since I was young."

Then she turned to James and said "Last time I did something like that. I was just a kid."

"Yes, I know, me too." Said James as he helped his wife down onto the blanket and stretched out along besides her, holding her hand.

James then began to point out the constellations, talking about the stars, like he was professor or an authority on them Cindy listened, knowing he didn't know what the hell he was talking about, but not wanting to burst his bubble or ruin the moment, she pretended that he did.

They laid there for hours looking up at the stars contemplating on whether there was life out there. Cindy feeling very comfortable, began to get sleepy. Laying her head on her husband's chest. James, seem like he could talk for hours and never be tired. Cindy did her best not to let him see her trying to nod off, but finally he caught her dozing.

James stirring around, woke her, and he said. "Let's go to bed. I'm tired." Not really feeling that way. But not wanting to make her feel uncomfortable because she was.

James got up first and helped his wife to her feet. Grabbing the pillows and blanket, they walked back into the room, James tossed them on the bed and said "I've got to go to the bathroom. I'll be right back."

Cindy sat down on the side of the bed. Being so used to conserving water at home, routinely hollered,

"Don't flush it, I've got to use it too."

James looked at her and shook his head, walking into the bathroom. A few minutes later he returned only to find his wife slumped over sideways on the bed. James walked over and shook her saying, "Cindy honey, you still have to use the bathroom?"

Cindy opened her eyes and looked at him and set up with his help, nodding her head yes. James helped her to her feet and walked her into the bathroom, placing her down on the toilet. Cindy sat there silently, with her eyes closed, rocking back and forth and finally she reached up and got the roll of paper rolled it around and tore a piece off reached between her legs and wiped herself dropping it into the toilet.

James wondered *"How was that even possible? She's not even awake."*

James reached down and grabbed her by the shoulders, getting her to her feet. He flushed the toilet and helped her back to the bed, Cindy pulled off her night close and crawled underneath the covers, curling up in a ball. James watched her for a few minutes. Then suddenly, she sat upright in bed, saying,

"Honey, please don't be mad, I know you probably wanted to make love, but I'm so tired."

Jane said "It's all right. I understand lay back down."

Cindy asked, you're not mad?"

"Now honey, get some sleep." Said James trying to reassure her, he wasn't angry.

"But aren't you coming to bed?" Asked Cindy worried that he might be in fact mad and not want to be around her.

"Yes, I'm going to check and make sure the doors locked. I'll be right there."

"Okay honey, night. I love you." Said Cindy half asleep.

"I love you too baby sweet dreams." Said James as he got up and walked over, checking the door, making sure that they were in fact locked. Then returning to the bed. Cindy, was fast asleep, so he stretched out next to her and stared at the ceiling.

Until finally his eyelids begin to get heavy and he fell fast asleep. The next morning, he woke up alone in the bed. He set up and called his wife saying,

"Cindy where are you"

"I am out here, honey," She answered, here on the balcony."

James got up and walked out onto the balcony with her and asked "What are you doing?"

"Oh, I'm just watching this beautiful sunrise and thinking how wonderful it is to have this time alone with you."

"I know it's been a long time, since we spent so much time together especially alone." Said James lowering his head.

"I was watching you sleep, this morning and I thought to myself how much I love you James, I really do love you. Your wonderful father to our boys and I couldn't ask for better husband."

"Thank you honey." Said James "I love you too, what would you like to do today?"

"I don't know how bout we go downstairs to the restaurant and have breakfast.

Then Maybe we can walk around town to see some of the businesses here." Said Cindy. Obviously, getting bored and not wanting to stay in the room.

James said "That sounds like a good idea," going in the bathroom to get dressed.

A few minutes later he returned dressed and ready to go.

Then it was Cindy's turn, she went into the bathroom, explaining to him,

"I'll only be a minute."

And true to her word. In a few minutes, she emerged from the bathroom dressed and eager to start their day. The couple started out of the room, making sure they had their key cards and went downstairs to the hotel restaurant. They had a complimentary breakfast buffet,

Cindy said. "Look at all this wonderful food. Have you ever seen so much?"

"It is pretty amazing, so many things I don't even know what are," commented James.

Then they both sat down and had a good breakfast together sampling a little bit of everything there was. Finally, they both were so full they could hardly move.

James looked at Cindy and asked,

"Now what would you like to do honey?"

"Let's walk around town some." Said Cindy, hoping that he wasn't ready to go back to the room.

James eagerly agreed. Wanting to spend more time with his wife. They spent the whole day going through this little shop and then that one walking around the town. Getting to know some of the local people. Finally ending up back at the hotel. James said as they were heading back into the building,

"I'm tired and I don't believe I can walk anymore, but haven't we had a wonderful day honey? "Yes, I can't remember the last time I had such a wonderful day with you," explained Cindy smiling at him.

"I know baby, I have been so busy I haven't spent very much time with you, or the boys." Said James as they entered the elevator going up to their room.

"It's not your fault honey, "Cindy said as she followed him into the elevator.

"We really been struggling last couple years. But maybe all that's over with now we can enjoy life and each other more, oh honey, I'm so excited at the very least, maybe I can help you to raise your boys ensuring that they have a happy life and all the things that they could ever need or want."

"Cindy honey, you probably shouldn't get your hopes up too high." Said James as he walked into their room, letting the door close behind them.

"I mean all the lawyers said. was that it was an inheritance, it might not be that much and the estate might be some old rundown something, but we could sell it and I'm thinking maybe I can build you a better home. I see you from time to time looking at our neighbors in their brand-new fancy homes and I watch you looking at people riding around in nice cars."

"Oh James, I don't need all those things, I've got you and the boys. That's what makes me happy." Said Cindy trying to reassure him that there wasn't anything for him to worry about.

James looked at his lovely wife saying,

"Honey, I love you with all my heart and I thank God every day for you and my boys. I want to grow old and gray with you. I can't imagine my life without you in it Cindy."

James looked deep into her eyes, they both leaned forward and kissed each other.

James ran his hand up the back of her neck and under her hair, pulling her little body close to him. The room became very warm, they were overwhelmed by emotion, as they were kissing and caressing each other. James ran his hands all over his wife's beautiful body and down her back, cupping her butt, in his hand.

He then raised her up off the floor, with her back against the wall. They both were breathing heavily kissing each other. James pinned her to the wall with his body, as she wrapped her legs around him. Cindy started kissing his neck working her way to his chest, pulling at his buttons on his shirt with her fingers on both hands, she got the first two buttons undone on his shirt, as she dropped one of her legs to the floor to steady them. She began kissing his chest, running her face. Through the hairs on it.

James put his hands on both sides of her head underneath her hair as he held her head close to his chest. She kissed her way down, dropping the other leg, slowly lowering herself to the floor, pulling at the remaining buttons, till finally opening his whole shirt. James put his arms back and let it fall to the floor as she began tugging at the snap on the top of his jeans. Rubbing her nose, face and cheeks all over his strong, muscular stomach and biting him, until finally managing to un-snap his jeans with her teeth.

James reached down, grabbed her. By the shoulders and pulled her up to her feet. Kissed her tenderly holding her head in his hand, rocking it back and forth as he kissed her deeply. Their tongues intertwined. He kissed her chin and down her neck, working his way around her neck to her shoulder she tilted her head to the side and with one hand, pulled her hair over her other shoulder, so that James could get to it. He pulled the collar of her blouse over and very sensuously, he began to kiss them. Cindy could feel her legs getting weaker as he kissed his way down to her chest.

James slid his hand up underneath her blouse, to unhook her bra, tugging at it from the front relieved her breast, from their enclosure. He caressed and kissed each one of them all over.

Cindy's whole body trembled and jerked. Each time his lips touched her skin. She began breathing even more heavily, falling back against the wall. As he worked his way down her muscular tight tummy lowering his self to the floor. He then kissed and nibbled at her navel button. Taking the tip of his tongue and encircling and probing at it tenderly, until finally he stood to his feet, reached down and picked her back up off the floor in his arms and carried her over to the bed. Continuing to kiss her all over her body James kept thinking,

"How beautiful she was and how wonderful she felt in his arms."

They made love for what seem like hours. Afterwards, they held each other, the rest of the day, holding hands, letting their fingers intertwine. With Cindy laying in front of him. James moved her hair to the side kissing her on her neck and laid his head down on top of her. Cindy, playing with his fingers." Said to James

"I love you so much and you make me very happy."

Then, while holding her in his arms, they both fell fast asleep.

• • •

The next morning, James was awakened by his wife moving around still in his arms. He opened his eyes and gazed lovingly at her. She smiling at him asking, "Good morning, how did you sleep sweetheart?"

James replying to her "Like a rock honey." "What time is it?"

Cindy said "It's about 7 o'clock."

"We've got to get up and get ready to go." Said James.

Cindy said "I know I was just enjoying laying here with you.

"I know baby. I don't really want to get up either. But we've got to, the limousine driver said he would be back to get us about 8:30. So that doesn't give us very long to get ready." Said James reluctantly.

Cindy said "I know honey."

James asked his wife, "What's wrong honey?" "You don't sound that exited anymore."

"I am James! But! I'm also a little frightened." Said Cindy closing her eyes and taking a deep breath, letting it out slowly.

James asked her, looking confused

"Whatever in the world for?"

"Because I don't really know what to expect," explained Cindy.

"It's all going to be alright baby. Remember, I'm here with you." Said James trying to put her mind at ease.

"Yes, I know and I thank God for it. I don't think I could do this without you James."

"Yes, you could, you don't give yourself enough credit, you're a lot smarter than you think you are baby." Said James while sliding his feet off the side of the bed."

James reached over, patted his wife on her little but, saying, "Come on baby get up, we've got to get ready," as he got up and walked into the bathroom looking in the mirror at his reflection, he thought

"I looked like the hell."

He then turned around and climbed in the shower. A few minutes later, Cindy walked in the bathroom, open the shower door and asking, "Is there room for two in there?"

"Sure! Climb on in." Said James as he moved to the side, letting his wife under the warm water with him and closed the shower door.

They soaped each other's bodies up and played around a little, but they both knew they did not have much time, so they climbed out, dried off and got ready to go. James asked her, looking at his watch,

"Well are you ready?" "It's almost 8:30."

"Okay! Let's go." Said Cindy while walking to the door.

James checking to make sure he had the hotel room key cards. Satisfied that he did, they went out, letting the door close and lock behind them. They went to the elevator and headed downstairs to the front lobby and waited for the limousine driver to arrive.

A few minutes after eight, James noticed a long black car as it pulled into the front entrance of the hotel. It was in fact their driver, he pulled up to the couple got out walked around to open the back door four them. While they climb in James smiling at him saying,

"Good morning Willy, it's nice to see you," "How have you been?"

He answered him, saying, "Good morning, sir and ma'am, I can't complain."

Then he closed the door and walked around, got back in the limousine and drove them across town to the professional center, where the lawyer Marcus Wilcox's office was located, the driver then got out, walked around to the back of the limousine and opened the door for them saying, "I'll be waiting here for you when you return, to take you back to your hotel."

James said to him as they climbed out, "Thank you Willy, we shouldn't be that long"

Then they headed into the building. Inside the lobby was a large desk with two women sitting behind it side-by-side. The couple walked over to the desk. One of the receptionist's asked "Can I help you sir?"

James said "Yes ma'am, can you tell us what floor, Marcus Wilcox's office is on?"

"But of course, it's on the fourth floor. Take the elevator around the corner. Go up to the fourth floor and in front of the elevator you will see his secretary's desk."

"Thank you, ma'am." Said James.

Than he and Cindy, walked around the corner and got in the elevator, heading upstairs to the fourth floor. When the elevator doors opened, there a few feet away was a big oval shaped desk, with a distinguished looking woman sitting behind it. James walked over to her, saying,

"Good morning, I am James Parker, this is my wife Cindy Parker and we have an appointment with Mr. Wilcox this morning."

The secretary said. "I will let him know you're here." As she picked up the phone and saying,

"Yes Sir, a Mr. and Mrs. Parker, are here to see you…, and pausing for only minute she said.

"Yes Sir." Then she hung up the phone saying, "He'll be right with you. Please, have a seat."

CHAPTER 5

James and Cindy walked over and sat down in a couple of chairs. The excitement was almost more than Cindy could stand as she sat there holding James hand as tightly as she could. Then in a few minutes, a tall heavyset man came walking through a door next to the desk, walked over to James sticking out his hand, saying, "Good morning, Mr. and Mrs. Parker, I am Marcus Wilcox, please follow me to my office if you will."

The couple followed him down the hall to his office, sitting down in front of his desk.

Mr. Wilcox said. "It's nice to finally meet you two. I trust you had a good flight and you're enjoying your hotel accommodations."

"Oh, yes Sir!" said Cindy. "They're treating us like royalty."

"Well ma'am and a sense, that's what you are, Mrs. Parker. You just have become a very wealthy woman."

Cindy squeezed James hand, smiling at him. James repeated

"Wealthy woman, how wealthy?"

"Well Mr. Parker, your wife now is worth millions of dollars, $375 million, to be exact"

"375 million! Dollars!!" yelled James excitedly.

"Yes, she has just inherited $375 million and an estate worth, 10 times that amount." Said Mr. Wilcox, looking at the couple. "I don't understand." "How could this be?" Asked James in disbelief.

"Well as I indicated to your wife on the phone, we would go over the details here in my office let's get right to it.

Mrs. Parker, your birth mother and father were Stephen and Ginger Summerhill. Your uncle Charles was the brother of your father's father.

"You mean I have a great uncle?" said Cindy. Interrupting him feeing confused.

"You had a great uncle." Said Mr. Wilcox. Here look, perhaps this will explain it better for you. James and Cindy came closer to his desk, as he unfolded a document with a diagram outlining The Summerhill family bloodline.

• • •

| **MARGARET & GEORGE SUMMERHILL**
WAS THE FATHER AND MOTHER TO
ROBERT
ALL- DECEASED |
|---|

| MAGGIE & **ROBERT** SUMMERHILL I
BOTH DECEASED |
|---|

| BEATRICE & **ROBERT** SUMMERHILL II
BOTH DECEASED |
|---|

| **KEITH** & KELLY SUMMERHILL. HAD TWO SUN'S **CHARLES** & **DAVID**
BOTH DECEASED |
|---|

| **DAVID** & MARRY
SUMMERHILL
BOTH DECEASED |
|---|

| **CHARLES** SUMMERHILL (ELDEST)
INHERITS SUMMERHILL MANOR FROM **STEPHEN** & GINGER
SUMMERHILL AFTER **DAVID** & MARY UNTIMELY DEATH.
BOTH DECEASED |
|---|

| **STEPHEN** & GINGER SUMMERHILL THE BIRTH FATHER & MOTHER TO **CINDY**
BOTH DECEASED |
|---|

CINDY WAS **ADOPTED** BY LARRY & STEPHANIE COLLINS

CHARLES DIED, CINDY'S GREAT UNCLE.

THAT MADE CINDY THE ONLY LIVING BLOOD RELATIVE, OF THE SUMMERHILL FAMLY, AND THE SOUL HEIR OF THERE LEGACY, AND WEALTH.

as you can see your great uncle was sole heir of the Summerhill estate. But now that he's passed away. That leaves you as the sole heir and all its inheritance, now Mrs. Parker I understand this is a lot for you to take….," said Mr. Wilcox.

"Yes, it is! I didn't even know that I was adopted." "You sure there's no mistake?" said Cindy Interrupting him once more.

"No ma'am, I am certain about my findings. I researched this for months, now trying to find an heir to your uncle's estate and you are all that remains of the Summerhill family. With that - being - said. all I need you to do is sign some legal documents, accepting the terms of the Will and transferring the estate over to you."

James asked him "Terms, what are the terms?"

"Well in every Will there are guidelines to follow and in this case, the old man has protected the mansion. Here I'll read them to you, I Charles Thomas Summerhill the third, being of sound mind and under witness. Do hereby bequeath all my belongings, wealth and possessions to my sole heir, upon my death. Under the terms and conditions that they dwell within the manor and maintain it. They cannot remove or sell any items, inside or on the grounds of the Summerhill estate. If they do so, they hereby lose possession of the Summerhill Manor, its wealth and all its entirety,"

James said "So let me get this straight, what you're saying, is she will not get her inheritance and all her uncle's wealth, unless she lives in the Summerhill mansion, and maintains it."

"That's correct, those are in fact, the terms and conditions, of the Will. Set aside by her uncle to protect the manor." Said Mr. Wilcox trying to be as clear as he could with the couple.

"Can we see it before she signs anything?" Asked James still trying to make sense of all of it.

"But of course, Mr. Parker. I would not expect anything less, please if you would follow me." Said Mr. Wilcox, getting up from his desk.

James and Cindy, following behind him went to the elevator heading down to the lobby.

James asked as they were heading down,

"this manor! Is it some old rundown dwelling that needs a lot of work to restore it?"

"Not at all, although it's been quite some time since anyone has been in the manor and I imagine it is probably dusty and could use a good cleaning. I do assure you it is fully intact." Said Mr. Wilcox. As the elevator doors opened to the lobby.

Walking out of the front of the building and over to the waiting limousine, that the couple had arrived in earlier, Mr. Wilcox said. "Good morning William, take us to the estate If you would please,"

"But of course, sir." Said the driver as he opened the back door for them. Then after closing the door behind them, he returned to the driver's side getting in, he headed to the Summerhill estate.

Cindy asked, "How far is it?"

"It's about 45 minutes from the town, answered Mr. Wilcox.

They drove through the country. Cindy could not help but notice how beautiful everything was and she pointed it out, again and again, to James.

Who was feeling overwhelmed with all that he had heard about the money and the manor. He began to wonder if it would be possible to live there. After all, it would get them and the boys out of the big city and away from the crime life. That they undoubtedly would become a part of. If they remain in Detroit.

Then the limousine started down a gravel road winding up the mountain. Mr. Wilcox looking out the window saying, "Now from this point on, the roads can get kind of treacherous. And we do have an occasional rock slide coming down the mountain, but if you take your time and be very careful. It's really no big deal."

Finally, they arrived in front of two large iron gates, with the name Summerhill Manor inscribed on metal plates enclosed in them. Beside the driveway coming out of the ground, was a post with what appeared to be a small metal box, with a keypad attached to it. Mr. Wilcox had the driver stop a few feet away, getting out he walked over to the keypad and entered the code. In doing so, the two iron gates opened. Then he got back into the limousine and they continued driving through them up the driveway, heading to the mansion. All along the driveway, there were large trees on both sides, they came together creating and an effect of a tunnel. As they drove through the rows of trees they finally came to the circular driveway in front of the mansion.

It was a big beautiful old historical place. That seemed to go on forever. The sheer size of it overwhelmed both James and Cindy

Cindy said with excitement

"This is not a house is a castle."

Mr. Wilcox said "In a way, yes, you're right. I know it is a bit overwhelming."

James said out loud, "That's an understatement. How do you maintain something of this magnitude?"

Mr. Wilcox said.

"With a lot of help, which with your inheritance. You will have no trouble in finding plenty of."

As they got out of their luxurious limousine and walked up to the front of the estate, the pure splendor of the place was unmatched, to anything that either James or Cindy had ever imagined. There was what appeared to be a set of beautiful marble steps, leading to the entrance way, with two large magnificent, old colonial style pillars towering over them and a breezeway encasing two of the largest wooden doors that they had ever seen, in front of the mansion.

Marcus unlocked them and swung them open. Standing in the foyer straight across from them was a staircase going up to the other floors. Off to the right side of the staircase with an opening leading into a large room with what appeared to be a marble fireplace, huge in size and there standing in the center of the room was a life-size statue of what appeared to be a beautiful woman, beside it, a large reclining chair. Mr. Wilcox said "This was the main room of the mansion; your uncle Charles was a bit of an eccentric old man. He never came down off the mountain. He stayed here all alone in this mansion, surrounded by his artifacts and his statue. They said that he went out of his mind and that he would actually talk to his statue."

Cindy said "Well I can tell you now, this thing has got to go."

Mr. Wilcock said "I'm sorry, Mrs. Parker, but you cannot do that. The terms of the Will plainly state that you cannot remove or sell anything in or outside of the mansion."

"Will, can I at least put it out in the yard where it belongs?" Asked Cindy

"If you don't remove it from the property or sell it. You're still in your guidelines of the will." Said Mr. Wilcox.

Cindy said. looking at Mr. Wilcox,

"That's good, because I won't that thing out of my house."

James said. "My God, this place is huge."

"Yes, like I told you, it can be a bit overwhelming." Said Mr. Wilcox, but it is a beautiful old place would many rooms. Some of them I can tell you I've never seen the old man closed off most of the house years ago, far as I know no one's ever been in them, do either of you like to read?"

Cindy answered him, saying, "Oh yes!! I love to read,"

"Follow me he said as he went down the long corridor, which came, to a large wooden pocket door that slid open into the wall. As they walked into a huge room with the upper-level, which was the library, wall-to-wall books and more books surrounded them with an enormous wooden table in the center of the room. This is the drawing room, library if you will. Of the Summerhill mansion. Some of these books are dated back to the 1800s, the whole history of the Summerhill family and their legacy is undoubtedly located somewhere in this library." Said Mr. Wilcox.

Cindy obviously feeling overwhelmed said. "My God! I've never seen so many books,"

"Mr. Wilcox said. so, young lady, what do you think, can you live with the terms of the Will?"

"Well Mr. Wilcox I have to talk this over with my husband, I can't rush into a decision like this and it will be life altering."

"Well how much time do you need?" Asked Mr. Wilcox.

"I don't know, James what you think about all of this?" Asked Cindy

"It is a bit overwhelming, but I think you're right. I think we need to really sit down and talk about this. It's going to change our lives forever, it's not a decision that we can rush into. I'm sorry, Mr. Wilcox, but we will need some time."

"That's quite all right. I fully expected this and I do understand. Let's go back to my office and I'll had the driver take you back to your hotel, you guys discuss this, sleep on it even, then get back to me when you have a decision, so that we can finalize everything."

James looked over at Mr. Wilcox saying, "Thank you Sir, just give us a little while and will let you know."

Mr. Wilcox headed out of the mansion with James and Cindy, following behind him. When they got back into the limousine. He said. "William take me back to my office and take the Parkers back to their hotel."

When they got back to his office He got out and leaned down, looking at the couple saying, "Let me know what you all decide."

James said. "We will and one more thing before you go, would it be possible for us to have a key so that we can go walk around the manor on our own?"

"But of course, here's the key's and this is the code to the gate. The driver will give you his personal cell phone number if you want to go up to the mansion call him and you'll come pick you up at your hotel." Said Mr. Wilcox, handing everything to them.

Once again James said to him, "Thank you, Mr. Wilcox,"

"That's quite all right and like I said. please, when you come up with the decision, let me know." Said Mr. Wilcox as he shut the door, to the limousine turned around and walked into the building. They pulled out of the driveway heading to the hotel.

CHAPTER 6

When they arrived, the driver walked around and opened a door for the couple. They climbed out and He said.

"Here is my card. It has my personal cell phone number on it. If you need the car, don't hesitate to call."

"Thank you, Willie yes, we'll be calling you if you don't mind? Because we might want to go back up to the manor and walk around on our own." Said James handing him a tip and taking his business card.

"You're quite welcome." Said William walking around the limousine to get back into it.

Cindy and James turned around and walked into the hotel, through the lobby, over to the elevator headed up to the room. Neither one of them said anything. They were both deep in thought, trying to figure out what the other one was thinking. When they got back to the room.

James walked over and sat down on the bed, thinking, *"My God! It's worse than I thought all that money and a mansion."*

Cindy walked over and sat down beside him saying, "Honey, please talk to me. Tell me what you think we should do."

"I don't know. I guess we should try and think of it as good and bad. Get a piece of paper and a pen and write down on one side, all the reasons to do it and on the other side all the reasons not to, perhaps that can help us decide." Said James.

"Do you have a piece of paper and a pen?" He asked.

Cindy walked over and looked in her bag because. She always keeps a notepad with her in case there is something that she needs to jot down, she got it out and brought it and a pen back over to James asking

"Will this work?"

...

"Yes, that will be fine." Said James taking the paper and pen. Writing number **One,** on the piece of paper, then he paused, thinking about it for a minute. Cindy said. "I know that I could help you raise the boys, giving them all the things we never had and really feel like I'm their mom. How's that for number **One?**"

James looked at her saying, "Okay then number **Two,** will never have to pay rent again."

Cindy reached over and touched James arm saying, "One thing's for sure, we can get the boys out of the city and away from the gangs there. That they would undoubtedly end up getting into and ruining their lives."

"Okay then that would-be number **Three." Said** James agreeing with his wife.

"Here's another one James, we can send the boys away to college, making sure they have a good education and a good start in life, I guess that's number **Four,**"

"Well his number **five,** People will treat us like royalty.

"How's this for number **Six,** James. We'll have the money to do anything we want to go on vacations, help friends and family, anything.

"Yes, that's a good one honey. How about this for number **Seven,** Cindy. We can get out of the city and away from all the people, traffic and chaos that follows it."

James honey, "How about the simple fact that the mansion and the grounds around it are absolutely beautiful and secluded, quiet and there is no one to tell us what we can and can't do on our very own property that alone makes it almost all worthwhile.

"You're right, honey that is definitely number **eight." Said** James.

"Here's one Cindy we will definitely spend more time together and with the boys. I think that Classifies as number **nine.**"

"James honey, let's face it, it's beautiful up there and the people are so nice. It's like a whole different lifestyle, like nothing, either one of us has ever known.

"Yes, I guess we can call that number **ten." Said** James putting down the ink pen.

"Okay, I'll read it back." Said James as he was picking up the paper

Wyatt Allen

"1) you can help me raise the boys giving them all the things we never had and really feel like you are their mom,
"2) We would never have to pay rent again.
"3) We can get the boys out of the city and away from the gangs.
"4) We can send the boys away to college, making sure they have a good education and a good start in life.
"5) We will live like kings and queens.
"6) We'll have the money to do anything we want. Like going on vacation and help our friends and family.
"7) We can get away from the rush of the city and all the people.
"8) The mansion itself is beautiful and the grounds around it.
"9) We will spend a lot more time together and with the boys.
"10) It is beautiful up there and the people are all so nice.

CHAPTER 7

"Okay, that's 10 reasons why we should do it. Now let's see how many we can come up with, that says we shouldn't." Said James as he wrote saying, "Number **One,** I just was not raised that way, the man supposed to take care of his wife and family, not the other way around and after all it is your money and inheritance not mine."

"James don't be silly what's mine is yours, you know that. But any way, number **Two,** we've got to move away from Tracy and all our friends." Said Cindy

James looked at her saying, "Okay, number **Three,** I have made a lot of acquaintances through my business, people count on me. I have made a name for myself."

"Number **Four,** the boys will lose their friends and if we pull them out of Detroit school, it will be hard for them to start over." Said Cindy.

"Well they will make new friends honey." Said James trying to comfort his wife.

"Yes, but they will probably hate me for it." Said Cindy, dropping her head.

"Well number **Five,** I guess the main thing for us to think about would be were going to have to live a life, we're not accustomed to under somebody's thumb for the rest of our lives. If we accept this." Said James trying to make it clear.

"I don't understand." "What do you mean James?" Asked Cindy with confusion in her voice.

"Well take the money for instance, I'm sure whatever we want to spend the finances on, will first need to go through Mr. Wilcox, if I'm understanding this right." Said James trying to explain as best he could.

"You mean I have to go ask him whenever I want money, like for groceries and get my hair done or by a new pair of jeans?" Asked Cindy getting upset.

"If I understand this right, yes, that's exactly what I'm talking about." Said James trying to make her understand.

"Surely not! I mean after all it's my money! I should be able to do with it whatever I want." Said Cindy getting even more upset.

"It is definitely something we need to talk to Mr. Wilcox about." Said James, looking at they're not to do it list.

"Yes, that alone would be reason for us not to do this James I am not going to live underneath somebody's thumb, the rest of my life." Said Cindy getting angrier at the very thought of it.

James looking at her side saying,

"Well honey, I am getting kind of hungry." Then he asked,

"What do you say we order some room service and curl up on the bed, watch some TV and don't think about this anymore for a while?"

Cindy, nodding her head saying, "Yes that sounds like a wonderful idea and I like to take a shower, it has been an overwhelming day as I need to unwind."

"Well sweetie, you take a shower and I'll order us some dinner." Said James as he was picking up the phone.

"What do you have in mind?" Inquired Cindy.

"I'm thinking I'll order us, some seafood. I saw it on the menu the other night, a seafood platter for two, with lobster tail and three different variations of shrimp, steamed scallops, clam strips, hush puppies, French fries and I'm going to get us something to drink,"

"Oh!" James that sounds wonderful!" said Cindy as she headed to the bathroom to take a shower and relax.

James ordered their dinner, then he walked out on the balcony, sitting down in a chair, watching the people going about their everyday lives, at the bottom of the hotel. Cars coming and going, people walking back and forth, undoubtedly headed to different destinations. James watched them as he waited for their dinner to arrive.

Trying to unwind and relax himself, because he was feeling overwhelmed by the day's activities and the decision that they had to make. He began to wonder what Cindy was thinking, about as she was taking her shower.

"*Perhaps she is thinking the same thing that I am.*" He thought.

Cindy, finishing her shower, climbed out and was looking at herself in the mirror. She was in fact thinking of all the day's activities and the decision that had to be made. But she was also thinking, "*About her true parents and how it was that people of their magnitude could give up their child.*" "*What prompted them into thinking they had to give her away?*"

"*They obviously came from a very wealthy family and could easily afford a child.*"

The thought of it saddened her. Then she began to think back "*When she was a girl, of 14, her mother and father made her give her child away, but she came from a poor family and her only being 14 herself felt like she had no choice. But she wondered about **Sabrina**, her baby girl from time to time somewhere in this world.*" As a tear rolled up in her eye, she placed her hand on her stomach. Feeling the loss of her child from so many years ago, and as those memories ran to her head, she continued to get dressed for the evening. Putting on a sheer nightgown. That had little lacey straps for her shoulders and was silky in texture. Cindy was somewhat of a tiny woman. A little under 5 feet, maybe 115, pounds. the sheer little thing hung down almost to her ankles and cling to her little frame because she didn't quite get dried off, it is low cut in the front, exposing quite a bit of her cleavage and her nipples stuck out from the transition from the hot water in the cool air in the room, so you could easily see them. Cindy dried off her hair and brushed it out, walking out into the room.

James was sitting on the balcony watching the people, he looked up at her coming toward him, smiling at her he said. "Sometimes I forget just how beautiful you are."

Cindy walked over to the bed and picked up a rope slipping it over her arms and shoulders, to hide herself, so that she could go out on the balcony with him. James got to his feet, walked over and hugged her, kissed her tenderly on the lips. Handing her the tip money for when their dinner arrived saying, "Now I'm going to take me a shower and relax, I won't be long."

Cindy said "I'm going to call Tracy and check on the boys. Do you think that I should say anything to her about this?"

"Not yet, honey, let's decide what we're going to do okay" said James pulling his shirt from his jeans heading to the bathroom.

"But she'll want to know something," explained Cindy.

"Tell her we met with the lawyer and he went over everything with us and...," James paused for a minute, looked down at the floor. Then he said. "You know what, on second thought, if you want to tell her you can. After all, she is your best friend and it will affect her as well."

"Thank you, James." Said Cindy smiling at him reaching for her cell phone."

James walked into the bathroom to take a shower Cindy dialed Tracy's number. It rang a couple times, finally she answered it saying, "Hello."

"Hey Tracy, it's me,"

"Well hey girl so what was going on?" Asked Tracy with excitement in her voice. Happy to hear from her friend.

"Well, we did meet with the lawyer and I do have a fairly large inheritance and estate to consider,"

"I don't understand consider." "What is there to consider?" Asked Tracy with confusion in her voice.

Cindy said "Well under the terms and conditions of the Will, we have to live here, in the Summerhill manor and maintain it,"

"And that's a bad thing why?" "I mean sweetie, you're up in the mountains and you're out of Detroit away from his city. The people and the crime here. I bet you, the only trouble somebody gets into up there is when they get in a fight at the local bar." Said Tracy trying to make her understand.

"Yes, it is quite different than living in the city. The people here are so nice and my God Tracy! They're treating us like royalty. The hotel is beautiful and so is my manor. I can't wait for you to see it." Said Cindy with excitement in her voice. "Is it a large inheritance?" Asked Tracy trying to understand her confusion.

"Tracy, its $375 million! And my estate, the lawyer says is worth 10 times that amount,"

"My God Cindy! You are like royalty." Said Tracy with excitement in her voice.

"Yes, it's a bit overwhelming, for the both of us." Said Cindy confirming her thoughts.

"Obviously, I can understand that." Said Tracy with jealousy in her voice.

"Well anyway how are the boys?" "They are not giving you any trouble, are they?"

"You mean the little monster and his brother? They are doing fine, My God, Cindy they fight all the time for the littlest things,"

"I'm sure I don't have to ask who the little monster is. And yes, I know Trace they drive me crazy with all of that,"

"You know honey that will be a good opportunity for them as well. With that kind of money, you can set both - of - them up for life, my next question would be, when I can move." Said Tracy trying to make light of it.

"We haven't really decided what we're going to do yet." Said Cindy

"WHAT!!" why is there even a question to it, my God girl! You're talking about $375 million and a beautiful estate what is there to decide?" Asked Tracy trying to understand.

"Well, trace, it would mean I have to move away from you." Said Cindy trying to make her understand one of the reasons for her confusion.

"Oh honey! I can come and visit you guys and you can come and visit me. You can't let that be a deciding factor." Said Tracy, trying to put her mind at ease.

I know Trace, it's more than our wildest dreams. This kind of thing doesn't happen to people like us." Said Cindy starting to show some degree of emotion.

"No sweetheart," it doesn't and yes, I'm sure it is a bit overwhelming for the both of you. But think about your boy's future, you know what's here in Detroit the crime rate climbs higher every day. The gangs are all around so it's only a matter of time before the boys are introduced into that. Listen to me. Sweetie both you and James are good people and God watches out for good people. Perhaps this is his way of assuring you your future." Said Tracy as she was really trying to be a good friend and make her understand.

"Tracy I love you." Said Cindy I better get off here thank you so much. Kiss the boys for us. Tell them we love them and miss them,"

"I love you guys too and Cindy, whatever you decide, sweetheart, I'm here for you." Said Tracy have a good night.

"I know Trace. You've always been there for me. Thank you again, have a good night." Said Cindy as she hung up her phone, letting everything that Tracy had said to her run through her mind.

Suddenly there was a knock at the door. Cindy, re-fastened her road to cover her breasts, walking over she opened it. There again was that tall thin man, from the other night with the hotel uniform on saying, "Good evening ma'am, I have your dinner here, where would you like me to place it?" He asked while pushing the little cart inside the room.

"I'll take it." Said Cindy handing him his tip.

"Thank you, ma'am, enjoy your dinner." Said the man as he walked out of the room.

"Thank you." Said Cindy as she closed the door behind him. Turned around and pushed the cart out onto the balcony waiting for James to emerge from the bathroom. A few minutes later he appeared clean and with his hair still damp in a pair of boxers, asking,

"Was that someone at the door?"

"Yes, our dinner is here I put it out on the balcony like last night." Said Cindy as she walked back into the room.

"Okay honey, did you call Tracy?"

"Yes, I did and she thinks we are crazy if we don't do it. She said we should think about the boy's future and how it will affect their lives." Said Cindy looking at him.

"But we are thinking about the boy's future, and our own..., honey, I don't want to rush into anything. It's going to change all of our lives." Said James dropping his head looking down at the floor.

"I know James, but I really think it would be for the best."

James looked at her and smiled, saying, "It sounds like to me. You have already made up your mind and you want to do this."

"Yes, I do honey, but only if you want to, because I'm not doing anything without you." Said Cindy looking at him, eager for his reply.

He looked at her with a puzzled look on his face and asked, "Even if it means giving up all that money and the estate?" Asked James once again, lowering his head in disbelief.

"Yes, because all the money in the world doesn't mean anything if you can't be happy... and you and the boys make me happy." Said Cindy as she was trying to reassure him.

"Well, let's eat our dinner and enjoy the evening together and don't think about this anymore will deal with it tomorrow,

"I wish I could do that James, I can't honey, it's all I can think about right now it's the not knowing what to do. That makes it so hard." Said Cindy trying to make him understand.

Let's for a little while, not think about it and enjoy our dinner. I'm very hungry and it's getting cold,"

"Okay honey, I will try my best." Said Cindy walking out on the balcony and lifting the lid off their dinner saying, "It does all look wonderful."

"Yes, it does, I can't wait to sink my teeth into it." Said James eagerly.

They set there and had a nice dinner together and although they did mention it a couple more times, they really did try and shy away from deciding right then at that moment.

Jane's got up and started to walk inside. He turned around, looked at his wife saying, "Cindy I love you with all my heart and if this will make you happy, truly happy, then okay, honey tomorrow we'll talk to Mr. Wilcox, about the financial part of it, making sure that we understand all of it and if you think we can live with the decision? Then let's do it." Said James trying to make his wife happy and put her mind at ease.

Cindy ran over and put her arms around her husband and hugged him as tightly as she could, saying,

"Oh James, you really want to honey?"

"I want to make you happy and if that's what is going to make you happy, then yes, I want to." Said James smiling at his wife and very tenderly kissed her on the lips. Then he turned around and walked into the bathroom. Cindy put the remainder of their dinner in the refrigerator and cleaned up their mess off the balcony, walked over, dropping her nightgown on the floor beside the bed and climbed into it, waiting for her husband to return.

Quite some time past and Cindy climbed out of the bed, walked over to the bathroom door knocking on it. Asking, "James, are you all right, honey?"

"My stomach is a little upset. I guess something I ate didn't agree with me, you go on to bed. I'm going to be a while." Said James.

"Okay honey, if you need me I'm right out here." Said Cindy as she walked back over and climbed into bed.

Cindy feeling concerned about her husband and not really wanting to go to sleep without him. Did try her best to fight it and stay awake. But she was very tired and emotionally worn out. Her eyelids got heavier and heavier, till finally she fell fast asleep. When James came out the bathroom. He noticed his wife sleeping soundly, not wanting to wake her. He slipped into the bed beside her and pulled her close to him, holding her all night.

The next morning the couple woke up and looked at each other saying, "Good morning,"

Cindy once again said. "I am hungry, let's go downstairs to the hotel restaurant and have breakfast,"

James said. "Then I'm going to call for the limousine driver to take us to Mr. Wilcox office and we'll find out where we stand in all of this,"

•••

James got his cell phone and the man's card calling him. Saying,

"Willie, this is Mr. Parker, we need you to come and get us this morning and take us to Mr. Wilcox office, okay, thank you." Then James hung up the phone turned around and said to Cindy,

"He said he'll be here within the hour, so we better get dressed honey."

The couple got up and dressed. As quickly as they could and headed downstairs to have a quick breakfast and meet the limousine driver. He picked them up in front of the hotel and took them to Mr. Wilcox office.

When they arrived, they walked inside, went up to the fourth floor and over to Mr. Wilcox's secretary's desk. James asked, "Would it be possible for us to speak to him this morning?"

The secretary said "Give me a minute, as she was picking up the phone and said "Mr. Wilcox, the Parkers are here to see you...,

"Yes Sir,"

She hung up the phone and saying, to the couple

"Go on in."

"Thank you, ma'am." Said James as he and Cindy walked down the hall to Mr. Wilcox office. Went inside and set down in front of his desk.

CHAPTER 8

Mr. Wilcox said "Good morning, have you made a decision?"
"Well, there are a couple of things we like to ask you about." Said James.
"But of course, you can ask anything,"
"About the financial part of it. Does this mean anytime we need money for anything, we must go through you? Asked James.

"Not at all, this is how it will work, upon the time that all the documents are signed by your wife, the remainder of the money is in an account underneath the Summerhill name and I will open up a separate account in both yours and your wife's name. Once the estate is transferred over, I will deposit $1 million into that account to do with whatever you wish. You can use the money to maintain the mansion or whatever you like, if you use the money to maintain the mansion, I will replace it, keep all the receipts and turned them over to me prior to the agreement of the Will and every year after that. As - long - as you both live, I will deposit another $1 million into that account and like I said. the money is in there to do with whatever you like,

"You mean we can go on vacations, help families and friends, that kind of thing?" Asked Cindy.
"It's your money. You can give it away if that's what you want." Said Mr. Wilcox.
James asked, "But what if we decide we don't want to live in. The manor for whatever reason."
"Well if that's the case, the Summerhill manor and the estate will be going into probate and eventually become the property of the state." Said Mr. Wilcox.

"What if we transfer all the documents into my wife's name and you open this account placing $1 million in it like you said and then we decide Six months down the road, we don't like it there and want to leave. What happens then?"

"Well under the agreement of the Will, you have to live in the manor and maintain it. If you do so you accept all responsibilities and take care of the mansion and if you do that, you get the inheritance, but if you leave the manor than, once again, it will be going into probate and ultimately end up going to the state."

"What about the money that's in our account, will that be froze?" Asked Cindy.

"Not at all, you can take the money remaining in the account and do with it whatever you will, but there will be no more." Said Mr. Wilcox.

"Okay but what if something happens to you?" Asked James

"Well Mr. Parker. I am but one lawyer in a large firm, retained by Charles Summerhill to take care of his affairs. If something happened to me. The firm will simply appoint another attorney on your behalf, James looked over at his wife and she nodded her head yes. Then he said. "All right what all does she sign?"

Mr. Wilcox walked over to a filing cabinet and got all the documents together and brought them back over placing them on his desk. Saying, "Okay she signs here, here initials here, here, here, signs and dates it here and I sign it here as a witness. We need one more witness, hold on a second."

Mr. Wilcox picked up the phone and called his secretary saying, "Mary, would you step back here for a minute please?" Then he hung up the phone.

In a few minutes, his secretary came walking in. Mr. Wilcox said we need another witness on this document, sign it right here please. Mary picked up the pen and signed her name.

"Okay that's it." Said Mr. Wilcox as he held out his hand. Then he said. congratulations, Mr. and Mrs. Parker, I hope you'll be very happy with your decision. Give me a couple days to take care of recording the deed and open the bank account. When did you want to head back to Detroit?"

James said. "We are going to go back to the hotel pack and head home today, but if you don't mind. She wants to go out to the manor before we leave and take some pictures to show her friends and the boys when we get back."

"But of course, William will take you wherever you wish to go. Oh, yes and before I forget, the gardener and his sons are in the process of removing that statue out of the house upon your request ma'am, I don't know if they've done it yet, but it should be gone by the time you return. You guys go ahead on out to the mansion, by the time you get packed your tickets will be waiting for you, when you arrive to the airport just give them your name, same as before. Have a safe trip home and I look forward to seeing you when you get back." Said Mr. Wilcox, while shaking James hand.

James said. "Thank you for everything,"

"Yes, Sir thank you very much." Said Cindy. Absolutely bubbling over with excitement.

"You're quite welcome and once again, congratulations." Said Mr. Wilcox, one last time as he walked the couple to the door.

James and Cindy walked out of Mr. Wilcox's office, went downstairs, where the limousine driver was waiting for them, he was standing by the car, watching as they came out of the building. He reached over and opened the back door. As they started to climb in. James asked, "Willie would you be so kind as to take us back to the estate please, we would like to take some pictures."

The limousine driver as he shut the back door said. "But of course, sir."

When they arrived, to the metal gates.

James got out, punched in the code, that Mr. Wilcox, had given him, earlier that day. After doing so the gates opened and they drove up to the manor,

The driver got out and walked around to the back of the limousine to open the door for the couple James said. "Willie, we should not be very long. She wants to take a few pictures to show our friends when we get home."

The driver, while nodding his head yes said. "That's quite all right, take all the time you need sir."

James and Cindy got out of the limousine, Cindy took her digital camera out and started taking photos of the front of the manor. Then they unlocked the door and walked inside. Cindy started taking pictures of all the other rooms when they walked into the main part of the house, there was that statue still standing there. But there was a dolly attached to it. Cindy looked at James and asked him, "Would you do something for me?"

"Of course, honey anything." "What is it?" Inquired James eager to please his wife.

Cindy while pointing at the statue said. "I want that thing out of my house. I want to take some pictures in this room without it in them, do you think we can move it?"

"I don't know honey, it looks awfully heavy." Said James looking at the statue.

"Can we please try James?" pleaded Cindy.

"Well I guess we can try, if that's what you really want." Said James trying to please her.

•••

Taking a hold of the dolly he pulled back on it, letting the statue, lean back against him.

Cindy got hold of the other side of the dolly and together they started to pull it to the doorway, leading out to the garden. As they were pulling it out, the weight of it got them off balance and caught Cindy's hand in between the doorway and the dolly, smashing the blood out of three fingers. James upon seeing this asked,

"Oh! honey, are you all right?"

Not wanting to say anything to him, because she knew he would undoubtable want to stop and she wanted that thing out of the house. She answered saying, "I'm fine."

And continued to pull the dolly.

Blood dripping from her fingers running down the side of the statue. Finally, they manage to get it, outside the doorway, onto the landing leading down to the garden. James stopped pulling the dolly looked around saying, "This is far enough honey, the gardener and his sons can place it wherever they want in the garden."

"As - long - as it's out of my house I am sure I don't care." Said Cindy helping James set it up right.

James upon seeing all the blood on the side of the statue and realizing that Cindy's hand was hurt more than she let on." Said "Cindy why didn't you tell me how bad that was?"

Then not being able to find anything else he pulled off his shirt and wrapped her hand. In – an - attempt to stop the bleeding.

James said "Hand me your camera and I'll take a couple of pictures of that room for you, so we can get out of here and take care of your hand."

Cindy handed him the camera. As they were walking back inside, he took a few more pictures of the stairwell and of that room. He then turned around and took a couple more pictures of the garden and the mountains in the distance. James asked, "Are you all right honey?"

"Yes, I'm fine, it's not that bad, really!" said Cindy as they walked back through the house and out the front door, letting it close and lock behind them. The driver was standing beside the limousine. He reached over and opened the door for the couple and as they were getting in James said. "Willie take us to the hotel please."

"Yes Sir." Said their driver as he closed the door behind them and headed back around to his side of the luxurious vehicle.

When they arrived at the hotel. The driver got out, walked to the back of the limousine and once again opened the door for the couple. James said. "Willie we've got to go upstairs and pack and then we need to head to the airport, we don't have that much, so it shouldn't take very long." "Could you wait he asked?"

"Yes Sir, I'll be waiting right here, take your time." Said the driver closing the door.

Then they walked into the lobby and over to the elevator going up to the room. When they got to the room Cindy went into the bathroom and ran warm water on her fingers. They had stopped bleeding, she told James,

"It really wasn't that bad, they were more pinched than anything else."

Cindy walked over to her bag because being a mother of two boys she always carried Band-Aids for that kind of thing. She bandaged up her fingers and started getting her things together. James also packed his bag and looked around the room one last time, making sure they were not leaving anything

Behind. He looked at his wife and asked her.

"Okay honey, are you ready?"

Cindy nodded her head yes. Handing her bag to him, as they walked out the door, letting it close and lock behind them, they went back downstairs to the lobby to turn in their room keys. The hotel clerk said. "Please if you would sign here Sir."

James signed their names and handed the hotel clerk their keys, the clerk said. "Thank you, sir. We do hope you have enjoyed your stay here with us and we do hope you will come again."

Cindy smiling at him said. "Oh yes" the rooms were magnificent and the food was absolutely wonderful."

"Well ma'am we are glad you enjoyed it and please do come again." Said the hotel clerk handing them a complimentary package which undoubtable had a few coupons and other various types of information. The couple walked out the front of the hotel. True to his word, the driver was standing beside the limousine. He reached over and opened the door for them. They got back into the limousine and headed to the airport.

CHAPTER 9

Back at the manor the statue, was still standing on the landing leading down to the garden with Cindy's blood all over the side of it. When suddenly, the blood absorbed into it and Margaret opened her eyes for the first time in over 100 years. She watched as the old gardener, Joe and his two sons, Carl and Sam, arrive coming back to finish moving her to the garden at Cindy's request. Joe upon seeing the statue standing outside asked out loud,

"Now how did that thing get out here?"

Then the three of them walked over, just looking at the statue, Joe headed out into the garden area to pick the perfect location to place her. The two boys began talking about Margaret. Sam, the younger of the two boys said. "What a beautiful woman she must have been, if the statue was created in her image."

"Yes, and look at that killer body." Said Carl reaching down and grabbing his crotch.

"She almost looks lifelike." Said Sam.

"Yes, she does." Said Carl. Running his hands all over her breasts, fondling them.

"What are you doing?! Stop that Carl," yelled Sam.

"Why she just made of stone." Said Carl still fondling her breasts.

"Still, it's not right, don't do stuff like that to her." Said Sam in discussed with his brother. "What's wrong little brother, haven't you ever touched a woman's breasts before? Will hear is your chance." Said Carl grabbing them once again.

"You know the thing is to have such a beautiful body and face, people say she was an evil bitch. She treated people like dirt, she thought she was better than everybody around her." Said Carl, looking disgustedly at the image of Margaret's face.

"Well, I got something for you, Miss high and mighty." Said Carl as he unzipped his pants and peed, all over her laughing.

"What are you doing? Yelled Sam stop that right now, or I'm going to tell dad."

"Whatever, what's gotten into you, I told you, she is just stone." Said Carl zipping up his pants.

"I don't care, you still should have respect." Said Sam, looking shamefully at his brother.

"Respect...! For this evil bitch, you don't know what the hell you're talking about." Said Carl, looking at Margaret's image, face-to-face.

"Anyway, whatever happened to her?" Asked Sam.

"People say someone killed her, but no one really knows, the body was never found. She just disappeared one night. But it couldn't have happened to a more deserving evil bitch." Said Carl fondling her breasts once again.

"Carl I'm serious. If you don't stop doing that. I'm going to tell dad." Said Sam

"Tell dad-what!!?" Asked Joe the old gardener as he came from the back of the estate to where the boys were.

Sam looked at his brother Carl and then at his dad, saying, "Nothing. He just picks on me." Said Sam, dropping his head.

"You stop picking on your brother, both of you get over here help me move this thing, I found the perfect spot for it." Said the old man.

The old man and his youngest son Sam, leaned the statue back against them. Sam got hold of the loose part of the strap that was dragging on the ground behind them. Carl walked along beside the statue steadying it while they pulled it down into the garden area and faced it toward the mountains.

Joe and Sam were standing behind the statue holding the dolly, Carl, being the strongest of the three leaned the statue toward him. The old man, warned his sons, saying, "All right boys, this thing is very heavy, so be careful."

"I got it Dad, pull the dolly out." Said Carl, balancing the heavy statue toward him.

The old man grabbed the dolly, while Sam took hold of the strap and released it from around the statue. As the old gardener pulled the dolly out from underneath it, Margaret shifted all her weight onto Carl.

Being unable to hold her, he fell backwards and she fell on top of him, crushing the boy to the ground. Joe and Sam rushed over and rolled the heavy statue off the young boy, but it was too late. The impact of all that weight crushed his chest in.

Blood was puddling up in his eyes and gushing from his mouth, Joe grabbed his cell phone calling 911 for an ambulance. When it arrived, Sam was sitting on the ground, holding his brother's hand, trying to talk to him, the old gardener Joe was beside his self in worry.

The paramedics climbed out of the ambulance and rushed to the boys' side. They determined that he was bleeding internally, so they put him in the ambulance as fast as they could and rushed him to the hospital. The doctors did everything they could, but to no prevail. His injuries were too great and the boy died.

• • •

"Why didn't he listen to me?" "I told him to stop doing all those things to her, but he just would not listen to me, so she killed him." Said Sam, holding back the tears, over the loss of his brother.

"Who killed him?" "What are you talking about?" Asked Joe in grief.

"It was the statue dad, she killed him. He kept fondling her breasts and he peed on her, so she killed him." Said Sam shaking his head and repeating over and over to himself.

"Why didn't he listen to me?"

"No one killed him son, it was an accident, a horrible accident, you're just out of your head, not thinking clearly." Said Joe to his son.

CHAPTER 10

When James and Cindy arrived at the airport. They got their bags out of the limousine, James thanked Willie and handed him a tip saying, "We'll see you when we return."

The driver said. "It's been my pleasure sir. Have a safe trip back to Detroit?"

James and Cindy turned around and walked into the airport terminal. After standing in line for some time, they finally made it to the ticket counter. James said. "Good afternoon, I am James Parker, this is my wife Cindy Parker and we are supposed to have tickets reserved for us, heading to Detroit."

The man behind the ticket counter looking at his computer saying, "Yes sir," "Do you have some form of identification?" James and Cindy both presented their driver's license, to the man after carefully looking them over, the man said "OH! Yes, there you two are. Please sign here." Handing James a piece of paper. After James signed it, the man handed him their tickets.

James looking at Cindy saying, "We have a little while before we board the plane. Why don't you call Tracy and let her know we are on our way home and should be there in a couple of hours."

Cindy said. "That is a good idea, and I want to make sure that she has both boys there and ready to go. Because the last time that she and I talked, it sounded like Billy has a girlfriend and he could be with her, or one of his other friends. I just really want to go get them and go home James. I have missed them so much and I know that you have too."

"Yes, I have Cindy, but I don't want to just run in there and get them." "Don't you want to spend a little time with Tracy also?" ask James, with cornered in his voices.

"Of course, I do James, but we do need to talk with the boys, about what we are going to do. Remember, we are going to take them out of their school and away from their friends. I am sure that they are not going to like it." Said Cindy lowering her head.

"Well anyway honey, go-ahead and call her and let her know." Said James.

Cindy got her cell phone and dialed Tracy's number. It rang a couple of times when Tracy acer it saying, "Hello"

"Hey Trace, we are at the airport, about to live coming home, we should be there in about two hours or so I can't want to see you and the boys, I have missed you all so much." Said Cindy with excitement in her voices.
"We have missed you to honey, we'll be waited four you to arrive, have a safe trip home see you soon." Said Trace also filling excitement.
"Okay, we about to board the plane, love you, by for now." Said Cindy, hanging up the phone.

Then an announcement came across the intercom, in the airport terminal alerting them that their flight was about to leave.
James said. "Come on honey, we need to go." The couple grabbing their bags rushed to their gate to board their plane.

The flight was pretty much the same as before, in what seemed like just a few hours later, they were back in Detroit, at the airport. Cindy was bubbling over, with excitement all the way there. When they arrived, the couple went straight to the truck and headed over to Tracy's, excited to see her, the boys and tell them about their inheritance and the estate.

• • •

James said. "You should probably call and make sure they're home, she may have taken the boys somewhere."

"That's a good idea." Said Cindy while reaching for her phone and dialing Tracy's number.

It only rang a couple times and Tracy picked it up saying, "Hello"

"Hey Tracy, it's us, are you guys at home?"

"Yes sweetie, we're here, I told the boys you are on your way and they're anxious to see you."

"Yes, we're excited to see them as well and tell them about the estate have they been good?"

"Well know boys will be boys. But yes, all in all, they had been good. How far away are you guys?" Asked Tracy with excitement in her voice.

"We are just leaving the airport now, we should be there momentarily,"

"Okay we'll be waiting. You guys be careful." Said Tracy with even more excitement in her voice eager to see her friend and hear all about their trip.

"Okay Tracy, thank you, we'll see you in a few minutes." Said Cindy hanging up the phone. As she turned and looked at James saying, "Yes they're at home. She says the boys are excited to see us, but I have been thinking James. They've got friends here and it's really going to be upsetting for them. I mean to pull them out of their school and take them away from their friends. They are not going to be very happy about that." Said Cindy with concern in her voice.

"Families do this kind of thing all the time. After all, they are kids, they'll get over it." Said James with authority in his voice.

"I know James, but this is my fault and I don't want them to hate me for it." Said Cindy with even more concern.

"They're not going to hate you and after all, remember you're going to be able to give them things that they have only dreamed about,"

"You mean we can, don't you...?" "Both of us are going to be able to give them things. But I want them to love me for me, not just because I can buy them ever thing they could won't." Said Cindy, feeling even more concerned.

"They already love you honey, you are there Mother and they might be upset for a little while, but like I said they will get over it. After all, it's not like we can leave them here and move away." Said James trying to make her understand, as he was pulling into Tracy's driveway.

Tracy and both the boys came out of the house. The boys ran straight up to their mother and hugged her. As they begin to tell their parents about all the things they did with aunt Tracy while they were gone.

"You guys come on in. I know you must be tired after your flight and I want to hear about everything." Said Tracy overwhelmed with excitement.

The couple followed Tracy into the house. Cindy reached into her pocket to get her camera to show Tracy and the boys some of the photos that they took of the mansion and the grounds around it.
Tracy noticing that Cindy fingers were bandaged ask her,
"What happened to them?"

Cindy said. "There was a statue in the middle of a room on our estate. While James and I were removing it from the house I smashed them."
Tracy looked at her with confusion.
"It's a long story I will tell you about later, look at these beautiful photos of our mansion." Said Cindy as she started flipping through some of them in her camera. Showing, Tracy and the boys.
Although the boys seemed somewhat interested in the pictures at first. It wasn't long before they got bored with them.

James sitting in a chair getting very comfortable, watching in silence.
Tracy asked,
"When are you guys going to be moving up there?"
That's when Billy asked,
"What does she mean moving up there?" "You mean we are moving to North Carolina?" "I don't want to move the North Carolina, what about my school and my friends?" said Billy getting upset.
"Billy I'm sorry honey, but we have to move up there, I have to live in the Summerhill Manor to get my inheritance." Said Cindy trying to make him understand.
"I don't care about your old inheritance!! Why do we have to move? It's not fair." Said Billy stomping his foot.
"That will be enough of that young man, you're moving and that's

final! I don't want to hear another word about it." Said James pointing his finger at his son.

Billy looked at his dad with tears welling up in his eyes. Then he ran outside, without saying, another word.

Upon observing his brother's outburst of emotion. Michael asked, "What's wrong with Billy?"

"He hates me." Said Cindy. Lowering her head.

"No! He does not Cindy, he's just mad, he'll get over it. I told you when he gets moved he will make some new friends." Said James once again, expressing his authority.

Michael ran outside, after his brother. A few minutes later he came running back in. Saying,

"Yep. He hates you Mommy."

"Michael, don't say things like that," snapped James at him.

"But daddy that's what he said. I heard him." Said Michael not knowing any better and trying to explain himself.

"Michael honey, why don't you go outside and play with Billy." Said Tracy smiling at him.

"Okay said Michael running over to his mommy saying,

"I don't hate you Mommy. I love you all this much," he said holding his little arms out as far as he could, then hugging her.

Cindy hugged him back. Saying, "I love you too baby, now go play."

Then all three of them watch Michael as he ran outside to play with his brother.

"I knew it. He is going to hate me." Said Cindy with tears welling up in her eyes.

Tracy reached over and put her hand on her arm, saying, "Oh honey, he's not going to hate you. He might be mad for a little while, but he'll get over it, like James says when he gets moved he'll make some new friends. I wouldn't worry about it."

"That's what I have been trying to tell her. Maybe she'll listen to you." Said James getting upset.

Tracy, putting your hand to her mouth said. "Oh, you know what, I think I know what it is? He's met a girl in his science class, he talks about her all the time. All the boys think she's the prettiest girl in school and she likes him,"

"Oh, no James! His first love, now what am I going to do?" "He will really hate me now." Said Cindy dropping her head about to cry.

"Will what can we do Cindy?" "You've already signed the papers. So now we've got to live there. No!! That's enough, I don't want to hear another word about this. He is going to have to get over it. I'm sorry, but we can't live our lives to suit him. He's 11 years old, they'll be plenty of time for girls." Said James getting more and more upset so he walked outside.

Tracy looked at Cindy, with her head still down now shaking it and saying,
"He doesn't understand. I want so much for the boys to love me, I'm not their mother and I can never take her place, but like I said I want them to love me."

"Cindy honey, James is right, you need to do what is best for the boys. And you know what that is. You've got to get them out of this city and away from the gangs around here. And like James said you cannot live your life to just suit them. You must consider everyone involved. Now I know from what you tell me and from those beautiful pictures. that you all are going to have a wonderful life up there. think everything through and…," Tracy paused for a minute and then said

"You know there are only a few more weeks of school left and if you two would be willing and this is just a suggestion mind you, I could keep the boys here with me, till school is out that would give you all a chance to get settled in. like I said. in just a few more weeks' summer will be here and school will be over. Then I can bring the boys up to you, that way you will not have to come back and get them and I could see your beautiful place and spend some time with you guys." Said Tracy trying to help the situation.

"Oh Tracy! We couldn't ask you to do that and anyway I don't know if, James would even go for it, but thank you for offering." Said Cindy smiling at her.

"Like I said it is just a suggestion you've got a lot to do and if the boys were here with me, they wouldn't be underfoot, while you guys are getting settled and like I said. they can finish school,"

"You sure you wouldn't mind?" Asked Cindy really giving it some thought and wondering if it would be best for everyone involved.

"Of course, not, you know I love those boys almost like they were mine and I love both of you too. I don't want to see something like this come between you two, when I can help." Said Tracy trying to reassure her.

"Tracy I love you so much, you are closer to me than if you were my sister, all I can do is talk to James about it and see what he says." Said Cindy, trying to be optimistic about her question

"Okay you want me to go with you out to talk to him, maybe between the two of us, we can get him to understand?"

"No, I'll talk to him." Said Cindy as she got up and walked outside to find James.

He was sitting in his truck in the driveway with forehead down on the steering wheel when Cindy came walking up and asked him, "Can I talk to you?"

"Sure honey, what is it?" Asked James.

"I was talking to Tracy and she suggested that if we were willing, she could keep the boys until summer break. That would give us a chance to go get settled in and that way we wouldn't have to take the boys at a school. Then when summer break comes, she'll bring them up to us and spend a couple of days. But I told her I need to talk to you." Said Cindy eagerly waiting for a reply from her husband.

"We can't ask her to do something like that." Said James once again lowering his head to the steering wheel.

"She really wants to James, after all she lives alone and the boys are company for her." Said Cindy trying to plead her case.

James still hanging his head down, thought for a minute saying, "It would make things easier on everybody involved."

"Yes, honey I think it would. James, I don't want the boys to hate me because I take them out of school and make them move away from their friends." Said Cindy trying to make him understand how she was feeling.

"Well let's think about it a while. We got a week to make up our minds what we're going to do." Said James not wanting to make a quick decision.

"Okay honey, I'll tell Tracy that we are going to think about it, I'll get the boys So we can go home, we've got a lot of packing to do in only a week to do it in." Said Cindy while climbing out of the truck.

"Yes, we do and I need to call Mr. Carmichael and let him know we are moving. And what do you think about us having a backyard barbecue in a couple of days and inviting all our friends. I also would like to invite some of my customers and let them know they must find somebody else. But I do want them to know how much I appreciate working for them," James with remorse in his voice.

"That's a good idea honey and I was thinking maybe we'll have a yard sale and whatever we don't sell, we will give away." Said Cindy smiling at him.

"Only you will be worried about making money with millions of dollars in the bank." Said James shaking his head at his wife.

• • •

Cindy smiled at him. Turned around and walked back inside. A few minutes later both she and Tracy emerged from the house calling the boys,

"Billy, Michael, it's time to go, come hug your aunt Tracy and thank her for keeping you," yelled Cindy.

Michael came running around the house, up to Tracy and hugged her thanking her for letting him stay with her. Billy, came reluctantly around, still pouting, saying, "Thank you for keeping us." As he walked to the truck

Tracy asked, "OH, OS THAT'S, IT...! I don't even get a hug?"

James said to Billy, "Young man. Get over there hug her and thank her properly,"

Billy said "Yes Sir." As he reluctantly turned around and walked back over to Tracy and hugged her, saying, "Thank you for keeping us."

Tracy said. "You're very welcome, cheer up, things will work out you'll see."

Billy said. "No!! They won't, my life is ruined and it is not fair." As he turned around and walked back to the truck and climbed in.

Cindy looked at Tracy and smiled, shaking her head as she hugged her neck, saying,

"We'll talk to you later, in a couple of days were going to have a barbecue out back, you are going to come, aren't you?"

"Of course, I will, but I'll see you before that. I mean you are going to need some help packing, aren't you?"

Cindy said "Well yes, but you've done so much for us already. I hate to ask,"

"Nonsense, that's what friends are for sweetie, I'll see you in a little while." Said Tracy

"Okay we'll see you later then said Cindy as she walked over to the truck and climbed in?

James hollered out the window, saying, "See you later Tracy, thank you for everything."

Then they drove away, heading home.

On the way, there Cindy said. "We need to go by a liquor or grocery store and get some boxes."

James said. "There's a place up here on the right. Bob's all night liquor, I'll stop in there and see if he has any,"

Pulling into the liquor store parking lot. James said. "I'll be right back," As he got out and went inside.

A few minutes later, James came back saying,

"The man behind the counter said to go around back to the dumpster. We can have whatever boxes we find."

James pulled around back to the dumpster. There were boxes sticking out all over it and a whole big pile of them that were already broken down. James and Cindy, got out and started gathering up the boxes. James got the whole pile of broken down ones, and threw them in the back. They both climbed back in the truck. Cindy said. "Those are enough boxes to pack up everything we have."

"And then some." Said James cranking up the truck.

When they got home. The boys climbed out of the truck. Michael ran inside. Billy started to leave the yard. James hollered at him,

"Don't go very far we need to talk to you two in a while."

"I'm going to go down to Tyler's house." Said Billy, not even turning around as he broke into a

Run, heading to his best friend's house down the road. Cindy looked at James and asked,

"He still mad, isn't he?"

James walked past her heading into the house,

"Saying, he'll get over it."

Cindy stood there for a few minutes staring off into space. Then she followed James into the house. James walked into the kitchen and opened the refrigerator stood there for a minute, looking inside.

Cindy walked up behind him and asked, "What is it honey?"

James answered her, saying, "I am trying to find something to drink."

"Would you like me to make some tea?" Asked Cindy.

"Would you? I would really appreciate that honey." Said James shutting the refrigerator door. Cindy walked, across the kitchen and started getting a pot down to boil some tea bags."

James stood quietly in the corner of the kitchen, watching her and looking around.

"You know, I'm not even really sure what we're going to pack. I mean we don't need anything out of the kitchen were not taking any furniture, so what do we pack?" Asked James with confusion in his voice.

"Well honey, I guess we'll take our clothes, pictures off the walls, my what knots, things like that,"

"I'm going to go pack up all my hunting and fishing things and my tools. I guess we really need to sit down and talk about this and how we're going to move our thing Cindy." Said James getting more frustrated.

"James honey, there is no need to get upset we'll take what we need, whatever, we don't want to take will buy new. I'll tell you what, Tracy will be here in a little while. She and I will worry about packing, you pack whatever you like. Pack up your computer and all those hundreds of movies and videos that you got. We will take care of the rest after all, there's really no hurry. We've got a whole week. Nothing must be done right now, why don't you watch some TV and I'll make you something to eat to go with your tea. I think there's might be some turkey meat. How would you like me to make you a sandwich?" Asked Cindy trying to comfort her husband.

"Yes please, that sounds good, your right honey. I'm still a little bit overwhelmed by everything. Maybe I do need to sit down and relax for a while." Said James walking into the living room flipping through the stations on the TV, finally settling on, an old Western.

Then in a few minutes Cindy came walking into the living room carrying a big glass of tea with a sandwich and handed it to James.

James reached up and took it from her saying, thank you well, I guess you won't be doing this anymore."

"What do you mean by that?" Asked Cindy feeling confused.

"We will probably have a maid and a butler, someone like that to prepare our meals, for us you won't have to do it anymore." Said James taking a bite of his sandwich.

"I don't know what you mean, I'm still going to take care of my family, I won't have somebody doing that." Said Cindy, feeling hurt and confused.

"Why not honey, you don't have to, now we can pay somebody." Said James.

Not realizing he was hurting his wife's feelings and making her feel unappreciated.

"I might have someone help me clean and take care of the place, but they're not going to take care of my family. I'm still going to cook our meals and take care of you and the boys. I'm not going to be one of those rich snobs that has everybody waiting on them James!" said Cindy, feeling angry and hurt, as she started to walk away.

James reached out and grabbed her arm and stopped her saying,

"Oh honey, I didn't mean it like that. I was just saying, you don't have to if you don't want to, we can afford to have someone do those things, so we can spend more time together and do things together as a family.

Maybe you can get a hobby to take up a lot of your extra time, that you will undoubtedly have, and let someone else do all the cooking and cleaning that kind of thing, like they do on TV." Said James as he was making a poor attempt to explain his self.

"NO! I won't have that and I can't believe that you would think I would." Said Cindy pushing his hand away from her arm and walking back into the kitchen feeling hurt.

"Oh honey, don't be like that." Said James to his wife as she walked away.

Cindy, looking out the window, saw Tracy arriving as she pulled into the driveway.

Getting out of her car and walked up onto the porch knocking on the door. Cindy hollered

"Come in Tracy."

"Hey guys what is going on?" Asked Tracy noticing the look on Cindy's face.

Cindy looked at her, with a tear in the corner of her eye and lowered her head. Tracy walked closer to her and asked, "What's wrong?"

"James said something hurtful to me." Said Cindy. Looking at Tracy holding back the tears. "Really like what?" Asked Tracy concern for her friend.

"He thinks when we move up there that I'm going to hire a maid and a butler, someone to cook and clean, so I don't have to do it anymore." Said Cindy trying to explain.

"Okay I don't understand, what's wrong with that, I know I would." Said Tracy.

"I'm not going to have someone do all those things and take care of my family. I don't care how much money I have. I'm still a mother and a wife and I have a family to take care of." Said Cindy getting very upset that Tracy was taking his side.

"Cindy honey, I'm not saying, that you're not a mother and a wife, but, my God girl! You have the money to pay someone to help you with those things. You know what I would give to be where you are right now? You have two great boys, a husband that loves you and now all the money in the world a beautiful mansion and you're going to live on top of a gorgeous mountain. What do you have to be upset about? You should be on cloud nine and excited about the life, that is a head of you." Said Tracy. Obviously feeling jealous of her friend.

"You're right Tracy, but the thing is, I don't know how to act. I never had money I don't know how I'm supposed to be. I felt threatened that someone else will be taking care of my family and me. I don't want to be one of those rich snobs that thinks the world owes them a living. Because I got money, doesn't mean I must change, does it?" Asked Cindy getting very upset.

"No honey of course not, that doesn't mean you have to change you can still remain. Your lovable sweet self. It means you won't have any more worries, like I told you before you can travel. You can do things as a family. You can help out your friends, put your kids through college and enjoy your life." Said Tracy trying to make her understand.

"I guess you and James both the right, James says I can get a hobby but like what?"

"I don't know. Maybe you should try painting, or work in the yard you got a beautiful garden. The point is, you can do anything you want to honey and you could have anything you want. Have the life that dreams are made of,"

Cindy looked at her as Tracy took her hand in hers saying, "Now take your little self in there, kiss your husband. Tell him you love him and let's start packing."

Cindy walked back into the living room, turned sideways and set down in her husband's lap, put her arms around his neck, kissed him, saying, "James I'm sorry I love you and I can't wait to get our life started up there in that beautiful mansion."

James looked at her and said "I love you too Cindy. I think we both are a little overwhelmed. Eventually it will all sink in and maybe we can get back to a normal life."

Cindy looked at him saying, "Honey I don't think our lives are ever going to be normal again."

"You're probably right they're not. But together we'll make the best of it." Said James as he leaned forward and kissed his wife tenderly.

Cindy asked, "Do you need anything else," as she climbed out of his lap.

James said "Not right now, as he reached up and patted her butt, thank you for asking."

"Okay then Tracy is here and we're going to start packing." Said Cindy smiling at him.

"Okay honey, don't let me get in the way, I'm just going to sit here and watch some TV, try to unwind and relax."

"Okay if you need anything let me know." Said Cindy walking back into the kitchen with Tracy.

Tracy smiled at her saying, "There, now don't you feel better?"

"Yes, I do, thank you Trace." Said. Cindy smiling at her.

Tracy put her arms around Cindy saying, "Now let's get to that packing what all do you want to take?"

"Me and James, were talking about that, we're not sure what to take, we don't need anything out of the kitchen and we're not taking any furniture, so if you see anything you want, it's yours,"

Tracy looked around the room and then at her, asking "Okay then what are we supposed to pack,"

"Well I told James we'll take pictures off the wall. My watt knots and our clothes, that kind of thing." Said Cindy. Looking at Tracy.

"Let's take a box and go from room to room and start packing." Said Tracy, grabbing a box.

They went from room to room, packing one box after another and stacking them up, over by the doorway in the kitchen. They even made their way around in the living room working all around James, who had fell asleep in his chair watching TV. Till finally they begin to get hungry. Tracy said. "You called the boys in and I'll go get us something to eat. What sounds good to you?"

"Well, there is a place down the road that has some pretty good chicken and I think you get three side orders like corn, mashed potatoes and gravy coleslaw, macaroni and cheese, baked beans things like that," explained Cindy.

"Okay I'll go get us some chicken and a few side orders and I'll be right back." Said Tracy, grabbing her purse, walking toward the door.

Cindy said. "Hold on, let me give you some money."

"No this is my treat." Said Tracy." Heading out the door and letting it close behind her, she got in her car and backed out the driveway and headed down the road, to get them some dinner. Cindy picked up the phone and called down to Tyler's house Tyler's mom, Debra answered the phone saying, "Hello."

"Hi Debra this is Cindy Is Billy down there?"

"Oh, hi Cindy Yes, he and Tyler are playing in his room,"

"Please tell him to come home. It's dinnertime,"

"I'll send him write home and by the way, if you don't mind me saying, so Billy told us that, you're moving away. It's really going to be hard on the boys separating them. He said you all are moving up into the mountains."

"Yes, I inherited a place up there and the only way I get it is if we move there," explained Cindy,

"Well I must say me and Paul are going to be sorry to see you guys go and I know Tyler is really going to miss Billy,"

"Yes, I know and Billy's going to miss him to, but they can still be friends, Billy can come visit Tyler and he will be more than welcome to come see Billy anytime he like's." Said Cindy.

"Oh, yes and by the way, were going to be having a backyard barbecue in a couple days and I hope that you and Tyler a long with Paul can all come. We are just going to have a few friends get together and James is going to invite some of his customers. Basically, to tell everybody what we're doing and say goodbye, like I said we hope you guys can come." Said Cindy, waiting for a reply.

"Yes, we would like that. We can see you guys before you go. About what time will it be?" Asked Debra.

"Thursday, round 6:30, is about what time we will eat. But you guys can come over anytime you like," explained Cindy.

"Oh, that's great Paul should be home by then, I'll make my chicken casserole and bring it, we'll be looking forward to seeing you guys then Cindy, I'll send Billy home,"

"Thank you, tell Paul we said hey, have a good night." Said Cindy as she hung up the phone. Cindy turned around and James was standing behind asking,

"Who was that?"

"Debra and Paul Tyler's mom and dad. That is, it was Debra, I called to see if Billy was down there and asked her to send him home if he was, and I invited them over to the barbecue. I told her it would be Thursday round 6:30 when we ate, but they could come over anytime they like, is that all right honey?" Asked Cindy realizing that they had not even decided on what day they even going to have the barbecue, let alone the time.

James stretched and yawned saying, "Yes that be fine."

He looked around and asked where Tracy was?"

"She's gone to get us some chicken, I tried to give her some money, but she wouldn't take it. I'm really going to miss her James,"

"Yes, I know, you will it's understandable that you miss your friends and your life here, honey, it's all you've known for years now." Said James as he turned around went down the hall toward the bathroom.

Cindy just set down at the kitchen table fiddling with her phone. In a few minutes, Billy came in the door. Cindy said.

"Go get washed up, your aunt Tracy is gone to get us something to eat."

"I'm not hungry." Said Billy, shuffling his feet, sitting on the arm of the couch.

"You do what I told you, get in there and get cleaned up." Said Cindy in a stern voice.

Billy said "Yes ma'am." And went stomping off, passing his dad in the hallway. James looked at him as he was walking by. Coming back to the kitchen and asked

"What's wrong with him?"

"He hates me James! I knew he would." Said Cindy with tears in her eyes.

"Honey we've been through this, he does not hate you, he's just mad, he'll get over it,"

Cindy looked up and out the window because she heard a vehicle driving in the driveway. It was Tracy returning from the store. James said to his wife,

"I'll go give her a hand,"

As James went out on the porch he hollered
"You need any help?"

Tracy said. walking around to the passenger side of her car.

"No, I've got it."

James walked out into the yard and said "Here, let me get that." reaching for the packages

"I got some sandwich meat and a couple gallons of tea and a gallon of milk, some cereal for the boys. I didn't think you guys had left much to eat, when you went on your trip.

"You didn't have to do all this Tracy." Said James. Feeling embarrassed.

"I wanted to." Said Tracy. Closing her car door with a couple other packages in her arms.

James and Tracy walked up to the porch and into the house. James looked at Cindy saying, "Look at all of this."

Cindy said. "Tracy, you shouldn't have done that.

"Honey like I told James, I didn't think you guys had much to eat, you are going to be here a few more days. Besides, I wanted to," explained Tracy as she walked by Cindy and set the groceries down on the table.

Cindy reached over and hugged her neck, saying, "Thank you."

Then the two of them began to put the groceries away.

Tracy asked "Where are the boys?"

"Michael's playing a video game in his room and Billy just went stomping off down the hall. He's still mad at me." Said Cindy dropping her head.

"It'll be all right, he'll get over it. By the way, have you two gave any more thought to my offer?" Asked Tracy eagerly awaiting a reply from either one or both.

Cindy looked over at James for confirmation. As he said "Tracy, we can't ask you to do that for us."

"Nonsense. I love you guys and I want to help. The boys will be quite all right. I'll take good care of them." Said Tracy trying to convince them.

"That goes without question, we know that you will, but it's a lot to ask." Said James.

"Look! You know that I love those boys. You've got your hands full, with everything you must do here and I'm going to help as much as I can, plus you got more to do when you get back up there. So please let me help you guys," pleaded Tracy with tears welling up in her eyes.

Cindy walked over and put her arms around her saying, "Of course we'll let you help us your part of our family. Don't you ever forget that right James?"

"Exactly you're a big part of our family and always will be and we want you to come up there and spend as much time with us, as you can spare." Said James looking directly at Tracy.

"Oh, you guys can count on it." Said Tracy. Wiping the tear from her eye and hugging Cindy.

"Now we better eat this chicken before it gets any colder." Said Tracy unwrapping her packages.

James walked into the hall and yelled!

"Boys get in here, it's time to eat."

Michael came running down the hall and into the kitchen, he pulled out a chair and sat down.

Billy came down the hall reluctantly and asked, "Why do I have to eat dad? My stomach is bothering me and I don't feel good."

"It's just your nerves you'll be all right, you haven't eaten anything, now get in there." Said James with a Stern voice.

Tracy and Cindy both started dealing out the dinner, fixing the boys a plate,

Michael hollered, "I want a leg and some macaroni and cheese."

Cindy walked over and set a plate with a little bit of everything on it in front of him saying,

"Eat whatever you want,"

Tracy made Billy, a plate and set it down in front of him Cindy said.

"Make yourself one and sit down, I'll get mine and James."

Tracy made herself a plate turned around and joined the boys, sitting across from them. James walked into the kitchen and poured himself a glass of tea. Came over and sat down at the table, Cindy handed him his plate and made herself one, they all sat comfortably enjoying their dinner Cindy was playing airplane, with his dinner. To get him to eat. Billy just sat quietly staring at his still upset.

Cindy noticed that Billy was taking a fork and just pushing his food around on his plate. Obviously deep in thought. Looking over at James, clearing her throat. She tilted her head, casting her eyes at the boy. James looked at him and then at Tracy. She smiled and squinted her eyes wrinkling her nose. James said. "Boy's me and your mom and your aunt Tracy have been talking. We have decided that, when we go back, were going to leave you two here with your aunt Tracy to finish school."

Billy looked up from his plate at his dad hanging on his every word. As James continued saying, "In the summer, when school is out she's going to bring you up there for us."

"Really, you mean I don't have to go now and I can finish school with my friends?" Asked Billy with excitement in his voice, as he jumped up from the table and ran over and hugged his dad.

"Don't thank me, thank your mom and your aunt Tracy, this is their idea."

Billy ran over and hugged his mom and said "Thank you."

Cindy said. "You're welcome, but you boys better be good and don't give your aunt Tracy any trouble at all."

"Oh, I won't." Said Billy as he turned around and grabbed Tracy and hugged her, saying, "Thank you, thank you."

Tracy said. "See I told you things would work out."

Michael now was just sitting quietly at the table, looking down at his food. James asked,

"Now what's wrong with you?"

Michael looked up at his dad said. "I want to go with you and mommy."

Cindy got up from her chair, walked over and knelt down beside him and said "Honey, you'll be coming up there soon enough, but it's important that you finish school and before you know it. Summer will be here and you, Billy and aunt Tracy, all are going to come up there and will have a wonderful time I promise."

Michael put his arms around his mom and hugged her, asking,

"You promise?"

"Yes baby, I promise." Said Cindy hugging him tightly and rocking him back and forth in her arms

"Now go thank your aunt Tracy, for letting you stay with her."

Michael got up and ran over and climbed into Tracy's lap, kissing and thanking her. Tracy wrapped her arms tightly around him, rocking him back and forth, saying, "You are so very welcome sweetie now go finish eating before your dinner gets cold."

Michael climbed down off Tracy and ran back to his plate. The boys were giggling and playing across the table, as happy as they could be. James just watched them shaking his head, looking at his family. Tracy and Cindy grasped each other's hands on the table and squeezed them smiling at each other. The rest of the evening. The boys played, Tracy and Cindy continued packing and James returned to the living room to watch TV.

Till finally it was bed time for the boys. They hugged Tracy's neck, thanking her once again and ran off to bed. Tracy said. "Yes, I guess I better be going too, it is getting late and I've got to work, but I'll be back over soon as I get off."

As she stood up and started toward the door. With Cindy, close behind her. Cindy hugged her and said "Thank you again."

"You're very welcome sweetie, I'll see you tomorrow," Tracy said as she walked out the door heading out to her car. She got into it, cranked it up and headed home, Cindy locked the door and went back into the living room climbing into her husband's lap. Who was sleeping in his chair as she touched him? He woke up. Cindy looked at him saying, "Thank you honey, you made the boys and Tracy very happy, I love you so much James and I would be so lost without you."

"I love you too baby." Said James as he kissed his wife tenderly.

Then James just stood up with her still in his arms and carried her back to the bedroom. He very gently laid her down on the bed and began kissing her all over. Working his way down her neck as he raised her up off the bed toward him. He started undoing her bra.

Cindy said. "Wait a minute, no, honey, I'm hot and sweaty I've been packing all day, I need to take a shower."

But James just ignored her, as though he didn't hear and continued to undo her bra, reaching around rubbing his hand across her flat tummy and cupping one of her breasts in it. Cindy struggled to get away. But James held her tightly until finally she snapped at him saying, "No! I told you I'm nasty and I want to take a shower."

She pulled away and climbed off the bed, she scurried into the bathroom and slammed the door. James laid there for a minute, staring up at the ceiling. Then he slid over to the side of the bed and sat there thinking about the way she acted. He stood up, pulled off all his clothes and climbed into the bed watching for her to return as he waited his eyelids got heavier and heavier. Finally, he fell asleep. A few minutes later, Cindy emerged from the bathroom, hair still wet from the shower, but her body was dry. She climbed into the bed beside her husband and reached over and touched his side asking,

"Honey are you awake?"

James snapped at her, saying, "I am now. What do you want?"

Cindy said. "I thought you wanted to...?" And paused for a minute.

Once again, James snapped at her asking, "What! You thought I wanted to do what?"

"Oh nothing..., good night honey." Said Cindy as she rolled onto her side facing away from her husband. James laid his head back down mumbling something to himself.

Cindy asked. "What did you say?"

James raised his head up, looking at her and said "I'm dirty, I haven't had a shower."

And laid his head back down on the pillow. Cindy understood, why he was so angry, but she still did not think it was warranted, because all she wanted to do was be fresh and clean for him. For the first time since they have been together the couple went to bed angry at each other and it really, truly bothered Cindy.

But they both allow that to happen. The next morning when they woke up. Neither one of them really did not say a whole lot to each other as they went about their day. James, seem to want to keep to himself, as he rummaged through his things, trying to the side on what to take and what to leave behind. Cindy, went about the grueling task of packing up the boy's things. All except what they were going to take too Tracy's. The day seemed to drag out, till finally it was time for Tracy. Cindy was glad to see her when she arrived, she grabbed her and put her arms around her neck, saying, "I am so glad to see you."

Tracy asked, "What's wrong?"

"It's James. He's acting so strangely, is as if he doesn't want to be around me at all." Said Cindy, looking like she was about to cry.

"What happened?" Asked Tracy with confusion in her voice.

"Last night after you left. I went in and got into his lap and thanked him for letting the boys stay with you. I told him how much I loved him,"

"What did he say?" Asked Tracy still not understanding.

"He told me how much he loves me too. Then he picked me up and carried me back to the bedroom and laid me down on the bed, wanting to make love, but I stopped him." Said Cindy, dropping her head, looking down at the floor.

"Why did you do that?" Asked Tracy now really feeling confused.

"Because we had been packing all day, I was hot and sweaty and I hadn't had a shower yet. I felt nasty and couldn't really get into it. But he didn't care, he kept on trying till finally I snapped at him pulling away, running into the bathroom. After my shower, I came out and he was already in the bed and asleep. I woke him up thinking that he might still want to make love, but he only snapped back at me. He was very angry." Said Cindy with tears in her eyes.

"I'm sure everything will be all right. He's just going through a lot. You both are. But all he's ever known is taking care of you and the boys. I think he's feeling like you won't need him anymore. That's probably making him feel like less of a man." Said Tracy trying to help her understand.

"But of course, I need him. I love him I would be lost without him and I told him"

"Well sweetie give him some time. I'm sure everything will work out when he gets through this big move. When you get back up there and settle in. Things should return to normal. Maybe even better, because you'll be able to spend a lot more time together,"

"That's one of the things that is worrying me. What if, because we do spend more time together, we come to realize that we're not so compatible after all? And we start to get on each other's nerves. What do we do then?"

"That's not going to happen. You can't even think like that. Like I said. you both are under a lot of pressure. Now let's stop thinking about this and get some more packing done,"

"You're right, Tracy I know that James loves me. We had a good time when we were up there. Thank you Trace, you know, I don't know what I would do if I didn't have you to talk to." Said Cindy as she grabbed a box.

"Right there's something else to consider. Sweetie, you do have me to talk to and James has no one. All the things that he's going through in his mind about the move, his inability to take care of you, he is keeping everything bottled up inside because he doesn't have anyone to talk to about it." Said Tracy trying to help her to understand a little bit about what her husband might be going through.

"You're right, I didn't consider that, James really doesn't have any friends. He pretty much well keeps to himself and I don't guess he feels like he can talk to me about any of it. I wish that he could, but I bet he doesn't think he can." Said Cindy as she was starting to understand.

"Like I said just be a little bit patient. When this is all over, you'll see he'll get back to his lovable self and you guys will all have a happy life together."

"will you Tracy, like we said. you are a very big part of our family." Said Cindy trying to include her.

Just then James came walking in the house and asking

"Hey you two, what do you think? A 12 x 6 trailer, you think I can get all those boxes in something like that?"

Cindy looked at Tracy and asked "What you think?"

"I think so James, they should all fit," answered Tracy.

"That's what I was thinking too." Said James as he turned around and walked back out.

Tracy looked at Cindy smiled saying, "See, he's not mad honey, he's just got a lot on his mind. He's obviously trying to set up some way to move your things,"

Cindy. Closing another full box and taping it shot said. "You're right, I just need to be a little bit more sensitive to his feelings,"

Finally, she and Tracy packed the last box. Other than what they were going to need was left out. They both sat down in a chair at the kitchen table, feeling exhausted. Tracy said. "Well, I've got a few things I need to take care of. I'm going to head home, but I'll see you tomorrow. I'm going to come and help prepare things for the barbecue if that's all right, honey,

"Of course, Tracy, thank you again." Said Cindy, hugging her neck and walking her to the door,

"Tell the boys, I love them and I'll see them tomorrow." Said Tracy heading out to get in her car in drive home.

As she walked down the steps. She passed James standing in the yard. Tracy raised her foot and kicked him in the butt. Saying, "I'll see you tomorrow, try to behave yourself."

James smiled at her and said "Good night trouble. We'll see you tomorrow."

Tracy climbed into her car and started to back out of the yard. Looking out her windshield, she waved goodbye to James and drove home.

James walked inside and stood beside Cindy at the kitchen table. Cindy looked at him, asking,

"Are you still mad at me?"

James said "No you've got to forgive me. I just got a lot on my mind and a lot to do."

"I know James and I'm sorry honey. Is there anything I can do to help?"

"Now I'll take care of it. At least I can still do that." Said James looking down at the floor.

"James I am sorry. I just don't tell you enough, you do so much for me and I don't know what I would do if you didn't. I couldn't do all this by myself. I wouldn't have a clue where to even start. But you do and I love you for that." Said Cindy as she got up and walked over to him and hugged his neck.

James just stood there, as she hugged him. Then said. with a condescending voice

"Yes right! You don't give yourself enough credit. You can do a lot more than you think you can, I'm beginning to realize you don't really need me as much as you think,"

"Honey your wrong. I need you more than you know. What do I got to do to convince you James? I would be lost without you,"

"Well anyway, I have ordered a U-Haul trailer for Friday. It is 12 feet long by 6 feet wide that should be plenty of room for all our boxes, close and things. I'll pull it behind my truck and we'll just drive back up there. I know it's a long way, but I don't see where we have a choice. That's the only way we can move all our things and I can take my truck with all my tools,"

"You see, that's what I'm talking about James, I wouldn't know how to go about that,"

"All you got to do is pick up the phone and order it Cindy, anybody can do that." Said James, interrupting her getting upset.

"James Please, there is no need to get upset. I'm just trying to show you how much I do need you, what do I have to do?" Asked Cindy about to cry.

James said "I'm sorry Cindy. I don't know what's wrong with me. I feel so lost inside. I need..., He paused for a minute and said "Never mind, I'll be all right, don't worry about it."

"James No, please honey talk to me. It's all right." Said Cindy. Reaching down and taking his hand in hers.

James pulled his hand away saying, "No I can't...," then he paused for a minute. Turned and started to walk away, got a few feet away stopped, turned back around and looked at her, saying, "I told you, it'll be all right." Then he turned back around and walked down the Hall heading to the bathroom.

Cindy laid her head down on the table, feeling like she was losing him. She started to cry because she didn't know what to do. As she set back in her chair with a tear running down her cheek. She started thinking. *"I wish I never decided to do this, why can't we just be happy like we were?"*

Then she said out loud,

"God, what am I going to do? I don't want to lose him."

The boys came running in the house from outside, they saw their mom, sitting at the table crying. Both walked over to her.

Billy asked "What's wrong mom?"

"I'm just thinking about everything and how much I'm going to miss your aunt Tracy and everybody," answered Cindy wiping the tears from her eyes.

"Then don't go." Said Billy, not understanding.

"I wish it was that simple honey, but it's not. I have already signed all the documents, we have to go now." Said Cindy trying to make them understand.

James came walking in the kitchen saying, "I'm getting kind of hungry. What do you guys think about us ordering a pizza?"

The boys started jumping up and down saying, "Yay - yay - yay, can we, can we?" Asked both boys at the same time, looking at their daddy. "It's up to your mom."

The boys ran over to her. Billy asked "Can we Mom?"

Then Michael asked, "Oh can we, mommy." "Can we?" "I love pizza."

"It's all right with me. What would you like on it the usual?" Asked Cindy, reaching for the phone and looking at James.

"That sounds good honey, don't you think so?" Asked James as he smiled at her.

Cindy looked at him with confusion, thinking, *"He is acting so strangely, one minute, it seems like he's mad at me and the next minute it seems like he is not, I just don't understand."*

Still, not wanting to question his change in attitude toward her. She just smiled at him and ordered the pizza. When she hung up the phone.

She told the boys to,

"Go wash your hands and get ready, the pizza is on the way."

Cindy looked at James and said "It will be about 30 minutes and they said it'll be $18."

James walked over closer to her, reached in his back pocket and got his wallet and took out $25 and handed it to her smiling. Then he turned around walked back into the living room and got back in his chair in front of the TV. Cindy just stood there, holding the money in her hand not knowing what to say about the way he was acting. She walked over and sat down at the kitchen table. A few minutes later the two boys came down the hall and sat down. Cindy got up and got them a paper plate and a glass of tea with some napkins and waited for the pizza to arrive. Several minutes passed by, till finally there was a knock at the door. Cindy walked over and opened it their pizza had arrived, she paid the man with a tip. Thanking him. Turned around and close the door behind her. The boys were all excited sitting at the table. As she walked over with the pizza sitting it down opening the box. She put a piece of pizza on the plate for both. Then she put a piece on another paper plate for herself and hollered into James saying, "The pizza is here. Are you going to come in here to eat with us, or do you want me to bring it to you?"

But there was no reply from him. she hollered once again asking, "James honey, did you hear me?"

James hollered back saying, "I would really like to watch my show. Could you bring me a piece and a glass of tea please?"

Cindy put a piece of pizza on a paper plate and poured him a big glass of tea and took it in there for him. Handing it to him, James never taking his eyes off the TV reached for it, saying, "Thank you."

He took the piece of pizza in his hand took a bite of it and set it back down on the plate. Cindy just stood there beside his chair, looking down at him. Once again James not taking his eyes off the TV. Took a second bite of his pizza. Cindy stepped backwards, turned around and walked back into the kitchen with the boys and set back down at the table. The boys were cutting up and playing Cindy was deep in thought about what was wrong with James. Michael finishing eating a piece of pizza getting to the crust. He threw it over at Billy, hitting him in the head Billy looked at Cindy saying, "Mom. Tell him to stop."

Cindy looked over it Michael saying, "Michael, you stop that right now. Don't play with your food."

"Yes ma'am." Said Michael.

The boys continue to eat, finally finishing up asked, "If they could go out and play for a little while before it got dark."

Cindy agreed, telling them,

"For a little while, but don't go far. Then you come in and take a bath and get ready for bed"

The boys got up and ran outside. Cindy gathered up the paper plates and threw them in the garbage can, putting the remainder of the pizza on the counter. She walked back over and sat down at the table watching James from the kitchen thinking. *"She really didn't know what was wrong or how to fix the problem. She felt alone and confused. She never realized that this would affect him so strangely because if she had known, she never would've agreed to it. She just wanted things to get back to the way there were. But she also knew that it couldn't."*

CHAPTER 11

Cindy finally decided it was time to try to talk to James. she got up and walked into the living room. He was flipping through the stations trying to find something on. Cindy asked,

"James, can I talk to you please?"

James while continuing to flip through the stations asked, "What is it, did the boys do something to upset you?"

"No, it's you." Said Cindy looking at him.

James looked over at her, still holding the remote control out in front of him pointing at the TV asked, "Me! What the hell have I done to you?"

"Please James, put the TV control down and talk to me," pleaded Cindy.

"Fine, okay, there the TV is off. Now what are you talking about?" Asked James looking at her.

Cindy kneeled down beside his chair saying, "I don't know what's wrong James, your acting so strangely, I thought we had this all worked out. I thought that this is what we both wanted."

"Oh yeah, sure Cindy. I want to give up my business, I want to go up there and live off you for the rest of my life." Said James angrily.

"Please don't get upset, talk to me," pleaded Cindy once again.

James said. lowering his head, looking at the floor

"What is there to talk about other than what I just told you?"

"You're not telling me anything. You're not going to be living off me, don't you understand. That place and the money. All of it is as much yours as it is mine honey. We can make a better life for ourselves and the boys, we can go anywhere we want, we can have anything we want to gather." Said Cindy trying to make him understand.

"James did not say a word. He just looked down at the floor listening to her.

"I love you and the boys, you all are my life. Don't you understand, I feel like you're pushing me away and it hurts me more than I can tell you. I need you right now more than I ever have." Said Cindy about to cry.

James still looking at the floor said. "Cindy, anything that you need from this point on in your life. You can pay somebody to do it for you. What do you really need me for?"

"My God! James, you're my husband and I love you. Not a day goes by that I don't think about you. I laid their filling so alone last night next to you. Wanting you to say something, or just hold me in your arms. I'm sorry I never should've pulled away from you, I just felt so nasty because I was hot and sweaty from packing all day. I wanted to be fresh and clean for you." Said Cindy trying to explain herself.

James didn't say a word as he continued looking down at the floor and listening to her.

"I know you don't think I need you and that you are feeling like you're not going to be taking care of me anymore. But my God! Honey. What I need most from you now, is for you to hold me and tell me you love me, let me know I can count on you to help me through all of this. You know when we got married we promised that we would always be there for each other and that we were going to grow old and gray together, until death do us part. Well, I meant that and no amount of money in this world is ever going to change that for me." Said Cindy with tears in her eyes.

James still looking down at the floor said. "Well, all I wanted to do was hold you and make love to you. A spur of the moment thing. I felt the need to be with you and show you how much I love you. I didn't care if you were dirty or not, that did not matter. But what did and does, matter is the way that you pulled away from me. That hurt me, it made me feel like you didn't want me. I'm already feeling like you don't need me anymore Cindy and last night I felt like you didn't want me anymore either." Said James finally looking up at her.

"But honey your wrong, I told you I felt nasty and dirty. I could smell myself. I was hot and sweaty and stinky. I didn't realize how much you needed to be with me at that moment. Had I have known that it would have been different. I would've ever pulled away from you. I love you James. With all my heart." Said Cindy. Reaching out for him.

James got up out of his chair, reach down and helped her from the floor looked at her and said "I love you too Cindy. I'm just...," James paused for a minute.

Cindy said "It's all right, honey talk to me. Please tell me how you feel."

James said. "I just feel..., He paused again and said I mean I'm feeling..., it's hard to describe it. I feel like less of a man. I feel like I'm not doing what I'm supposed to do, like taking care of you and provide for you a home and all the things that go along with it. Yes, you're my wife and I am supposed to do all those things and more. If I'm any kind of a man." Said James starting to get upset again.

"Honey, you're more man than I have ever known and you're still going to take care and provide for me, it's going to be a lot of work to take care of that mansion and the grounds around it. I thought that we, you and I was going to do it to gather the place is huge. You saw it. Can you imagine what it'll take to take care of that place? I can't and you think I'm not going to need you. Like I said. I need you more now and I'm going to need you more than I ever have before to help me with all of that. But it's not just for me. James it's for us. I wish I could get that through your thick head. It is going to take the whole family to take care of that place." Said Cindy trying to make him understand.

•••

"Well, you are right about one thing, it is a huge place and if we don't pay somebody to take care of the ground and the maintenance around it, it will take a lot of work just to maintain it. But to be quite honest with you Cindy, I thought you would just pay to have it done."

"No honey, I want us to do it, you and I together,"

"Well okay then. I guess I better take all my tools and I'll probably need to buy some new ones." Said James getting a little bit excited. Finally starting to understand.

"Honey, we can buy all the tools you could ever want and I like to get you a new truck." Said Cindy smiling at him.

"No, I'll keep my old girl. She's been a good track. We have been through a lot together. She and I and she's never let me down. I can't just abandon her,"

"Will why don't you keep her for work and buy yourself a brand-new one. To drive around town and go places like that?"

"I don't know. Maybe later, but right now I'm just worrying about getting us and all our things back up there,"

Cindy could see that he was finally starting to feel better with the situation, so she turned her attention to the boys who were still outside. It was starting to get dark and it was time to call them in because she knew that they would not come in on their own.

"Well, I better call the boys in and have them get their bath and get ready for bed." Said Cindy as she turned around and started to walk away.

James grabbed her arm and stopped her saying,

"Thank you, baby, you made me feel a lot better."

"Good I'm glad, you really had me worried, I love you and I want to do whatever it takes to have a happy family." Said Cindy, hugging his neck and kissing him.

Cindy turned around and walked to the back door, calling the boys telling them

"It's time to come in and take their bath."

The boys came running to the porch from out of the dark. First Michael and then Billy, ran up on the porch, passed their mom and into the house. Cindy turned around, closed and locked the door behind her, she watched the two of them chasing each other down the hall fighting over who is going to take the first bath.

"I'm taking my bath first." Said Michael shoving Billy into the wall, running into the bathroom and slamming the door.

Billy said. "Mom tell him to let me take my bath first, he takes forever."

Cindy walked down the hall and knocked on the door saying, "Michael let your brother get his bath first."

"Mommy, why does he get to go first?" Asked Michael opening the door and folding his arms, stomping his foot.

"Because I said so, now young man, get in there with your daddy until he takes his bath." Commanded Cindy.

"Yes ma'am." Said Michael running down the hall, sticking out his tongue at his brother.

Billy punched him in the arm as he passed him in the hall, Michael grabbed his arm like he was in pain and acting like he was going to cry. He ran over to Cindy saying,

"Billy hit me and broke my arm."

Cindy picked him up in her arms and yelled at Billy asking, "Why did you hit your brother in the arm?"

"Because he stuck his tongue out at me," answered Billy

"I did not. He's lying." Said Michael and the two boys started arguing back and forth.

"That's enough, what are you two fighting about now?" Asked James as he came walking in there to find out what it was all about. "What's going on?" He asked angrily looking at the two boys.

"I was going to get my bath and Michael stuck his tongue out at me so I hit him in the arm." Said Billy knowing better than to lie to his dad.

James walked over and looked at Michael's arm. Saying, "I think you might live,"

Then he walked over and smacked Billy in the back of his head with his hand saying, "You stop hitting your brother and get in there and get your bath."

"Yes Sir." Said Billy. Glaring at Michael.

Michael smiled deviously and stuck his tongue out again at his brother.

But this time James saw him do it, so he said. "And you, young man. Stop messing with your brother and keep that tongue in your mouth if you want to keep it." Said James walking back into the living room, returning to his chair.

"Yes Sir." Said Michael as he dropped his head turned around and put his arms around Cindy's neck, laying his head on her shoulder. Cindy rocked Michael in her arms and asked him,

"Why must you two fight all the time?"

"He starts it." Said Michael. Looking at his mama.

"Its things like this that make me worry about leaving you two, with your aunt Tracy, you guys don't fight like this around her, do you?" Asked Cindy, looking at her youngest son.

"I don't mommy, but Billy does, he fights all the time with me." Said Michael, trying to be as convincing as he could.

"Oh, but you don't have anything to do with that, do you?" said Cindy, putting her forehead to his looking directly into his little eyes.

"No mommy. I try to be good all the time. But he hits me and bites me and he calls me names and gets on my nerves." Said Michael, looking at his mama.

A few minutes later the bathroom door open and Billy came walking down the hall to the kitchen, Cindy told Michael to "Go take your bath baby."

He climbed down off her lap and ran down the hall past his brother. Billy continued into the kitchen, went to the refrigerator to get something to drink. Cindy asked.

"Billy why must you fight with Michael all the time?"

"Mom, you have seen it. He starts it, shoves me into the wall sticks his tongue out at me."

"I was telling him its things like that, makes me worry about leaving you too, with your aunt Tracy." Said Cindy, looking at him.

"Well, why don't you take him with you?" Asked Billy. While pouring himself something to drink.

"Young man, because he needs to go to school the same as you. No if I'm going to take one of you. I'm going to take both of you." Said Cindy angrily.

"Oh man, he's going to make you change your mind, isn't he?" Asked Billy getting upset.

"No, he's not making me think about changing my mind. You both are. I'm not going to have you acting like that with your aunt Tracy, the first time I talked to her and she tells me and she will tell me make no mistake about it, that you guys have been acting like that fighting, hitting each other, anything like that and I'll take you out of school and make you come up there with me so fast your head will spin, do we understand each other?" Asked Cindy angrily.

"Yes, ma'am but what if it's all him, what if he does…, I mean, why should I get in trouble for something he did?" Asked Billy.

"Billy, it takes two to fight, like tonight. he stuck his tongue out at you, it didn't mean you had to hit him, ignore him. He is just a little boy and he's your brother. Now, come give me a hug and go to bed,"

Billy walked over and hugged Cindy saying, "Please mom. Don't let him ruin this for me."

"Like I said. honey, he's not ruining anything, but don't you ruin it for yourself." Said Cindy, hugging his neck.

"Yes ma'am, good night mom, I love you." Said Billy, hugging her back.

"Good night son. I love you too, now go tell your father good night,"

Billy walked into the living room and looked at James. He was sound asleep in his chair, so he whispered to Cindy saying, "He's sleeping." and turned around and went down the hall to his room.

A few minutes later, the bathroom door swung open against the wall and here come the holy terror Michael, his clothes were sticking to his body, because he didn't fully get dried off and his hair was still wet. He ran into the kitchen to hug Cindy's neck and tell her good night asking her,

"Will you tuck me in mommy?"

"Of course, I will Baby, but first we've got to at least get your hair dry." Said Cindy as she was picking him up and carrying him back to the bathroom to dry his head.

She put him down on the floor and grabbed a towel. Kneeling beside him, she dried his hair. When she got done, stood back up, reach down and picked him back up in her arms and started to his room. Michael said. "I want to kiss daddy good night."

"Well when Billy went to tell him good night. He was asleep in his chair. But we'll see if he's still asleep." Said Cindy, carrying her little troublemaker in her arms.

When they got to the living room. Sure enough, James was still asleep in his chair. But Michael wanted to lean down and kiss him anyway. Cindy leaned him over so that he could kiss his daddy, which of course woke James. He reached up and started tickling Michael sides. He was squirming in kicking his legs, which almost made Cindy drop him. Michael said. "Good night daddy, I love you,"

James replied by saying, "I love you too Good night, you little monster, sleep tight."

• • •

"Don't let the bedbugs bite." Said Michael talking to his daddy as Cindy was carrying him down the hall over her shoulder. When she got to his room. She tossed them on the bed. He stood up and bounced up and down on the bed a couple of times, then he fell back down on the bed, landing on his back. Cindy grabbed him, pulling him to her, she started tickling him on his side. Michael was giggling and squirming, trying to get away from her. Till she finally said. "Okay munchkin, get under the covers time to go to sleep." Said Cindy as she rolled down the blanket and sat down on the side of the bed. Michael climbed under them headfirst spun around and came back out playing. Cindy tucked the covers around him, kissed him, saying, "I love you, you little monster."

Michael curled his fingers showed his teeth and growled at her playing monster. Cindy said

"Go to sleep, you little mess," and kissed him a second time on the forehead.

As Cindy got up and started to leave his room. Michael said. "Mommy, I will do my best not to let Billy fight with me."

"That would be good baby," Cindy said as she walked out of his room, closing the door and headed back into the living room with James.

CHAPTER 12

James just watched her as she came up the hall with a sad look on her face. Cindy looked up at him saying, "I sure am going to miss my boys."

"I know honey me too, but it won't be long and they'll be up there and we will be ready for them." Said James as he walked over and wrapped his arms around her.

"Are you about ready for bed? Or do you need to take a shower?" Asked James snickering at her.

"Very funny." Said Cindy. Reaching out to hit him in the arm.

"Although actually I do need to take a shower. You want to take one with me?" Asked Cindy smiling at him wiggling her butt, walking down the hall to the bathroom.

"Thought you'd never ask." Said James pulling off his shirt, following right behind her.

When they got to the bathroom, Cindy reached past the curtain, to turn on the hot and cold water both, adjusting the temperature, letting it run for a few minutes. She pulled off all her clothes and climbed in the shower waiting for James to join her.

James said. "I'll be right with you. I have to pee." As he lifted the lid on the toilet, he did so. Then, without thinking he flushed it. Cindy, underneath the hot water screamed and jumped out of the shower standing there, dripping on the floor, looking disgustedly at James saying, "You did that on purpose!"

James pulling off the rest of his clothes giggling at her." Said "No honey, I'm sorry. I promise you, I did not!"

Cindy was standing there half scalded, dripping on the floor looking at him. As he was giggling at her, waiting for the toilet to fill back up. Finally, it did. she climbed back into the shower, with James right behind her. He grabbed a wash rag, soaped it up and began rubbing it all over her little body. Cindy turned around, looked at him saying, "I still think you did that on purpose, but honey that does feel good."

James was rubbing the wash rag across her shoulders and the back of her neck. Pulling her close to him feeling her tight little muscular body pressed up against him. Her body was slippery to the touch from the soap. He began rubbing her body next to his. The soap ran down between the two of them. Between the warm water and her tight little body pressed up against him, it noticeably excited him. She looked down at his muscle, which was reacting to her touch. James pulled his beautiful little wife closer to him and began kissing her. Letting the warm water hit both on top of their heads, running through their hair and down the lengths of their bodies. He took his hand and begin rubbing her body all over from the back of her neck to her heart-shaped little butt. Cindy ran her hands down. His muscular back, letting her fingers. Follow the crease of each individual muscle. James turned her around, facing away from him, she put her arms on the wall as he raised one of her legs slightly off the bottom of the tub. He very gently and tenderly accepted the invitation from her body. They made love in one position, then the other, fulfilling each one's desires and wishes. Expressing all the love that they both had for each other in multiple ways. Until finally feeling the climax of satisfaction, that ultimately follows when two people become one with all that they must offer each other.

They both climbed out of the shower, drying off, slipping on their night clothes, and then made their way to the bedroom. Removing their clothes and climbed under the covers. They held each other for the rest of the night until the next morning.

Cindy was awoken by all the noise coming from the kitchen. The boys were obviously up making themselves some breakfast. She slipped out from underneath James's arm and put on her night clothes and a robe. Heading out to see what they had gotten in to. To her surprise, they were dressed for school and sitting at the table eating a bowl of cereal that Tracy had bought for them. Upon seeing her. Michael got up from the table ran over and hugged her. Saying, "Good morning mommy."

Cindy hugged him back saying, "Good morning baby."

Michael ran back over and continued to eat his cereal. Billy Asked, "What they were going to do today?"

Cindy answered, saying, "We're going to have a barbecue, I've invited Tyler and his mom and dad. They said they were going to come. Your dad has invited some of his clients and aunt Tracy is coming over later to help out."

"That sounds cool." Said Billy getting up from the table, replacing the milk in the refrigerator. Billy walked over and hugged Cindy saying, "Well, I better get to the bus stop. I'll see you later mom."

As he turned around, grabbed his book bag, slipping it over one shoulder, then the other and headed out the door.

"You finish eating your cereal, I'll get dressed so I can take you to school." Said Cindy. Looking at Michael as she turned around and started down the hall heading back to her room to get dressed.

Cindy slipped on her bra, a pair of old jeans and an oversized T-shirt. Walked over and leaned down and kissed James. Then she started to leave the room. As she did. James asked, "Where are you going honey?"

"I'm just going to run Michael to school. I'll be right back." Answered Cindy walking back over and kissing him one more time.

"Okay, honey, be careful." James said as he laid his head back down on the pillow, feeling very comfortable and not wanting to get up yet. Cindy started out the door, she stopped, turned around and asked

"Honey, what all do I need to pick up for our barbecue? And I need some money." Said Cindy as she was walking back into the room.

James rolled over and looked at her for a minute, then he slid his legs off the side of the bed, sitting there, he stretched, yawned then stood to his feet, walking across the room and getting his pants. He took his wallet out. Opened it and handed Cindy $150. Saying,

"I guess pick up some hot dogs, hamburgers, cheese, buns for the both, oh yes and some kind of salad. I'm going to tell everybody they can bring a dish of something if they would like. But they don't have to. Al get some soft drinks, potato chips. You know, honey stuff like that. You want me to come with you?" Asked James reluctantly slipping on his jeans.

"No that's not necessary. You've got to get out the barbecue grill and clean it up. I can handle it." Said Cindy kissing him once more. Then heading out the room and down the hall, where Michael was patiently waiting. She looked at him and smiled, noticing he had placed his bowl in the sink and was sitting on the couch with his shoes on but untied. Cindy walked over. Kneeling in front of him to tie his shoes, saying, "That's my big man all ready to go to school!"

• • •

Michael looked at his mommy with pride from what she had said to him and watched her as she playfully showed him how to tie his shoes, saying,

"You have two little fish's, this little fishy swam into a circle, that little fish swam through the circle. Then both little fishy swam apart, then this little fishing made another circle, but this time that little fish swam around the circle, making his own circle and swam through it, then they both tried to swim away with the two circles came together and caught the two little fishes. There you go, your shoe is tied." Said Cindy playfully, now you try."

Michael tried several times, until finely the two little fishes were caught and his shoe was tied. He giggled in pride, hugging his mommy because he had tied his own shoe.

Cindy grabbed the truck keys as they both headed out the door, taking Michael to school.

As they drove Michael asked question after question about the mansion and the people in the mountains up there. Cindy did her best to answer his questions and keep her mind on the road at the same time, till finally saying, "Don't worry honey, you'll get to see all that for yourself soon enough. All I can really tell you baby it is beautiful up there. There's woods and trees and animals and we have in the beautiful garden. Maybe you can help mommy plant new flowers in the garden. I'll even let you plant some of your very own and we will call it, Michael's flower garden!" said Cindy as she was trying to get him to feel more excited about coming up there.

And she did, the more she talked about it, the more excited Michael became until finally saying,

"I wish I could come with you now mommy." Said Michael bubbling over with excitement.

"I know baby, but it's very important that both you and Billy get to finish school, it won't be long." Said Cindy as she pulled up in front of the daycare/pre-school that Michael had been attending.

She put the truck in park and shut it off, saying, "Come on my little man, I'll take you to your class."

Cindy got out and walked around to his side of the truck, unbuckled his seat belt, taking him by the hand they walked together into the school.

CHAPTER 13

James got his phone and started calling people to invite them to the barbecue, like he had told Cindy, he told them they could bring a dish, but explaining they did not have to, only if they wanted to. Then James called Mr. Gilmore and invited him and his wife, Mr. Gilmore agreed that they would be there around six James then called Mr. Carmichael the landlord. His phone rang a couple of times and finally, Mr. Carmichael answered the phone saying, "Hello"

"Mr. Carmichael. This is James."

"Yes. James what can I do for you?"

Well, Sir, my wife has inherited a large estate, in North Carolina, per the will, she does not get the estate in less she lives in a mansion that goes along with it, so we're going to have to move up there."

"Well congratulations James, it could not have happened to a more deserving couple, I'm sorry to see you go but, very happy for you both!"

"When are you all leaving?"

"That's something we would like to talk to you more about Sir, I'm hoping you and your wife can come to a barbecue that we're having tonight around 6:30,"

"I don't see why not; would you like us to bring anything?"

"I'm telling people they can bring a dish of some kind. If they like, but they don't have to,"

"James we're looking forward to it."

"Thank you, Sir, we'll see you then. Goodbye,"

After James finished calling and inviting all the people he intended to. He got dressed and went outside to get out the barbecue grill and clean it up for the night's event, looking it over. He thought,

"It is not too dirty this shouldn't take long at all."

After about an hour of cleaning the grill thoroughly, he pulled it up onto the deck and placed it in one of the corners. Then he put together a makeshift table constructed of several concrete blocks stacked on top of one another and a piece of plywood, he had left over from one of his jobs, Then James walked into the house and got one of Cindy's good sheets out of the linen closet, spreading it across the plywood, then he went into the kitchen and found Cindy and Tracy had left two whole stacks on paper. Left over from last year's barbecue. He placed them along with his cooking utensils, ketchup, mustard, salt and pepper in a whole stack of napkins out on his homemade table, leaving plenty of room for other dishes that someone may or not bring with them. James stood back and admiring what he had done said to himself

"Now what's wrong with that?"

He looked down at his watch, it was only 9:00 in the morning and so he went inside, trying to find something to eat for his breakfast. As he did. He looked out the window and saw Cindy come driving up in the driveway, so he walked out to his truck to help her bring in the groceries. Cindy said.

"I think I got everything were going to need."

"I'm sure you did honey, you didn't happen to get something for breakfast, did you?"

"As a matter of fact, I did. I got some eggs, turkey bacon, bread and I also got you a jug of orange juice." Said Cindy, feeling quite pleased with herself.

"Thank you honey, I'm very hungry." Said James. Following her into the house, carrying some of the bags of groceries.

"Let me put some of this stuff away and I'll make us some breakfast." Said Cindy smiling at him, putting the bags down on the table.

James started looking through the bags and helping her put stuff away. Each time they would come across an item for the barbecue. He set it aside. Finally finishing unpacking the groceries.

He looked at all the items that she had gotten saying, "Honey, it looks like you got everything and even a few things I didn't ask for. You did well." Said James, hugging his pretty little wife.

"Well, out of curiosity I checked that account and Mr. Wilcox had indeed place the money in it for us. here's your $150 back honey, we have plenty of money. Now, for whatever we need and I came across a few things. I thought that might go well with the barbecue. Plus, I got a couple stats of paper cups and three different kinds of soft drinks because

I wasn't sure what people would like and we still have plenty of tea." Said Cindy with pride.

"I see that sweetie. Like I said. you did well." Said James, as he patted her on her butt.

"Oh by the way honey, the table and everything looks great, I think we'll have plenty of room for everything. Even if someone does bring something with them." Said Cindy as she was walking out on the deck with James.

"Now why don't you go watch TV, I'll make us some breakfast." Said Cindy hugging his neck and kissing him.

"Do you need some help?" Asked James. Still holding her in his arms, looking down at her.

"No, I've got it, you go relax, you get to do a lot of cooking tonight." Said Cindy as she turned around walking to the counter and giggling at him.

James reached out and popped her on the butt saying, "Hey, don't think you're going to get off that easily you're going to help out too."

Then he turned around and walked back into the living room, got in his chair, turned on the TV and started flipping through the stations trying to find something to watch, waiting for his breakfast.

When Cindy finished making it. She called James saying, "Honey, its ready, come and wash your hands. Let's eat before it gets cold."

James came in the kitchen. Walked over to the sink and washed his hands, sat down at the table with her. They had a nice breakfast together. James got up, leaned over and kissed his wife very tenderly thanking her for breakfast.

• • •

As he started to walk back into the living room the phone rang. James picked it up, saying, "Hello,"

"Mr. Parker, this is Marcus Wilcox,"

"Good morning Mr. Wilcox, what can I do for you Sir?"

"I'm sorry to inform you, but there has been an accident out at the mansion."

"What?!" "What happened?" Asked James. Looking over at Cindy.

Cindy could see the tragic look on James's face, so she asked very quietly,

"What is it honey?"

"Mr. Wilcox said "The gardener and his two sons were moving that statue out into the garden, at your wife's request and I don't really know all the details, but from what I understand the strap broke or something and the statue fell on one of his sons killing him."

"Oh, my God!" said James sitting down at the table with even more of a tragic look on his face.

Cindy was about to lose her mind, wanting to know what was going on she asked again.

"James what is it honey?"

But James just held his hand up at her not saying, a word. Because he couldn't tell her what was going on and listen to all the details from Mr. Wilcox as he said. "Although it was an accident, it did happen on your estate, so it was my duty to inform you and of course I'm taking care of all of the arrangements for the boy and his burial services. I feel that is the least we can do for them and I thought that you and your wife might permit me to make some sort of small donation to the family."

"Yes Sir, but of course, matter of fact, we would like to make a large donation to them. Let me talk this over with my Cindy and I'll call you back and please give our condolences to the family."

"I'll do that, I am sorry to be calling you with this news, but I knew you would want to know and it is my job." Said Mr. Wilcox with remorse in his voice.

"Oh but of course, sir, thank you very much and like I said. let me discuss this with Cindy, about the amount and we'll call you back."

"Mr. Parker, I'll be in my office. The rest of the day,"

"Thank you again sir. Goodbye.

Cindy not being able to stand it any longer. Asked, "James what is it?"

"One of the gardener's sons was killed trying to move that statue, off the landing down into the garden, it somehow fell on him or something."

"Oh, my God! James is there anything we can do?"

"Mr. Wilcox is taking care of all the funeral arrangements and we are helping the family out as much as we can, because it did happen on our estate. He felt that we would want that."

"But of course, James, we want to help out any way we can. Don't we?"

"Yes of course we would Cindy and He also asked, do we want to donate to the family? I told him yes, we would, but I would need to discuss the amount with you."

"How much do you think honey?" Asked Cindy? Looking at James.

"Cindy, they just lost their son. No amount of money, we give them, can never replace him, but I think it should be the largest donation that we can make. We're talking about a human life."

"I understand. James what are you thinking?"

"I think we should at least offer them $1 million, Cindy, Mr. Wilcox can take care of all of the financial arrangements for us. It would help the family out considerably."

"Yes, honey I think so too. My God! James, it makes you look at how short life really is."

"Yes, it does." Said James calling Mr. Wilcox back to tell him that they want to donate to the family to help out."

It rang only a couple of times and Mary, Mr. Wilcox's secretary answered, saying,

"Hello, Mr. Wilcox office. How can I help you?"

"Yes ma'am, this is James Parker, would it be possible for me to speak to Mr. Wilcox?"

The secretary said. "Hold please."

"Hello Mr. Parker. What did you guys decide?"

Well Sir, I spoke to Cindy. And we would like to donate $1 million to the family. Can you take care of all the legal and financial documents for us?"

"But of course, James, if I can call you by your first name and let me just say that's admirable of you both."

"Thank you, Sir, and yes, please do so, Mr. Wilcox like I said. we went to help out as much as we can."

"I'll take care of all the arrangements and please call me Marcus. Do you want the family to know, who you guys are and what you've done for them? Or do you want to remain anonymous?"

"Well I don't know Sir, what do you Think...? We should do?"

"James, you and Cindy, are going to donate $1 million to the family even though it was an accident. No fault of yours or no legal obligation. I think that the family should know the kind of people you two are, to agree to give such a generous gift."

"Okay then yes Sir, you can tell them and like I said. please if you would give our condolences and let us know if we can help out in any other way."

"I'll do that James and God bless you and your wife, Good bye for now."

James hung up the phone, standing there looking down at the floor, trying to imagine what that father must be going through to lose one of the sons. Cindy walked over and put her arms around his neck as though she knew what he was thinking and they just held each other for a minute.

James looked at Cindy and sighed saying, "I can't imagine what that man must be going through. If I was the loose one of my boys. I would..."

"I know James, I can't even begin to think about it." Said Cindy. Interrupting him and lowering her head, because she couldn't even bear to hear him say the words.

"Will hopefully the money will help them out a little. But like I said. it can't ever replace their son. Still, perhaps that can help somewhat." Said James. Knowing that if something like that had ever happened to him. That no amount of money could ever end his pain and suffering over the loss of his son. But al still feeling that they need to do something for the family.

"Yes, I know honey and I feel somewhat responsible. I mean, if I hadn't wanted them to move that statue. It would never have happened." Said Cindy, feeling overwhelmed with guilt.

"You can't blame yourself honey, how could have we known something like that was going to happen. I wanted that thing out, of the middle of the house myself." Said James trying to comfort his wife.

"Well maybe if we were there, we could have helped somehow I don't know. James, I feel so guilty almost as though I killed the boy myself." Said Cindy still riddled with guilt.

"Cindy, it's nobody's fault. It was just a horrible, tragic accident." Said James as he was trying to comfort his wife even further and perhaps his self a little bit as well.

The rest of the day, they pretty much will have kept to their selves. James went about packing some more of his things and doing one little thing after another, to prepare for the barbecue later that evening. Cindy cleaned in the house. Most of the shelves were empty and bare. she wiped them and the walls down, where the pictures had hung, with the warm soapy rag. Trying to stay busy and not think about the tragic accident that had occurred at her estate. Until finally it was time for the boys to come in from school.

Cindy grabbed the truck keys, saying, to James,

"I'll be back in a little while, I'm going to get Michael. As she kissed him. Going out the house, Cindy got in the truck and drove away. Shortly after that, Billy came in, having gotten off the bus. Upon seeing him. James felt the overwhelming desire to hug his son and tell him he loved him. Billy was quite confused about the way his father was acting, but didn't say anything he just hugged him back. Saying, "I love you too dad."

James asked him, "Do you have any homework?"

Billy answered him, saying, "No Sir."

Then they both just stood silently. Neither one of them, knowing what to say to each other, until finally, Billy broke the silence by saying, "Well, I'm going to go outside and play."

James said. "Okay, but be careful and don't go far. Remember, we're having a barbecue tonight."

"Yes Sir." Said Billy. Happy to be removing himself from such an uncomfortable situation.

As Billy was running out the house. James could hear him and Michael already fighting about something. A few minutes later, both Cindy and Michael, came in the house. Michael ran over to his dad handing him some artwork that he did in class today. James said. "That's really good. Give it to mommy and when we get up there, we'll be sure and hang it on the refrigerator."

Michael ran over to his mommy. Handing her the artwork saying, "I'm going to go outside and play with Billy."

"Okay, but you try not to fight about everything and I have already told Billy. Now I'm telling you, don't go very far." Said James. With authority in his voice.

CHAPTER 14

Cindy looked out the kitchen window. Because she heard a car drive up. It was Tracy coming to help prepare some of the dishes they were going to have for the barbecue and when Tracy walked in the house. Upon seeing Cindy, she could tell right away something was wrong. she took Cindy to the side and inquired about what was troubling her. Cindy told her about the death of the young boy at the estate and how it happened. She could not believe her ears saying, "How tragic that must be for the father."

"I know that's what James said too. All I could think about was, I can't imagine what it would be like if that would've been one of my boys." Said Cindy.

"I know, that would even devastate me." Said Tracy lowering her head.

"I told James. It makes you really look at life and realize just how short it can be." Said Cindy   "Yes it does," agreed Tracy. Walking back out the door. Cindy chasing after her asking where are you going?"

"I've got a few things out here in my car. Want to come give me a hand?" said Tracy. Smiling at her. Cindy asked, "What have you done now?" following behind her.

When they got out to the car the back seat was full of groceries Tracy open the door and started handing bags to Cindy. As she asked "What are you doing?"

"I just got a few things to help out with the barbecue." Said Tracy

Cindy said. shaking her head,

"A few things, looks like you bought out the store,"

Tracy said "No but I know you guys didn't have very much."

"Honey Tracy, you shouldn't have done this, that lawyer Mr. Wilcox placed the money in the account so we have plenty of money. I'm going to pay you for all of this." Said Cindy, feeling embarrassed.

As they both walked back to the house with their arms loaded down with groceries. James met them up on the porch,

"Asking what are you two doing?"

"Go out there and look in her car James." Said Cindy. Tilting her head toward it.

James walked out to Tracy's car. There were still several bags of groceries. He turned around and looked at both

"Asking what is all of this?

Tracy, answered him saying, "Well I didn't think you guys had that much for the barbecue."

"Remind me to whip her butt." Said James grabbing the rest of the groceries out of her car and shoving the door shut with his foot.

Tracy and Cindy, walked into the kitchen and sat the groceries down, on the table. Then the both, started unloading their packages. Tracy got hot dogs and some of those frozen hamburgers already made up. all James had to do was grill them and she also bought stuff to make a salad and a few things for the kids.

"What are we going to do with all this Tracy? You know, we are leaving tomorrow." Said James as he was coming in the house.

"Well I thought whatever doesn't, get eaten tonight, I will just take back home with me, for the boys," answered Tracy trying to explain herself. "Actually, that's a good idea." Replied James

Tracy pushed out her bottom lip pouting and asked, "Does that mean I'm not going to get my butt whipping," James just smiled, shaking his head at her and walked outside to fire up the grill.

Cindy opened one bag that had several plastic containers with lids asking,

"What are these for?"

"Oh, that's just what we can put the leftovers in tonight and I'm sure there will be some," answered Tracy taking one of them.

"And we can also place the food in them, after it's been cooked like this." Said Tracy as she spread napkins across the bottom.

Cindy took a platter and started opening packs of hot dogs and placing them on it. Tracy did the same with the already prepared frozen hamburgers, straight out of the box. The girls carried them out to James at the grill. It was already hot enough, so he began placing them on it so that they could slowly be cooked. From time to time he checked on the grill rolling the hot dogs around and flipping the hamburgers.

As James cooked, the guests started arriving, first Tyler and his parents, from down the road. Then Mr. Gilmore and his wife Tina, showed up shortly after that, Mr. Carmichael along with his wife, Beatrice. Throughout the night a few other customers that James had worked for also showed up. Some stayed for quite a while, others only for a short time. The night went well, everyone laughed and had a good time. Many of them were bragging on James, saying, how much they appreciated him and how sorry they were to see him go. But they were all happy for both James and Cindy.

The last of the guests were leaving, thanking both Cindy and James for an enjoyable evening, wishing them luck and a happy life. Till finally all that remained behind were Mr. Carmichael and his wife Beatrice. James, Cindy and Tracy were entertaining them in the living room and the boys were playing outside. Then Mr. Carmichael said. "Now that we've got you by yourselves,

We would like to discuss some things with you."

"Sure, Mr. Carmichael, what's on your mind?" Asked James sitting next to Cindy.

"While talking to you earlier this morning, you indicated to me on the phone that you are not taking any of your furniture or appliances."

"No Sir, we're not going to need anything like that." Said James interrupting him.

"James please. Hear me out. We would like to return your rent to you plus your deposit because you just payed it and you are not going to be here and you are leaving these items behind." Said Mr. Carmichael getting out his wallet.

"Well Sir, we thank you, but that's not really necessary." Said James looking at Cindy, feeling a little embarrassed.

"Please both my wife and I would like to do it for you. Although we're sorry to see you guys go we couldn't be happier for you two." Said Mr. Carmichael handing James the money.

"Will sir, we really do thank you and let me say how much I appreciate the two of you working with us and being so understanding throughout the years." Said James taking the money and shaking Mr. Carmichael's hand. Because although they obviously did not need the money, James knew that if he did not take it, it would just embarrass the couple.

"You're quite welcome James my wife and I both could tell you two were good people and everybody needs a helping hand from time to time in this world." Said Mr. Carmichael as he and his wife stood up, hugging the both, like parents. As Beatrice was hugging Cindy, she said. "You two be sure and stay in touch with us, let us know how you're doing from time to time."

Cindy agreed, saying, "You can count on it, and you two must take a little time and come up to see our place in the mountains."

Beatrice turned to her husband, asking "We would love that, wouldn't we honey?"

Mr. Carmichael, nodded his head, saying, "Yes once you guys get settled in, let us know and we'll come for a visit and once again we wish you both all the happiness in the world!"

Then Beatrice said. "It's getting late honey, we need to get home and you need to take your medicine."

"Yes dear, we're leaving right now." Said Mr. Carmichael as James and Cindy walked them to the car. Telling them goodbye once more and thanking them, watching as they drove away.

Cindy and Tracy both pondered about the grueling task, of cleaning up and placing all the leftover food in those containers that Tracy had purchased. She commented saying, "See I knew it. I've known you all for many years now and we've had several functions like this and I know James always cooks more than what anybody could ever eat."

"You're right, as usual Tracy. Well, I'm glad we got to do this because it will be quite some time before we are able to do it again." Said Cindy. Looking at Tracy with tears welling up in her eyes.

"You'll see honey, that it won't be long before, Summer will be here and will be together again, it's for just a little while." Said Tracy, putting her arms around her, trying to give comfort.

But at last it was more than both could bear and they both started crying, holding each other saying, how much they are going to miss each other.

James walked in the room and asked, "What's all the fuss about?"

Tracy reached for him and pulled him to them, saying, "Come here your big lug I'm going to miss you too."

They all three hugged each other. Obviously already feeling the loss, till finally Tracy said. "Well I better get this food home and let you guys get some sleep. You've got a long drive tomorrow. But before I go, now what we're doing is. You two are leaving in the morning, after you send the boys to school, right? And I pick them up?"

"Only Michael. He gets out about 2 o'clock and Billy will ride the bus. He would just get off, over by your house. Instead of coming all the way here." Said Cindy as she was trying to confirm their plan.

"I got it, you guys be careful and call and let us know you're all right and drive safely." Said Tracy hugging the two of them, one last time.

Then she walked over to the table, picked up her containers and they watched as she walked out the door heading to her car to drive home.

Cindy wiped the tear from the corner of her eye turned and looked at James saying, "My God! James I'm going to miss her so much!"

"I know, she kind of grows on you, but we'll see her soon enough, along with our boys, like she said the time will pass quickly." Said James trying to comfort his wife.

Then routinely they got the two boys ready for bed and then themselves. But this night, they laid in the bed, holding each other thinking of what was ahead of them. James asked her,

"Are you frightened?"

"Maybe a little. I think it is more the excitement of venturing into the unknown." Said Cindy. Looking deep into his eyes.

"I know what you mean. It's going to be a long night and a long day tomorrow." Said James as he was pulling his wife as close as he could, tenderly kissing her and urging her to try to get some sleep.

Cindy turned on her side, lying in his arms and did after some time finally fall asleep. James laid there, watching her sleep. Going over in his mind the task ahead, until he also finally fell fast asleep.

The next morning the couple woke early, so that they could together properly, tell both the boys goodbye and get them off to school. Billy hugged both his mom and dad saying, I love you and I'll see you both this summer and darted out the door to catch the bus. Michael hugged his mommy saying,

"I love you mommy and you better be good and don't fight with daddy or give him any trouble."

Cindy said. "I won't. You, come here, my little munchkin." As she hugged his neck. She almost squeezed him in half. Michael hollered,

"You're killing me to death."

James literally having to pull him out of her arms, saying, "He's turning blue honey," and then he kissed her saying, "I'll be right back. After I drop him off at school. I'm going to get the trailer."

"Okay honey." Said Cindy holding back the tears, so that Michael would not see her cry.

But as soon as they got out of sight. Cindy began crying uncontrollably as she finished packing the few little things that they had left out. She felt like her heart was breaking and it was almost more than she could bear. A couple hours passed and she began to wonder, where James was. With no number to call or any other way that she could get in touch with him. All she could do was bear it and wait for him to arrive. Finally, she saw his truck coming down the road and she watched as he backed the trailer

Right up to the deck. James got out of the truck, saying, "It took forever for them to give me this trailer. The lady could not find anywhere in the computer, where I had reserved it. After some time, she finally did find my paperwork and then the traffic was a bitch. All the way here, I am so glad to be getting out of this damnable city."

As Cindy was helping James open the back of the trailer. He could tell she'd been crying so he said to her tenderly.

"I wish there were some way I could make this easier for you. I hate seeing you all upset like this."

"I'll be alright as soon we get on the road." Said Cindy as she started helping James carry the boxes out, placing them in the trailer. Cindy carried them out one by one, stacking them on the back of the trailer. James strategically and carefully stacked each one. Trying his best to make them as secure as possible for the long journey ahead of them.

Till finally they had all the boxes loaded into the trailer along with everything else they were going to take. Which consists of some of James tools that were too large to place in the back of his truck. He also had two large toolboxes from out of the garage. James and Cindy placed them against all the boxes and put a ratchet strap across the trailer securing the whole load, then they both walked back into the house. Going from room to room to verify that they were not leaving anything behind.

Once they were both confident that they had everything, they climbed into the truck and headed down the road leading to one of the major main highways that would ultimately take them up to North Carolina and to what was to be their new home,

CHAPTER 15

Finally arriving at the double iron gates, marking the beginning of their new life in a new place and ending a trip on the highway that neither one of them expected to take so long. James punched in the code and opened the double gates, then continued to the mansion. James looking over at Cindy saying, "I am utterly exhausted from that long drive. What do you say we try to get a good night's sleep and start unpacking tomorrow?"

Cindy agreed, saying, "I know I'm tired too. I'm sure we can find a bed somewhere in which to spend the night."

The couple unlocked the door and ventured into the mansion, James reached for a light switch. To his surprise the power was on, and the more switches he engaged, more light flooded the rooms.

They made their way to the staircase and started climbing it, looking for a room with a bed in it. It didn't take long, the first door they came to was open. There was a huge bed, inviting the couple to spend the night.

James being so exhausted from the long drive, slipped right into it. Having no trouble getting comfortable and falling asleep. Cindy, on the other hand, noticed that there was an eerie quiet throughout the mansion. That was disturbed by an occasional creaking sound, as the wind was whistling through the halls. She began to see figures peering back at her from out of the dark, frightened she reached over and woke James saying,

"There's something in the room with us. It's watching me from over there in the dark."

James raised his head and looked toward the dark corner that she was pointing at. Not seeing anything. He tried to dismiss it by telling her.

"It's a new place and it's just your imagination getting the better of you. Then he urged her to get some sleep. James laid his head back down, and in no time at all was deep in another slumber. Cindy just could not shake the feeling that something was watching her from the dark, making her hair stand up on the back of her neck. From time to time, she could see it moving over in the corner and it truly did scare her. Then suddenly, she was feeling the urge to use the bathroom and there was no way she was going alone! she woke James once again, saying, "Honey. Honey."

"What is it now?" Asked James. Not really awake yet.

Cindy said softly, "I have to pee."

"Then go pee." Said James raising up and looking at her.

"Would you go with me?" It's dark and I don't want to go alone." Said Cindy obviously feeling frightened.

"Oh honey, you'll be alright. I'm tired and need to get some sleep." Said James really - not wanting to get up just to take her to the bathroom.

"Please James, come with me, I'm scared?" pleaded Cindy tightly grabbing his arm.

"My God Cindy! come on, let's go so we can get some sleep." Said James, pulling away from her as he reluctantly climbed out of the bed, putting on his slippers, because the floor was cold.

"Thank you honey." Said Cindy tightly grabbing his arm once again, walking slowly with him down the hall to find the bathroom.

When they got to it, James reached inside the doorway and turned on the light.

"Okay, now hurry up, so we can get some sleep." Said James. Feeling like a father taking his daughter to pee.

Cindy poked her head inside the room. Although there was some light in there, it was dim and there were shadows in the corners. Cindy still feeling frightened, turned to James and asked,

"Will you come in here with me please,"

"You have got to be kidding me Cindy! You want me to hold your hand too?" Asked James starting to get frustrated with his wife.

"James please I'm scared. Like you said it's a new place. Please, honey?" Pleaded Cindy once again.

James looking at her, realizing that she was truly frightened, softly said.

"I'm sorry. It's all right, I'm right here and yes, I'll come in there with you."

"Thank you, James." Said Cindy with relief in her voice.

James followed her into the bathroom and stood against the wall. She sat down and peed. When she finished. He took her by the hand and they walked back to the bedroom together. They climbed back into the bed. James pulled her close and held her tightly against him, saying,

"Now honey, I'm right here. I won't let anything happen to you. So please try to get some sleep." Cindy feeling safer now with her husband's arms wrapped around her and having relieved her bladder, finally was, able to relax and fall asleep.

The next morning. James was awoken by the pain in his arm from his wife's body lying on it all night. Although it did hurt considerably he did not want to move it and disturb her. Instead, he just laid there, holding and watching his beautiful little wife sleeping soundly.

Although his arm was in agonizing pain, he tried to ignore it. Now, because it was daylight outside, the light filled the room. For the first time, he got a good look at it. They were sleeping in a big, beautiful, old magnificent, colonial style bed. With curtains that pulled close all around it. On the walls hung several old pictures of landscapes. The room was huge in size and over in one corner was a dressing table with a large oval shaped mirror and with what appeared to be carefully preserved. On top of it was a silver handle brush and several bottles of many types of perfume, covered in dust. In front was a little red velvet covered stool.

Over in another corner hanging on a hook was what appeared to be a woman's robe. James began to realize that they must be in the bed that belonged to the mistress of the house. Because everywhere he looked in the room were more and more of a woman's things. His arm now was getting to the point where he could barely stand the pain. Finally, Cindy began stirring. He saw this as the opportunity to wake her and put an end to the agonizing pain in his arm, by saying, "Good morning sleepy head. Did you sleep well?"

Cindy slowly opened her eyes answering him by saying, "Good morning honey with a soft voice and asked what time it was?"

James hoping that she would get off his arm said. "I don't know, why don't you find your phone and look?"

Cindy sat up, relieving the pressure off his arm. Climbing out of bed she began digging in her purse to find her phone to see what time it was. James, unable to move his arm on his own reached over and grabbed it with his other hand, pulling it close to his side and as the blood came rushing back into it. He experienced an additional throbbing and agonizing pain that almost brought him to tears. Till finally, he began to feel a little relief and could move it. Cindy, turning around to tell him what time it was. Noticed him holding his arm,

"Oh honey, I'm so sorry, why didn't you move me off - of it?" Asked Cindy as she walked back over and climbed in bed taking his arm in her hands and rubbing it.

"Because you had such a hard time getting to sleep, I didn't want to wake you," explained James. Feeling more and more relief as she rubbed his arm, helping the blood to flow back into it.

"Thank you that does, feel so much better. What time was it?" Asked James smiling at her.

Now feeling the full use of his arm and hand. Reaching out and grabbing one of her naked breasts. Because she was holding his hand close to her chest as she rubbed his arm. Cindy smiled, pulling her breast out of his hand, saying, "Not time for that. We have a lot to do." She said

Dropping his hand.

James chased her off the bed with it, trying to grab her tight little butt saying,

"Come back here."

Her little butt, barely escaped his hand. James laying sideways across the bed, reached his arm and hand out of the side of the bed toward her whimpering and wiggling his fingers saying,

"Let me feel it."

Cindy giggling playfully said. "No."

"Come on let me feel it, just for a minute." begged James playfully.

Cindy walked back over to the edge of the bed, backing up to his hand, with her a little butt. Saying,

"Just for a minute, then we've got to get up." as she placed her butt cheek in his hand.

James grasped and squeezed it, trying to get a good grip to pull her back to the bed, but it was too firm, so it slid out of his hand, as she pulled away giggling at him, saying, "Now come on honey..., get up you know we've got a lot to do."

And tossing his pants at him, playfully."

James reluctantly set up sliding his feet off the side of the bed and down to the floor, playfully saying,

"You never let me have any fun."

Cindy looked to him, giggling saying, "Oh really, well we'll just have to see about that later, that is if you're a good boy!" Pulling back on her jeans, having already put her bra and T-shirt on.

James playfully said "Yes ma'am, jumping to his feet and pulling on his pants."

When the couple finished getting dressed, Cindy started downstairs, eager to get their trailer unloaded. As she was heading downstairs, the door right by the stairwell, slowly opened in front of her, causing her to freeze in her tracks. Cindy tried to call James, but frightened from what she had just witnessed could not get the words out or move. James came walking out the bedroom, saw her standing at the stairwell asking, "What is it honey?"

Cindy very slowly raised her hand and pointed toward the open door saying, "That door just opened by itself."

James walked past the stairwell to the room with the open door and looked inside saying,

"There's nothing in here, honey, nothing."

"But don't you see, the door is open. We haven't been in that room yet. how did the door, get open?" Asked Cindy. Obviously frightened.

James reached down and grabbed the doorknob and pulled it shut. Then he took the palm of his hand pushed on the door it. Easily unlatched and opened.

"It looks like the latch is broken and I guess the wind blowing down the hallway opened it." Said James trying to explain it to her.

"But James, I didn't feel no wind in the hallway." Said Cindy. Obviously not convinced.

"Well there's not anything in here now." Said James grabbing the doorknob and pulling the door shut.

Then he walked past Cindy. Going downstairs. Saying,

"I'm going to unload the trailer."

Cindy stood there looking at the closed door thinking,

"Maybe, James is right. Maybe it is just my imagination running away with me."

Starting down the stairs. She heard the door and latch and swing open very slowly. she froze in her tracks once again, turned facing the door, looking at it. Feeling a breeze on her face, she dismissed it, thinking to herself,

"James was right. It's the wind." And she continued down the steps.

Then to her amazement, she heard the door hinges start to squeak. Again, freezing in her tracks, she turned toward the door and watched it close and latch by itself. Cindy took off running down the stairs to find James, both scared and excited. She ran outside, where James was unloading the trailer saying, "The door closed and latched by itself," Okay, opening with the wind, that's one thing but closing and latching by itself? "Asked James with curiosity. "Come on James something's going on here!" Said Cindy.

"Oh, honey come on." Said James as he walked past her. Heading upstairs once he got to them, they climbed them together. James walked to the door and pushed on it with his hand. Easily opening it. About halfway, they just stood there for a few minutes as they watched the door. Then suddenly, it began to move slowly at first and then a little faster, till finally, it closed and latched. James turned to her. He looked saying, "See Honey in these old houses, things get off balance." "The door is just out of balance, it won't stay open," "The wind opens it by pushing on it, once it stops, the door will automatically close back in the weight of it, causing it to latch." Said James obviously feeling like he's right, trying to convince her.

Then suddenly while they were both standing there, the door unlatched and swung open. Cindy said. "James. I don't feel a breeze."

"Give it a minute." Said James stepping back realizing she's right and there is no breeze.

But this time the door didn't close by itself. They watched it for several minutes. Still nothing James. Feeling a little uneasy reached down, grabbed the doorknob and slammed the door shut, saying,

"I don't have time for this and neither do you. We've got a lot to do, we can play with the door later."

James walked past her heading downstairs to finish unloading the trailer. Cindy still not convinced that it was the wind. Decided to just dismiss it and go help James finish unloading the trailer. Cindy looked at James asking, "What do you think honey, should we stack everything in this room over here and go through it later, so we can get the trailer unloaded, take it and drop it off?"

"That sounds good to me and we can get something to eat while we're in town." Said James as He unlatched the back of the trailer door opening it.

Cindy standing at the back of the trailer. As James opened the door said. "Looks like everything rode alright, you did a good job loading it."

James smiled at her, saying, Thank you ma'am."

As he started to release the ratchet strap holding the two large toolboxes. Cindy. Upon seeing what he was doing said. "Hang on a minute I'll give you a hand with that?"

As she grabbed the other side of one of the large toolboxes. Together they carried it into the house, placing it against the wall in one of the rooms. Then they got the other one, placing it beside the first one. After they had both toolboxes safely in the house, they began removing the boxes from the trailer, one after another, till finally the trailer was empty and the boxes were safely and securely stacked in the room to be gone through later. Cindy said. "Give me a minute please, I need to go to the bathroom before we go."

She turned around and ran upstairs heading to the bathroom. James yelled,

"Get my wallet and truck keys! They are right there on the nightstand beside the bed!"

As he was closing the door to the trailer, latching and securing it. A few minutes later, Cindy came back downstairs, carrying her purse asking, "Are you ready to go honey?" Handing him his wallet and keys.

James taking them answered her, saying, "I guess so if you are?"

Cindy followed him out the mansion, letting the door close and lock behind them, climbed in the truck and headed in to town to take the trailer and drop it off. As they were driving Cindy asked, "So where is it that we have to drop the trailer off?"

"At the airport. It's the only rental place around here," answered James.

They arrived at the airport to drop off the trailer. James said. "Honey you wait right here. This won't take long, then we can go get something to eat."

He got his paperwork and when inside. A few minutes later, James came back out, saying, "Okay where would you like to go get something to eat?"

"Let's go back into town and see what we can find!" said Cindy all excited.

"But honey, let's grab just a little something for now, I'm too excited to eat a lot."

James reached down and cranked his truck up and headed back into the town. James spotted a little restaurant with a drive-up window on their way. As he drove up to it, he turned, looking at Cindy said.

"Well, I've got to eat something. I'm hungry."

While driving up to the window, he noticed a billboard with a menu on it. He stopped his truck beside it for a few minutes looking it over. After discussing the whole menu, they finally settled on a couple of breakfast sandwiches and a couple glasses of sweet tea. James drove up to the window, a young woman looked to be in her 20s asked "Can I help you Sir?"

James ordered their breakfast and what seem like just a few minutes the young woman came back with

Their order.

James payed her for it. Thanking the young woman and drove away. James and Cindy ate their breakfast as they drove looking at all the beautiful sites surrounding the mountains. They drove for hours taking it all in, till finally Cindy said. "Well honey as much as I hate to, we need to get back to the mansion and start trying to organize some of our things."

When they got back to the estate. They worked together. Going from room to room, dusting, cleaning and admiring all the old beautiful things still left in the mansion that were now theirs. The more and more, they cleaned it, the more in love they both fell with the old place. James looked at Cindy saying, "You know honey, this is a big, beautiful, magnificent old place."

"Yes, I know James, I can't believe that we are really here and this big beautiful place is all ours and we have all the money that we could ever need to maintain it!" Sometimes I think I'm just dreaming and I think to myself if I am, I don't ever want to wake." Said Cindy polishing on some of the old furniture. James walked out of the room that she was cleaning in, going across the hall to two big beautiful solid wood pocket doors and slid them open. Just on the other side was a huge, magnificent room. Inside was a wooden bookshelf, a big oval desk in the center of the room and a fireplace. On one wall was an old couch with wooden arms and legs that curled back. He had undoubtedly found the study,

He hollered to Cindy saying, "Honey, come here and look at this!"

Cindy came running out of the room. She'd been cleaning and into the study, looking around, she said. "Oh, my God, what a big beautiful room!"

"I know, isn't it?" Asked James with excitement in his voice as he continued to say "I think it's the study, honey, if you don't mind, I'd really like to have this room for my very own." Said James like a little boy just picked his bedroom.

Cindy pulling open the curtains to let some light into the room said. "Honey, the whole house is yours as much as it is mine."

"I understand that Cindy. But please honey, I'd really like to have this room as my own private place where I can go to be alone from time to time," and just, I don't know, think about things." Said James trying to convince her.

"But of course, James if you want this room all for yourself, I don't mind honey, you can have anything you want." Said Cindy walking over and kissing him very tenderly.

The couple worked on the mansion, most the day, only stopping briefly around lunchtime returning to the same restaurant with the drive-through window ordering a few hamburgers, French fries and something to drink. They returned to the mansion to eat their lunch.

• • •

They continued cleaning till finally was getting dark and they were both extremely hungry. This time. James said. "Let's go into town and see if we can find us a nice place to have dinner."

Cindy agreed. Walking out of the mansion, letting the door close and lock behind them. They got in the truck and headed back into town although they passed several fast food places, none seem to be what they wanted. Then Cindy noticed a sign saying, "Betty's family diner."

she pointed it out to James asking, "You want to try that place there?"

James looked over to where she was pointing saying, "Sure, why not, a little place like that usually has some really good food."

The couple pulled into the driveway, got out and went inside. It was your average little diner, about 15 or 20 tables, with a couple of booths and a counter with a few stools in front of it and on the side of it was a set of double doors. Obviously going back into the kitchen area. When they first came in the front entrance, by the door was a sign saying, please seat yourself. So, they walked over and found, a nice booth back in one of the corners and sat down. As they did an older lady, come walking over to them handing what appeared to be a couple of dinner menus saying, "Hi, I'm Peggy your waitress." Then she asked "What Can I get you to drink?"

Both Cindy and James ordered a glass of sweet tea, asking, can we have a couple minutes?" Peggy said. "I'll bring that right on out to you, take as much time as you need Sweetie."

Cindy looked over at James saying, "Oh honey, there's some really nice stuff on here and it's not very expensive."

James looked at her and giggled, saying, "Like that would matter and yes, you're right. There are some really nice things on here."

"What are you going to have?" Asked Cindy. Who obviously could not make up her mind, with so many good choices?

"I think I might have this chicken dinner plate. It comes with three sides and a salad." Said James pointing it out to her on the menu. "Wow that does sound good! I think I will too." Said Cindy folding up her menu.

when Peggy returned with their drinks, a couple being close-by ordered the same dinner, with the three sides being. Macaroni and cheese, mashed potatoes with gravy and baked beans and a chef salad. With ranch dressing. Peggy asked them,

"Would you like your salad before dinner, or after?"

James looked over at Cindy for confirmation saying, "I guess we can have them now if it's no trouble?"

Cindy nodded her head yes.

"It's not no trouble at all sweetie." Said Peggy "I'll be right back."

A few minutes later, true to her word. Peggy returned with two extra-large salads and two small containers, of ranch dressing,

"My God!" said James. "These things are a meal on their own."

Peggy looked at them and smiled, saying, "Yep, we try to make sure folks get their money's worth around here."

"You sure do, thank you very much ma'am." Said Cindy looking down at her enormous salad.

"My pleasure dear, if you don't mind me asking? Ain't never seen you two around here before just passing through, or visiting some folks?" inquired Peggy.

"Oh, no we live here now. We inherited a place up on a mountain," answered Cindy, with pure excitement in her voice.

"Well I reckon I'll be seeing a lot more of you two." Said Peggy smiling at them.

As she turned and started to walk away... But paused for a minute and walked back over to the table asking hang on a minute. Where did you say, your place was? That is, if don't mind me asking?" inquired Peggy.

"Not at all." Said Cindy "We inherited...THE SUMMERHILL MANOR."

• • •

"Perhaps you've heard of it?" Asked James. Noticing the look of fear on the woman's face.

"Most people around these parts know that place." Said Peggy sitting down beside Cindy whispering.

"You two really going to be living there? Inquired Peggy.

"Yes, ma'am that is some of the stipulations of the will. That we lived there and maintain the place," why is there something wrong?" Asked Cindy, waiting to find out what the woman had to say next.

"Well I for one am glad somebody's gone be taken care that old place. It sure is beautiful, I have only seen it once and that was from a distance." Said Peggy.

"Yes, it is beautiful and I might be looking for some help." Said Cindy. Watching for the woman's reaction.

James on the other hand wasn't saying, anything. He was just eating his salad, watching and listening to the two of them talking,

"Well like I was saying, it sure is a beautiful place and I'm sure there isn't nothing to all the stories. Folks have been saying, about it all these years." Said Peggy as she started to get up.

"What stories?" Asked James finally speaking up.

"Well I haven't never seen nothing myself, but folks around these parts, say, the place is haunted, by Margaret Summerhill." Said Peggy whispering

"Who was that?" Asked Cindy hanging on every word Peggy was saying,

"Well back in the 1800s, Margaret Summerhill had the Summerhill mansion built. Her husband colonel George Summerhill had it done for her. They say a lot of folks got killed building it. Which isn't hard to believe, because that was quite common back in those days. They also had a bunch a slave living on the place to work the fields and take care of her and the estate. Margaret was a tyrant of a woman, evil in nature. She was ruthless and cruel to the slaves.

She was one of those women that thought she was better than everybody else. Her daddy owned a railroad and they always had money."

"Whatever happened to her that makes people think she's haunting the mansion?" Asked James. Interrupting Peggy.

"Well one night after the colonel had left her. Margaret Summerhill come up missing and no one never found out what happened to her, she just disappeared."

"That still don't say why she would be haunting the place." Said James, interrupting her and getting frustrated.

"Some say. She was killed and the body was buried somewhere up on the Summerhill estate and she isn't, at rest and that's why she haunts it, but some say she just run away back up to her daddy because of something. The colonel done it to her, then he went away. But isn't nobodies that really know. All folks can do is speculate." Said Peggy getting up to go see if their dinner was ready. James looked over at Cindy, who was deep in thought and asked, "all this talk is really starting to scare you, isn't it?'

But before she could answer Peggy came walking back saying, "It isn't quite ready yet, few minutes more."

"James I don't know, about living in a haunted mansion. What are we going to do?" Asked Cindy. Obviously, getting more and more frightened.

"Okay well you know all these old places like this are supposed to have ghosts, I remember when I was a boy in school. There was an old rundown shack down the road from my house. Everybody said it was haunted and we were all scared to death of it, as kids. But when I got older and a lot smarter. Going to high school, Tina Wilson. The prettiest girl in the whole school, told me that she would kiss me in front of everybody. If I would spend the night in it. Well you know I wasn't going to pass that up, so I did. I spent the night in it, and about 2 o'clock in the morning.

I think it was, couple my buddies decided, they were going to play a prank on me and try to scare me out of it. By making noises and running around in the dark. But it didn't work out. I spent the night in the old place and nothing got me. But you know what the worst thing of all was, I never did get my kiss from Tina." Said James laughing.

"What I'm trying to say is all these places that are supposed to have ghosts and be haunted. There's usually a reason for it and can be explained. All this is just kid stuff and people letting their imagination run away with them." Said James trying to put Cindy's mind at ease.

"Will kid stuff or not, there has been some tragedy at that place and some unexplainable accidents." Said Peggy "Just a few days ago, the man that used to maintain the grounds there had one of his sons killed by a statue falling on him or something."

"Yes, we know." Said Cindy. Lowering her head. "They were moving that statue for me. I feel somewhat responsible for the boy's death."

James putting his salad fork down hard enough on the table to make a noise saying,

Honey, I told you it was just an accident. It's nobody's fault. Unfortunately, things like that happen in life."

"Did you know him?" Asked Cindy looking at Peggy.

"No I didn't know him, but he did come in here from time to time with both his little brother and father," answered Peggy looking at Cindy.

Just then a man's voice hollered,

"Order up," as he hit a little bell.

Peggy while getting up from the table said. "Well that will be your dinner. "As she walked back to the pickup window to get it.

"I don't know, honey, I think there might be something to what the woman said. I could've sworn something was staring at me from the dark corner last night in that room." Said Cindy even more frightened than before, to the point that her hands were trembling.

"Cindy honey, even if we do have ghosts in the mansion. Ghosts can't hurt you there just spirits.

They can make you hurt yourself by being afraid of them. But they cannot physically hurt you." Said James like he was some sort of a paranormal professional.

"But how do you really know that James?" Asked Cindy. Lowering her head.

"I don't really, I have just seen a lot of shows on TV about that kind of thing. Now I know some of them are made up just for TV. But others like documentaries. I think you can pretty much well believe that kind of stuff." Said James trying to explain himself.

"Nevertheless, if you don't mind, I'd like to find a different room to sleep in tonight maybe one closer to the bathroom." Said Cindy looking at him,

"Okay honey, when we get back will find one." Said James trying to put her mind at ease. As Peggy came walking up, bringing their dinner on a big tray. James looking at it all said. "My God! You could feed an army with all of this. You people really believe in putting out the food. Don't you?"

Peggy smiled saying, "Like I said. we want to make sure folks get their money's worth around here. Will there be anything else?"

"Yes ma'am, could I have some more to drink?" Asked James, finishing off the last little bit of tea out of his glass.

"Sure, thing sweetie." Said Peggy as she was turning a look at Cindy asking "Would you like for me to top that off hon?"

"Yes ma'am, if you don't mind?" Asked Cindy. Handing her the glass.

As Peggy reached for the glass, she noticed. Cindy's hands were trembling. she asked

"Are you all right my dear?"

James said. taking Cindy's hand in his, holding it tightly and smiling at her,

"You have got to forgive my little wife. She's very sensitive and scares easily. The thought of us living in a haunted mansion is almost more than she can bear."

"Oh honey, I wish I would've known that. I never would have said nothing." Said Peggy with a concerned look on her face.

"She'll be all right, I'm right here with her and soon she'll find out there isn't anything to be worried or scared about." Said James as the very tenderly touched the side of Cindy's face smiling at her.

"You two are absolutely adorable. I am so glad you stopped in here tonight and I got to meet you. I hope I'll get to see more of you two." Said Peggy as she went to get them some more to drink.

"Are you going to be all right, honey?" Asked James as he picked her hand up and gently Squeezed it.

"Yes James, if I have you I will be fine." Said Cindy smiling at him, raising and very tenderly kissing the back of his hand.

"I'm right here. eat your dinner, and don't worry, everything's going to be all right." Said James once again, squeezing her hand in releasing it.

Cindy finally calmed down and they both sat there and enjoyed a very nice dinner laughing and making plans on their new future together at …THE SUMMERHILL MANSION.

• • •

CHAPTER 16

Earlier that day Tracy drove to Michael's school to pick him up because it was almost 2 o'clock. As she walked inside. She noticed Michael was sitting in a chair in the corner. Obviously, in trouble and she wondered about what. School was out and most of the kids were already gone. Tracy walked over to Mrs. Sweeney Michael's teacher asking, "What has he done now?"

The teacher looked up from her desk, recognizing Tracy from other previous times that she had picked Michael up, saying, "He pulled Mary Sycamores hair today and punched Peter Walker in the arm. As a matter of fact, I've had quite a bit of trouble with him and I was hoping, that Cindy could shed a little light on the subject for me."

"I can do that," whispered Tracy, leaning closer to her desk.

"She and James inherited a place up in the mountains and they left the boys here with me, so that they could finish school. You, see I'm sure he's just rebelling." Said Tracy looking over at Michael.

"Well okay then yes, that does explain it. Children, especially little boys tend to strike out at everyone around them in situations like that, to tell you the truth it puts my mind at ease. I was afraid that Cindy and James might be going through a divorce, or separation something like that." Said Mrs. Sweeney would relief in her voice.

"Oh no, nothing like that. They're quite happy together, starting a new life somewhere else, kind of makes me envious of them." Said Tracy, reaching out her hand for Michael to come to her. "But I will tell them about how he's acting up in school."

"No there is no need to do that. Times like this we just have to be a little bit more understanding with our children." Said Mrs. Sweeney looking at Michael.

"Yes, I know you're right. But I'll talk to him about pulling the girls' hair." Said Tracy, taking Michael's hand saying, "Will see you tomorrow.

"Michael,'" said Mrs. Sweeney. "You be good, everything's going to be all right."

But Michael did not say anything, he just wrapped his self around Tracy's arm holding it close to him.

"Well anyway." Said Mrs. Sweeney "Thank you for letting me know Tracy."

"You're quite welcome." Said Tracy smiling at her. Looking down at Michael saying, "Tell Ms. Sweeney goodbye and you'll see her tomorrow."

Michael looking down at the floor, holding Tracy's arm to him, saying, "Goodbye Ms. Sweeney will see you tomorrow."

Tracy smiled at her saying, "We'll see you."

As she turned around, took Michael by the hand. They walked out of the classroom and got in her car, she buckled Michael into his seat. Then she got in herself, looking over at the boy.

He was just sitting there, looking down at the floorboards of the car. Tracy said. "You know it is going to be all right." and reached out and touched him on the shoulder.

"I miss my mommy and daddy." Said Michael just about in tears.

"Oh honey, come here." Said Tracy reaching her arms out. Michael undid his seat belt and climbed over the console of her car and into her lap, wrapping his little arms around her. Tracy, held him and rocked him for a few minutes, saying, "I know baby, I miss them too, but it is going to be okay and in no time at all. School will be over and you get to go up there and see your new home." Said Tracy trying to comfort him.

"Hey, I've got some shopping to do. What do you say you and I go do some grocery shopping? Then will go get Billy when he gets off the bus, and go have some ice cream. Would you like that baby?" Asked Tracy, holding him close to her and continuing to rock him.

Michael didn't say anything, he just nodded his little head yes. Then Tracy said. "Okay baby, climb back in your seat and put your seat belt on." As she reached up and cranked her car, putting it in drive. She pulled away from the school. Heading to the grocery store, when they arrived at the store Tracy got a buggy and asked Michael

"You want to ride in it?"

Michael snapped at her, saying, "I'm not a baby. I can push the buggy."

"Well excuse me little man," she said playfully.

"Can you think of anything you want?" She asked him, as she headed down the candy aisle.

Michael just looked down at the floor shaking his head "no". Continuing to push the buggy.

"You know I haven't been feeling well today. I wonder if there might be something in here that might help me feel better." Said Tracy. Scratching her head and looking up at the ceiling.

Michael pointed to a great big bag of chocolate candy saying, "I bet that would make you feel lots better aunt Tracy."

"You think so?" she asked, reaching up and grabbing a big bag of chocolate.

"Let's give it a try."

"And you know what else?" said Michael walking down the toy aisle over to the hot wheels, reaching up and taking one down, handing it to her saying, "Hot wheels always makes you feel better. Anyways, it makes me feel better all the time." Said Michael smiling at her.

"Oh, it does, well, I for sure got to give that a try." Said Tracy smiling at him.

"Now you know what else might be nice Michael?" She said "I bet you Billy is feeling bad too, maybe we should get him one. What do you think?" Asked Tracy looking down at him.

"Yes, because I know hot wheels sure do make you feel better all the time." Said Michael looking up at her and smiling.

"Okay if you think so. But let's get one, just like yours, so he won't fight with you about it." Said Tracy. Walking back over to the hot wheels.

"Yes, because I told mommy, I'll try not to let him fight with me all the time while they're gone." Said Michael following along behind Tracy. As she said.

"That's a good idea.

• • •

Now tell me about why you pulled Mary's hair today." Said Tracy, reaching for something on the shelf.

Michael looked down at the floor and while he was shuffling his feet said.

"Cushing made me do it."

"Oh, I see, she made you do it." Said Tracy looking at him. "Well how did she make you do it?" She asked while putting her groceries in the buggy.

"Because she's a stupid head, and she all the time be pinching me, and kicking me, and you know what else? She pulls my hair too..., She just a stupid head!" Said Michael trying to explain himself as innocently as he could.

"Maybe she just likes you, and she does that kind of thing because she likes you and you know what I think? I think you like her too! "Said Tracy. Walking to another aisle.

"No way," yelled Michael "Girls got cooties, I don't want no cooties on me! She's just a stupid head! That's all it is." Said Michael. Continuing to push the buggy for Tracy.

"Well I'm a girl, does that mean I have cooties?" Asked Tracy looking down at him.

"No, you are a grown-up girl." Said Michael "You done gave your cooties away to somebody."

"Oh, is, that, right?" Asked Tracy. Grabbing and tickling him in the aisle.

"Well come on you little monster, I am done and we've got to go get your brother." Said Tracy.

Grabbing her last package off the shelf, putting it in the buggy, heading to the checkout counter.

Michael continued pushing the buggy out of the store and over to the car. Tracy opened the back of it and placed all the groceries in it and headed to go get Billy.

When they arrived at the bus stop. Several kids got off and then Billy came to the car and climbed in, saying, "Hey aunt Tracy!"

"Hey honey, how was school?" She asked while pulling away from the bus stop. "I told Michael, we would go get some ice cream. How does that sound to you?" She asked, looking at him in the rear-view mirror.

"That sounds good." Said Billy looking out the window.

Michael turned around and looked at his brother, saying, "Aunt Tracy and I got you a hot wheel to make you feel better."

Billy looked at him in confusion saying, "Well okay. Thank you."

"You're very welcome sweetie," Tracy said as they pulled up in front of a little ice cream stand that was down the road from her house. When they arrived, they all three climbed out. Tracy walked to the window to order the ice cream. The boys dug in the grocery bags, looking for the hot wheels. Upon finding them Michael grabbed the both at the same time. Tracy turning around to find out what kind of flavor they wanted.

She could see that they were fighting in the car, so she hollered over to them saying,

"Hey you two stop fighting long enough to tell me what flavor you want."

Michael said. "I want chocolate."

Billy said. "Me too, please ma'am."

Tracy turned back around and told the lady in the window.

"Three chocolate ice cream cones please." Feeling embarrassed for making her wait. Tracy got the ice cream cone and walked back over to the car asking, "Now what you two fighting about. I got you the same car. How could you be fighting over that?"

"Because one's red and one's blue and I want the blue one." Said Billy trying to get it from his brother.

"Oh, my God! You can't be serious, hand them both here and take your ice cream cones." Said Tracy as she handed their ice cream cones to them and asking Billy to hold hers. Then taking the two cars, one in each hand and holding them behind her back switching them from hand-to-hand. Then she held them out in front of her saying, "Choose one!"

Michael pushing Billy out of the way saying, "Me first!"

As he stood in front of Tracy looking at both of her hands, she said.

"Well come on, we don't have all day, pick one." Said Tracy really feeling agitated.

Then he finally picked her right hand. Tracy held it out in front of him and the other out in front of Billy, opening them both at the same time. Billy got the blue car and Michael got the red one.

Michael dropped his head pushed out his lip saying, "I wanted the blue one."

"Fair is fair, that's how it just worked out. Now take your cars and stop fighting the both of you." Said Tracy as she got her ice cream cone back from Billy which was starting to melt.

They walked over and sat down at a little table that was in front of the stand. Michael still pouting, was letting the ice cream drip on his red-hot wheel Tracy trying to take his mind off it asked,

"Hey how would you guys like to have pizza for supper tonight?"

Both boys excitedly yelled "Yes can we?"

Michael said. oh please, aunt Tracy I love pizza!"

Tracy seeing the opportunity to get some type of control over them and feeling quite pleased with herself because of it and the fact that she did manage to take Michael's mind off the color of the car said.

"If you two are good and stop fighting!"

"Okay." Said Michael "I won't let Billy fight with me, no more again." As he started to lick his ice cream cone and being is good for the moment as he possibly could.

"Okay boys, let's head to the house." Said Tracy walking toward her car, saying, "I've got groceries to put away. You two could play for a while before supper time."

Then all three of them, got back in the car and headed to Tracy's house. When they arrived, the boys being as good as they possibly could, helped her carry the groceries in and then went about their way trying to get some playing time in before it got dark. Till finally Tracy walked to the back door, saying, "Boys come in and get your hands washed and get ready for supper. I have already ordered the pizza and it is on its way."

Both the boys came running toward the house. Michael arrived at the door first. But Billy be in bigger and faster, shoved him out of the way, busting through the door. when Michael got inside, he ran over and hit him. Billy turned around and shoved his little brother down on the floor, but that only angered Michael further, so when he got back to his feet. He ran up behind Billy chasing after him in the hall and grabbed two handfuls of his hair, pulling it Billy turned around once again and shoved him to the floor. Tracy just stood there watching the two of them. Shaking her head as they were fighting, running down the hall, bickering about who is going to get into the bathroom first. Billy ran into the bathroom and slammed the door in front of Michael He grabbed the doorknob hollering,

"Let me in, stupid head." Kicking the door. He hollered. Once again,

"Stupid head, let me come in."

But Billy just ignored him, till finally he opened the bathroom door and Michael ran inside. Although Tracy could not see what was happening. She did hear smacking sounds come from the bathroom, as Billy, came walking out and down the hall to the kitchen. She just shook her head, looking at him as he sat down in the chair at the table and ask, "Why must you fight with him so much? He is so much smaller than you and you're supposed to be his big brother who loves him and takes care of him. I wish when I was growing up, I would have a big brother to look after me."

"But he starts it all the time, aunt Tracy you saw him pull my hair." Said Billy trying to look innocent.

"Yes, but I also saw you shove him out of the way coming in the door and then again on the floor." Said Tracy looking at him, not buying his innocence.

"But he's just a butthole and wish I didn't have a little brother." Said Billy. Looking at the table.

"Young man, don't you ever, I mean ever let me hear you say that again, do you understand me." Said Tracy, very angrily pointing her finger right at Billy. Then she passed him. Going down the hall to find out what was taking Michael so long. When she got to the bathroom.

She knocked on the door asking "Michael honey, are you all right?"

But there was no reply from the bathroom. Tracy reached down and grabbed the doorknob turned it walking inside. She saw that Michael was sitting on the side of the tub holding his little face. Michael looked up at her with tears in his eyes saying, "I want my mommy and daddy."

Tracy walked over to him and knelt on the floor and put her arms around him, holding him tightly for a few minutes. She leaned him back, looking at him saying, "I know baby, it's going to be all right. Let me see."

When Michael took his hand down you could see a red full imprint, of Billy's hand on the side of his cheek. Tracy looked at the red weld on the boy's face, shaking her head she said. "Oh, baby hang on a minute."

She stood to her feet and got down a wash rag out of a linen cabinet that was right beside the tub. Then she reached over to the sink, turned on the cold water, holding it under the water for a few minutes soaking the rag. She rang the excess water out of the rag. Then folded it a couple of times and placed it on the side of the boy's face, saying, "Their baby. Does that feel better?"

Michael didn't say anything, he just nodded his head yes. Tracy held him for a few minutes with the cool rag on the side of his face. Then she said "Okay My little man, go run in there and get up to the table. The pizza should be here any minute."

Michael hugged her neck, saying, "I love you aunt Tracy."

Tracy, with a tear in the corner of her eye, hugged him back as tightly as she could. Then she continued to say.

"I love you too baby. Now you go get to the table, I'll be right there."

A few minutes later Tracy came walking down the hall with an angry look on her face, looking directly at Billy saying, "Billy, look at the side of your brother's face. Look what you did. You listen to me young man. Don't you ever, I mean ever hit your brother like that again. If you do, I will call your mom and I will tell her. She's already told me that if I have any trouble with either one of you. For me to call and tell her and she will pull you out of school so fast your head will spin and bring you up there with her. You ever hit your brother like that again, so help me God! I'm going to call her. You understand me?" Asked Tracy, with a very angry voice.

Billy lowered his head and said "Yes ma'am."

"Now you tell your brother, you're sorry for hitting him in the face." Said Tracy feeling very agitated with the boy.

Billy looked at his little brother saying, "I'm sorry for hitting your face Michael."

"It hurts really badly, I'm just a little boy, but I guess it's all right." Said Michael. Fidgeting with his hands on the table.

The rest of the evening. The boys got along a lot better, although they did bicker back and forth. They didn't really fight. Even after the pizza arrived. While they were eating, the phone rang. Tracy walked over and picked it up, saying, "Hello, hey girl how are things going up there on your mountain?"

The boys realizing that Tracy was talking to their mother jumped up from the table and ran over to her side begging for the phone. Michael was jumping up and down in one spot, wanting to talk to his mama.

Tracy said. "Well I better let you talk to these two."

First, she handed the phone to Billy. He took it, saying, "Hey mom. What are you all doing?"

"Well right now, me and your dad are having dinner at a little diner we found up here," answered Cindy and asking, "Billy, are you guys being good for your aunt Tracy?"

But he did not answer her. He just stood there holding the phone. Cindy asked once again more forcefully this time,

"Billy answer me, are you too given your aunt Tracy any trouble?"

"Yes ma'am," answered Billy, knowing better than to lie to his mother. "We're fighting a lot and I showed Michael down on the floor and slapped him." Said Billy, lowering his head.

"Let me speak to your aunt Tracy right now." Said Cindy very angrily.

Billy turned around to hand the phone to Tracy. Michael was jumping up and down, wanting to speak to his mother and reaching for the phone yelling,

"Give me the phone stupid head."

Billy holding the phone out of his brothers reach, yelled

"No!! Mom says she wants to talk to aunt Tracy, not you."

Then he handed the phone to Tracy.

"Yes honey, what it is?" Asked Tracy concerned for the boys.

"Those boys giving you a hard time?" Asked Cindy, feeling embarrassed.

"No more so than usual,"

"Billy told me, he shoved Michael on the floor and slapped him." Said Cindy feeling like she has really burdened Tracy.

"Well yes, he did, but I got on to him about it and I don't think he'll do it again.

"Tracy honey, why don't you let me take them out of school and bring them up here with me? I didn't mean for you to have to deal with all this.

"Don't be silly. They are just boys and believe it or not, they are a lot of company for me. I've been feeling really alone lately and there..., She paused for a minute, well, like a said there a lot of company for me honey." Said Tracy hoping that she wouldn't take the boys.

"We'll all right, if you're sure. But if they get any worse, you've got the promise me you'll let me know." Said Cindy trying to do what was right for everybody.

"But of course, I will, sweetie and I must tell you I've got a little man here is about to die if he doesn't get to talk to you soon." Said Tracy, smiling at him handed him the phone.

Michael took the phone and said "Hi mommy, what are you doing? Do you miss me? I miss you with all the world." Said Michael holding the phone with both hands to his little head.

"Hi baby, yes, mommy does miss you and so does daddy,

"I love you. Mommy."

"I Love you to baby. Are you being good for aunt Tracy?"

"Well course I am. I'm not letting Billy fight with me. No more. Where is daddy?" Asked Michael. Still holding the phone with both hands. "He's over at the table eating baby," answered Cindy.

"Tell daddy, I love him and I miss him." Said Michael holding the phone to his little head.

"I will baby, I love you and try not to fight with Billy and mind your aunt Tracy." Said Cindy. "Isn't it a about your bedtime? Let me talk to your aunt Tracy baby and you go to bed. Sweet dreams, remember you be good for aunt Tracy and mommy and daddy love you."

"Okay mommy, you be a good. I love you." Said Michael starting to hand the phone to Tracy pulled it back to his little mouth quickly saying, "Goodbye." As he continued to hand the phone to Tracy.

"He's just a sweetheart. I love him to so much." Said Tracy to Cindy on the phone.

"Yes, I know I miss them both, but Michael is my heart. I miss you too Tracy, I can't wait for you to come up here and see me." Said Cindy as her voice cracked and tear formed in her eye.

"I know I miss both you guys. Like I said if it weren't for the boys. I would be all alone. thank you again for letting me keep them. Even if it's just for a short while." Said Tracy with her voice also cracking about to cry.

"You're very welcome honey and thank you again for taking care of them, you have a good night. I love you Tracy." Said Cindy hanging up the phone.

As Tracy hung up. She looked at the boys saying, "It was time for bed."

The boys went to brush their teeth and climbed into their beds. Tracy told them both good night. Especially little Michael she hugged and kissed, saying, to him.

"Good night baby if you need me I'm right down the hall."

As she went and curled up on the couch with a good book, called **The Soul Collector**, by a new author named, **Wyatt Allen**, and a glass of white wine, trying to unwind and relax after what undoubtedly was a very hectic day. Between her work and the boys fighting so much, plus, the fact that she wondered about Cindy and James and what might happen now because when Cindy told James about the boys fighting.

He could still want to come get them. It all overwhelmed her. Tracy feeling very alone. She began wondering to herself,

"If she was always going to be."

With a heavy heart and in despair. She stretched out on the couch and fell into a deep sleep

CHAPTER 17

After James and Cindy finished what undoubtedly was the most memorable dinner that they had in a long time. They thanked Peggy for an enjoyable evening and good conversation, tipped her and went out and got back in the truck heading home. Cindy sat quietly looking out the window, knowing that sooner or later, James would ask how the boys where. She wondered to herself,

"Should I tell him, about the boys fighting and how much trouble, they are giving Tracy?"

She knew although the boys were company for Tracy, and she felt like she needed them. James would undoubtedly want to go get them. she struggled with the idea of not even telling him, till finally James looked over at her and asked, "how are the boys? Are they giving Tracy any trouble?"

Being confronted with the question directly Cindy knew better than to lie to him. she swallowed real hard, lowered her head saying, "Yes honey they are, they're fighting a lot and Billy, shoved Michael to the floor and slapped him." Then she said. quickly. But Tracy told me she got on to him and she didn't think that he would do anything like that again."

James stared out the window the truck shaking his head, until finally he said. "I knew they couldn't behave, that settles it. I'm not going to burden her any further with our responsibility. We'll go back down there and get them. The hell with it and I'm not going to arguing about this. There our boys and I am not going to have them do her like that." Said James with anger and disappointment in his voice.

"James honey, it's only the first day. It's going to take time for them to get used to the situation. Besides Tracy asked me please not two. The boys are company for her and she told me she's really starting to feel alone." Said Cindy, trying to calm her husband and hoping that he may reconsider.

James stared out the window obviously, in deep thought continuing to drive home. When he got to the main gate. He punched in the code and continued up to the mansion, driving up in front of it. He shut the truck off and sat silently there for a few minutes, then finally looked over at Cindy saying,

"Maybe you're right. I don't want her to be alone, but I don't want to burden her with our boys, I'm afraid they're just not going to behave Cindy."

"Honey, let's just give it a little while longer. I'm going to be calling her and check in on them every night and she promised me that if it gets any worse, she would tell me."

"You believe her, you think she would tell you, knowing that it would get the boys took away from her?" Asked James. Obviously, in doubt.

"James honey. Tracy would not betray our trust in such a way, no matter what. I believe that with all my heart." Said Cindy, looking directly at him.

James looked down at the floorboard of the truck took a big breath and let it out slowly, saying,

"All right, we'll give it a while longer. But if there are any more incidents like this and they continue to give her any more trouble. Cindy so help me God! We are go down there and get them." Said James trying to be accommodating.

"Thank you honey. You'll see it's all going to work out." Said Cindy smiling at him. "Anyway, it won't be that long. Before we know it, school will be out and the boys will be on the way up here, along with Tracy and I for one can't wait for that day."

"I know honey, then we can be a family again and hopefully we'll all be happy here. I know it will take some time for the boys to adjust, but I think ultimately we will all find happiness here." Said James climbing out of the truck.

"I hope so. James is going to be a big change for them, as it is for us." Said Cindy walking around the back of the truck.

Cindy paused for a minute, staring at the doorway of the mansion. Looking at it, remembering all the things that Peggy had told her that people were saying, about the place. James unlocked the door, turned around, noticing his wife just standing there, asked, "What is it honey, are you all right?"

Cindy, looking at him and asked, obviously feeling frightened,

"Do you think there is anything to although stories about this place?"

"Oh honey, it's going to be all right. Even if there is remember what I told you ghosts can't hurt you, there are just spirits and don't forget I'm right here with you and I won't let anything happen to you." Said James walking back out to his wife. Taking her hand in his, leading her into the mansion.

"I mean, look at this place. Cindy, you just said this afternoon, how beautiful this place was and how it was like a dream. Now ask yourself, are you going to let the stories of ghosts and the ramblings of an old woman scare you out of here.

"No, you're right James, this is my home now and I'm not going to let anything like that make me uncomfortable here, or scare me out of my birth right home." Said Cindy getting angry.

"We didn't just buy this place off the market. Cindy this is your home, your family came from here. You have the right to live here, just like all the other Summerhill's." Said James as he was really trying to pump her up so that she doesn't feel afraid.

"You're right James, I got a right to be here and live here." Said Cindy really feeling agitated.

"That's my girl." Said James.

"Now let's go find a bedroom next to the bathroom like you want. Then we will take us a nice shower and get ready for bed. We got a lot more cleaning and unpacking to do tomorrow and I'm very tired."

● ● ●

Both went upstairs, searching the rooms. They found one right next to the bathroom. There was even a door, leading from their room into it. Then they went back to the first room, gathered up all their stuff and moved into the room. That they had just chosen. Then they got a change of clothes and headed to the bathroom. When they got there.

They climbed in the shower together. Soaping each other's bodies up.

They begin kissing and caressing each other. In between the warm water, in the shower and the tenderness they were showing each other. They both felt the desire to make love.

Holding each other kissing and loving on one another. James turned her around facing away from him, as she put her hands on the shower wall. Once again, letting his manhood accept the invitation of her body in the middle of their lovemaking they noticed to the clear shower curtain the bathroom door opening very slowly back against the wall by itself. Cindy frightened, pulled away from James catching her breath asking "Honey, did you see that?"

James Feeling a little bit agitated, from the interruption snatched open the curtain, looking at the door saying, "it's nothing honey we must not have shut the door all the way."

Then he pulled the curtain back shut, still feeling anxious. He reached for her, trying to pull her close to him but the moment was gone along with the mood for her. she said to him,

"James I just can't, that scared me."

"But Cindy, it wasn't nothing, we just didn't close the door, that's all it was, or it was the wind." Said James getting more frustrated by the minute.

"I'm sorry James. Please try to understand, I just can't now." Said Cindy, climbing out of the shower and drying off, leaving James standing under the water still noticeably excited.

He Finished washing his body off, climbed out the shower and dried off without saying, a word to Cindy. Put on his clothes and walked out heading to the bedroom. When he got to the bedroom. He pulled off his clothes and climbed in bed, rolling onto his side. Cindy came walking in and sat down on the side of the bed saying, "Honey, I'm sorry that scared me James and I just couldn't after that."

James raised his head looked up toward her saying, "Don't worry about it. It's over now, so just come to bed and let's try to get some sleep, we got another long day ahead of us tomorrow."

Cindy feeling better about the situation, because he was an angry. Pulled off her clothes and climbed in bed next to her husband. Snuggling up against him asking, "Honey, you sure you're not angry?"

James did not reply to her question. Cindy raised up, looking over his shoulder shaking him gently asking again,

"James honey, you sure you're not angry with me?"

James took a deep breath and while letting it out slowly." Said. "No, I'm not angry. I'm just tired. Now go to sleep."

Cindy while still looking over his shoulder asked, "Will can I at least have a kiss good night?

James rolled over and kissed her. Like a mother would sending her son off to school. Rolled back over saying, "Now go to sleep."

Cindy looked at him, lying there with his back to her saying, "You are..., still mad at me, aren't you?"

James took in another breath, let it out slowly saying, "No Cindy, I told you I'm not mad, but I'm going to get that way, if you don't lay down and let me get some sleep."

Cindy stretched out beside her husband, lying there looking up at the ceiling. Feeling so distant from him, wishing to herself that she would have never pulled away from him in the shower. Being tired herself. Her eyelids begin to get heavier and heavier, thinking about it. Till finally she did fall asleep.

Cindy was awoken in the middle of the night, from a loud noise. That seems to be coming from downstairs, she had unpacked a digital clock radio, sitting it on the stand beside the bed. she could easily see that it was 3 o'clock in the morning. Once again, she heard the noise.

Feeling frightened she reached over and shook James saying, in a whisper,

"I heard a noise downstairs,

But there was no reply from him. Shaking him even harder. Said in a little bit louder whisper,

"James, I think there's somebody downstairs."

But still no reply from him. Cindy got up out of bed, put on her robe and very slowly walked across the room. Poking her head out the door. Looking down the long dark hallway. She heard the noise again, for the third time. Cindy's heart raced in her chest and being overcome by fright she turned around and ran. Jumping back in the bed beside James shaking him with both hands saying,

The Summerhill Manor Blood Curse

"James please am scared, I think there's somebody downstairs."

Finally, without even raising his head. James took in a deep breath and wall blowing it out asked,

"What is it honey?"

"I heard a noise. I think there's someone downstairs." Said Cindy, once again, in a whisper.

James raised his head and looked at her, asking, "Wait!!?" "What did you say?"

"I think there's someone downstairs, I heard a noise," whispered Cindy obviously feeling frightened.

James. Realizing this climbed out of bed, slipped on his pants. Cindy said.

"Wait a minute." As she got out the flashlight from the nightstand and handed it to him.

Saying, "Be careful."

James whispered, "You stay here, I'll be right back."

"Not on your life." Said Cindy. Grabbing his arm clinging to it.

"All right, fine. But stay out of the way." Said James. Starting out of the room to investigate the noise.

Then the couple walked down the hallway to the stairwell, James stop for a minute at the top of the stairs to see if he could hear the noise. Cindy clinging tightly to his arm." Said. "I'm scared James."

James. Putting his finger to his lips, making a shih sound saying, in a whisper, "Listen."

The couple stood there in the dark for a few minutes James not hearing a sound took a deep breath and while letting it out said. "I don't hear anything, I'm sure it was nothing."

Then he turned around and started to walk back to the bedroom. Suddenly there was the noise again, coming from downstairs. Cindy feeling frightened, as James froze in his tracks, with her still clinging to his arm, she said. "There it is again."

James just looked at her, turned around and started down the stairs with her clinging tightly to him, shining the light out in front of them. The sound seemed to be coming from one of the rooms next to the entrance. As they got closer to the doorway, there was the sound again. It sounded like paper rustling from somewhere in the room. When they got to the doorway. James pulled Cindy off his arm and said in a very quiet whisper.

"Stay right here."

Cindy shaking all over nodded her head, obviously frightened. James reached down and took hold of the doorknob turning it very slowly, although it made a slight creaking sound. He managed to get it completely turned and suddenly, he shoved it open and busted into the room, only to see a window was cracked and papers were blown all over the floor. Cindy poked her head inside the room asking, "What is it?"

James walked across the room and pulled the window too, latching it, saying, "It's just an open window, lowering paper all over the floor."

"James, I close that window. I know I did. I closed all of them, before we went to bed." Said Cindy trying to redeem herself.

"You mean before we went to the restaurant?" Asked James reminding her.

"That's right. We did go to the restaurant and right to bed. When we got home." Said Cindy, feeling embarrassed realizing it was her fault.

"Yes, you must have undoubtedly left this window open." Said James stretching.

"I'm sorry James." Said Cindy now really feeling embarrassed.

"Well I'm going back to bed. Are you coming?" Asked James yawning.

Cindy nodding her head yes once again, saying, "Honey I am sorry for waking you up, but I did think I heard someone." Said Cindy still feeling embarrassed and trying to explain herself.

"It's all right honey, let's just go back to bed." Said James scratching his butt. As he walked back to the stairwell and up to their room.

Explaining to her.

"It just goes to show you honey. Most of the noise is that you hear like that and some of the actual hauntings. That people think they see in old places like this one. Can be explained with ease and there's nothing really to be frightened of." Said James trying to calm her down a little.

Cindy following close behind him, hanging her head, thinking, *"I really did think I heard someone."*

When they got to the room they both climbed back into bed and in no time at all with fast asleep

The next morning, Cindy woke up alone in the bed. she got up and got dressed, went downstairs to find James. Not seeing him, she thought,

"He must be in his study doing something."

She walked over and knocked on the door asking, "James honey. Are you in there?"

But there was no reply. she tried to pull the doors open to go inside. But they were locked from the other side Cindy realizing he must be in their knocked asking again,

"James, are you in there? Open the door."

But still there was no reply from the room Cindy stepped back, looking at the door. Thinking, *"Maybe he's not in there?"*

she walked out the front of the mansion to look in the yard and around the truck. Not seeing him, she came back in the house thinking, *"He's got to be in there. Why won't he answer me? And why does he have the door locked?"*

But this time. When she got to the study, both doors were pulled open and James was not in there. Suddenly, he came walking up from behind her, which startle her. Cindy jumped grabbing her chest yelling,

"James...! You scared the hell out of me. What are you trying to do? Give me a heart attack? Hey, why wouldn't you open the door and let me in? And why did you have it locked?

"What are you talking about honey, I've been working in the kitchen. I found it by the way and you are not going to believe it." Said James with surprising his voice.

"You weren't just in a study?" Asked Cindy obviously not be leaving him.

"No honey, I told you, I've been working in the kitchen, come here, I'll show you." Said James turning around and walking through two double doors.

With Cindy following close behind him, saying, "James you had to be in there. The doors were locked from the other side."

Honey I'm telling you. I wasn't in the study. I've been in here since I got up this morning, look at this place." Said James as the both walked into a huge massive kitchen.

With to walk in coolers, full of frozen food. But obviously, Mr. Wilcox must have placed there for them and a gas stove with about eight burners on it. Cindy could not believe her eyes. That kitchen was bigger than their whole house, there was every kind of pot and pan you can imagine in every kind of cooking apparatus known, the main two great big ovens a huge counter made from butcher's block. The couple just stood there in awe over the massive size of it.

"It took some doing, but I got the gas turned on and lit all the burners." Said James, with his hands covered in charcoal. Wiping them with a rag.

"Now, what were you talking about? Asked James and confusion.

"The study, when I got up I went looking for you in it, but the doors were closed and locked from the other side." Said Cindy still not quite believing his story.

"Come with me." Said James as he walked ahead of her back through the double doors to the study. Once they got there. James walked into the room. With Cindy, close behind him and slid the pocket doors shut saying, "Honey, these doors don't have a lock,"

Cindy walked over and pulled them shut and opened them looking on both sides. She could not believe her eyes. Yes, there truly was no way to lock those doors. She turned around, looked at James saying,

"That can't be. I just tried to open them. They were closed and would not open."

"Cindy honey the only way to keep these doors from opening is if you hold them shut. And you saw what I have been doing all morning. Now I will say this one more time. I was not in the study this morning." Said James trying to convince her and feeling frustrated by the fact that she did not believe him.

"Okay honey, I believe you, it's just bizarre. I can't figure it out. I know I tried to open the doors and if you weren't in here, then what was holding the door shut?" Asked Cindy, looking directly at her husband waiting to hear what he thought.

"I don't know Cindy. The only thing I know it wasn't me." Said James as he turned around and walked back to the kitchen.

Cindy slid the pocket doors closed and open one more time. Watching how easily they did slide. Deciding to just dismiss it and get on with the day, but as she turned around and started down the hallway. She heard the doors close back behind her, turned around and looking at them, seeing that they were in fact closed made the hair stand up on the back of her neck. Walking back over to the doors she reached down and with little effort slid the doors open. She thought about telling James, but he would just say that they closed by themselves.

Because the house was off balance or it was just the wind. Realizing this fact, she simply turned around and walked back down the hall, heading to another room to continue cleaning.

But really, not putting it out of her mind totally she did think about it throughout the day, as she cleaned trying to figure out what may have caused it. James would join her from time to time for the rest of the day, the couple claimed on the house till finally, once again begin to get hungry and decided to go to their favorite little restaurant and have dinner.

Cindy while going upstairs to get ready saw the door from the other morning open in front of her, but not wanting to deal with it at that time just dismissed it and continued to the bedroom. She grabbed a quick shower and slipped on her clothes coming out of the bedroom with a towel still drying her hair. She walked to the landing and hollered down to James asking, "Honey, aren't you going to take a shower, before we go?"

But there was no reply from her husband downstairs, so she hollered once again. A little louder this time asking, James, "Honey, did you hear me?"

While Cindy was looking down the stairs, James appeared from out of the hallway asking, "What did you say?"

"I was asking whether you are going to take a shower, before we go get something to eat." Said Cindy while still drying her hair.

"No I think I'll just take one when we get back," answered James looking up at her.

Cindy while turning around to go back into the bedroom to finish getting dressed. Out of the corner of her eye and passed the edge of the towel while it was still moving from her drying her hair. She thought she saw someone enter that room. Startled, she paused for a second, then walked down to the open door looking inside. But there was no one in there. Standing there for a minute, with a towel in her hand, she thought, *"James must be right, my imagination is really getting the best of me,"*

Cindy then turned around and closed the door. While walking back to the bedroom, she was continuing to dry her hair and finished getting dressed to go to dinner. As she came downstairs ready to go. James met her standing in the hallway and commented on how nice she looked.

The couple then left the mansion, closing and locking the door behind them, got in the truck and proceeded into town.

"Honey, if you don't mind, I really don't want a lot to eat tonight. That place is overwhelming. They just give you too much food. What you say we just grab a quick bite to eat and go back home, curl up on the couch and light a fire. In that big old marble fireplace of ours?" Asked James smiling at his little wife.

"Oh honey, that sounds wonderful. We haven't had a whole lot of time together lately, but I do need to call Tracy and check on the boys." Said Cindy getting her phone.

As she dialed Tracy's number. She looked over at James saying, "Don't worry, I'll only be a minute honey."

It rang a couple times and then Tracy answered it, saying, "Hello"

"Hay trace it's me. How are the boys? Not giving you any trouble I hope." Said Cindy, waiting for a reply.

"Oh no, not at all. A matter of fact, the getting along too well, makes me leery. Kind of like watching the calm before the storm, I know that something is going to happen. I just don't know what or when." Said Tracy giggling.

"Well can I speak to them?" Asked Cindy, eager to talk to her sons.

"They are outside playing, I'll see if I can find them." Said Tracy going to the back door.

Cindy could hear her over the phone hollering for the boys, then she said. "Well, honey, I got one of them. Michael's coming in a run." Said Tracy, handing him the phone.

Michael out of breath from running saying, "Hi mommy, what are you doing? You'll never guess what, I got to ride a pony and Pet the animals and everything."

"I took them to the zoo," hollered Tracy over the phone, interrupting him.

"I love you and I miss you terribly us. Do you miss me?" Asked Michael still trying to catch his breath.

"Yes, baby I do miss you very, very much and so does daddy and that's wonderful that you got to ride the pony and Pet all the animals and you know what else, I am very proud of you Michael, you and Billy Both. Because you are getting along and not giving your aunt Tracy any trouble.

"But of course, not, I told you I want at Billy fight with me, no more again and aunt Tracy won't have us on her nerves." Said Michael holding the phone with both hands, talking at it.

"Will that's wonderful baby. Do you know where Billy is?" Asked Cindy, hoping she could talk to him.

"He's outside talking to that dumb old girl. You know what Mommy, Billy is going to get cooties from that dumb old girl. Because you know why, I saw her kiss him and he's going to get cooties." Said Michael in a whisper over the phone.

"You did, yep, I guess you're right. He's going to get cooties all right." Said Cindy giggling with him.

"I am going to go play some more. I love you and tell daddy, I love him with all the world." Said Michael as he handed the phone to his aunt Tracy running back outside.

"He's a mess, isn't he Cindy?" Asked Tracy giggling.

"Yes, he is and you're spoiling him rotten. I knew you would. You're going to have them both, especially him so rotten. They'll be no living with them when they get up here." Said Cindy. "Do you know anything about this girl? He said is kissing on Billy?" Asked Cindy with a little bit of concern in her voice.

"Well I think he's talking about Billy's girlfriend, but I sure didn't know she was kissing on him." Said Tracy. Feeling a little concerned. "I guess I'm going to have to keep a closer eye on that boy, I mean we wouldn't want him to get cooties." Said Tracy giggling. "Oh yes by the way, I don't know if I told you, but. Michael told me. I don't have cooties anymore because I'm old and I must've given my cooties away to somebody by now." Said Tracy. Laughing out loud.

"Yes, he is a mess, my God! I miss them so much and I miss you to trace." Said Cindy as her voice cracked, while she was holding back a tear.

"I know honey, I miss you too. Both of you." Said Tracy also trying to hold back the tears. "How are things going up there by the way?" She asked, trying to change the subject.

"Oh Tracy, wait till you see this place, it is magnificent. A little creepy at times, there are some strange things going on here. But James is right, it's just all my imagination." Said Cindy really - not wanting to get into it. With James sitting right beside her.

"Really like what?" Asked Tracy? With concern in her voice. "Something to do with you and James?" She asked really feeling concern not getting a reply from Cindy right away.

Cindy holding the phone in silence finally said. "Yes, we're going to dinner. James is right here beside me, then she turned the James and said Tracy sends her love."

"Tell her I love her and miss her too." Said James while driving.

Tracy also sitting in silence. Just holding the phone listening to Cindy finally saying, "Okay, I understand you can't talk right now, can you?"

Cindy, feeling frustrated because she wanted to explain in more detail what she was feeling. But also, not wanting to ruin the evening that they had just planned said. "Well, I guess if Billy's not going to come in and talk to me, please tell him we love him and we miss him, if you're going to be around. Maybe I can call and talk to you tomorrow and we can catch up on a few things." Said Cindy trying to let Tracy know that they would continue their talk later.

"Okay honey, we love you have a good night and perhaps we can talk tomorrow good night honey." Said Tracy trying to let her know. She understood.

"Good night traces, Kiss the boys for us when you put them to bed and thank you honey." Said Cindy as she hung up the phone. Cindy sitting there in the silence, looking out the windshield of the truck as they were driving. James looked over at her, reached out and took her hand in his saying,

"You know honey, if it will make you feel better about things. You can call and talk to Tracy about them. I do understand." Said James bringing her hand up to his lips and kissing it.

"Thank you honey." Said Cindy sliding across the seat next to him so that James could put his arm around her. " what do you feel like eating?" Asked Cindy looking at her husband.

"I don't know baby you pick something." Said James, allowing her to make the choice hoping that she pick something good.

"Well let me see. I know the other day when we were driving through town I saw a lot of fast food places and I think I noticed a pizza sign. How does that sound?" Asked Cindy, waiting for him to reply.

"Oh yes" that does sound good. Not a whole lot to eat and we can just take it back home and Bill that fire, curl up in front of it. With the pizza and enjoy each other's company. Yes, that is a good choice honey." Said James quite pleased with her with excitement in his voice.

James headed into town to find the pizza place. Upon finding it, the couple went inside and ordered a pizza to go. It took some time, but finally it was done. They paid for it and headed back to the mansion to build the fire that they discussed earlier. When they returned to the mansion.

Going inside James did in fact get a nice roaring fire going, then the couple, curled up on a huge couch that they had uncovered earlier that evening and eight their pizza, making plans for their future there in the mansion.

There were a few slight changes James would like to make. He clarified them with her. She simply agreed to his every plan so that he would fill more inclined to be there at the mansion with her. Some of them were a little far-fetched, but she looked at him and smiled as he started laying out the plans and the changes that he wanted to make.

The mansion was silent, all except the crackling of the fire. As the couple laid there, holding each other. Cindy began to get a chill all over her body. James could feel the coolness of her skin, not wanting to leave the fire. He said. "Honey, you're freezing hold on a second,"

Then he got up and got the sheet that was covering the couch.

Earlier that day, shook the dust out of it and climbed back on the couch, wrapping it around the both. In no time at all Cindy was warm and toasty next to her husband's body as he held her in his arms, watching the fire crackling away. They both sighed a sigh of relief as a calm fell over the moment.

Cindy looked up at James and kissed him tenderly saying, "You know honey, I think we really will be happy here. The place is beautiful. We have each other and soon the boys will be here. What more could we want?"

James took in a deep breath and while letting it out slowly saying, "Yes I know baby, I feel like sometimes it's almost too good to be true."

"I know what you mean, it really is like a dream except for a few little creepy things to bring me back to the reality of it all in all I do feel very lucky to have inherited such a beautiful place upon a mountain."

Then they just lay there, watching the fire, holding each other from time to time they would kiss and looked lovingly into each other's eyes. Cindy feeling so comfortable lying on her husband's chest felt herself starting to do and although she was tired and would like to go to bed, she didn't want to break the moment of them being together. James. Feeling the same things. Al said nothing and just laid there, holding his beautiful little wife watching the fire burned away. Till them both slipped off into a deep sleep, holding each other.

Then suddenly, they were both awoken at the same time, by a loud noise coming from upstairs. Sounding like a door slamming shut and it's startled them both.

Cindy said. "Let me guess. That was the wind slamming the door shut upstairs, right?"

"In a matter of fact, it probably was." Said James just trying to dismiss it as such and the fact that the fire had burned away and it was truly getting cold in the house James looked down at her, saying, "Let's go to bed."

Cindy nodded her head and then they both got up and went upstairs to their room. James, not wanting to get into the bed dirty, decided to take a shower Cindy so exhausted she could hardly hold her eyes open and the fact that she had called into that warm comfortable bed was too much for her

she slipped off into a deep sleep, only to be awoken by the sound of movement in the room looking through her half-closed eyes. She saw a figure moving in the dark at the foot of the bed and dismissed it as being James coming out of the shower.

she simply closed her eyes and started to slip back into a slumber. Only to once again being awoken by James. Opening the bathroom door and the light flooding the room startling Cindy. That's when she realized that the figure she had seen earlier was not James. Cindy Setup in the bed looking at him and asked, "Where you Just in here?"

James looked at her and yawned saying, "No honey, you saw me come out of the bathroom. What are you talking about?"

"I could've sworn I saw someone walk by the end of the bed. I thought it was you." Said Cindy with her eyes closed.

James stretched out beside her while closing his eyes said. "Oh honey, can we give the ghosts arrest tonight I'm very tired and would like to try to get a good night sleep without you hearing something bumping in the middle of the night, you must have dreamed it."

Cindy said without opening hers,

"You're probably right. Good night honey."

"Good night baby." Said James rolling on his side.

The next morning. James was awoken by Cindy. Jumping up and running into the bathroom. By the time, James reached the bathroom door. He could hear her getting sick and knocked on the door asking,

"Honey, are you all, right?

But there was no reply from her, then he could hear her as she was getting sick once more. James

Knocked on the door, asking again, "Cindy, honey, are you all, right?

Cindy snapped at him, saying, "Does it sound like I'm all right?"

"Is there anything I can do for you?" Asked James. With concern in his voice.

"No Something I ate is not agreeing with me." Said Cindy trying to explain it.

"You think it was that pizza?" Asked James trying to help her figure it out.

Cindy flushed the toilet and came and opened the bathroom door, looking at him and asked,

"I don't know. Are you feeling bad?"

"No honey I'm fine." Said James looking at her as she was wiping her face with a cool rag.

"Then I guess it wasn't a pizza." Said Cindy as she walked past him. Going back to the bedroom. "Why don't you lay back down for a while till you start to feel better?" Asked James following

Her back over to the bed with concern in his voice.

"That's just what I'm going to do." Said Cindy climbing back into the bed.

"Would you like me to go get you something cold to drink asked James sitting down on the side of the bed next to her.

"Maybe a cold glass of water." Said Cindy looking at him.

"Okay honey, I'll be right back." Said James as he got up from sitting on the side of the bed and headed downstairs to get her a cold drink of water. When he returned, Cindy, was fast asleep. Not wanting to disturb her. He covered her up and sat back down on the side of the bed, watching her sleep

James got up and went downstairs into his study, he was rearranging some of the old books that have been left on the shelf.

When he came across a very old and fragile ledger belonging to George Summerhill. He very carefully opened it contained within it were notes from George, to his self. About the manner and as he further looked through the ledger, he came a cough old photograph of the manner in all its beautiful glory. With a man and woman standing in front of it and that is when for the first time. James got a look at Margaret. He became captivated by her photo.

Although she was some distance away from the camera and it was quite an old likeness of her. It left an impression on him. He found his self-longing to see more photographs of her. So, he began digging around, some of the old books contained on the shelf. He did in fact, come a crossed several photo albums with even more photos of the wants beautiful woman. Margaret. He turned, page after page of the album learning more about the Summerhill's and deeper into the album James came across a full likeness of Margaret. He thought,

"My God! She truly was a beautiful woman."

James could not take his eyes off her. He seemed almost memorized by her eyes, looking back at him from the photo. He walked over and sat down behind his desk and just stared at the likeness of Margaret. There was something almost hypnotic about her photograph that seem to draw him in, causing him to lose track of time. He began to wonder what she truly was like, so he got up once more, searching the shelves, eager to find more out about her.

with that in mind he combed every shelf, nuking Carney throughout the study, he finally came upon a stack of old ledgers, some belonging to George. Others were from other family members. Some of George ledgers dated back to when he was just a lad attending school. James began to read the whole life story of George Summerhill, because back in that time. That's what most men did. They kept a ledger, writing down everything that they did and that happened to them.

Sometimes the ledgers would, lay out a man's whole entire life history. From the time, they were children up into the time. They could no longer write. There, it all was laid out in front of James, but it wasn't George that James was eager to find out about, it was Margaret.

he searched through the ledgers hoping to find one for her, but there were none to be found. Although he did come upon one, where George had written about his first encounter with Margaret Peabody. James red where George wrote,

"I met the most beautiful woman, I think that exist in this whole world. The very line of her, the color of her skin, the links of her long hair. The curvature of her body and the sparkle in her eye. All of them seem to captivate me and the only thing I could think about was, when would be the next time I see her. That's why I'm setting out to somehow make this woman my own. Her father's, one of the richest men in Washington. Owning a railroad. He knows crooked politicians and judges and he his self, is a tyrant of a man. It is hard for me to imagine a man of his stature, having such an enchanting daughter. But still I had to somehow make her mine. I'm going over to see her tomorrow and ask her if she'll write to me while I'm away at war. My goal is to climb as high in rank as I possibly can so that her father will show favoritism upon me when I returned home after the war."

Upon searching that ledger. James came upon a stack of letters from George to Margaret. Blinded with a red velvet strap, James. Very gently pulled the strap loose from the letters got one out and begin reading it. The letter was written by George while he was away at war. George wrote,

"My dearest Margaret. I killed a young man today, just a boy really. I watched the life leave him at my hands. I have so much blood on them. That even after they are cleaned, I still can see it and it is my hope and desire to somehow find some good in all of this that we are doing. My darling. It is my hope that when the war is over to make you my wife and having a wonderful life with you and in doing so somehow sponge away all the blood and that you can somehow, help me to overcome the nightmares and forget about some of the horrific, terrible things that I have done."

James just sat back in his chair. Replaying in his mind all the things that he had read in the way that George talk to Margaret. From time to time he would pick up the photo of her and gazing into those hypnotic eyes. James spent the better part of the day reading through the ledgers and some more letters that George had written to Margaret about how much he loved her and couldn't wait to get home to her, one made an impact on him, saying,

"Oh, my darling, this is truly the gateway of hell. So much blood and guts. I watch men fall all around me from both sides. If it were not having the thought of you and how much we loved each other. To help me through these days, I truly feel sometimes it would be more humane, to take my revolver and blow off the top of my head. But my love, I do have you waiting for me to return home, that thought alone, my darling helps me through another bloody day. I'm a lieutenant now my love, not that I wanted that rank, but I was next in line and I can't describe the feeling of watching these young boys, being blown to bits, by cannon balls and shot down in the beginning of some their lives, under my command. Several times now, I have literally had to march them to what ultimately was their death. But sometimes amongst all the blood and guts, something happens to remind us what we're fighting for. A young boy under my command, got a letter from home from his new wife, saying, that a baby has been born. It was a healthy little boy, they would both be waiting for him to come home, that reminded us why we were fighting. Because we believe what we were doing, is right in the eyes of God. But you still must question it. How could God let such horrific things happen to......?"

There was no more writing of that letter. James searched frantically through the letters, trying to find the continuance of that particular one. But there were none. James noticed a letter that appeared to have droplets of blood on it so he read it. The letter said.

"My dearest Margaret. It's been quite some time since I received a letter from you. I hope all is well, is still the same hell here. I'm a lieutenant colonel now, just another rank with another name. I'm still in the middle of all the blood and guts my darling. It is my hope and wish that you have not abandoned me, because it is the thought of you and our life together. They keep me going. One of my youngest captains. Is starting to question the existence of God. He came to me wanting counseling on the subject. What do I tell him, my dear? I told him what I tell all of them. They were doing the right thing, God is on our side. It's hard to watch these young boys, fighting because they're told to. Because a lot of them don't really know why they're fighting. Some are just following others to their death. My darling. I see their faces when I close my eyes at night. I feel their pain. I hear their screams. I smell death every day now and that unforgettable smell of rotting flesh. I had discovered the higher up in rank to go, the less you fight. Instead, you must send others to their death. If you make a good decision. You may get a handful of them back. You make a bad one and all will be lost, but you yourself sit back and watch it unfold in front of you. Please, my darling right to me. Let me know I still have something to come home to.

Then suddenly from the corner of his eye. He noticed one of the letters stood out more than the others. It was dirty and looked like it had been balled up in and straighten back out. It, too, was covered with blood. James began to read it. It was obviously written by a broken man. Not only filling in despair. But in fear for his very soul. The letter said.

"My dearest Margaret. I still have not received any letter from you, all is but lost. There is only a handful of us left now. So many have died. So much death and despair. I keep trying to find a shred of hope to cling to. But there is none. I held that young man. That recently had a child born, in my arms this morning and watched him die. It made me begin to wonder, what his wife and baby was going to do, without their father. So many sons and fathers have died in this damnable war. I find myself wondering if it was even worse it? So many times, I told these children of God. That we were fighting because we believed it was the right thing to do, but I don't know anymore. My darling. All I really want to do is come home to you now. But there are so few of us left, I am beginning to wonder if I'm even going to be able to. I can't even begin to describe some of the horror that I've seen. I am no longer looking at one side or the other. My darling, I look at this war and I wonder how one human being could do the things to another in the name of what they believe. I'm a colonel now, my dear and I'm sure in the eyes of your father and men like him, that will probably stand for something. But they're not crawling around in all this blood and guts, like I am. I watch these young men, boys really go to their death, day after day. I truly feel like this war has broken me, not receiving a letter from

You any longer. Makes me wonder, is there any hope at all left……,"

When James got done reading the letter. He set back in his chair, letting all the information that he had just obtain run through his mind. Then James heard what sounded like a woman calling him in the distance, so he got up to go check on Cindy, as he walked toward the stairs. He heard it once again, it was a woman calling his name off in the distance. Only it seemed to be coming from outside somewhere, James thought,

"Now what is she doing outside. I thought she was sick?"

As he continued to the back of the house. Her voice seemed to be coming from the garden area. When James got there, there was no one. All he saw was a landscape and several statues, including the one that killed the boy. But Cindy was not there. He stood there for a minute waiting to see if he could hear. Calling him again, but there was nothing. James turned around went back into the house and upstairs to check on her. Cindy was not in the bed. he called to her.

"Cindy, honey, where are you?" Asked James concerned for her.

Then the bathroom door open. Cindy came out obviously still not feeling well, asking, "What is it?"

James asked her "Were you just outside in the garden?"

Cindy, while climbing back into the bed, saying, facetiously

"No does it look like I could go out to the garden?"

James paused for a minute, then said. "That's funny. I could've swore I heard you call me from the garden."

Cindy once again facetiously said. "Maybe it was the wind."

James just looked at her saying, No really, honey, I'm serious. I thought you were in the garden calling me."

"James I've been right here all morning. I'm so sick, I sure don't feel like getting out and playing with you in the garden." Said Cindy laying back down. Placing a wash rag over her eyes.

"Anyway, can I get you anything?" Asked James. With concern in his voice. "I mean, are you hungry, or would you like something cold to drink?"

Cindy answered him feeling guilty for the way she spoke to him, saying,

"No honey I'm sorry, I just don't feel well, but thank you for asking."

James smiled at her, reached out and touched her on the leg saying,

"All right, honey try to get some more rest, if you need me I'm just downstairs in a study."

"Thank you, James. Maybe I'll feel better in a little while." Said Cindy curling up in a ball.

James just stood there for a minute, looking at his little wife.

Then he very quietly turned around and eased out of the room, so as not to disturb her. James was thinking. As he was going back downstairs,

"Now I know I heard someone call me." Then he paused for a minute, thinking, then said out loud. "I know what it was, it was Cindy's ghost, either that or my imagination is running amok same as hers. At any rate, it was quite strange."

Then James returned to the study and continued his search to find out more about the elusive Margaret. He searched through all the boxes, drawers and shelves. Hoping to find more treasures. Then at last. He found what he was looking for.

CHAPTER 18

There in a Crimson colored, covered diary, were all of Margaret's thoughts. James picked it up Very gently and brushed the dust off it. Holding it like a priceless heirloom. He just couldn't believe his eyes. Then he very gently opened it and began reading all about the elusive woman.

As James read her inner thoughts. He started feeling somewhat connected to her, dabbling in her mind. She starts out innocently enough, talking about her day and some of the wonderful things happening in her life and then as though a black veil had been drawn. Her thoughts become sinister and cold. Without feeling almost as though something, evil had entered her mind and then......!

James was interrupted by the sound of a woman calling his name once again, he listened there it was again seeming to be coming from everywhere, as though it was in his head.

He very gently closed the diary. Standing to his feet. He went out to investigate where the sound was truly coming from.

Cindy woke up in the bed alone, feeling better, so she got up and slipped on a rope and went downstairs to find James. Going from room to room. But James was nowhere to be found. She looked out front. He wasn't there either. Then she walked to the back of the house to the garden area. As she came to the large glass door leading out onto the landing. She saw James standing beside a statue. The same one that they had removed from the house and killed that boy.

Cindy eased out onto the landing and call to him and although he was just a few feet away. It was as if he didn't hear her. she called to him again, saying, "James, can you hear me?"

He just stood there staring at the face of the statue still not getting a reply from him. She approached him out into the garden and touched him on the shoulder. He jumped, startled and ask, "What the hell are you doing?"

"James, didn't you hear me call you?" Asked Cindy, feeling a little startled herself.

"No I didn't hear you call me." Said James angrily.

"What are you doing? Why are you standing here looking at that statue?" Asked Cindy with confusion in her voice.

Cindy, noticing that it was in fact turned facing the house and she had requested that it be facing toward the mountains saying, "Why is this stupid thing turned toward the house? It's supposed to be facing the mountain."

James staring at the statue answered her, saying, "I don't know. You know, whoever she was, she was a beautiful woman."

Cindy, looking at the statue, not believing what she just heard him say Feeling a little bit of jealousy." Said to her husband,

"If you say so, but damn thing gives me the creeps."

Then she turned around and walked back toward the house, heading upstairs to get dressed. After getting dressed she came back downstairs, looking for James.

He was still standing in the garden staring at that statue and she could not believe it, so she walked out to the landing. Once again saying, with a Stern voice

"Are you going to stand there all day and stared at that stupid damn thing, or are you going to help me finish cleaning our house?"

James did not reply. He just stood there staring at the statue. Then Cindy hollered once again now really beginning to get frustrated with him saying, "James."

But still she got no reply from him. So once again, she approached him out in the yard and touched him on the arm, saying, "James."

He suddenly jerked his head around and looked at her, his eyes were dark. His face was distorted and he said with a cold, angry voice,

"Woman, what the hell do you want?"

"From the look on his face and the fact that she could not believe the way he had just spoken to her scared her, so she asked in a very calm voice,

"What's wrong with you?"

"What wrong with me? I'll tell you what's wrong with me all you do is nag, nag, nag, now what do you want?" Barked James once again.

Cindy not believing the way he was speaking to her. Didn't say anything, she just turned around and walked back into the house. Feeling hurt and confused. Replaying over and over in her mind not only what he said. but the way he said it. Cindy went about cleaning feeling so hurt, she just couldn't believe it was happening. From time to time she looked out the window. She watched her husband standing in the yard just staring at that statue, all day long.

He stood out there without moving a muscle. Cindy began to get hungry, but she was truly afraid to say anything to James because there was obviously something wrong with him, the way he looked at her. hateful it truly did scare her, so she decided to leave him alone and go into the kitchen and see if she could find something to eat. Fortunately for her. Mr. Wilcox had not only had the freezer fill full of food. But all the cabinets and Refrigerator had plenty to eat in them as well. Cindy found some sandwich meat in the refrigerator and some bread. she made herself a sandwich and she brewed a couple tea bags in a little tiny pot on the stove and made a pitcher of tea. Then she found a place where she could stare out the window and watch her husband, unbelievably just standing in the yard staring at the statue. Cindy ate her sandwich and drank her tea. Watching him, feeling helpless, because she truly did not know what to do.

Upon finishing her sandwich. She thought,

"Maybe I should go see if he wants a sandwich he's got to be getting hungry. He's been standing there all day, just staring at that thing. God, what is, come over him, I've never seen James like that and it scares the hell out of me."

Cindy thought about it for a few minutes and then she decided no, she would just leave him alone and she went back to cleaning on her house. The day seem to slip away and it started getting dark outside. Cindy walked to the back door, looking out at James just standing there, obviously fatigued as he began to rock back and forth and looking like any moment he could fall over.

She thought about saying, something to him, but she was still frightened from earlier, so she just turned around and went upstairs to get her shower.

Cindy pulled off all her close and climbed into the shower standing there underneath the hot water, she felt like crying, she never felt so alone and distance from James and she really did not know what to do. She thought about calling. Tracy and talking to her about it, but it would only worry her. Cindy finished her shower and dried off her body slipped on her night close and went back downstairs, one last time she looked out the back door. It was pitch dark outside. she turned on the outside lights. They were bright, illuminating the whole backyard including the garden area and there to her utter amazement, James was still standing beside the statue against her better judgment. She eased out onto the landing holding onto the railing. She said in a very calm voice,

"James honey, please come inside. You're scaring me."

But there was no reply. He stood there staring at that statue about the fall. Cindy could not believe her eyes and she began to fill frustrated with him. she turned around and very slowly walked back into the house. Leaving the outside lights on. She went upstairs and climbed into bed, laying there, she began to cry because she didn't know what to do. She was scared and felt so alone. Cindy cried herself to sleep.

Only to be awoken in the middle of the night by feeling James climb in bed beside her. This truly did frighten her. Cindy, felt like getting up and running out of the room, or at least turning on the light, but she was afraid of what she might see. she just turned on her side with her back to him and pulled the covers tight up to her chin, then suddenly James put his arms around her and pulled her close to him. Cindy truly feeling confused.

Didn't know what to do, her husband's arms felt wonderful wrapped around her, but the way he was acting scared the hell out of her. All kinds of thoughts ran through her mind as she laid there, with his arms wrapped around her to her eyelids got so heavy. She could no longer hold them open and she slipped off into a deep sleep

The next morning, Cindy woke up next to James. She rolled over and looked at him. James opened his eyes smiled at her and asked,

"Good morning baby. Do you feel better today?"

Cindy look to him with confusion saying,

"Yes, I do, how you feel today?" she asked.

"I feel all right. I'll be glad when we get this place cleaned up, my God! It's huge. You sure you don't want to hire some extra help? Just to get it cleaned up. I mean." Said James sliding his legs off the side of the bed and sitting up.

"No honey, I want us to do it." Said Cindy feeling very confused.

Not being able to stand it any longer. She looked at James asking,

"James what the hell was all that about?"

James turned around and looked at her with confusion and ask,

"What you talking about honey?"

"Yesterday you would that damn statue. You said some really hurtful things to me." Said Cindy about to cry.

James looked at her obviously confused asking,

"Cindy what the hell you talking about honey, what statue?"

Cindy, feeling frustrated jumped out of bed and said angrily,

"You know damn well what I'm talking about yesterday you stood outside all day into the night staring at that damn statue you snapped at me. You said. all I do is nag, nag, nag, you scared me James, I thought you were going to hurt me,"

"Oh honey, I would never hurt you, I love you, Cindy, I think you're confused honey, you were sick all day yesterday you never got out of bed. I came in and checked on you a couple times. Cindy baby, you must've dreamed it." Said James trying to put her mind at ease.

"It seems so real. James, I thought., Cindy paused for a minute. Then she asked "It was a dream?"

"Yes honey, it was just a dream, I cleaned on my study and fiddled around in the house and you slept all day, I came up a couple times and tucked you in and ask you if you are hungry and if you wanted anything to drink, don't you remember me bringing you back glass of water? Asked James pointing over to the nightstand.

There was a glass that was half empty with water in it. Cindy looked down at the floor and she got dizzy, catching herself at the end of the bed and sat down, realizing that it was just a dream. She said as her voice cracked about to cry.

"I'm sorry honey, but it seemed so real"

But she also felt relief. Realizing that James really did not talk to her like that. It was just a dream. Cindy reached over and put her arms around James thanking and kissing him.

Then the couple got up and got dressed and went downstairs. James asked.

"Cindy what would you like to do today?"

Cindy said. "We've only got one more room that needs to be cleaned downstairs. Then we got to go start on the upstairs."

The couple walked down the hall coming to two huge wooden doors with brass handles and swung them open and there, on the other side was another huge, massive, magnificent room, with gorgeous chandelier hanging in the center of it and what appeared to be a grand piano covered in dust. Giant windows that had to be 11 feet high with long curtains. James said.

"My God! I wonder what this room was for."

"I think it must've been a music room honey." Said Cindy, pulling at the windows curtains to let in some light.

"You mean like a ballroom where people come to dance and party, things like that?' Asked James helping her to open the windows.

"I think so. My God! You could've put our trailer and yard in this room." Said James looking at what appeared to be a marble floor.

"James this is without a doubt the most beautiful room I have ever seen in my entire life." Said Cindy so excited. She was about to pee her pants.

When they finally got all the windows open and the light filled the room shining on the chandelier reflecting all around the room they both just stood there in awe over the beauty of it all.

Then James looked at Cindy and asked,

"Honey, what are we going to do with this room?"

"I don't know. James, I don't know what you're supposed to do with a room like this," answered Cindy. Feeling absolutely overwhelmed.

Just then they heard musical chimes ringing throughout the whole mansion. They looked at each other. James said.

"What the hell is that?"

"I don't know honey." Said Cindy, feeling just as confused.

Then they both heard the faint knocking at the front door.

James said. "Wow that must've been the doorbell." As he headed toward the front of the mansion to the door to see who it was.

As he got to the front door. He opened it and there stood Mr. Wilcox.

"Oh hello, Mr. Wilcox, how are you doing sir?" Asked James reaching out to shake his hand and saying, "Please do come in."

"Hello James, I just thought I'd stop by and see how you guys are coming along." Said Mr. Wilcox.

By then. Cindy had gotten to the front door, saying,

"Hello Mr. Wilcox, how are you doing sir?"

"Hello Cindy, like I was telling James, I just stopped by to see how things are going and please if you would call me Marcus." Said Mr. Wilcox, smiling at her.

"Well it's a little slow, but things are starting to come together. Please want you come in and sit down?" said Cindy, leading him to, what they think is the sitting room.

"Yes, the place is pretty big. You know, of course, anytime you get ready, you can easily hire on some help this place is way too big for you two, to manage on your own." Said Marcus.

"Yes, we know, we just found what we think might be a music room. I was telling Cindy. We could have put our whole trailer and yard, both in just that room." Said James. Obviously feeling overwhelmed.

"Well there is. Some of this house, you could just shut down and close off that way it won't be so overwhelming." Said Marcus.

"We haven't even found all of it yet." Said Cindy giggling with excitement.

"Oh by the way we want to thank you for stocking the freezer and cabinets full of food." Said Cindy smiling at him.

"Well I didn't figure you guys would have time for all of that, just moving in and you're quite welcome, although there are some really good places around here to get something to eat." Said Marcus.

"Yes, we found one of them already, called Betty's family diner. But that place is hazardous to your health." Said James rubbing his belly.

Marcus look to him saying, "Oh yes I know exactly what you're talking about, they give way too much food out, but it is good."

James patted his belly again and said "Yes it's too good. We were just discussing that the other night, I ate so much. I looked like a beached whale and Cindy looked pregnant."

Then all three of them started laughing, Marcus asked,

"By the way, don't you two have kids where are they, if you don't mind me asking?"

"Not at all. A friend of ours is keeping the boys until summer break so that they can finish school. Cindy was afraid that if we took him away from their friends and out of school. They would hate her." Said James looking over at her and smiling.

"That was a good idea that would give you a chance to get settled in. How old are they?" Asked Marcus.

"Well Billy's 11 and youngest Michael, he is 6 and he is hell on wheels." Said James laughing about it.

"But both my boys are good kids. That's one of the blessings about moving here to get them out of the city of Detroit, away from the gangs and the crime." Said Cindy. Thinking about them. I really do miss them and can't wait for them to get up here, I think they're going to love it."

"Well you live on a beautiful mountain there are lots of woods, they can explore and there's a creek down in the bottom that dumps into a huge lake, full of fish down in the Valley. I must show you some time." Said Marcus. "I mean, I've lived here all my life. I know where pretty much everything is having been here as a boy. Speaking of boys, I have a son he is 12 maybe when your boys get here. I'll bring him over and who knows, they might hit it off."

"Oh, that would be wonderful Marcus, I told Billy when he got here he would make new friends." Said Cindy. "Hopefully they will? Who knows, they might become best friends."

"Do you like to do any hunting James?" Asked Marcus.

"I love the bow hunt," answered James "But we live on a wildlife reserve, don't we?"

"Yes, but it's your mountain if you want to hunt it There's no one to stop you." Said Marcus. "And if you do maybe I can come along and hunting with you. I love the bow hunt myself." Said Marcus.

"Wow that be cool and yes, of course, Marcus, you're more than welcome, to go hunting by yourself or I would love for you to go with me." Said James.

"Are you married?" Asked Cindy. "I mean, does your wife like to hunt and go fishing?"

"Wendy, she likes to fish, but not much into hunting" said Marcus "But she does like to fish,"

"Wendy is that your wife's name?" Asked Cindy curiously.

"Yes, she's my childhood sweetheart, we went to school together fell in love, we went to separate colleges, but when we got back home and we got back together. I don't think either one of us has ever dated anyone else." Said Marcus pulling out his wallet to show them a photo of his wife."

"Maybe you two can come to dinner sometime. God knows we got the room." Said Cindy. Laughing out loud.

"Yes, I'm sure Wendy would love that. I know that I would. This is a big beautiful place I've always loved it." Said Marcus. Confirming their invitation.

"After we get settled in and I get everything organized. We will definitely have to get together and I'll show you and your wife all around." Said Cindy trying to make him feel welcome.

"That would be wonderful." Said Marcus "Well I guess I better be going. I just wanted to stop by and check on you guys." Said Marcus getting up from the couch.

"Oh, yes and I also wanted to tell you that your gift was greatly appreciated. They wanted me to tell you thank you and it helped more than you could realize and they also wanted to know if perhaps they might come and thank you personally they asked me to ask you, not knowing whether they would be disturbing you are not said Marcus. Looking at James and Cindy, waiting for confirmation,

"But of course, you tell them that there are more than welcome and that if we can help in any other way not to hesitate to let us know." Said James. With Cindy wright behind him. Confirming it.

"I will tell them. James and Cindy, thank you both and God truly will bless you for help in that family." Said Marcus walking to the front door.

James put his arm around Cindy saying, "God has already blessed us

Marcus in many ways. You take care and come back to see us anytime and bring that lovely wife and son of yours."

"We will do it and you two take care." Said Marcus turning around and heading to his car.

James and Cindy returned to the music room and begin cleaning. Then suddenly, they heard the chimes once again.

"Marcus must've forgot something." Said James

As they walked back to the front door and opened it, but there was no one there.

"That's strange." Said James scratching his head.

Cindy said "Maybe it was the wind."

"Very funny." Said James as he closed the door and went back to the room to finish cleaning.

Then once again they heard the chimes from the doorbell. Only this time James went to the door by his self, leaving Cindy in the room alone. Cindy felt a cold chill come across your body, as the hair stood up on the back of her neck, while she was standing in the huge room. She walked over to the piano and begin to try to clean it. She raised the lid and propped it open, with its stand. Cindy begin dusting the piano all over, waiting for James to return. She was holding onto the side of it, as she very gently took a soft rag and begin to wipe the dust off it. Cindy got the eerie feeling, that someone, or something, was in the room with her. She begins to get frightened and as she turned around to look across the room, the lid from the piano came slamming down, just missing her hand. At the same instant James came walking back into the room saying, "I think I know what it is, after all these years no one has been pushing the button to ring the door chimes. When Marcus did, it must now be sticking." Said James quite pleased with himself that he had figured out what it was.

Cindy on the other hand struggled, with the thought in her mind.

"Should she tell James what just happened to her, or keep it to herself."

Realizing he would just probably dismiss it and not take her seriously. She decided to keep it to herself. The rest of the day they cleaned on the room. Without any other incident occurring. But in the back of Cindy's mind, she couldn't forget the encounter. Each time James would lead the room, she would follow him not wanting to be left alone in them.

They cleaned the whole entire room, it seemed like it took the better part of the day. But finally, they were done, the room was magnificent and immaculate. With the marble floors and a grand piano now dusted and brought back to its beautiful luster. The light coming through the windows filled the room and once again James turned his Cindy and asked,

"Honey what are we going to do with this room?"

"I don't know James, but isn't it beautiful said Cindy with the excitement overwhelming her.

Then she said.

"My God and my tired." "I know honey so am I, what do you say we go upstairs and get a quick shower, then head into town to our little diner, to have dinner?" Asked James heading out of the room.

"That sounds good to me," answered Cindy following James upstairs to their room.

The couple got a change of clothes. Then went into the bathroom, to get a shower. While they were in their soaping each other's bodies up although they were naked and it had been a long time since they made love, they were both just too tired. neither one of them really didn't seem to want to get into anything, they just finished their shower, got dressed and headed into town to have dinner.

When James and Cindy arrived at the restaurant, James came around to open the door for her. Cindy standing up beside the truck, felt dizzy and had to sit back down on the seat. James concern for her asked, "Honey are you all right?"

"Yes, just give me a minute please," answered Cindy starting to feel better.

"Of course, baby take all the time you need. A matter of fact let's just go back home." Said James feeling concern for his little wife.

"Don't be silly I'm fine." Said Cindy standing back to her feet." Anyway, I'm hungry."

"Well alright baby if you're sure." Said James taking her by the arm to help her inside.

"James please I am not an invalid." Said Cindy feeling embarrassed pulling her arm away from him and walking on her own.

"I know honey I'm just concerned about you." Said James opening the door for her.

"I know James I'm sorry the whole thing is just embarrassing. I obviously have overdone it to day. I just want to have a nice dinner, then go home and curl up on the couch and watch a movie with you." Said Cindy trying to explain herself.

"Okay baby that does sound nice. But if you start to feel bad, or dizzy again, let me know." Said James obviously still feeling concern for her.

"Don't worry honey I will." Said Cindy smiling at him.

Peggy upon saying, the couple come inside. Waived at them from across the room. As she walked over saying, "Have a seat guys I'll be right with you."

James led Cindy to a nice comfortable quiet booth, over in the corner of the restaurant. The couple both sat down and waited for Peggy.

True to her word, in a few minutes she came walking up, with two menus, handing them to James and Cindy saying, "Good evening you to, how are things going? I mean have you guys got all settled in?" Asked Peggy eager to hear what they had to say.

"Well we got a lot of the place cleaned up. Oh, my God! Peggy some of the rooms in that place are magnificent and they are huge. We were just discussing today what we're going to do with a lot of those rooms." Said Cindy bubbling over with excitement.

"Yes, I imagine it is all a bit overwhelming. Why don't you guys think about turning that place into a hotel, or maybe even a bed-and-breakfast is beyond me. I know that's what I would do." Said Peggy getting out her notepad to write down what they might want for dinner.

James looked over at Cindy commenting on her suggestion saying, "You know that's not a bad idea, God knows we've got the room. We could hire on a little's staff to help with the guest and cook the breakfast.

"Well I don't know James it could be something to think about." Said Cindy looking at him and then at Peggy.

"I know that's what I would do sweetie." Said Peggy then she asked "What would you guys like to have for dinner tonight?"

Cindy said. "I would like….,"

Then suddenly, she put her hand over her mouth jumping up from the table. Obviously headed to the bathroom, but as soon as she got to her feet, she collapsed in the floor. James rushed to her side asking, "Oh my God! Cindy honey are you all right?"

But there was no reply, she had passed out unconscious. Holding her in his arms James looked at Peggy and asked, "Please would you call me an ambulance?"

"But of course, sweetie." Said Peggy scurrying to the back of the restaurant, to get to the phone as quickly as she could. A few minutes later she returned saying,

"They're on their way. What could be wrong with her?" Asked Peggy obviously feeling concerned for her.

"I don't know Peggy, wish I did. When we were coming in, she felt dizzy and had to sit back down in the truck. She said she thought she just overdid it today." Said James holding her in his arms waiting for the ambulance to arrive.

"I'm sure that's all it is." Said Peggy trying to comfort him.

"I don't know," she has been under a lot of stress with all this. Between leaving the boys behind and all the cleaning on that place. Plus, she is convinced it is haunted and she keeps having bad dreams. I don't know maybe it's all just too much for her." Said James starting to rock her in his arms.

Just then the ambulance came pulling up with their siring on. Two paramedics came rushing inside, asking James several questions,

"Like how old she was, how long has she been un-conscience and had it happen before?"

James told them, about the dizzy spell she had, just before coming in the restaurant. Then he went on to say, that he thought she may have overdone it today, cleaning on their estate. One of the paramedics said. "That's right. You two are the couple that have inherited the Summerhill manor, aren't you?"

"Yes, we are," answered James then he asked "What's wrong with my wife?"

"That's what we're trying to find out Sir, please if you would stay back out of the way."

Said one of the paramedics. Then one of the paramedics radioed to the doctor. At the hospital, he said. "Transport her as soon as possible to the hospital."

One of the paramedics, told James the doctor, wants us to bring her in, to examine her. He's very concerned, about the fact of her still being unconscious. James told the paramedics that he would follow them. they wheeled Cindy out on a gurney and put her in the back of the ambulance, heading to the hospital, as quickly as they could. With James right behind them, being very careful not to lose them. Because he in fact did not even know, where the hospital was. When they arrived at the hospital, the ambulance backed in.

James parked his truck and rushed into the emergency room. The nurses stopped him from going back, as a wheeled Cindy down a long hallway and out of sight, leaving James standing alone in the room.

James walked over and said down, in the waiting room. He struggled with the idea of calling telling Tracy. But he also knew he would just worry her and James in fact wasn't that type of man. He was the stronger quiet type that keeps to himself kind of person.

he figured he would just wait to find out what was wrong with Cindy before he called her. The hours passed by so slowly. All kinds of thoughts ran through James head, as he sat quietly in the corner watching people come and go.

Till finally James noticed a doctor walking to the desk. One of the nurses behind it stood to her feet and pointed over at James. The doctor walked toward him. James got up and met the doctor in the middle of the room the doctor said. "Mr. Parker I am Dr. Collins; your wife is resting comfortably..."

"Just tell me what's wrong with her doctor." Said James interrupting him.

"Well that's what I want to talk to you about can you tell me what she's been doing the last

couple of days?" Asked the doctor.

"We inherited a place here in the mountains and we been cleaning on it." Said James trying to answer his question.

"Now when you say cleaning, you mean with cleaning solutions, such as warm soapy water, things of that nature right?" Asked, the doctor would be concerning his voice.

"Yes, sir we both have," answered James trying to make sense out of all of it.

"What kind of cleaning solutions chemicals has she been using?" Asked the doctor once again we concerning his voice.

"Well some type of polishing oil, for the woodwork and she's been mixing bleach and water with some type of soap in a box, I am not sure just what it is." Said James now getting very concerned.

"Mr. Parker your wife should not be exposed, to any type of cleaning solutions such as that not in her condition and I'm sure that ultimately is why she's been passing out." Said the doctor filling like he had discovered the cause.

"Her condition, I don't understand doctor, what condition?" Asked, James with confusion.

"Mr. Parker your wife is pregnant, I thought you knew that Sir." Said the doctor with confusion.

"Why no!!" Neither one of us did. Is that why she keeps getting sick in the morning and has lightheadedness and can't seem to get enough to eat?" Asked James starting to understand.

"I'm sure it is Mr. Parker, you should really try to keep her from using any type of cleaning solution and stay off her feet as much as possible. Is times like this, we really must take care of our wives. Try to be more understanding to her needs, she's got to be going through a lot of different types of things. Such as mood swings, hot and cold sweats that type of thing.

Is this your first child?" Asked the doctor.

"It is her first child. I've got two boys from another woman, she died several years ago, since then Cindy has become the mother to my two boys." Said James trying at the doctor's question best he could.

"Well looks like your two boys are going to have a brother or sister, I assume having just moved here you don't have a regular doctor yet?" Asked the doctor.

"No sir we haven't had time to find one," answered James.

"That's understandable well there is a very good, OB-GYN on staff here at the hospital, I highly recommend her if you would like all have her call Cindy and they can set her up an appointment." Said the doctor.

"Yes, sir thank you very much, I'm sure Cindy needs to see someone soon as possible because we had no idea what was going on with her." Said James still trying to convince the doctor.

"I have Dr. Kerman give her a call as soon as possible." Said the doctor.

"You said Cindy is resting comfortably can I see her?" Asked James would be concerning his voice.

"But of course, follow me all walk you back." Said the doctor as he turned around and headed down the hall, with James close behind him. As they went to the double doors, about three quarters of the way through the hall, they came to the area where Cindy was. To their surprise, she was sitting up in the bed. Upon seeing James, she smiled saying, "Hey honey."

The doctor said. "Hello little lady welcome back, how is you feeling?" Asked the doctor as he walked over and took her vital signs.

"I want to go home." Said Cindy

"Well I don't see any reason to keep you, your vital signs are normal and he seemed to be feeling better, although I must tell you young woman you need to leave those chemicals alone for a while." Said the doctor removing the blood pressure cuff from her arm.

"Is that why I'm passing out?" Asked Cindy looking at the doctor.

"Yes, that and…, the doctor paused for a second and looked over at James saying,

"I think I'll let your husband tell you."

Cindy looked at James with confusion and asked, "Tell me what honey?"

"Well baby looks like we might have to hire some extra help to finish cleaning that place after all at least for a few months anyway." Said James looking over at the doctor and smiling at him.

Cindy tilted her head sideways looking at James filling very confused asking,

"I don't understand, what are you talking about James?"

"Well baby you can't be around any kind of cleaning solution and you need to stay off your feet as much as possible at least for about another, what would you say doc? For maybe five months." Said James smiling at her.

James what do you talk…ing… Cindy paused for a minute smiled from ear to hear put her hand over her mouth saying, "Oh my God! James! You can't be serious. Oh, my God!! Tears of joy started forming in her eyes.

Both James and the doctor were smiling from ear to hear Cindy looked at one and then the other and said again with tears of joy rolling down her cheek,

"Oh, my God!"

James walked over to her put his arms around her and held her kissing her very tenderly, Cindy looked at the doctor and asked, "How could this happen?"

The doctor said. "Well I've got some videos on it and I hear you can download quite a bit information, from the Internet." Said the doctor smiling at her.

"Now listen young lady, I told your husband there is a very good OB-GYN, on staff here at the hospital. I am going to call and talk to her on your behalf and have her get in touch with you, so you can set up an appointment and get you and your baby checked out." Said the doctor looking at her. Then he turned around, while walking out the door he said. "I'll go take care your paperwork, you take care yourself little lady and that baby."

"Oh, I will and thank you very much doctor." Said Cindy smiling at him.

You're very welcome young lady, you make yourself an appointment and take care of yourself." Said the doctor as he walked out the door.

Cindy placed her hand on her belly and smiled saying, out loud for the first time,

"My baby."

Then Cindy looked at James and asked would concerning in her voice,

"Oh, honey is this all right with you?"

"Well it's a little late if it's not." Said James condescendingly, of course it is baby I love you Cindy and no matter what it is boy or girl, I'll am going to love it to."

"Oh James, honey I love you so much." Said Cindy wrapping her arms, tightly around him saying, "We're going to have a baby, a baby, can you believe it James? A baby." Just then a nurse came walking in, bringing the paperwork for Cindy to sign. she could go home and she also had two prescriptions. One was for her anxiety, the other was to help her sleep. After Cindy finish signing the papers, she got in a wheelchair and James pushed her to the front of the hospital. Then he went out to the parking lot to get his truck. James drove around to the entrance to get her. On the way driving back home Cindy was just sitting quietly rubbing around on her belly, smiling from ear to hear obviously deep in thought. James looked over at her and asked, "Honey are you hungry, we never did get any dinner."

"No actually I'm not hungry I just want to go home and lay down." Said Cindy looking over at him.

"But you haven't eaten anything I remember you are eating for two said James smiling at her.

"Okay you're right we do need to feed the baby what sounds good to you?" Asked Cindy leaving the choice up to him.

"Well it is pretty late, art you supposed to be craving something?" Asked James looking over at her.

"Come the think about it, I would like to have some bananas, pickles and salary, dipped in peanut butter. "Oh Yes!! What really sounds good is sardines on crackers in between two pieces of white bread with mayonnaise" said Cindy rubbing her belly.

James just looked at her with a weird look on his face and his lip curled up and to the side saying, "That's the grossest thing I ever heard. So much for my appetite, you really want to eat that?"

"I'm sorry honey," whatever you want to get will be fine, if I eat something." Said Cindy trying to appease her husband.

"No" if that's what you want, I'll get it for you." Said James shaking his head with a funny look on his face. "There must be a grocery store somewhere in this town." He said. while driving along.

Cindy pointed out the window saying, "That looks like a little market right up there James."

"Yes, you're right I think it is honey. I'll pull in and grab some things, you just sit in the truck. I'll be right back." Said James pulling into the market and climbing out.

Cindy watched him as he went into the store thinking of a few other things that sounded good to her and she climbed out of the truck and followed him in.

James upon seeing her come in the store said. "Honey I thought you were going to wait in the truck?"

"I thought of a few other things, that sounded good to me." Said Cindy as she grabbed some marshmallows off-the-shelf. Then she walked over to a cooler and got some cottage cheese. Cindy made her way around the store, as if she knew where she was going. James just watched her, as she gathered up her items. Clinging to them like they were little treasures. When she finally got the last item on her self-made list in her head she looked at James and asked, "Are you going to get some things?"

"No honey I'm not the one with the cravings said James shaking his head as he looked over all her items.

"You really going to eat all this god-awful stuff?" Asked James with a funny look on his face.

Cindy just smiled at him as she grabbed a box of crackers off-the-shelf saying, "Yes I am, me and my baby. Oh, James isn't it wonderful? I can't believe it we're going to have a baby. I am so happy. I can't wait to call Tracy and tell her." Said Cindy just bubbling over with excitement.

"Speaking of Tracy I was thinking honey what if we were to ask her to come and live with us and be our nanny or something like that. That way she could help you with the boys, the mansion and now with the new baby" said James.

"Oh, James you think she would?" Asked Cindy with excitement in her voice.

"Well it would mean she would have to give up her job and her life there and start over

Again, here with us." Said James trying to make her understand.

"James honey," she doesn't have a life, when she brings the boys up there this summer and now that we're gone she truly will be alone." Said Cindy lowering her head.

"You to talk about it." I just want you to know that I'm all for it." Said James walking up to the counter with all of Cindy's items.

After the cashier got through ringing everything up, she looked at James saying, "That will be $172.12."

James looked at Cindy shaking his head and reaching in his back pocket for his wallet, saying, "Damn Honey!! You sure you didn't forget anything?"

Cindy said "Nope, I'm pretty sure I got everything I wanted."

James handed the cashier the money. As she was bagging up their items. Then he grabbed the packages and started out to the truck. Cindy followed along behind him. Already getting into a jar of pickles, which she had grabbed off the counter, before the cashier could bag it.

"James I love her so much," and she really would be a lot of help to me." Said Cindy looking at him, with tears welling up in her eyes. "But what if she won't James. What I do then honey?"

"Cindy I think she's going to be thrilled about the baby and coming to live with us in the mansion. Like you said. she will never have to be alone again." Said James trying to comfort her. As he drove up to their iron Gates and punched in the code. "I mean just talked to her about it honey and give her some time to think it over. Ultimately, I think she'll decide, this is best for everybody involved, including her. Then she can really be a part of our family." Said James further trying to comfort his little wife.

As they drove through the gates and on up to the mansion.

"I really hope so James." I miss her so much." Said Cindy climbing out of the truck.

"Will call and talk to her about it, I've got the groceries." Said James literally grabbing everything at one time. Waiting for Cindy to unlock the door of the mansion. Cindy unlocked the door, stepping over to the side. that James could continue in with all the groceries. As she grabbed her cell phone dialing Tracy's number. It rang a couple times and Tracy answered it saying, "Hello."

"Hey Tracy it's me, how is it going girl and how are the boys." Said Cindy bubbling over with excitement, about asking her. But al feeling a little frightened. Because she just might turn her down.

"Well I haven't killed them yet, if that means anything." Said Tracy giggling.

"Tracy I want to talk to you about something, very important honey. I need your full attention."

"You always have it." Said Tracy feeling apprehensive about what she was going to say.

"Well James and I were talking tonight and please Tracy hear me out honey before you ever say anything." Said Cindy.

"Sounds serious." Is that man upsetting you again?" Asked Tracy really feeling confused.

"No, he and I are getting along wonderfully. It's about you." Said Cindy not wanting to reveal her information just yet.

"About me, what could I have done?" Asked Tracy really feeling confused and a little bit frightened.

"Well it's more or less what we want you to do." Said Cindy still holding back.

"What do you mean honey?" Asked Tracy starting to get a little bit agitated.

"Please hear me out." Said Cindy like I said James and I were talking tonight. What would you say, if we ask you to quit your job down there and come move up here and live with us in this mansion? And be our nanny, or something like that. You could be so much help with this place, the boys and the baby. Oh, Tracy I really need you, I really need you to think it through and I hope you'll decide to. You know how much I love you." Said Cindy.

But there was just silence on the phone…, then Tracy said "I can't do that. That's your family. I couldn't coming impose on you…, Tracy paused for a minute. "Cindy, did you say what I think you said?" Asked Tracy with excitement in her voice.

"Please Tracy think about it honey, I really could use your help and James want you to. It was really more his idea." Said Cindy

"Cindy dad-gum you, answer me." Said Tracy with even more excitement in her voice.

Cindy could no longer contain herself she screamed into the phone saying, "Yes -yes –yes-yes, isn't it wonderful, were going to have a baby." Tracy please honey, I want to share it with you and I want to share my life and everything with you" said Cindy bubbling over with excitement.

But there was just silence on the phone again, Tracy wasn't saying, anything. Cindy asked, "Tracy are you their honey?" But still there was no reply. Cindy thought, *Maybe she hung up?* Asking one more time. "Tracy, are you still their honey?"

"Yes, I'm still here, I'm just taking it all in Cindy. I don't know if I could do that. I mean I love you and James and God knows I love the boys. But that would be me asking a lot out of you guys, I mean to take me in and share your life with me. I love you for even thinking about it. But I just don't know if I could do that." Said Tracy with her voice cracking.

"Tracy I love you, so much and I need you. I'm not trying to put more on you, then you can handle. But I really, really do, need you." Said Cindy also with her voice cracking.

"Well what does a nanny do?" Asked Tracy

"I think she takes care of the kids." But you wouldn't just be a nanny, you would really be a part of our family and you could share this life with me. I don't mean to sound hard about this Tracy. But honey, you don't have anyone and when you bring the boys up here this summer and now that we're gone from down there. You really will be alone. Neither I, nor James, want that. We both want you to come share our life with us and be a part of our family." Said Cindy with her voice cracking so much, it was hard to understand her.

"My God Cindy honey," I just don't know. Can I think about it?" Asked Tracy also feeling overwhelmed with emotion and slurring her words.

But of course, you can. Take all the time you need." Said Cindy now truly holding back the tears. But al feeling apprehensive to the fact that she really hasn't said no yet.

"Thank you, Cindy, and I love you honey." Said Tracy now crying.

"Upon hearing her cry Cindy started crying as well on the phone, telling her once again how much she loved and missed her.

"Cindy honey I hope you understand. But I really need to get off here now." Said Tracy

feeling so overwhelmed with emotion, that her hand was shaking, so much that she could hardly hold the phone.

"I do Tracy, just think about it honey." Said Cindy

Tracy asked, "Cindy you guys love me that much?"

"But of course, we do, don't you know that? And we want you to be a part of the family for real," answered Cindy.

"Well I will think about it, but like I said honey, I really need to go now. You take care and I love you, good night." Said Tracy hanging up the phone. As Cindy was putting her phone down she started thinking *"I hope she does, I really could use her help."*

Cindy walked back into the house and into the kitchen where James was. James asked "Well honey what she said?"

"She said she needs to think about it. Ho James what am I going to do if she doesn't want to?"

"Well honey guess we'll just have to make do. I'll help out as much as I can." answered James trying to reassure her.

"I know you will honey, but I really need her, I don't think she knows how much." Said Cindy with tears welling up in her eyes. James walked over and put his arms around her saying, "It's going to be all right."

"You look tired honey."

"Yes, I am but I'm also very excited." Said Cindy looking down and rubbing her belly once again.

"I don't know about you? But I'm going to grab me a quick shower and I'm going straight to bed." Said James yawning obviously feeling very tired as well.

"I'm right behind you honey. But I'm so tired, I think I'm going to skip the shower and go straight to bed" said Cindy stretching and heading to the stairs, following behind James.

"Well okay," but a shower might help you to relax and sleep better." Said James tugging at his shirt and pulling it off over his head.

"You're probably right." But to tell you the truth, I just don't have the strength, or the energy, to stand under a shower. I so just want to go lay down, it has been a long day and a very emotional one for me." Said Cindy once again yawning.

"Okay baby," you go stretch out. I'm going to go take my shower. I'll be right in there with you just as soon as I'm done and if you are in fact already asleep, I'll try not to wake you." Said James heading into the bathroom.

Cindy was awakened by a noise from somewhere in the manor. In the middle of the night. Feeling frightened she reached over and shook James saying, "Honey I hear something again." But there was no reply from him. Cindy, hearing it again and feeling even more frightened. She setup in the bed, behind her husband shaking him even harder saying, "James, I hear something."

But still there was no reply from him. It was almost like he was in a trance or something. Cindy just set on her knees behind her husband, looking down at him, thinking, *"Some help you are."*

She had also placed a flashlight in the nightstand beside the bed. Remembering this. She pulled out the drawer and got it. Gathering enough of courage and now armed with the light and not getting any help from her husband. Cindy decided to investigate the noise, on her own. She climbed out of bed, with that in mind.

Once again very slowly walking across the room to the doorway. Holding the light out in front of her. She poked her head out the door, looking down the long hallway, with the light in her hand. She shined it one way and then the other. Not seeing anything and gathering a little bit more courage. She stepped out into the hall. The floor was cold on her feet and there seem to be a breeze blowing down the hallway coming from, where undoubtedly a window had been left opened. Cindy's heart was really racing in her chest now. Because she truly was frightened. As she started to slowly make her way down the hall leading to the stairwell, shining a light ahead of her.

When she reached the top of the stairs. She heard what sounded like the whimpering of a woman. But it wasn't coming from downstairs. It was coming from a room at the other end of the hallway past the stairwell. she walked slowly toward the room a few feet away. She paused for a minute, so that she could be sure which room it was coming from. After a few seconds of silence, she heard it again. Confirming it was in fact the sound of a whimpering woman.

Coming from the room just a few feet ahead of her. That's when she realized it was coming from the same room that she and James had been investigating. Upon their arrival to the mansion, because the door would not stay shut.

Recognizing this a chill came over her body. Still feeling frightened, but also a little bit relieved because, *"After all it's just a woman whimpering and not some burglar that had broken in and was going to kill them in their sleep."* Then she thought, *"She's obviously upset. Perhaps I can help somehow."* she moved closer toward the doorway of the room that the whimpering was coming from. Cindy reached down and took hold of the doorknob when she did it dawned on her. *"How did she get into my house? Why is there a woman whimpering in a room in my house?"* Cindy thought. As she begins to fill little agitated at the thought of it continuing to turn the knob. She opened the door slowly shining the flashlight ahead of her. The door creak like it hadn't been opened in years. Cindy stepped into the room, asking, "Can I help you?" "What are you doing in my house?"

But there was no reply. She shined the light all around her. Finding the light switch. She turned it on. The light illuminating the room was just a dim glow. But she could clearly see there was no one there. Her heart was truly racing in her chest now as she begins to realize it was undoubtedly a ghost, in her house...,

Remembering all the things that Peggy the waitress at the restaurant had told her and James, frightened her, even more her hands begin to tremble, as they did the light was shaking out in front of her. She looked all around the room corner to corner. But there was truly no one in the room. Cindy turned around, looked at the doorway, with fear overwhelming her she thought, *"I just want to make it back to my bed, just let me get back to my bed."* Moving slowly toward the doorway leading into the dark hall. Cindy while going out the door, reached over and turned the light off. As soon as the light went out. She once again heard the whimpering of a woman, but this time it was right behind her. The hair stood up on the back of her neck and she got chill bumps all over her body. It was almost like she could feel someone breathing on the back of her neck. Cindy feeling overwhelmed with fear, broke into a run down the hallway, all the way to her room, slamming the door shut behind her. She jumped back in the bed beside James with the flashlight in her hand. She pulled the covers up over her head.

Then she heard the bedroom door knob Creek as it very slowly begins to turn. She pulled the covers down just enough that her eyes were the only thing poking out. Her whole body was trembling. She stuck her hand with the flashlight out from under the side of her covers and shined the light from it at the doorknob, watching it turning. Till the bedroom door slowly opened, creaking as it did. Cindy watched it from the safety of her bed. The more the door opened the more frightened she became, until she just could not stand it any longer. she pulled the covers back over her head. But she could still hear the door creaking as it continued slowly opening all the way back to the wall. Cindy truly was too afraid to look out from under the covers. Till finally she gathered up enough courage, to slowly pull the cover down and looked the door. It was slightly swaying very gently back and forth. The doorway was dark, leading into the hall.

She watched in fear for something or someone to come out of the dark. Once again, fear overwhelmed her, as she covered her head trembling all over her body. Cindy could fill a presence in the room with them. The thought of it made the hair stand up on the back of her neck and once again covering her body would chill bumps. She was so scared she could hardly stand it. But finally gathering up enough of courage to peer out from under the covers. In her disbelief, standing in the corner of the bedroom was a little black woman dressed in old tattered clothing with a white bandana on top her head. She looked like one of those slave girls from some of the old movies that she had seen. Cindy shined a flashlight at her, to try to get a better look at her face, but the light just passed through her shining on the wall. Cindy feeling so overwhelmed with fear.

She started to get lightheaded, feeling like she could pass out. Then the image of the girl moved toward her. Cindy pulled the cover back over her head and screamed as loud as she could. She was awakening by James shaking her and saying, "What the hell is the matter?"

Cindy pulled, the covers off her head and looked at James asking, "Where did she go?"

"You scared the hell out of me." Said James sliding his legs off the side of the bed, sitting upright. Cindy looked around the room and not seeing anything said. "I saw her James," right here in our room."

"Saw who?" Asked James turning around and looking at her.

"The ghost!!" I think she is a slave girl." Said Cindy. While looking around the room.

"Oh honey," you just had a bad dream." Said James trying to dismiss it as such. As he got up and started out the room. Cindy asked, "Where you going?"

James answered her saying, "I'm going to the bathroom and then down stairs and get something to drink, you want anything?"

Cindy shook her head no, as she watched him walk out the room. Noticing that she didn't have the flashlight and the fact that she didn't even have her robe on. She thought, *"James must be right, it must've been a dream, but it seems so real."*

When James returned to the room carrying a glass of water and climbed back into the bed. Cindy look to him saying, "I'm sorry honey, but it seems so real."

"It's all right," lay back down and try to get some sleep." Said James stretching and yawning, laying back down beside her.

"But honey, it was so real." Said Cindy with disbelief in her voice.

"You what a talk about it?" Asked James looking at her.

"No, it's late and I know you're tired. We'll talk about it tomorrow." Said Cindy as she curled up next to him. Replaying it in her mind. As they both settled back down and finally fell asleep. The next morning when they woke up. Cindy could remember everything like it had just happened. She told James all about it laying in the bed next to him. James without saying, a word set up right and slid his legs over to the side of the bed. Cindy set there, looking at him, waiting for response. James turned around, looked at her and said "Well that really is something," then he stood up, got his clothes and put them on and started out the room. Cindy said. "That's it? That's all you got to say about that?"

"Will honey, what you want me to say?" "It undoubtedly was a dream. After everything, that waitress at the restaurant told you and the fact that you're in a big mansion. That you know undoubtedly has a history. Your imagination is obviously running away with you." Said James trying to plead his case.

"James, I don't know what I want you to say. I just want you to try to be a little bit more understanding. Something happened to me last night whether it was a dream or not, it did happen and it scares me." Said Cindy getting very agitated, throwing on her close.

James walked over to her put his arms around her saying, "Honey I'm sorry, I am trying to understand truly I am. I don't know what happened to you last night. But I think it was just a dream, I really do and I don't think it's anything you need to be frightened of."

"You know what really frightens me the most. I couldn't wake you up. I tried it was like you were in a trance or something. Whatever it was. I had to deal with it on my own and that truly does scare me James." Said

Cindy. Pulling away from him. Walking out the room heading down the hallway toward the stairwell.

Cindy raised her head and looked toward the room from her dream and the door was standing open. She froze in her tracks, hollering with fear in her voice "James, James."

He came running out the bedroom, upon seeing her standing at the stairwell,

"What is it honey?" Asked James emerging from their room, with a look of concerned on his face

Cindy very slowly raised her hand and pointed toward the open door saying, "That's the room, from my dream. That's the room."

James walked past the stairwell to the room with the open door and looked inside saying, "There's nothing in here, honey, nothing."

"But don't you see, the door is staying open James. That's the same door that we couldn't get to stay open. When we first got here to the mansion, how is it staying open now?" Asked Cindy. Obviously frightened.

James reached down and grabbed the doorknob and pulled it shut. Then he took the palm of his hand pushed on the door it. Easily unlatched and opened. "Like we determined before, it looks like the latch is broken and I guess the wind blowing down the hallway opened it." Said James trying to explain it to her.

"Yes, but don't it strike you odd, that it just happens to be the same room that was in my dream?" Asked Cindy. Obviously not convinced.

"Well there's not anything in here now." Said James grabbing the doorknob and pulling the door shut.

Then he walked past Cindy. Going downstairs saying, "I'm headed to my study to finish cleaning."

Cindy stood there looking at the closed-door thinking, *"Maybe James is right and it is my imagination running away with me."*

Starting down the stairs. She heard the door unlatch and swing open very slowly. she froze in her tracks once again and turning to face the door, looking at it. Filling a breeze on her face, she dismissed it, thinking,

"James was right. It's the wind." As she continued down the steps.

Cindy had the overwhelming desire to talk about her dream, or whatever it was. She knew she could not talk to James. Because he would just try to explain it away and she really didn't think he was even trying to understand. But she also knew Tracey would. she thought about it for a minute and grabbed her cell phone, Dowling her number. It only rang a couple of times and Tracy answered it saying, "Hello this is Tracy can I help you?"

"Tracy it's me. Do you have a minute?" Asked Cindy hoping that she did.

"But of course, I do sweetie what's wrong?" Asked Tracy with concern in her voice.

"Something happened to me last night that I really need to talk about to you," answered Cindy.

"Okay sweetie." give me about 30 minutes. I'll take an early lunch and call you back. Can I do that? That way you will have my full attention." Said Tracy waiting for a reply from her.

"Of course, she can honey, I'm sorry to bother you. But I really need to talk to you about this." Said Cindy confirming Tracy's request to call her back.

"First, you're not bothering me." Like I said give me about 30 minutes and I'll call you back." Said Tracy trying to reassure her.

"Okay Tracy," thank you so much." Said Cindy would relief in her voice. Hanging up the phone, to wait for Tracy's return her call.

Being true to her word, exactly 30 minutes later, Cindy's phone rang and it was Tracy asking, "Now what's wrong honey? You have my full attention."

Cindy begin telling her all about everything. About the dream, or whatever it was and finding the door open at the top of the stairs the next morning and how strangely James had been acting. She finished up, by saying, "James says it's just my imagination running away with me."

Tracy just sat there in silence listening the whole time. Then she said. "Well honey is understandable that being in a big old mansion such as that and hearing about the history of the place from that woman at the restaurant and the fact that you are very susceptible two things of that nature, it is easy to see how it could be your imagination getting the better of you. But on the other hand, with the way that you said James had been acting and the unexplainable things happening all around you plus now a dream so vivid in your mind. I don't think we can rule out that it might be something else. I'll tell you what honey, if anything else happens, you be sure and let me know immediately. Because I have a friend, that is a paranormal investigator. A few years back the paper did an article on her and I followed her around for about two weeks I think it was...?"

"I remember that," you said even then you saw some unexplainable things, that made a believer out of you." Said Cindy interrupting her with excitement in her voice.

"Yes, I did," I saw some things, that still disturbs me to think about them, even today." Said Tracy confirming her belief.

"Well okay Tracy," if anything else happens, I will call you. Thank you so much honey. I don't know what I would do, if I didn't have you to help me through times like this." Said Cindy with relief in her voice.

"You are very welcome sweetie and you can call me anytime day or night. I really hope you know that Cindy. Oh yes, I want you to know, I am giving that a lot of thought. I'm not ready to talk about it just yet. I hope you can understand that." Said Tracy still feeling a little confused.

"But of course, Tracy take all the time you need. Just know that we do love you. Whatever you decide, nothing will ever change that." Said Cindy trying to put her mind at ease.

"Well honey I better get back to work. Keep me informed, on any new developments. Take care of yourself and that baby. I can't wait to see you, it won't be much longer now." Said Tracy with excitement in her voice.

"I know Trace I can't wait myself. I so miss my boys and you, more than you could ever know." Said Cindy with her voice cracking.

"Well honey like I said. it won't be much longer and we can talk about everything when I bring the boys up. But for now, I must get back to work. Give James my love and I'll talk to you later sweetie." Said Tracy trying to end the conversation.

"I will Tracy, kiss the boys for me and tell them both me and their daddy, love and miss them, with all our heart and. I'll talk to you later, bye for now." Said Cindy hanging up the phone. Cindy pause for a minute thinking, *"Should I tell James about the paranormal investigator and what Tracy said. or should I keep it to myself?"* Then she thought *"No he will think I'm crazy. I don't even think he believes me."*

And with that thought in mind she decided not to tell him.

Now not being able to clean, because she couldn't be exposed to the chemicals. She found herself with nothing to do.

Cindy thought, *"Surely it won't hurt if I go work out in the garden, or something like that."*

So, she went about getting some things together, to do that very thing.

CHAPTER 19

When Cindy was walking out the door, heading to the back of the mansion, her cell phone rang once again. Quickly as she could, she answered it thinking it might be Tracy, calling her back. But not really being sure, she just answered it saying, "Hello."

Then a woman's voice on her cell phone said. "Hello this is Dr. Kerman's nurse; can I speak to Mrs. Parker?"

Cindy said. "This is her how can I help you?" "Yes Mrs. Parker I am calling to confirm your appointment for 11 o'clock this morning." Said the nurse.

"Appointment, what appointment?" Asked Cindy with confusion.

"Yes, I'm sorry Mrs. Parker," Dr. Williams nurse from glory medical, upon his request, called and set up this appointment for you, to see Dr. Kerman she's a OB-GYN."

"Oh, that's right, he told me and my husband, he was going to do that for me. When did you say, my appointment was again?" Asked Cindy trying to confirm it.

It's for 11 o'clock this morning will that be alright with you man or would you rather reschedule?" Asked the nurse.

"Oh no, that will be fine. Is there anything I need to bring? Far as medical card, anything in that nature?" Asked Cindy digging in her purse to find it.

"Yes, ma'am we require your insurance card and two forms of ID. One has two have a photo and there will be a co-pay of $50 for today." Said the nurse.

"Okay you said $50 and 2 forms of ID, one with a pitcher and my insurance card. Is that correct?" Asked Cindy trying to confirm it.

"Yes ma'am," so we can go ahead and confirm your appointment?" Asked the nurse.

"Absolutely." Said Cindy eagerly.

"One more thing Mrs. Parker, the Doctor requested that you wear some type of loose closing. Because she is going to want to do an ultrasound on you. To check the status of the baby. She wanted me to be sure and tell you to do that." Said the head nurse.

"Okay," will see you then, thank you." Said Cindy Eager to know how the baby is.

James came walking up from behind her asking, "Who is out on the phone?"

"It was a nurse from the hospital. Confirming my appointment, with the OB-GYN, Doctor." Said Cindy trying to explain it.

"When is your appointment honey?" Asked James

"Today at 11 o'clock," answered Cindy.

"11 o'clock!!" That doesn't give you long to get ready. A matter of fact, we better head on over there right now." Said James pulling the keys out of his pocket.

"Yes, I know honey, give me a minute. I've got to change my clothes." Said Cindy scurrying back upstairs.

James hollered after her saying, "Honey you don't have time. We better get over there.

"James I have to," the Doctor asked me to wear something light. Because she wants to do an ultrasound. I'm going to put on a sundress." Said Cindy stopping just for a second to explain it to him.

James hollered up at her saying, "All right then, I'll wait for you in the truck."

James walked out and got in the truck, waiting for Cindy to emerge from the mansion. He did not have to wait long. As she walked out closing and locking, the door behind her. James got out and walked around to her side of the truck, opening the door for her. Explaining

"I'm afraid were going to be late."

Cindy said as James walked back around to his side of the truck as quickly as he could "I think you'll be all right honey. The nurse said that the Doctor is very anxious to speak with me."

"I hope you're right, but any rate, you know how I hate to be late." Said James driving just a little too fast, for those winding curves, trying to make up some time.

"Well is not going to matter if you kill us, before we get there." Said Cindy being slung around in the truck. "James please slow down your scaring me."

"I'm sorry honey, like I said I hate to be late." Said James slowing down a little bit but still driving faster than Cindy like and she was in fact relieved, to see the hospital up in the distance.

Jane said "Now don't be nervous honey, I am right here with you." As he came around and opened the door to the truck for her. James raced inside and straight up to the receptionist sitting behind the desk. Almost leaving Cindy at the door asking, "Where can we find Doctor…?" He paused for a minute, turned around and looked behind him at Cindy asking "What was her name again?"

"Dr. Kerman," answered Cindy walking up to the desk finally catching up to him.

James turned back around and repeated the name "Dr. Kerman," to the receptionist behind the desk.

She asked, "Do you have an appointment?"

"Yes, ma'am we do," it's for 11 o'clock, answered Cindy.

The receptionist looked at the clock hanging on the wall, saying, "Please sign the register and have a seat and will be with you shortly."

Cindy looked at James shaking her head saying, "See honey, you almost killed us for nothing."

James looked at his watch and then at Cindy asking, "Why do they even give you an appointment, if they're not going to bring you straight back?"

But before Cindy could even reply to that, a nurse came through the door saying, "Mrs. Parker."

Cindy stood up saying, "Yes ma'am that's me."

Then she and James followed the nurse back through the doorway and into a little room.

The nurse said. "Stretch out up on the examining table."

As she unzipped the back of Cindy's sundress and helping her pull it off her arms and down to her waist. Grabbing a bottle of some type of greasy liquid the nurse warned Cindy saying, "Now this might be a little cold." As she squeezed a bunch out on Cindy's belly saying,

"Okay the Doctor will be right with you."

A few seconds later, a tall thin, somewhat striking woman. With what appeared to be a caramel colored skin, came walking in the room introducing herself saying,

"I am Doctor Dorothy Kerman."

As she came in and set down on the stool and willed over close to Cindy. Saying,

"Now then let's see if we can see this baby."

Grabbing the ultrasound instrument, placing it on Cindy's belly. Rolling it around looking at the monitor. All three of them watch the monitor eagerly, as the image of a fetus. Became more and more visible. Both Cindy and James smiled with joy. Viewing for the first time, their unborn baby. The Doctor said "Well hello there."

As the baby's face came clear on the monitor. They could clearly see its little closed eyes, nose and mouth. Then the doctor moved the instrument around, finding the baby shoulders and arms, moving it down to its very tiny hands, counting each - and - every finger. Cindy held James hand as tightly as she could, overwhelmed by joy. Well peering at the monitor, watching her baby. Then the doctor moved the instrument further down saying,

"Let's see if we can see what you are."

All three of them stared at the monitor with anticipation. The image became clear and clear, the Doctor said.

"Well congratulations mommy, it looks like you have a little girl!"

At that moment, Cindy felt an overwhelming love from deep inside her heart. Unlike anything she had ever known. She stared at that monitor, watching that little life moving around, that was growing inside of her. The joy she felt so overwhelmed her, she could not help herself and began to cry. Even James wiped the tear from the corner of his eye. From being so overwhelmed by emotion. The Doctor took several images of the baby, with the machine for the couple. Then she hung the instrument backup and got some paper towels, cleaning all the greasy liquid from off Cindy's belly. Telling her that I want you to get plenty of rest, eat whatever it is you feel like you need to eat and drink plenty of liquids and do not overexert yourself."

Then James asked "Will climbing up and down stairs overexert her?"

"Will that all depends how many stairs?" Asked the Doctor

"There are 3 flights, going to the upstairs of the manor," answered James.

Suddenly the Doctor spun her head around and looked at James repeating with fear in her voice "The manor!" you mean the Summerhill manor?"

James looked at her, with puzzlement saying, "Yes! Why do you asked?"

The Doctor Not wanting to frighten the couple said. "Oh, it's nothing really, I'm just glad that someone is finally going to do something with that old big beautiful place. How did you to come to live there?" She asked trying to defuse the situation.

James looked at her for a few minutes, still puzzled by her response earlier, began to explain saying, "Cindy is the last known descendent of the Summerhill's. that being the case, she inherited the Summerhill manor and one of the stipulations to the will, is that we must live in and maintain it."

"I see." Said the doctor. "Well like I said it is a big beautiful place. Is it just the two of you? Asked the Doctor Now feeling fully convinced that she, had managed to change the situation and putting the couples minded at ease, from her earlier display of emotion.

"No ma'am, I have two sons that are still in Detroit. Being taken care of by a friend of ours. She's keeping them, so that they can finish school. This summer she will be bringing them up here." Said James still not really convinced by the Doctor.

"I see, well at any rate she should really take it easy. But just climbing a few flights of stairs, should not heard her." Said the Doctor finally answering James question.

"What about gardening? Can I go out in the garden to do some things?" Asked Cindy trying to find out what her limitations are.

"Long as you don't overdo it. I don't see where a little bit of gardening will hurt you. Cindy, you can do almost anything you like. I just really want you to take it easy with the baby." Said the Dr. expressing her concern.

"Oh, she will, you can be sure of it." Said James smiling at Cindy.

"Well okay then, I want to see you back, in about a week. I can check on the development of the baby and how you're doing as well." Said the Dr. "also I am going to give you a prescription to help you sleep. Only take it before you go to bed and I think you should set aside an hour, during the day. To take you a nap." Said the Doctor.

"I will doctor and thank you." Said Cindy pulling back on her dress over her shoulders, motioning for James to zip it up.

"Your quite welcome, now you're probably going to be having spotting, lower a domino pains, swelling in your legs and arms, mood swings and occasional headache, but these are all normal symptoms, so don't be alarmed. "But you have any heavy bleeding, get to the hospital as soon as you can. Now not trying to scare you, I just want you to really be careful this being your first baby." Said the Dr. smiling at Cindy.

Cindy lowered her head saying, "Well to be quite honest with you, this is not my first baby."

The Dr. with a puzzled look on her face, looked over at James saying, "Oh I'm sorry and I thought I heard you say that you, have two other sons. I just assumed that they were not yours to gather."

"No ma'am there not, the boy's mother died a few years ago, I am there stepmother. You see, I come from a very poor family. I had a child, when I was 14 years old. Now being so young and not really having anything. My parents thought it best, that I give it up for adoption." Said Cindy trying to explain.

"Oh, I see." Said the doctor lowering her head. this isn't your first child, then I guess you are fully aware of all the symptoms.

"Yes ma'am," but I was very young and to be quite honest with you, it was very traumatic for me. I tried to block out a lot of it. I mean I can remember some things, that happened to me, just not everything." Said Cindy trying to make the doctor understand.

"I have a question, asked James does she just have to take a shower, or can she get in a bathtub?"

"She can do what she wants. But in my opinion it would probably be safer, for her to just take a shower. For obvious reasons," explained to Doctor, as she was walking out of the room.

A few minutes later a nurse from earlier came walking in with the paperwork for Cindy to sign in her prescriptions saying, "The Doctor. Wants to see you back in a week. Be sure and stop by the front desk and make your appointment. As I had indicated on the phone to be a $50 charged today."

"Thank you, ma'am, will see you in a week." Said Cindy following the nurse out, with James close behind them.

They walked to the front desk. Cindy handed the receptionist behind the desk, at the front entrance her paperwork saying, "The Dr. wants to see me back in a week."

The receptionist took her paperwork looked at it asking "What's a good time for you ma'am? Morning or evening?"

Cindy looked over at James asking "What you think honey, in the morning sometime?"

"Yes, honey be fine whenever you want," answered James leaving the decision to be made by her.

Cindy looked at the receptionist saying, "Yes I think so sometime that morning, would be the best."

Then the receptionist typed all the information in the computer and handed Cindy her appointment card saying, "That will be $50 for today."

James reached in his back pocket and got out as wallet and handed the receptionist $50. The she handed him the receipt. Then the couple left the hospital heading home. Cindy was smiling from ear - to - ear, looking at the images of her baby from the ultrasound. Suddenly, she started crying James reached over and took her hand in his asking "What is it honey?"

"I can't help but think about Sabrina talking to the doctor brought up some old memories." Said Cindy blowing her nose in a paper towel.

"Honey the way I see it is, you were too young to be a mother at that time. Perhaps God is giving you another chance to be a mother again. Don't get me wrong, you're a wonderful mother to our boys. But now you get a chance to have a baby of your own. With me right beside you all the way. I know you're going to be a wonderful mother to our baby girl as well." Said James smiling at her bringing her hand up to his lips and kissing it tenderly.

The rest of the ride home they neither one said anything Cindy just stared off into space James would smile at her from time to time. Then James asked "Honey are you hungry?"

"Yes, we are starving," answered Cindy rubbing her belly.

In hearing that, James drove to the restaurant. When they arrived, he came around and opened the door for Cindy. Then the couple walked together inside. As they did Peggy saw them come in and rushed over and grabs Cindy hugging her asking, "What you find out? Are you going to be all right?" Asked Peggy obviously still concerned for her.

"Oh yes," I am wonderful." Said Cindy smiling at her.

"But what did you find out? I mean why did you pass out honey? Was James right and are you just trying to do too much?" Asked Peggy once again still with concern in her voice.

"Well yes in a way he was, but it is something else al" said Cindy not wanting to reveal her information yet.

"I don't understand honey, what did the doctor tell you was causing it?" Asked Peggy now realizing Cindy was holding back.

"The doctors said that it was pretty normal for…,"

"Pretty normal!" for someone to pass out at the dinner table? Those stupid doctors, half of them don't know what they're doing anymore." Said Peggy interrupting Cindy and feeling frustrated when hearing that. "I mean what's normal about it?" Asked Peggy still trying to understand.

"Like I was saying, he said it's normal for pregnant woman, after overdoing it all day cleaning and such as that to pass out like that." Said Cindy smiling from ear - to - ear.

Peggy said. "Oh, my God honey, you're pregnant? That's wonderful, congratulations and well yes that is understandable now you've got to take it easy and possibly hire someone to help you with that big old place.

"Well I am going to take it easy but I just not so sure I'm ready to hire anyone. I mean if I do take it easy, get plenty of rest and eat right, there's still a lot that I can do said. Cindy filling a little bit frustrated and if fact that it seems like everyone is telling her what to do.

"Honey they just want you to take it easy myself included, four the baby sake. I mean what if you would've passed out like that heading upstairs? You could've fallen down the stairs, possibly hurting yourself or the baby." Said Peggy trying to make her understand.

"I know what you're saying, Peggy…" Said Cindy

"Can we order something to eat? You girls can talk about this all you want afterword's. But please let me get something to eat." Said James interrupting Cindy feeling frustrated and obviously hungry.

"Oh, I do apologize sweetie what can I get you honey?" Asked Peggy pulling out her notepad and pen to take down his order.

"I think I'm going to have some of this fried chicken along with the macaroni and cheese and some dinner rolls and bring me a glass of sweet tea please mam." Said James closing the menu would relief in his voice that he was finally going to get something to eat.

"What about you sweetie?" Asked Peggy turning toward Cindy eagerly waiting to see what her choice might be.

"I think I have the same, but only can I have a big slice of apple pie some baked beans and oh yes one of those wonderful salads that you people make." Said Cindy rubbing her belly and not even bothering to pick up the menu.

"Would you like a glass of tea to go with that as well?" Asked Peggy once again waiting for Cindy to confirm.

'Oh, yes that sounds wonderful." Said Cindy eagerly.

"My God honey. Are you really going to eat all of that?" Asked James shaking his head.

"I told you we were starving to death," answered Cindy smiling at him.

Quite some time past, before Peggy returned to the table bringing their dinner. James not being able to finish his selection said, "I'll take the rested his home and you can eat it later."

As he motioned for Peggy to come over to the table, asking her for a to-go box. To take the remainder of his dinner home?

Then he watched in amazement, as Cindy devoured everything on the table in front of her. Then upon finishing her last bite, he asked her "Are you content, or would you like something else?"

"No, I'm quite satisfied. Now all I want to do is go home and lay down," answered Cindy getting up from the table. Come on honey, I want to say goodbye to Peggy and then just go home." Explained Cindy as she was yawning.

Then she and James both hugged Peggy, handed her a tip and explain how they will see her next time.

Peggy said "Now honey I'm serious, you go home and take it easy, remember you have to think about the baby now."

"Don't worry I am deathly thinking about the baby and I will take it easy. Good night Peggy." Said Cindy hugging her neck one last time, before she and James walked out of the restaurant heading home. On the drive home Cindy was sitting quietly, staring out into space. James being concerned for her asked, "Are you all right honey, you're not starting to feel bad, again are you?

Cindy replied saying, "No I'm just really tired, I can't wait to get in that bed, I'm tired and full as a tick."

"I know even you should be able to sleep like a baby tonight." Said James looking over at her.

"I hope better than last night." Said Cindy, trying to get comfortable in her seat.

James said. while driving up to the iron Gates and punching in the codes,

"It's just a little bit further honey and we can both get out of this truck and stretch out."

"What do we do it our leftover food?" Asked James.

"We probably shouldn't have even brought this, home." Said Cindy repositioning in it on the seat between them.

"I don't think it will hurt anything to leave it out," she continued to explain.

"Maybe your ghost will be hungry." Said James facetiously giggling at her.

"That's not funny, James don't joke about that."

"I'm sorry honey. Just poking fun at you. I didn't mean anything by it," explained James trying to redeem his self. As they pulled up in front of the mansion. James said. "Finally, we're home and I can't wait to get in there and go to bed, the hell with the food."

Climbing out of the truck they went into the mansion. James turned around and locked the door behind them turning out the lights as he followed Cindy heading upstairs. They went straight to the bedroom, pulled off their clothes and climbed into the bed.

In no time at all James was fast asleep. Cindy on the other hand, would doze off, but then wake back up again, she did this several times till finally she fell into a deep sleep. Then suddenly, she set up in the bed, swung her legs over the side and put on her robe. Getting the flashlight out of the nightstand, she went out the bedroom walking down the hallway with the flashlight shining ahead of her. Cindy looked up and their standing at the top of the stairwell was the slave girl that she saw the other night in her dream. Cindy, thinking that she was dreaming now had no fear.

"After all, it's just a dream," she thought, following the slave girl down the stairwell and out the mansion, going into the garden area. It was

raining and lightning was striking all around them. There was mud all over the ground and Cindy was walking in the mud trying to follow the girl, she climbed the hill shining the flashlight in front of her as the lightning would strike she could see the girl, about 50 foot or so ahead of her climbing the hill with ease.

Cindy was slipping in the mud, but finally she did manage to get to the top of the hill and there in front of her was a well-covered in vines and weeds. All around it the slave girl standing beside the well pointed at it and disappeared, right before her eyes. Cindy drew closer to the well, because she could hear the faint crying of what appeared to be a baby coming from the deep dark hole. Cindy leaned over, looking down into the dark hole of the well trying to shine her flashlight to see the bottom, but she couldn't. It was too far down.

Then suddenly something, or someone shoved her and she went over the side of the well. Falling further and further into the darkness. Till finally splashing down in the water at the bottom of the well. Cindy Claude at the walls, trying to find some way to climb out but she couldn't, so she screaming for James, as loud as she could, or anybody to help her. Scared and cold and soaking wet. She started crying as she continued to scream for help, calling James or anybody then suddenly the flashlight started flickering because she had gotten it wet. Cindy was scared to death and she thought,

"Oh, my God! No. If I lose my light. I will be in total darkness." That would be more than she could bear."

But there in the bottom of the well, the light went out. She could not see anything but total darkness, all around her she screamed at the top of her lungs, saying,

"My God James! Please help me."

She looked up and every time the lightning would strike it would light up the top of the well and she was screaming as loud as she could for James or anybody to help her, as she did

Lightning struck and lit up the sky above her, she saw a figure staring down in the well at her. Then down in the darkness she heard a baby crying right next to her and in the dark hole with no way out. She felt something or someone touch her and she let out a bloodcurdling scream. Once again, James woke her up, asking,

"What is the matter with you? You did it again, you scared the hell out of me."

Cindy was sitting up in the bed trembling and crying uncontrollably, James put his arms around her, saying,

"It's all right. I'm here, I'm right here with you."

James was holding her in his arms, rocking her as Cindy was still crying uncontrollably and her whole-body trembling. Once more James said with a soft voice,

"It's all right honey it was just a bad, dream. Just another bad, dream."

Cindy feeling safe and comfortable, started to relax. Because her husband had his arms around her. Starting to doze off again. James stretched her out, covering her up and laying down beside her, watched over her as she fell back into a deep sleep. The next morning. When Cindy woke up. She was soaking wet and her feet were covered in dried mud. This truly scared her. So, she screamed for James waking him up asking, "What is it honey?"

"Look at my feet." Said Cindy as she pulled the covers away.

James with a puzzled look on his face asked, "Where did all the mud come from?"

"I don't know, if it was real, or just a dream." Said Cindy starting to tremble.

"I don't understand. Cindy where did the mud come from?" Asked James looking at her scratching the side of his head, once again with a puzzled look on his face.

Cindy begin to tell him about her dream and as she told him. James sat quietly, listening to her every word. Till she finally finished saying, "So I must've sometime last night gotten up and walked outside in the mud."

"But honey, there is no mud outside. It hasn't rained in days." Said James, feeling even more confused and wondering where in fact the mud it came from?

"James. How can that be?" Asked Cindy, even more confused. Then he was.

"I don't know and less…," He paused for a second bin angrily continued to say, "You think this is some kind of a joke and sometime during the night, you went outside and I don't know, ran the hose in the garden or something like that, to make the mud. Cindy if you did that? There's something seriously wrong with you. I mean trying to make me believe in this cock and bull story of yours, is one thing. But to go outside and do this, you need help." Said James climbing out of bed.

"James I can't believe you would think I'd do that, for what?" Asked Cindy with tears starting to well up in her eyes.

"Oh, I don't know, maybe because you want me to believe this place is haunted and that there is something going on here. Maybe you're so eager for me to believe it, that you would do this." Said James with a cross voice, shoving his legs into his jeans, first one and then the other, not even looking at her. Cindy jumped out of bed and ran into the bathroom crying uncontrollably, slamming the door behind her. James walked over to the bathroom door speaking to her through it saying, "Cindy maybe you don't even know you are doing these things? Maybe you're doing them subconsciously?"

"Go away James, just go away and leave me alone," she said with a hurt voice.

"Cindy am sorry honey I just don't know what's going on I...,"

"Go away James," yelled Cindy interrupting him.

James turned around and went downstairs to his study. Cindy sitting on the side of the tub washing the mud off her feet. With the words at James just said to her, playing over and over in her mind. Crying and feeling all alone. hurt inside that he would even think that of her. She felt like her heart could burst. From the waves of pain, that she continued to feel thinking about what he had said. When she finished washing the mud off her feet, she dried them off. Going back into the bedroom, still feeling so hurt inside the she could hardly stand it. She remembered what Tracy had told her that if anything else happened? To be sure and call her. Cindy got her cell phone and doubt Tracy's number. It rang just a couple times. Tracy answered it sitting at her desk at work saying, "This is Tracy can I help you,"

"Tracy it's happened again." Said Cindy now really starting to cry.

Tracy said. "Honey it's all right, calm down tell me what's going on."

Cindy started to tell her all about the incident last night and waking up with mud on her feet the next morning and the way that James acted and the things he said and oh how hurt she was inside, that he would even think that,

Tracy just sat quietly listening to her every word, until she saw her opportunity to say, "Cindy listen to me, there is obviously without a doubt something going on in that house, involving that slave girl. I'm going to help you. You are not alone in this honey. I'm going to call my friend and tell her everything. She'll know what to do. Try to calm down, give me a little while. I'll call you back later, after I talk to her and tell you what she said."

"Okay Tracy, I don't know what I would do, if I didn't have you to talk to. I think I would go crazy. Thank you for helping and believe in and me." Said Cindy starting to feel a little better.

"You are quite welcome honey, you can always call me, no matter what. Now just hang in there and wait for my call,"

∙ ∙ ∙

Cindy starting to in fact feel better, decided she would go try and talk to James. she headed downstairs to look for him. Heading down the hall toward his study. She started to call his name. Not getting a response, she made her way to the double doors just outside of it and open them. Poking her head inside she called him once again saying, "James are you in here?"

But there was no reply. Then to Cindy's disbelief she noticed that statue that were standing out in the garden, over in one of the corners of the study. Cindy could feel the anger boiling up inside her. Standing there staring at the image of the woman. Cindy thought *"How did he get that thing in here by his self?"*

Now with the anger welling up inside of her like a sickness, she slams the double doors to the study shot and continued her search for James. Going from one room, to the other. Not finding him in the house, she slowly but surely made her way out to the garden. Walking past the area where the statue had been standing, Cindy looked at the empty space shaking her head feeling even more anger, as she continued her search for him.

But still once again he was nowhere to be found. Cindy made her way back into the mansion. Upon arriving inside she finally saw James coming down the Hall toward his study. Now boiling over with more anger than you would think humanly possible.

Cindy lashed out at James saying, "Why did you bring that damn thing backing this house?"

"What the hell are you talking about?" Asked James reacting defensively to her tone.

"Don't you dare act like you don't know what I'm talking about, that stupid statue standing in your study? Tell me James why did you bring it back in his house?"

"I thought I told you to stay out of my study," barked James shoving her to the side walking into it.

• • •

"James what has gotten into you?" Asked Cindy feeling more scared then confused. Because of his reaction to her question.

Then turning around slowly with a cold almost empty look on his face. "I'm not going to tell you again to stay out of here do you understand me." Said James slamming the door shut between them and avoiding her question. Cindy stood there with a mixture of emotions of anger, pain, fright and disbelief, running through her mind, all at the same time. A part of her felt like snatching those double doors open and demanding he get that thing out of her house and tell her what is going on. But another part of her felt scared.

Because she really wasn't sure anymore what James would really do? without saying, a word, she walked slowly away down the hall and back upstairs to their room. Standing at the foot of the bed for a minute, replaying what happened in her mind, that cold look upon James's face, scared her beyond belief.

Cindy continued to walk slowly over to the side of the bed and sit down, still staring off into space and filling confused and unsure what to do. Leaning forward she placed her hands. On both sides of her face, spreading her fingers apart, letting them slide against the scalp on her head, as the hair drooped down over her hands. Holding her face she began to cry, filling so overwhelmed with emotion, she felt sick to her stomach.

Then almost to the moment, that Cindy was feeling broken and bewildered. Her cell phone rang, giving her a ray of hope, that it might in fact be Tracy calling her back. Cindy could not get it fast enough saying, "Tracy please tell me that you."

"Yes, honey it's me, I talked to my friend, she has agreed to call you and see if she can help, it will probably be later today and when she calls you honey, tell her everything. Including the way James is acting, it could have some bearing on the situation." Said Tracy trying to make sure she understands all the details, she continued to say, "Now honey I know this is going to be hard for you and I wish I could come up there and help you.

But it's not quite time for the boys to be out of school. Soon as it is I will be there. But in the meantime, you must trust in my friend and try to do what she tells you, she's dealt with this kind of thing for many years now, so believe me she knows what she's saying,"

"I will Tracy and thank you so much, I've got to tell you James is really starting to scare me, it's as if it's not even him." Said Cindy trying to make Tracy understand the situation.

"Well honey I don't want to scare you further but it just might not be." Said Tracy with fear in her voice. Upon hearing that, the realization of the situation settled in Cindy's mind and a chill ran up her spine. Cindy swallowed real hard and then clearing her throat she asked "Tracy, do you think he would hurt me?"

"No, I could never believe that of James. If I thought that for one second, or you are in any danger. The hell with the boy's school I would get them and come up there as fast as I could." Said Tracy trying to put Cindy's mind at ease. Then Tracy continued to say, "All though, I do think that things are only going to get worse, if something isn't done. That's why I've called my friend, like I said she knows exactly what to do."

"What's her name?" inquired Cindy.

"Ashley Michael's and I have already told her everything I know; the rest is up to you sweetie." Said Tracy. Then she continued to say, "I trust her and I'm more than confident that she can help you with whatever's going on there."

"I hope so Tracy, thank you honey, being able to talk to you is helping me more than you know. I love you and thank you again." Said Cindy hanging up the phone.

CHAPTER 20

Later, that morning, Cindy still trying to keep busy and her mind off - of everything. Continued cleaning the mansion, although she was just doing a light dusting, waiting for the phone to ring.

And just when she was about to give up and called Tracy to see what the holdup was. Her phone did in fact began ringing. Cindy couldn't answer it fast enough, saying, "Hello."

A woman's voice began coming from her phone amount of the silence inquiring, "Is this Mrs. Parker?" Cindy answered her saying, "Yes, it is,"

"Mrs. Parker, or can I call you Cindy? This is Ashley Michael's, I'm Tracy's friend."

"Yes ma'am, please do. I have been expecting your call." Said Cindy with excitement in her voice.

"Well Cindy, please tell me what's been going on and for how long?" Inquired Ashley

"Two be quite honest with you, I started noticing things the first night we were here. I tried to tell my husband, but he just said it was my imagination running away with me. Or the wind, he never has believed in this kind of thing and he says that if it is a ghost, it can't hurt me anyway. I didn't have anything to be afraid of." Said Cindy.

"Do you think it's just your imagination?" Inquired Ashley

"No ma'am, I believe in ghosts, plus there something wrong with my husband." Said Cindy trying to answer her the best she could.

"When you say, there is something wrong with your husband, do you think that because of the way he's acting, or some of the things he says?"

"Yes ma'am," answered Cindy.

"Well which is it? Tell me more about that," inquired Ashley

Then like turning on a switch, Cindy began to tell her about how James had been acting. From the time, he stood out there all day and night staring at that statue and the things he said to her on up to the incident this morning with the statue in the study.

She also told her about both dreams she had about the slave girl and how she woke up the next morning soaking wet with mud all over her feet and how James had accused her of doing that to herself to make him believe the mansion was haunted and there is something was going on. Then she told her about what Peggy the waitress at the restaurant had told them about Margaret, as Cindy revealed her information Ashley sat quietly listening to her every word. When Cindy finished telling her everything she knew.

Ashley said. "Well it sounds like to me, that there is deathly something going in involving the slave girl and the well, but what I can't understand, is how that could be affecting your husband. There must be more to this than we know. Mrs. Parker, Cindy, I would like to bring my team out to your home and investigate. Would that be possible?" Inquired Ashley.

"Oh, yes anything you need and thank you so much." Said Cindy with relief in her voice.

"Don't thank me yet, we still got to find out exactly what we're dealing with, then we can determine the situation and how to deal with it further. But I am confident that we will in fact find something." Said Ashley.

"God I hope so, I am starting to feel like I am losing my mind and not getting any help from my husband, I can't tell you how much I appreciate you helping me." Said Cindy with relief in her voice.

"Well I am going to try to do my best to get to the bottom of this, I and my team should be there in the morning try to rest easy and I must tell you Miss Parker it might be best if you do not alert your husband to the fact that we are coming." Said Ashley.

"I don't understand why I shouldn't tell my husband." Said Cindy.

Because Miss Parker, like I said we don't know what we're dealing with and I don't want to frighten you. But let me say your husband might not be himself. If that's the case, he would undoubtedly have tried to put a stop to our coming at all. for now, I think it's best if you do not say anything to him." Said Ashley.

"I understand, to tell you the truth I would be a little scared, because I'm not quite sure what he would do." Said Cindy.

"Don't worry Miss Parker will be there shortly and will know more about what we're dealing with and we will find a way to put a stop to it." Said Ashley trying to reassure her.

"Yes ma-am and thank you I look forward to meeting you and your team both." Said Cindy.

"Well we've got to get our equipment together and get on the road if we are going to be there by morning. Don't worry Mrs. Parker you're not alone in this and will see you shortly." Said Ashley ending the conversation by hanging up the phone.

Cindy just stood there holding the phone in her hand thinking, *"I wish I understood more about, when everybody keeps saying, that James might not be his self. What do they think he's possessed or something? I've seen shows like that on TV, but I never thought something like that could happen to us."*

Cindy then placed her phone in her pocket and went about dusting the mansion letting everything play over in her mind. As she begins to get hungry she wandered, *"Should I go see if James might want to go to dinner?"* Then she thought, *no abettor just go in the kitchen and find myself something and leave him alone."*

Cindy made her way to the kitchen and then in fact fined several things she wanted to eat. While preparing them, the overwhelming sense of loneliness and confusion, seemed to consume her, she found herself *"Wishing that it was already morning and that they were there to help her."* But it was not to be. Now that she had eaten something she began to get tired, so she decided she would just go take a nice hot shower and lay down.

After her shower, she stretched out on the bed wondering to herself *whether - or - not James was even coming in there?* She turned all the lights to the mansion out and just laid there in the darkness frightened and thinking, *"If he did would he be his self or something else?"* That thought alone scared her, she begins to wonder if her eyes got heavier and heavier, *"If I go to sleep will I have another one of those dreams? And if so what would it be about?"*

The next morning Cindy awoke without incident, although she was relieved of that. Turning her head, she noticed James was not lying beside her, realizing this fact she wondered, *"If he had even come in there at all,"* She lay there staring off into space filling like she was losing her husband and feeling powerless to do anything about it, she reached over and grabbed James pillow pulling it close to her breast. Bearing her face deep within it she began to cry, while holding it she slipped back into a deep sleep.

• • •

CHAPTER 21

Suddenly Cindy was awakening by James bursting into the room, asking with a Stern voice, "Cindy who the hell are all these people out here?"

"Their paranormal investigators James, I know you don't believe it. But there is something going on here and they've come here to help me with it." Answered Cindy climbing out of the bed and putting on her close.

James stood there staring at her with an angry and distant look on his face, then he asked with a condescending voice, "Are there no limits that you are not willing to go with this charade?" He continued to say with even more of an angry tone,

"Well you have your fun, but you tell them to stay the hell out of my study and leave me alone."

Cindy just look to him filling hurt and confused, as he seemed to look right through her. Then he turned around and walked away, obviously heading to his study.

Cindy followed him out of the room, heading downstairs to greet her guest. Half way down the staircase she heard the pocket doors on his study slam shut.

Making her way to the front entrance of the mansion. She opened the door and there standing in front of her was a tall woman, with long blonde hair, that looked to be in her late 40s, or early 50s, broad shoulders and her face look like she had been out in the sun too much in her younger days.

Her hair was all messed up and she looked tired. Matter of fact the whole team did. They look like they had just drove right through the night.

Cindy said. "Please everyone come on in, my name is Cindy."

"Good morning Mrs. Parker, I mean Cindy, I am **Ashley Michael's** this is my team **Joe**, **Robert**, **Jessica**, **Terry** and that young man coming in the door right there is **Paul**,"

"Well good morning everyone I can't tell you how happy I am to see all of you, please come and make yourself at home, you all must be hungry, when she gets settled in, we can go into the kitchen and I can find you all something to eat." Said Cindy trying to be accommodating.

"That sounds great Mrs. Parker." Said Joe. But please let us get all our equipment in first and unpack."

"But of course, please follow me upstairs, I have plenty of rooms one for each of you if you would like." Said Cindy turning around to lead them upstairs.

As they got to the top of the stairs Cindy pointing at the room that was in question and said to Ashley, "This room right here is where one of the first encounters happened,"

"Is at the room that you are telling me about?" inquired Ashley.

"Yes mam, that's the room I heard the whimpering woman in the next morning after my dream or whatever it was the door was open and nor I or my husband had been in there." Said Cindy with the frightening look on her face.

"Jessica, make a note of that, I deftly would like to set up a camera in this room." Said Ashley.

"Yes ma'am," answer Jessica.

"Yes, and I think we should put one at each end of the hall and another one pointing down at the staircase." Said Robert looking at Ashley and waiting for confirmation.

"There are several rooms and areas that are going to need to carefully be watched in this mansion." Said Ashley looking back at her team. "I want everything we have infrared, motion detectors, alpha waves detectors, heat signature detectors, I want it all here, I promise you, were going to find out what's going on in this place."

"Terry, are you picking up anything?" Asked Ashley,

"There's been a lot of tragic things happen in this place, I since confusion, pain, despair, loneliness and loss and is something else." Said Terry holding her head and stomach both.

"What is it Terry?" Asked Ashley

"There is a dark presence here it's angry and it wants revenge," answered Terry falling back against the wall catching herself.

"Is she all right?" Asked Cindy.

"Yes, she'll be fine, Terry is my gifted medium, she picks up on spirits and other paranormal activities, she can somehow channel their energy." Said Ashley putting her arms around Terry.

"Can I get her anything a bottle of water, or something cold to drink?" inquired Cindy, wanting to help the girl.

"No, I'll be all right please just give me a second." Said Terry taking a breath and letting it out very slowly. Then suddenly, she turned white as a ghost in pure fear ran across her face and her whole body began to tremble as she said. "Oh, my dear God!"

"Ashley having never seen that before and being concern for her asked, "What is it Terry?"

With the color starting to return to her face and now being able to catch her breath said. "I don't know, it's gone now is as if, something, for just a few seconds came into the room I don't know what it was, it was cold and empty inside it was evil Ashley pure evil. But it's gone now said Terry catching her breath and saying, "I will take that bottle of water now if you don't mind?"

"But of course," Said Cindy scurrying downstairs to get her a bottle of water.

As Cindy was coming back up the stairs with a bottle water. She could hear the team whispering back and forth to one another. But she couldn't make out what they were saying,

When she came into the room they were silent, that made her feel uneasy she could tell they were trying to keep something from her, so she inquired on what it was by saying, "Please don't spare me, tell me what's going on I need to know."

"Well to tell you the truth Cindy, were not really sure. Terry has never picked up a presence like that, or acted in that manner and it is quite frightening, there is something we not sure what it is yet, but there is definitely something sinister about this entity." Said Ashley unmistakably with concerning her voice.

"Will, can you make it go away?" Asked Cindy wringing her hands and swallowing real hard.

"That's what we're here for honey, we will find a way." Said Ashley trying to comfort her.

But first we've got to find out just exactly what we're dealing with."

Terry said. "It knows we're here and why, I suggest that we sleep in teams and no one moves throughout this place alone.

"Terry, you have never said anything like that before, how dangerous is this entity?" Asked Ashley obviously concerned for her team safety.

"To be quite honest with you ma'am I'm not sure, I sense anger, hatred, despair. It wants revenge for something, only on not sure just what." "Is it that slave girl that I've been having dreams about?" Asked Cindy.

"No, it is not a spirit but something else, it's watching us right now, it knows our fears and it will try to use them against us." Said Terry looking at the whole team. As she continued to say the only thing I can tell you for sure is that, it does not want us here and it will try to stop us." Said Terry looking over at Ashley.

"Okay team, were obviously dealing with an entity that none of us have ever dealt with

before. this calls for a vote, on whether we figure this. Or we think it is more than we can deal with and we leave this thing to continue haunting and ultimately destroy this family." Said Ashley feeling even more concern for her team.

"Well I for one, am for continuing the investigation, I know it's dangerous and I know it's more than what any of us have had to deal with in the past. But, if we let this thing run us off without even trying, then we all might as well put away our cameras and seek other alternative jobs." Said **Terry** looking at the whole entire team as she was speaking.

"I agree with Terry, we can't tuck our tails and run away from this thing, I vote we keep going." Said **Joe** picking up a piece of equipment.

"Hey guys this is our job, this is what we do, we investigate the paranormal it's always dangerous and we never really know what we're dealing with, but we always seem to come out on top. Because we work well as the team." Said **Robert** also picking up a piece of equipment.

"Well what do you two think?" Asked Ashley looking over at Paul and Jessica.

"Well ma'am I work for you, to whatever you think." Said Jessica lowering her head.

"No Jesse, this is not a decision I can make for you, I cannot ask any of you to put yourself in harm's way I will not do that." Said Ashley looking at Jessica.

"Okay then I think we should go ahead with the investigation and help these poor people." Said **Jessica** also grabbing a piece of equipment.

"Paul I guess it's up to you, the vote has to be unanimous either we all go, or we all stay" said Ashley waiting for confirmation.

"Okay sure, lay it all off on me, let me just say this, I believe in this team and I believe in what we're doing and I for one think we can overcome any obstacle put in our path. I say the hell with this thing and let's find a way to stop it." Said **Paul** making the vote unanimous.

"Okay then, let's do it. Robert, you and Joe, take care of the cameras above the stairwell and down each hall and in the room where there was first activity and put some motion detectors at the foot of the stairs so we can get it coming or going. Paul, you and Jesse, set up the monitors. Now guys I want everything we have in here, the full gamut. We've only got a couple hours before it gets dark and I would love to have all of this set up and ready to go.

Terry and I are going to be one investigation team, Robert you and Joe, will be the other one, Jesse you and Paul monitor everything and keep in contact with the teams. Al I know we are not supposed to bother Mr. Parker in his study. But I would like a camera pointing down the Hall toward it. Oh yes, I would like to have another one out in the garden pointing at the well. Okay guys let's get cracking, if we all pitch in and work as quickly as we can, we can do this." Said Ashley trying to boost her team's morale. Cindy watched the whole team from a distance and helping from time to time by carrying something or polling accord, anyway she could. Till finally everything was in place, Ashley after doing a final check on all the monitors and cameras praised her team by saying,

"Well done guys I knew we could do it."

Paul came walking in, with two large cases. Upon seeing them Cindy looked on with in puzzlement. Ashley noticing this opening one of the cases and asked, "What you think of these, there my own design?"

"What are they?" Asked Cindy curiously.

"Come here and I'll show you." Said Ashley opening the case.

"I had these made especially for this team, they are made from some very light material." Said Ashley pulling a series of cameras, on what appeared to be a metal frame, out of one of the cases and placing it over Cindy's had and onto her shoulders, buckling it behind her back. As she went on to explain,

"You see, here on your right shoulder facing directly behind you is this camera and on your left shoulder facing directly in front of you is this one and right here is where the monitor is mounted, with another camera directly above and pointing down at it. Then you have this headset right here." Said Ashley as she strapped it to Cindy's head pulling and tightening the strap asking, "Is that too tight?"

"No actually it's quite comfortable." Said Cindy moving her head from side to side. A matter of fact the whole thing is. I can hardly feel the weight of it even."

"That's because of this little design here." Said Ashley as she showed Cindy the part that came down and placed across her belly supporting the weight.

"Now each one of these cameras hold a four-hour charge and with this design you can see in front and directly behind you, the camera on your head, sees everything you see and it's all monitored and recorded, not only by the investigating team, but also by the team members watching the monitors. They can see everything you do and you yourself can look down and see anything all the way around you as well. Then you have got this device here." Said Ashley strapping something to her wrist.

"What is that?" Asked Cindy again overwhelmed with curiosity.

"Well on this wrist, this device will pick up heat signatures and cold spots." Said Ashley smiling at her.

"Cool," commented Cindy looking down at it.

"Oh, yes all of our equipment is like this, is not only easy to use but it is high tech and on this other wrist this device detects alpha waves,

"Alpha waves, I heard you say that before, what is that?" Asked Cindy looking at Ashley.

"Sometimes entities spiritual and otherwise, give off alpha waves that we can't detect. But this device can and because it strapped to your wrist it leaves your hands-free to pick up something or carry another device like this." Said Ashley handing a little tape recorder to Cindy and continuing to say. This is a digital voice recorder, it can pick up sounds that the human ear can't, so while the investigating team walk throughout the area, we will attempt to communicate with the spirit and sometimes they communicate us back, but we can't hear them.

That's what this device does it picks up on sounds and hopefully voices from the entities that we encounter and that's pretty much it what's you think?" – Ashley smiling at Cindy looking like something from a science fiction show.

"I think it's all pretty cool I wouldn't mind doing it." Said Cindy looking at all - of the devices.

"It takes a long time to actually learn how to use everything. But you will get to watch, you can stay in the main room and watch the monitors. With Jesse and Paul, while we move throughout your mansion and you'll get to see everything that happens, to and around us and everything we see and hear. Although there is a degree of danger, from time to time, it's still quite exciting." Said Ashley starting to remove everything from Cindy.

"Yes, I can see that it is." Said Cindy once again looking over the equipment and watching as Ashley, Terry, Joe and Robert, strapped it all on getting ready to investigate her manor.

"Now if you will follow me, I'll take you to the main observation room, where all the monitors are set up and you can watch from in there, with Jesse and Paul." Said Ashley to Cindy.

Cindy followed along behind Ashley, eager to get the investigation going. As they went into the drawing room and there were four monitors set up with Paul and Jesse watching them. Ashley said as they came into the room,

"You can watch from here, Paul's monitoring the team members, what we see and hear he will too. Jesse is monitoring the upstairs and downstairs, also she's watching the garden area and all the motion detectors." Said Ashley starting to turn around and walk out she smiled at Cindy saying, "Enjoy the show."

"You can sit right here." Said Jesse pulling the chair upright between her and Paul.

"That way you can see both monitors and watch the show sometimes it can get quite exciting," Jessie continued to say.

"We have seen things that you would not believe."

"Yes, they were things that you, well you would just have to see them for yourself to believe it was real and even then, you would probably doubt it." Said Paul looking over at Cindy.

Then Paul continued to say "At any rate things are liable to get quite exciting knowing the history of this place and some of the things you've told us."

"What made you want to move into a place like this any way?" Asked Jesse with a confused look on her face.

"I inherited it and some of the stipulations to the will is that we have to live here." Said Cindy lowering her head.

"Why don't you just sell it?" Asked Paul.

"We can't sell it and we can't move anything off it either, more stipulations to the will." Said Cindy trying to make them understand.

"With all the things, you say are going on here, what makes it worth it?" Asked Paul with confusion in his voice.

"I also inherited $375 million along with it." Said Cindy once again lowering her head.

"Oh, I see." Said Paul as he looked over at Jesse.

Saying, "That is a lot of money."

"Yes, it is and besides that I really love it here, it is a big beautiful place, inside and out and if not for the obvious reasons, I think we could be quite happy here. That's why I'm hoping you guys can help me to figure out what this thing wants and maybe put a stop to all of this." Said Cindy looking at one of them and then the other.

"Well I'm sure were going to try to." Said Paul turning back around looking at the monitor, saying, "It looks like they're getting ready to start."

"Now when things really start to get interesting," Said Jesse turning back to her monitor.

Ashley said. "I am Ashley Michaels, heading the investigation team. It's 9 o'clock Friday afternoon, we are at the summer hill manner in North Carolina. The home of Cindy and James Parker, after careful consideration, along with the testimonial of Mrs. Parker, we have decided to go on with our investigation. We're going to try to contact the entity that is causing paranormal activity here at the manner and try to find out what it wants. Myself along with Terry my gifted medium on one team, and I have Joe and Robert, on another team.

Jesse and Paul two more additional team members, are set up in the drawing room of the manner. Paul is watching the monitor for the team members, he can see everything we see and hear everything around us. Jesse is watching the monitors overseeing the garden area, a downstairs hall, the stairwell and the hallway to the study. She is also monitoring the motion detectors. Now let's begin. Is there anyone here? We have come a long way to see you." Said Ashley quietly listening for reply. "We are here to see if we might can help you." Said Ashley. But once again there was just silence.

"I have helped in many other situations like this, can I help you? This is a digital recorder I'm holding in my hand, so that you can speak to us through it if you choose, please let me help you." Said Ashley once again eagerly waiting for reply.

Then suddenly breaking the silence was what appeared to be the whimpering of a woman. Terry looked at Ashley saying, "She scared."

"You don't need to be frightened of us, we're here to help, tell us what we can do for you." Said Ashley still trying to get a response. But there was still just silence.

"There's no need to be afraid, please let me help you," pleaded Ashley.

Then once again breaking the silence was more whimpering and what appeared to be a woman's voice mumbling something. Then there was just silence again. Terry looking over at Ashley and stumbling falling back against the wall holding her stomach and said "It's here."

On hearing that, the hair stood up on the back of Ashley's neck, as she considered the darkness with the dim glow, of the light from the cameras shining all around her. Ashley's asked "Why are you haunting these people in this place? Then she just stood quietly waiting for reply.

Breaking the silence once more, the team heard the clear words,

"Leave this place while you still can."

Making the hair stand up on the back of Ashley's neck again.

Then suddenly Paul excitedly asked "Did you see that?"

"See what?" Asked Jesse trying to look at his monitor.

"Come here look at this." Said Paul rewinding the recording on his monitor.

Both Jesse and Cindy, got up and move closer so that they could see Paul's monitor, as he was coming to the place in question.

"There, right there," do you see that behind Ashley?" Asked Paul excitedly.

"Oh, my God," it's right behind her." Said Jesse excitedly grabbing the Mike saying, "Ashley there's something right behind you, don't turn around just look down at your monitor."

Ashley once again with the hair standing up on the back of her neck and a tingling all over her head very slowly looked down at the monitor, she could in fact clearly see a dark image standing a few feet behind her. Although she could not make out any distinguishing features, it was clear to see that there was something standing in the shadows.

Ashley said very quietly into the two-way radio. "Yes, I see it,"

But before she could turn around to confront it and get a better look, it disappeared back into the darkness. Terry now being able to collect herself told Ashley "It's gone,"

"What was that?" Asked Cindy with a frightened voice.

Without answering her, Paul and Jesse just looked at each other.

CHAPTER 22

Robert and Joe made their way down to the music room, where the piano lid has slammed shut on Cindy. Opening the room Robert asked, "Is there anyone in here? We would like to try to communicate with you."

But once again there was only silence. The two boys stood quietly in the room listening for any confirmation reply. Upon not receiving one. Joe said. "There's nothing in here, let's go try somewhere else."

But before the two boys could leave the room a cold breeze blew across them moving the curtains on the Windows and they heard what appeared to be the whimpering of a woman. Robert asked, "What's wrong? Please let us help you. Are you the one that slammed the piano lid shut on Mrs. Parker? Why did you do that? Is there something you want her to do for you? Would you like to say something to us? We're here to help you?"

Paul was also watching them, when he saw what appeared to be a floating orb, in the back of the room, out of sight of the team. But he, could clearly see it on the monitor, from the light of the camera moving in the back of the room. he told the two boys saying,

"There's something moving around in the darkness a few feet ahead of you, it looks like…," he paused for a few seconds and continuing to say, "Yes I think it is, hey guys it is an orb."

Upon hearing that, they both struggled to see into darkness of the room and make it out. But not being able to see it Robert asked, "Would you like to say something to us? This is a digital recorder, with it we will be able to hear you."

But there was just silence.

"Say something to us," demanded Joe.

Then once again from out of the darkness breaking the silence, they heard what appeared to be the whimpering of a woman.

"What is wrong, can we help? I want to help you, please tell me what I can do to help you. Then all - of - a sudden, once again breaking the silence, they heard what appeared to be a voice speaking softly in a whisper, like underneath someone's breath. But trying his hardest they could they could not make it out. "What was that, we don't understand you? Please say it again, let us help you." Said Robert starting to get agitated, trying to get it to respond.

But there was silence. Both teams made their way around the mansion going from this room and then that one for several hours, trying to get a response. But as it got later and later, there was not another incident.

Finally, Ashley said over the radio, "Hey guys, I think that's enough for one night, let's make our way back to the drawing room and go over all the material and see what if anything we have."

Robert and Joe, made their way back to the drawing room first, having a shorter distance to go. When Ashley and Terry came in., they were all conversing back-and-forth starting to go over the video that they have captured,

"I see that there is definitely something standing behind Ashley." Said Robert was excitement in his voice. Paul then said "look at this that is definitely an orb floating in the back of the music room, a few feet ahead of you."

"Wow you're right, we did not see that, did we Joe?" Asked Robert waiting for him to confirm his statement.

"No, we do not see that, we felt a cold breeze blow across us in the room and we did in fact hear something, play the recorder Robert." Said Joe eagerly

Robert played the recorder as the whole team listen carefully to Joe said "Their do you hear that,

It sounds like the whimpering of a woman."

"Yes, we've heard the same thing earlier on, I think we got a recorded as well." Said Ashley with excitement in her voice "there's something else."

"What you mean? Asked Cindy starting to get even more" frightened.

"We recorded something else it was a voice. Clearly saying, leave this place while you still can." Said Ashley searching through her recorder to find a voice.

Upon finding it she played it out loud for the whole team, there "There is the whimpering of the woman said Ashley while holding the recorded so that the team could hear the woman,

Then suddenly to their disbelief a deep voice clearly stated over the recorder

"Leave this place while you still can."

Upon hearing that eerie voice everyone felt the effect but none like Cindy as she said. "I'll tell you guys I'm really scared."

"But don't you see it's trying to scare us, it doesn't want us here." Said Ashley,

"I think there's more to it than that." Said Terry finally speaking out.

"What do you mean Terry?" Asked Robert noticing the frightened look on her face.

"This thing is not a spirit, its ancient it's been here for a long time try to control your fear because it's feeding off - of it and gaining strength it has targeted you." Said Terry pointing directly at Cindy.

"Why has it targeted me, what does it want from me?" Asked Cindy now noticeably frightened "That right there, that's why it's targeted you, it knows you're afraid, you must try to control your fear, listen carefully to me Mrs. Parker, I mean Cindy, it's feeding off - of you, it has been ever since you've been here and it will try to use that against us." Said Ashley trying to make her understand.

"Well can you stop it?" Asked Cindy wringing her hands trying not to show fear.

"I don't know but we will try if you allow us to continue our investigation." Said Ashley looking directly at Cindy.

"But of course, I want you to try to find a way to get rid of this thing." Said Cindy with confusion, as she wondered why she would ask that,

Cindy continued to asked, when you said this thing has targeted me, doesn't want to hurt me."

"No, it can't hurt you." Said Terry looking at Cindy.

"But how do you know, how can you be so sure?" Asked Cindy looking for confirmation.

"Because Ms. Parker if it could hurt you, it already would have. Now like I said. it can't hurt you, but it can make you hurt yourself or others. And it's going to try to control you." Said Terry looking at Ashley waiting for her to confirm her statement.

"Yes, Cindy Terry is right it can't hurt you. But it can use your fear against us." Said Ashley again confirming Terry's belief.

"I don't understand how can it use me against you?" Asked Cindy with even more confusion in her voice.

"Because Cindy this is your house and make no mistake it does not want us here and it will try to get you to make us leave, it will lie to you not only will it try to scare you but it will try to turn you against us ultimately getting what it wants." Said Ashley trying to make her understand.

"Ashley I don't understand, why is it here, there has to be a reason for it, we know this from other investigations. An entity like this didn't just appear, it came from somewhere." Said Robert now also feeling confused.

"I don't know Robert, I don't know why it's here and I don't know why it remains here." Said Ashley also obviously feeling confused.

"It's always been here, its ancient and it stays here because of the spirit that is it not at rest here." Said Terry looking at both Robert and Ashley.

"Okay then that might be its undoing we could…"

"Ashley it's listening to us right now it has been." Said Terry interrupting her.

Ashley looking over at Terry then looking around the room said "I understand, hey guys what you say we jump into the Van and go to try and find something to eat, getting kind of hungry is there a place around here that might be open this time at night?" Asked Ashley looking at Cindy for confirmation.

"Well I don't know I'm sure we can probably find a place, but there's no need for that I have plenty of food in the kitchen we could simply…,"

"No I don't want to put you out, I think we'll all just jump in the Van!!! And you come along with us and we will try to find something." Said Ashley interrupting her placing her finger to her lips.

"Oh okay, if that's what you want to do, I'll come along, like I said there should be something open." Said Cindy nodding her head at Ashley letting her know she understood.

Then everyone went out the mansion, closing the door behind them and climbed into the Van heading toward town. As they got to the iron gates, Ashley said "Okay Paul pull over right here, I'm sorry everyone. But we needed to get out of the mansion. As Terry indicated it was listening to us, so no matter what we came up with, it would've already known." Said Ashley spinning around in her seat so that she would be able to see and talk to the whole team.

Continuing to ask "Does anyone have any suggestions, on how we might deal with this thing? Terry what are you, getting from it?"

"Well it is very cunning and like you said no matter what we would've came up with, it would've plotted against us, like I've indicated this is not a spirit were dealing with, it is something else. I must tell all of you, it's evil in nature and wants to destroy this family and it's keeping the spirit from being able to speak to us, we are a threat to it. I believe if we could somehow find out what the Spirit wants, undoubtable it is the slave girl that keeps trying to contact you Mrs. Parker. She wants or needs something from you and I don't know why but it has - to be you that puts her to rest. I know that much. Like I was saying, if we can put the slave girl to rest and break the hold that this entity has over her. I think we can get rid of it" said Terry looking directly at Ashley.

CHAPTER 23

"Well that settles it then, make no mistake about this, I do not like involving anyone other than our team, in situations like this. But these are special circumstances, so I must ask you Cindy to help us with this." Said Ashley, looking directly at her.

"Me, what can I do?" Asked Cindy feeling frightened and confused.

"While I have an idea, this thing cannot be two places at one time, so what I propose is that you go with Robert and Joe, to the back of the house. I think the music room is the furthest room away from the rest of the house, isn't it?" Asked Ashley looking at Cindy for confirmation.

"Yes, it is, but Ashley, I don't know if I can do this." Said Cindy lowering her head.

"Cindy, you have to. I just don't know any other way." Said Ashley getting a little frustrated with the situation.

"Go ahead with your plan." Said Robert eagerly awaiting to hear the rest of it.

"Well like I was saying, Terry feels that this evil entity will follow Cindy and try to get to her. What I'm proposing is, like I said it can't be two places at one time and if it follows you Cindy, to the back of the house. Then maybe we can talk to the spirit of the slave girl and find out what she wants, or needs from you. In doing so, we can be able to put her rest and ultimately get rid of the evil entity trying to destroy your family." Said Ashley looking directly at Cindy. Then she continued to say "So you see Cindy you have to do this. Paul and Joe will be right there with you the whole time, nothing is going to happen to you, remember what Terry told you: This thing, whatever it is can't hurt you."

"She'll be fine, will take good care of her, I won't let nothing happened to her." Said Robert continuing to get things together for the investigation.

"Neither will I, you'll be just fine will protect you with everything we got." Said Joe trying to put Cindy's mind at ease.

"Well ok, if you think this is the only way we can get rid of this thing. I can do it." Said Cindy trying to confirm the plan.

"The only other thing is. When, are we going to do this? I must leave that up to you all. But it is late, perhaps we should wait for tomorrow night." Said Ashley, leaving the decision up to her team.

"I for one, think we should just go back through tonight, strike while the iron is hot." Said Robert, while changing the battery on his camera harness.

"The thing that worries me is, if any of us talk about our plan, not only will it find out what were up to and try to stop us. It's a good bet it will keep the slave girl far away from us. With - that - being - said. I don't see where we have a choice, we've got to go back through their tonight. If our plan is going to work at all." Said Terry talking to the whole team.

"I agree with Terry, I mean think about how difficult it would be, not to talk about the plan. Or even thinking about it might give it away. After all we don't know, this thing might be able to get into our heads somehow, maybe even read our minds. no I don't think we have a choice either." Said Joe looking at Ashley.

"We'll all I know is, whether we go through tonight or tomorrow, doesn't matter to me. But I am getting hungry and would like to have something to eat and maybe even rest a little while to regain some strength, especially if we are going to do it tonight." Said Paul looking at the rest of the team.

"I've got plenty of food in my kitchen and I would be more than happy to make you all anything you'd like." Said Cindy trying to make them feel comfortable and welcome. "That sounds good to me, I'm getting kind of hungry to. But isn't this thing going to think it strange, that we leave to go get something to eat and we come back to raid the kitchen?" Asked Jesse, waiting for confirmation.

"We will simply start talking about how we couldn't find anything open, so it can hear us while we make our way to the kitchen." Said Robert trying to answer her.

"Jesse how do you feel about this, what do you think we should do?" Asked Ashley waiting for reply from her.

"I'm game for whatever it's going to take to help this family. I agree with everyone, I don't think we should wait either, too much could happen and something definitely needs to be done about this thing." Said Jesse answering Ashley.

"Okay Paul head back to the mansion will get us something to eat, rest for a little while and will take this thing had on and utilize the plan. I must tell you guys, I'm very proud of you, I really believe in this team and I think you guys are the greatest bunch of individuals I've ever known. No matter what comes our way you don't hesitate to take it on and it simply has been a pleasure working with all of you these years. You never fail to impress me, each one of you." Said Ashley talking to her whole team.

"I would just like to say that I think you're very intelligent and strong and an impressive woman, I've enjoyed working right alongside you and I for one am not afraid. Because of this team, I believe in it, I trust it and I know that no matter what we encounter, we can handle it." Said Jessica also looking at each individual member of the team.

"Let me just say, I seen a lot of things since I've been working with all of you. A lot of strange unexplainable things and sometimes scared me and made me feel very uncomfortable. Especially In the beginning. But as I've been working alongside of each one of you, gaining your trust and friendship. I to feel that there is nothing that we can encounter, which this team can't deal with." Said Joe voicing his opinion.

"Yeah-yeah- yeah, well if everybody's through tooting your horn can we get back to this task at hand? I'm getting hungry myself now and if this keeps up there is not going to be enough of room in this van for everybody's head." Said Robert voicing his opinion.

"Before we head inside. I just want to say, I can't thank you guys enough, I been dealing with this thing all alone. I think God for bringing you all here to help me with this. I can't tell you how much I appreciate it." Said Cindy smiling over at Ashley.

"It is one of the more difficult ones, there is no doubt about that. But I am confident that we can deal with this. like I said if we can find a way to put this slave girls spirit to rest, the entity will no longer have the power, or reason to be here and upon losing its strengths, should go away." Said Terry looking over at Ashley.

"You mean there's a chance that it won't?" Asked Cindy with fear in her voice.

"Cindy truthfully this thing has been here for a long time, it's ancient and we don't even really know what it is, were only speculating that it's the slave girl that is holding it here. So yes, I'm afraid there is a chance, it might remain here, even after the slave girl is put to rest, you do need to be aware of that." Said Ashley trying to make her understand. Then she continued to say, "But, I think it's very unlikely. I truly believe once we put the slave girl to rest, it will go away."

As they drove back up in front of the mansion Ashley said. "Now remember everyone, do not discuss the plan and try not to even think about it."

"The only thing I'm thinking about right now, is my belly. I'm hungry." Said Joe climbing out of the Van.

"I know what you mean, my stomach thinks someone slit my throat." Said Jesse smiling at Joe.

"Please everyone follow me, I'll take you to the kitchen, I have a huge refrigerator full of all kinds of food and almost anything you could want. Please make yourselves at home, help yourself to anything you desire." Said Cindy trying to make them fill comfortable and welcome.

As the team entered the kitchen, to their disbelief they saw a huge refrigerator, alongside two big freezers and a giant stove. Paul opened the refrigerator making a comment saying,

"My God! Would you look in this thing, I've never seen so much food. This isn't a kitchen, it is a supermarket."

"You think that's something, look in these cabinets. There is enough of food in here to feed a small country." Said Jesse looking over at Cindy.

"Please help yourself, to anything you guys want." Said Cindy smiling at them.

"I'm not looking to feed a small country, I'm looking to feed myself." Said Robert reaching past Joe and grabbing several packages of what appeared to be sandwich meat, in one hand and mayonnaise and mustard, with the other hand and he turned around and walked over to the table spreading them all out, as he said Jesse hand me a loaf of that white bread please."

Then Robert turned and looked at Cindy and asked, "Would you happen to have anything to drink?"

"Yes of course, I'm sorry, there's a couple pictures of Ice-T here, I'll get them for you." Said Cindy walking toward the refrigerator.

"No ma'am that's all right." Said Robert, as he turned around and ask Joe to hand him a pitcher of tea. Because he was still standing at the refrigerator, undecided on what he wanted. Joe not being able to make up his mind, turned around and noticed Robert and Jesse had already made a sandwich and seemed to be enjoying it. Upon seeing that he decided on one as well.

The whole team set down after making their choice on what they wanted to eat, sitting quietly. Then suddenly Paul yawned saying, "I got to tell you guys I'm sure glad I'm not the one is going to…,"

He paused catching himself before he revealed the plan. The whole team is looking at him with discussed? Robert just sat there shaking his head quietly looking over at Paul.

Paul shrug your shoulders saying, "Sorry."

After everyone had gotten through eating and had rested for quite a while. Ashley ask, "Hey guys is still early yet, what you say we do another walk-through?"

"At sounds like a good idea, we still have plenty of time for daylight." Said Robert agreeing with Ashley.

Them once again everyone strapped on their equipment, Jesse and Paul headed to the computers to monitor everything. Only this time Ashley turned to Cindy and asked,

"How would you like to try it?"

"Oh yes, you mean it?" Asked Cindy with excitement in her voice like a little girl at Christmas time.

"I don't see why not, come here and I will strap you in. You can do a walk-through would Robert and Joe. I want you guys to go back to the music room, shows Cindy how everything works out Robert." Said Ashley starting the plan in motion.

The three of them headed down the hall leading toward the back of the mansion, working their way slowly through the darkness. Till finally they came to the music room. Robert opened the big double wooden doors. As all three of them stepped inside the room, Robert turned on the recorder saying, "Where here again, would you like to talk to us? We have Mrs. Parker with us, would you like to tell her what it is that you want? Is there something you want her to do for you?" Then Robert turned his Cindy and said in a soft voice almost in a whisper,

"Try talking to her,"

Cindy said. "Hello, are you in here with us? Tell me how I can help you. I'm here and I have the recorder. Please won't you please tell me, how I can help you?

But there was only silence,

Ashley and Terry, were watching their monitors, waiting to see something happen in the music room. Terry looked over at Ashley saying, "She must be frightened, I don't think she's…,"

Suddenly Terry paused in the middle of what she was saying,

Ashley noticing this, looked at her with concern and asked what is it Terry?"

But she only stood there quietly staring off into space. Suddenly she said. "Oh, my God, it's in the room with them, God help them it's a lot stronger."

"Are they in any danger?" Asked Ashley with concern in her voice.

"No, not now, it's only watching and keeping the girl from talking to them, let's go to that room at the top of the stairs, where Mrs. Parker first had the encounter. For some reason that room has a very powerful significance to the girl." Said Terry as she started toward the stairwell.

Cindy was straining her eyes to see into the dark room, while Robert was trying to contact the slave girl.

Suddenly Robert and Joe, moved over to the other side of the room and appeared to be talking back and forth. Cindy struggled to hear them. But she couldn't understand what they were saying,

Then she heard Joe say "I've never seen Ashley let anyone joining our team like this."

"Yes, I know, I was thinking the same thing, I think it's because this woman has a lot of money and she probably offered Ashley a lot of money to let her." Said Robert snickering under his breath.

"Bet you we won't see any of that money." Said Joe glancing back it Cindy for a second.

"Of course, not, there's no telling how much money she's going to give her that we won't know anything about." Said Robert as he continued to mumble something under his breath at Cindy just could not make out, then they both started giggling.

"It's not like she'll miss it, how much money do you think she has?" Asked Joe with jealousy in his voice.

"You can bet it's more than will ever see in a lifetime." Said Robert trying to answer him quietly so that Cindy couldn't hear.

"Yes, she's probably one of those rich snobs born with a silver spoon in her mouth, thinking the world owes her a living." Said Joe disgustingly.

"I know these rich people, here bumps in the night and they call us to come fix the problem likely and got nothing better to do." Said Robert also disgustedly.

Cindy could not believe her ears, what she was hearing the things they were saying, about her how rude they were. Started her thinking, *"It's all been a front they had just been putting on airs, trying to get her to like them."* That made Cindy feel very uncomfortable, being in the same room with them. She felt like just walking out of the room, taken off that camera and making them leave her house. She just couldn't believe that they were talking like that behind her back. They didn't need to be there, they needed to get their stuff and go. Because there not doing any good anyway. She kept thinking about all the things they were saying, then she thought, *"They're just making matters worse so there is a slave girl spirit running around in the mansion, after all she's just a ghost can't hurt her* anyway." Then she thought, *"There obviously not going to do anything about it anyway,"* Then she thought *"I invite them in my home, feed and make them feel comfortable and welcome. Now she knows how they really feel about her."*

Cindy decided to say something to them so she said. "Hey you two I can hear everything you're saying,"

"Ma'am." Said Robert with confusion in his voice.

"Don't ma'am me I could hear every word you to, were saying, over there." Said Cindy disgustedly.

Robert with confusion in his voice said. "Ma'am we were not saying, anything."

"Oh, yes you were, I heard every word the both of you said. the two of you shouldn't talk about people like that. I'm not some rich snob and don't, I come from a poor family." Said Cindy angrily.

"Mrs. Parker I assure you we don't know what you're talking about." Said Joe looking at Robert.

"Yes, you do, I was standing right here listening. To the two of you talk about me and Ashley. I wonder if she really knows how you feel about her."

Mrs. Parker your mistaken we haven't said anything said Joe I promise you Mrs. Parker we haven't were trying to help you, why would we be talking about you and be trying to help you at the same time?

"Wait a minute, oh my God! I know what it is. It's trying to confuse you ma'am, it's getting into your head, it's making you see and hear things." Said Robert trying to help her understand.

"What you talking about?" Asked Cindy with confusion in her voice.

"The entity ma'am it's here in the room with us, like I said is trying to confuse you." Said Robert once again.

"I don't understand." Said Cindy starting to feel more and more afraid.

"It's trying to scare and confuse you, make you feel like everyone's against you because it wants to control your mind. You see, if it can do that, then you will do what it wants you to do, instead of what you-want. I promise you as God is my witness, we were not talking about you, or anything. We were standing quietly listen in for the girl." Said Robert doing his best to make her understand.

"I don't believe you." Said Cindy now filling even more frustrated, than frightened.

"Mrs. Parker listen to this, I was recording the whole time." Said Robert as he was rewinding the digital recorder, playing it back for her.

Cindy listened to a recording, at first, she heard everything they said as they came into the room. After that, to her disbelief there was nothing but silence. Till finally she heard her own voice say, I can hear every word you two are saying, Robert stop the recorder saying, "You see ma'am, if we had been talking about you, it would've recorded it." Said Robert still trying to convince her.

"I don't know I'm, I'm, confused I'm sorry." Said Cindy starting to understand and feeling embarrassed.

"There is nothing to be sorry about, it's trying to control you this is what Ashley and Terry were telling you, that it would try to get into your head and turn you against us. It doesn't want us here because were a threat to it. Stay close to us and you will see were not talking about you, were trying to help you and it doesn't want us to." Said Robert doing his best to put her mind at ease.

Then suddenly a cold breeze blew through the room, blowing Cindy's hair. As the double doors slammed shut to the music room.

Ashley and Terry made their way up to that room and when inside,

"You watched the monitor and keep an eye out for that thing, I'm going to try and talk to the girl, does it know where here and what we're doing yet?" Asked Ashley very quietly.

"No, it's watching the team." Said Terry considering the monitor.

Then Ashley asked, "Are you here with us? We don't have long, we set this up so that you might be able to speak to us and tell us what you want, what do you need Mrs. Parker to do for you?"

Then she along with Terry just stood quietly in the dark, holding the voice recorder out of fun of her, but there was just silence.

"I don't know how long will have two be able to talk to you, I know you're scared this will be our only chance to be able to help you, we've got it preoccupied in another part of the house so that you…," Ashley paused because Terry held her hand out in front of her, standing quietly as she looked at her and asked in a whisper, "Is it the entity?"

Terry shook her head no saying, "She's in here."

Upon hearing that Ashley said. "Talk to us, tell us what you want or need, we can help you, if you will just talk to us, what do you want for Mrs. Parker? We can tell her, why won't you…?" Once again Ashley paused because Terry held her hand out in front and interrupting her. Then suddenly breaking the silence they heard a woman's voice say **"MY BABY"** and several other sounds that they could not make out, as she held the recorder out in front of her. Then finally they heard the single clear word, **"WELL."**

Then suddenly Jesse said over the two-way radio startling Ashley and Terry both, "Ashley there's something going on in the garden, I see it what appears to be a missed over by the well,"

Ashley looking over it Terry she shook her head saying, "I don't know."

Then Ashley said. "We'll be right there."

As her and Terry made their way back to the drawing room as quickly as they could, Ashley came into the room she asked, "Where is it?"

"Right there." Said Jesse pointing to the monitor.

She and Terry both, looked at the monitor and you could clearly see a missed moving around the well. Ashley said "Come on let's get out there," with excitement in her voice.

Then as quickly as they could. While heading toward the garden area, Ashley asked Terry if the entity knew what they were doing yet.

Terry said "No I don't think so it's still just watching the team, trying to figure out what they're doing."

Arriving out in the garden they climbed the hill to the well. To their disbelief their standing beside the well was a transparent form. Which was the image of a slave girl, looking at the both - of - them. As she slowly raised her hand and pointed to the well, mumbling something in a whisper. Then disappearing right in front of them.

Suddenly Terry said. "Oh, my God! It knows Ashley. It's coming toward us."

Rushing back inside, she called to the other team members saying,

"Everyone get to the drawing room as quickly as you can."

Making their way down the hall leading to the stairwell, they felt a cold as ice breeze blow from out of nowhere and across the both. Causing them to stop in their tracks. Terry looked over at Ashley saying, "It's here,"

They saw a dark figure coming down the hall toward them, suddenly, the light started flickering from the camera and each time it would light up the hall. They could clearly see the dark image getting closer and closer to them. Ashley while clinging to the wall, felt what appeared to be a light switch, she turned it on. The bright light filled the hallway just before the entity got to them. The entity made. A low grumble growl as it disappeared.

Ashley and Terry, continued making their way back to the drawing room, while Cindy, along with Robert and Joe, came walking in asking, "How did it find out?"

"I don't know but it did I guess it just figured out what we were doing." Said Ashley with confusion in her voice.

"It's getting a lot stronger Ashley; therefore, it's beginning to be dangerous. It can almost take physical form, its drawing strength from our fears and there's something else feeding it. I don't know what but it's making it more and more powerful. If we can't put a stop to it soon, I'm afraid were not going to be able to at all." Said Terry with fear in her voice.

Upon hearing that, a chill ran across Ashley spine and the hair stood up on the back of her neck because she had never heard Terry speak in that manner and she was obviously frightened, then Ashley said. "All right everyone, time for another road trip."

Once again everybody walked out of the mansion letting the door closed behind them and climbed into the Van. Paul reached down cranking it up and drove out of the driveway heading toward the iron Gates, a few feet away from the gates Ashley said.

"Okay Paul pullover right here, well the good news is I think the slave girl tried to communicate with us. Playback the recording Terry."

Terry rewound the handheld recorder, at first there was nothing but silence then they could clearly hear a woman's voice say, MY BABY, PLEASE, MY BABY,

Ashley said. "That's while she was pointing at the well and disappeared right in front of us."

Cindy looked at Ashley was a surprised look on her face saying, "Oh my God! You don't think...,"

"Yes, I do Cindy, that's exactly what I'd think, the baby is in the well." Said Ashley interrupting her confirming her fear.

"What she wants is, for you to get her baby out of the well." Said Terry looking at Cindy.

"No," "I don't think I can do that. I mean how could I do that at?" "Please Ashley don't make me do that." Said Cindy with confusion and fear in her voice.

"Cindy, you have to, you the only one that can, I don't know why but it has to be you that does it. Maybe it's got something to do with the fact that you are a Summerhill? I don't know but for some reason she wants you to do this for her." Said Ashley, trying to make her understand.

"But how, do I go down in the well, oh my God! Ashley am scared, I don't think I can do that." Said Cindy with tears welling up in her eyes and with her bottom lip trembling she begin to ring her hands, fidgeting back and forth in her seat saying, under her breath "No, no, I just can't, please dear God no, I just can't."

Robert while looking over at Cindy, watching her staring out the window, mumbling to herself said. "My God! Ashley, look at her, she can't do that."

"She has to Robert that's what the girl wants." Said Ashley regrettably.

"Maybe one of us, can go down in the well and get the remains of the baby and give them to her, to present to the spirit of the slave girl." Said Joe trying to be sympathetic with Cindy's fear.

"That might work Ashley, because there's one thing we've got to consider. It's going to be dark down there and it will undoubtedly try to stop us if it can and with her being that afraid, it will only increase the danger. Whoever goes down in that well, cannot show any fear. Or they will not be able to remove the baby's remains and they might not be able to get out of there themselves." Said Terry looking over at Ashley.

"Yes, but what do we do with the babies remains, once we retrieve them from the well?" Asked Jesse trying to understand.

"That's a good question, what do we do with them?" Asked Paul with even more confusion.

Terry said "Somehow we've got to put the baby spirit to rest, then and only then will the slave girl be at peace having her ba…, Terry paused for a minute.

Ashley notice and asked, "What is it Terry?"

"I think I know what we have to do, we've got to find out where the mother is buried and then Mrs. Parker, Cindy, has got to bury the babies remains with its mother." Said Terry looking at Ashley.

"How are we going to do that? Asked Jesse with a confused look on her face.

"I don't know? Mrs. Parker I mean Cindy, you said this is an old plantation, right?" Asked Ashley trying to get Cindy's attention.

"What, I mean, yes, that's what the lawyer Mr. Wilcox told us, when we went over all the details of the mansion and my inheritance. Why do you ask?" Asked Cindy obviously confused.

"Because most plantations had slaves living on the grounds, I don't see why this one would be any different." Said Ashley trying to explain.

"Yes, so how can that have anything to do with where the mother is buried?" Asked Robert trying to understand were Ashley was going with that.

"Because Robert not only did they have slaves living and working on the plantation. But they also died here so that would mean...,"

"I see there's a graveyard somewhere on these grounds and you think that that's where the mother might be buried." Said Robert interrupting her starting to understand.

"Exactly, if we can find the cemetery where the slaves were buried and have Cindy bury the babies remains there that should put both of their spirits to rest for the slave girl to have her baby lying beside her,' said Ashley trying to explain further.

"Cindy, do you know if there is a graveyard or anything like that here?" Asked Ashley once again getting her attention.

"No I do I don't know," answered Cindy still filling very confused and frightened.

"What about this lawyer Wilcox fellow would he know?" Asked Ashley once again trying to talk to Cindy.

"I don't know, I mean maybe, I could call and ask I guess if anyone would know it would be him." Said Cindy trying to pull herself together and reaching for her cell phone, asking what time it was

Robert looked at his watch and said "My God it's almost 6 o'clock in the morning. I thought it was starting to get light outside.

"6 o'clock I can't call that man at 6 o'clock in the morning." Said Cindy putting her cell phone back in her pocket.

"6 o'clock in the morning, no wonder I'm so tired." Said Paul stretching and yawning.

"Yes, I'm sure we are all very tired, it has been a long night." Said Ashley also stretching in her seat. Then she said. while let's head back to the mansion everybody can lay down and get some rest, we will deal with this a little bit later today."

"Yes, if I'm going to go down in that well and I just assumed it was going to be me." Said Robert. Then he continued to say "I would prefer that it was daylight and I had a little bit of rest. I don't need much mind you, just a little."

"It being light outside will definitely give us an advantage." Said Terry also stretching and yawning.

"Yes, it will, all right Paul lets head back up to the mansion." Said Ashley turning back around in her seat.

When everyone got back to the mansion, they all climbed out of the Van and went inside, heading upstairs to their rooms. Terry looked at the team saying, "Remember everyone, were only going to get a few hours then we've got to deal with this thing while there is still plenty daylight outside."

"Don't worry I'll wake you all up in a couple hours." Said Robert heading along with Joe into a room next to the one that the girls were staying in.

"Cindy try to get some rest, Robert doesn't sleep very long, he's always been like that, he will definitely wake us all up in a couple of hours." Said Ashley looking over at her.

"I'll see you all in a little while then." Said Cindy heading into her room. Cindy noticing that the bed had not been slept in, as she thought about James. *"I wonder when we get rid of this thing, will I get my husband back. I miss him so much."* Then she thought, *"Maybe I should go check on him?"* After all she hasn't seen him in a couple days now, he hasn't even come out to eat anything. Then she thought, *"He might get mad. But I don't care, I got at least know he's all right."* she went downstairs and knocked on the study door saying, "James, James, are you all right?"

James answered her asking, "What, do you want!!?"

"I just wanted to know if you all right you have it came out to…,"

"Has the circus left town yet?" Asked James interrupting her.

"You mean the investigating team? No, they're still here, they, are just getting some rest it's been a…,"

"Go away Cindy and leave me alone." Said James interrupting her.

"James please honey you haven't ate anything I…,"

"Cindy I said go away," Yelled James interrupting her again and slamming the pocket doors shut in her face.

Cindy just stood quietly outside the pocket doors feeling lonely, scared and confused and unsure what to do. As she started to walk away she thought she heard James talking to someone, so she put her ear to the door, to see if she can make out what he was saying, then to her disbelief she heard him clearly talking to someone saying,

"Don't worry they're not coming in here, it's all right don't be frightened their…," He paused right in the middle of his conversation. Cindy stood quietly struggling to see if she could hear but it was just silence. Then suddenly, he swung the pocket doors open frightening her and stood there with a cold dark look in his eyes and asked "What are you doing?"

Cindy feeling startled, looked - into his dark cold eyes and asked "James who are you talking to?"

But he just seemed to stare right through her, with a piercing look that frightened her beyond belief. Then without saying, a word he slowly closed the pocket doors with a sinister looking grin.

Cindy truly did not know what to do. She stood there staring at the closed doors, afraid for her husband and wondering, *"What had come over him?"* she felt like running to tell Ashley what had just happened. But the thought of that to frightened her and she taught *"No it's best I just leave him alone."* Cindy very slowly turned and walked down the hallway heading back upstairs to their room. Upon getting there being tired herself, she stretched out across the bed, not even removing her clothing and slipped off into a deep sleep.

Only to be awoken in what seem like minutes later, by Ashley shaking her saying, "It's time let's get this over with so you can get your family back."

Cindy looked at her with confusion it was as though she already knew what had occurred with her in James earlier that morning. Then Ashley said "The boys, when in town to see if they could find a hardware store or something we need a piece of rope, so that Robert can climb down into the well."

"Yes, we don't have anything like that here, or if we do, I wouldn't know where it was." Said Cindy following Ashley down the Hall to the drawing room.

"I figured as much, that's why and the boys in the town. I'm sure they'll find something." Said Ashley walking into the drawing room. As she continued to say to the other team members,

"Hay guys, how was your little nap?"

"Not long enough." Said Paul stretching and yawning.

"I know what you mean, seems like I just laid down." Said Jesse shaking one leg and then the other, then polling her arms over her head and then backwards.

"Well guys we get this thing to deal with, we will take some time I think we could all use a nice long vacation." Said Ashley also stretching out her body trying to prepare herself for the task at hand.

"Yes, it will be my treat for all of you." Said Cindy smiling at them.

Just then Robert and Joe came walking in. Joe was carrying a sack and Robert had several feet of a large rope on his shoulder saying, "This is all we could find, it's big and bulky but it should be sufficient." Walking over and dropping it on the floor in a pile.

"We also got a couple of those headlights you know like the hunters use and some extra batteries." Said Joe dumping out the sack on one of the tables.

"I even got me a pair of waders, you know like fishermen where, because I figure there's going to be water in the bottom of the well and they should keep me somewhat dry." Said Robert unrolling them to show to Ashley.

"That's great guys where in the world did you find something like that, around here asked Ashley walking over and feeling the rubbery texture of the waders.

"From a little sporting goods store called, Bob sporting in hardware store, it's sure not like the big city around here, a guy can get used to this kind of life." Said Robert looking over at Ashley and smiling.

"Well alright then, looks like we've got everything were going to need. Robert, I want you to strap on a body cam to take down into the well with you. we can somewhat see what it's like down there." Said Ashley handing it over to him.

"Yes, I was going to suggest that we do that. After all I really have no idea what I'm going to find or what the conditions are going to be like down there for me." Said Robert taking the camera from Ashley in one hand and walking over and picking up the rope placing it on his shoulder. Then he grabbed his waders with the other hand saying, "Let's get this over with."

Upon saying, that he headed to the door, with the whole team following behind him. Ashley turned around and said "No, I need you two, stay here, Paul watch the monitor and Jesse you stay close to the phone unless something goes wrong.

"Yes ma'am." Said Jesse walking over and sitting back down.

"You're going to need all the help you can get, to lower his big old heavy butt, down in that well." Said Paul looking at Robert giggling.

"Very funny, if you prefer, I can just drop you on your head down in there." Said Robert glaring back at him.

"Come on guys there is no time for playing, we got to get serious about this. Paul, don't you take your eyes off the monitor. Robert let's go" said Ashley heading out the door.

• • •

The team made their way through the garden and up to the well. The sun was shining straight up overhead, with not a cloud in the sky. There was even a cool breeze blowing across the yard. Robert wrapped one end of the rope around the well, tying it off securely. Then he threw the other end over the side and down into the well. Watching it disappear into the darkness.

"You sure that's the way you want to do that? I mean climbing over the side and then down into the well. Maybe there is some way we can fix it, so that we can lower you down and pull you back out if you get into trouble?" Asked Ashley obviously concern for his safety.

"No, I'm afraid this is the only way I can do it. The little prick was right, I am probably too heavy for you all to pull out. If I get into trouble I'm just going to be on my own." Said Robert slipping on his waders.

Then Robert walked over and climbed up onto the side of the well taking the rope in his hands and easing his body over the side with his feet against the wall, with the rope wrapped around his waist and one of his legs, he leaned back letting his weight pull against the rope, testing its durability.

Looking over at Ashley, quoting a scene from one of his favorite movies Independence Day saying, **"Do me a favor, tell my family I love them very much,"** then he giggled. As he started to descend into the well.

Ashley looked over it Terry shaking her head. Terry said. "He is not afraid of anything, you know it?"

"I know, I would be, going down in that dark hole, but he's not," answered Ashley watching till he disappeared into the darkness.

CHAPTER 24

Then she turned to Cindy and said it would probably be a good time for you to try to call that Wilcox fellow, so we know what to do with the remains when he finds them."

"You really think he's going to find them, after all these years?" Asked Cindy once again getting her cell phone.

"I don't know, a lot of things depend on that. Like how much water than the bottom of the well. Whether the bones are all scattered out. I just don't know all we can do is hope." Said Ashley trying to answer her best she could.

Cindy dialed Mr. Wilcox's number and rang a couple times and finally Mary Mr. Wilcox's Secretary answered it saying,

"This is Marcus Wilcox office; can I help you?"

"Yes, ma'am this is Cindy Parker, would it be possible for me to speak to Mr. Wilcox? Tell him it's urgent."

"Hold on for a minute please Mrs. Parker all see if he's busy." Said Mary Mr. Wilcox Secretary.

"Good morning Cindy, how are you and James doing," inquired Mr. Wilcox.

"Were doing fine I've just about got this place in order, James is in his study working on something." Said Cindy putting on a front.

"How's that baby coming along," once again inquired Mr. Wilcox.

"Both me and the baby are doing fine." Said Cindy not wanting to reveal how she truly was doing.

"Will that's wonderful, Mary said that you're calling was urgent is everything all, right? What can I do for you?" Inquired Mr. Wilcox would be concerning his voice.

"Oh, yes everything is fine, I just was wondering, you said this used to be an old plantation, right?" Asked Cindy eagerly awaiting his reply.

"Yes, it was, I think they had something like 15 or 20 slaves working the place, at one time. A George and Margaret Summer hill, back in 1800s first build it. Why do you ask?" Inquired Mr. Wilcox, curiously. "No reason really, I was just wondering do you know what happened to them?" Asked Cindy once again eager for his reply.

"Well I think he died in the war or something like that and far as all the stories go she just disappeared one night, nobody really knows what happened to her. Some people even think she may be buried there on the estate somewhere. In the old slave, Cemetery, no doubt, Cindy while the questions are you sure everything's all right?" Inquired Mr. Wilcox obviously concerned.

"Oh, everything's fine Marcus, just trying to learn a little bit more about the old place. Did I hear you, right? Did you say there's an old slave Cemetery here?" Inquired Cindy even more eager for his answer.

"It's back in the woods, on the North end of the grounds I believe. Although you probably would never find it. Back in those days, they would just as soon dig a hole and throw them in it, if they buried them at all. Most of the graves were never even mark. They treated the slaves like animals back then. It's sad really, when you think about it." Said Mr. Wilcox with remorse.

"Yes, it is, hard to imagine any people being treated in such a manor." Said Cindy also with remorse. But any rate, I know you're a busy man and I won't keep you any longer. Like I said I was just curious, thank you Marcus and you must come out and see us." Said Cindy trying to put his mind at ease.

"All right then, if you're sure there is nothing wrong. Tell James I said hello and take care yourself and that baby. If you need anything Cindy, please don't hesitate to call." Said Marcus still's not quite convinced.

"Don't worry Marcus if something was wrong I would deftly call you." Said Cindy still trying to put his mind at ease.

"Well okay then, have a wonderful day Cindy, will talk to you later goodbye." Said Mr. Wilcox ending the call.

"It's over in the woods, on the North end of the grounds." Said Cindy confirming the whereabouts of the cemetery.

Ashley noticing a sad look on Cindy's face asked her,

"Are you all right?'

"I will be, it's just that so many things Marcus told me about the way slaves were treated, it really hurts my heart. Answered Cindy were remorse in her voice.

"Yes, I know, when the team was doing the research on this old place, to try to find out more about what we were dealing with. My God! Cindy, some of the horrific things that happened here, were unbelievable." Said Ashley just shaking her head.

"You mean with the slaves?" Curiously inquired Cindy.

"Not just the slaves, all the babies that died here to, in their crib for no reason. That alone hurts your heart." Said Terry looking over at her.

"What!! What babies, I don't understand." Said Cindy obviously confused.

"Oh, my God! Ashley, she doesn't know." Said Terry looking over at her.

"Doesn't know what, will somebody please tell me what you're all talking about?" Asked Cindy getting frustrated,

"You really don't know do you? Cindy, several babies have died here in this mansion, a matter of fact. No baby girl ever made it from the crib. That's why people have been saying, that the place was cursed. We just assumed you knew." Said Ashley curiously.

"Oh, my God! Oh, my dear God! No I had no idea, but that explains why my real parents adopted me out, it's not because they didn't want me, it was to protect me." Said Cindy with tears welling up in her eyes.

"You're right, they were trying to protect you from **THE SUMMER HILL BLOOD CURSE**." Said Joe looking over at Cindy.

"That means if we can't stop this thing…, Cindy pause right in the middle of her sentence and she said "Please dear God no, my baby girl," as she put her hand on her belly.

Ashley walked over and put her arms around her saying, "Cindy listen to me, don't even think that, we're going to beat this thing. Do you hear me? No matter what it takes, we are going to beat this thing."

• • •

Then suddenly, the sky started darkening up clouds formed from out of nowhere, blocking out the sun, the wind picked up from a slight breeze to about 15 miles an hour, blowing across the yard and hitting the team, then it started to storm. Lightning was striking all around them, rain began pouring down on them. Not wanting to leave Robert in the well during the storm. Ashley walked over to the side and called down to him saying, "Robert, it's too dangerous there's lightning striking everywhere and it's pouring down rain. You better come out."

But there was no reply from the well. She reached over and grabbed hold of the rope pulling on it. But it was loose just hanging there. Ashley called down to him again saying, "Robert come out of the well." Terry walked over and asked "is he coming out?"

"No I think it is too deep, I don't think he can hear me, do you sense anything?"

"No I can't sense anything I can't…, Terry positive then she said with fear in her voice,

"Ashley something's coming."

"From out of the well? Is a Robert? Asked Ashley looking toward it.

"From over there." Said Terry pointed straight out in front of them and down the hill leading to the well.

Then to their disbelief they saw a figure of a woman manifest itself from out of nowhere, coming toward them, carrying something. Although they could tell it was a woman, they couldn't really make out any distinguishing features. As it got closer and closer to the well, they moved back. Standing together with the rain pouring down on them, soaking them to the bone and with the lightning striking all around them that the figure of the woman stopped by the well.

Turned around looking toward the field she held something that appeared to be in feed sack in her hand. They watched as she stood there for a couple minutes. It sounded like a baby was crying in the feed sack lightning striking all around her, raising the baby up in the air over the Well. They heard a woman's voice crying and pleading coming from behind her. It was the slave girl finally gathering up enough strength to follow after her. She pleaded with the woman saying,

"Please don't kill my baby girl, I'm begging you, mistress, have mercy."

The woman turned and looked at her and said

"You can have somebody else's little bastard." Dropping the baby in the well.

The slave girl grabbed the side of the Well, looking down into the deep dark hole screaming

"Oh, my God and fell to the ground crying uncontrollably. The woman turned around and walked toward the mansion. The slave girl screamed at her, saying,

"You are an evil woman with a heart of stone."

Then disappeared right in front of the team's eyes,

CHAPTER 25

Robert slowly making his way down the rope, finding it harder and harder to hold onto. It was cold, nasty and slippery and smelled musty and old, the further down he went harder it was for him to hold onto the rope and keep his feet securely on the wall. Till finally he could hear the sound - of water underneath him, because he was knocking dirt off - of the size of the well and it was splashing down under him letting him know he was getting closer. Then he thought *"Thank God my arms are getting tired and don't know how much further I could've gone."* Paul was speaking to him through the two-way radio asking, "Are you all right, I'm only asking because it sounds like a freight train down there, or maybe a woman in labor."

"Shut up you little prick, or when I get out of here, I will put my foot in year ass." Said Robert finding it even more difficult to place his feet on the wall.

"How are you going to do that, sounds like to me you're going to need oxygen when you get out of there." Said Paul giggling at him?

"Shut up you little…, P-r-r-r-r-r-ick, yelled Robert losing his grip on the rope and falling ultimately splashing down in the water.

"Robert-Robert-Robert," yelled Paul but there was just silence.

Robert while going under the water, not only wet the two-way radio, but he also wet the camera, causing them both to fail. There he was, in the bottom of the well, no camera and no way to call for help if he needed it, he thought, *"I am literally going to kill him, when I get back out of here."*

Then he remembered, luckily, he put one of those headlights that they bought from the hardware store in his pocket. he got it out and put it on his head turning it on. Then he thought *"Although I don't have a camera or a two-way radio, at least I do have a light."*

Moving around in the water, he found the end of the rope, just inches away from the surface. Robert realizing there was several feet and not knowing how deep it was, new he was going to have to dive down and search the bottom.

Then taking a deep breath he headed down swimming with the light illuminating in front of him, not really being able to see anything. Till finally he reached the bottom, there was a rusty pale and several pieces of metal a few rots sticks, all sorts the debris he searched it with both his hands. Not finding anything and beginning to lose his breath. He made his way back to the surface. After doing this several times he began to wonder, *"How is he going to find the babies remains?"*

Then from out of nowhere he heard a sound of a baby crying, Robert looked all around him not seeing anything.

Then he heard it again, only this time it was clear to him, where it was coming from. It was in fact coming from the bottom of the well under the water.

Robert stuck his head under and there next to a big rock on the bottom was what appeared to be a faint glowing light coming from the ground. He swum down to it was with all his might, as he reached it he started digging with both hands, finding what appeared to be a feed sack. But it took quite some time to dig it up and he was out of breath.

Looking at it one last time and confirming that it was exactly what he was looking for. He then took off to the surface to get a breath of air planning to return to retrieve it. But on his way to the surface and just before he broke it, something or someone grabbed his legs and with a lot of force, pulled him back under the water.

Robert was trying to scream, grasping for air, fighting and kicking his legs. But the something continued to pull him down.

Through the murky water, he saw a dark figure that had a hold of his legs pulling him down. Robert kicked with all his might, but to no prevail. The thing was too strong and he was beginning to lose his strength. Each time he tried to scream he was taking in a lot of water, which was sure to drown him. It was almost like, he was being pulled into a whole that seemed to go on and on to the center of the earth. Getting deeper and deeper in the water now being out of both strengths and air he had all but given up.

Then once again to his disbelief he saw another figure manifests itself inform of him. It was a large woman he could clearly see her, she looks like an old slave woman coming towards him. Suddenly she grabbed the dark entity, causing it to let go of him. With the last little bit of strength, he had left in his body he forced his way to the surface choking and gasping for air, taking in one breath after another.

Grabbing the rope be started to climb fast as he could. But once again, he heard the baby cry. Which caused him to stop. Looking down at the murky water with a faint glow coming from beneath it he thought, *"Oh hell, I've got to get it."*

Then thinking that, he dove back into the water swimming past the large slave woman and a dark entity fighting over on one side of the well. She struggled to hold the entity as Robert swam past them, grabbing the feed sack as fast as he could. Then returning to the surface. Taking a hold of the rope, finding the strengths from somewhere deep inside him. Although he was tired and worn out he still managed to pull his self-up the rope to the surface. Grabbing the edges of the well he climbed out and collapsed on the ground.

Ashley came over to him and asked "Are you all right?"

"It almost got me, but a large older slave woman grabbed it and pulled it lose so that I can get away. I got it here are the babies remains." Said Robert pulling the feed sack closer to the side and handing it to her.

Ashley said "Joe stay here with Robert, Cindy let's go."

The storm was even fiercer now, the win was up to about 30 miles an hour they could barely walk through it, as they were trying to make their way to the woods, to find the old slave Cemetery.

Cindy and Ashley fighting the strong winds, lightning striking all around them just a few feet away finally made their way to the woods they found what appeared to be an old gravesite there were several stones standing straight up the only type of marker that they could see Cindy yelled "How are we supposed to find where the girl in this?

"I don't think it matters, we just need to bear the babies remains in hallowed ground, yelled Ashley. The storm was exerting even more force now.

Terry having made her way to the edge of the woods and was clinging to a tree, barely being able to hold herself down, yelling," "You must hurry its coming."

Upon hearing that, Ashley and Cindy dropped down to the ground and started to dig with all their strength and might digging a hole throwing the dirt behind them and to the side as fast as they could. "Hurry it's coming," holiday Terry once more.

Then as they pulled the feed sack over and placed it in a hole burying it. But nothing happened,

Cindy said "I don't know what else were supposed to do."

Just sin lightning struck the tree beside them and suddenly the winds died down and there standing in front of them was the slave girl, although she was in transparent form, they could clearly see it was her and she was holding her baby, she looked at Cindy and smiled then very gently dissipated right in front of them as she did, the wind subsided as suddenly as it came up. The dark clouds dissipated gave way to the sun shined a calmness seemed to come over the garden until there was no reverence of any storm. Ashley and Cindy just set there on the ground holding each other. Then Terry made her way over to them and said "It's over there gone."

"What about the entity?" Asked Cindy Eager to see what Terry said

"It appears to be gone to, I think we did it." Said Terry smiling at them.

Just then Robert and Joe came walking into the clearing, everyone was hugging each other obviously relieved because it was over.

"The slave girl is at rest and the entity was gone. Realizing this they made their way back to the mansion. Jesse and Paul's started gathering up all the equipment, everyone pitched in, taking down all the cameras and all the cables, motion detectors, everything.

Cindy for the first-time took a deep breath and said "I can feel it. Feels so much difference. It's like a brand-new home, I can't believe it it's actually over."

"Yes, maybe now you can get on with what undoubtedly is going to be a wonderful life, here in this big beautiful place." Said Ashley smiling at her.

"Yes, I must tell you I'm jealous as hell." Said Terry walking over and hugging Cindy's neck.

"Oh, you guys can come back anytime and stay if you like, that goes for all of you said Cindy looking at the whole team. "You better be careful on offering that some of us just might take you up on it." Said Robert also walking over and hugging Cindy. "Robert I can't thank you enough for going down and that well if it hadn't been for you doing that, I mean it hadn't been for all of you I just don't know what I would've done." Said Cindy once again looking at the team.

After helping load all the equipment in the Van. Cindy went into the kitchen and made them some sandwiches and got them all a bottle water for the trip home.

Then she walked over and handed Ashley a large package. Ashley looked at her and asked, "What is this?"

Cindy looked at her saying, "I want your vacation to be on me,"

"That's not necessary." Said Ashley feeling embarrassed.

"Please I want to do this for each one of you, when you're basking in the sunlight on a tropical beach somewhere and went you all to know how much I appreciate and love each one of you, thank you so much, for giving me back my home, in my life." Said Cindy with tears welling up in her eyes. "You're so welcome sweetie were glad we could help you," Cindy went around hugging everybody, Robert-Joe-Paul and even Jesse, then as she started to hug Terry she said. "Wait a minute, I think I left one of the detectors in my room."

Running back inside and upstairs into the room the girls were staying in. Coming back down the stairs, she heard the pocket doors slide open. Stopping in the hallway she asked "Mr. Parker, Mr. Parker is that you Sir?"

But there was no reply from him. Terry started down the hall toward the study and the open pocket doors. Drawing closer to them they slammed shut startling her. Gathering her courage, she walked over knocking and calling out Mr. Parker Sir. Still there was no reply. Eager to tell him that the entity was in fact gone she called out once again saying, "Mr. par………," Sensing something she paused she wasn't quite sure what it was but it frightened her. Terry felt a chill run up her spine the hair stood up on the back of her neck. Suddenly she began to feel sick to her stomach all she knew was she needed to get out of there as quickly as possible. Thinking that she turned and ran out of the manner and over to the side of the van. Breathing the fresh air and starting to feel better, she very slowly, without saying, a word to anyone, climbed into the Van. Ashley asked, "Did you find it?"

Terry just sat there not saying, anything, steering out into space.

Ashley looked over at Cindy saying, "Remember if you ever need us don't hesitate to call."

"I won't, and once again I want and thank you from the bottom of my heart, have a safe trip home." Said Cindy one last time.

Upon hearing that, Paul cranked up the van and everyone waved at Cindy, as they drove away heading down the driveway, toward the iron Gates, leaving the Summerhill Manor.

Cindy turned around and walked back inside. As she was entering the manor she looked up to see James standing there, with a cold distant look on his face just staring at her.

When suddenly, the front door to the mansion slammed shut, with tremendous force all by itself, right behind Cindy.

THE END, OR WAS IT?

SUMMARY

On top a mountain in North Carolina surrounded by hundreds of miles of beautiful countryside lies the Summerhill Manor. It's an old plantation that was once the center of society back in the 1800s, owned by George and Margaret Summerhill, which was maintained and cared for by their slaves. The plantation was a big part of the unimaginable wealth that gave Margaret Summerhill the standing in society she so desperately desired.

But after the war ended, something sinister and dark came over the Summerhill's, changing their lives forever. Now more than two centuries have come to pass, and a new chapter in the story of the Summerhill Manor is about to unfold.

Located in the big city of Detroit, a young couple struggles through life living from one paycheck to the next. But this couple's lives were about to change. Cindy, the wife of James Parker, was soon to discover that not only she was adopted from the wealthy Summerhill's, but that she was in fact the last living descendent; and she not only inherited their fortune, but their manor as well.

After Cindy and James travel to North Carolina to meet with lawyer Marcus Wilcox to claim the estate, they soon discover they've inherited much more than a beautiful plantation.

After several unexplainable events, James becomes withdrawn and cold. Cindy starts having strange dreams and turns to her lifelong friend, Tracy, for help.

Tracy is a reporter for a large newspaper in Detroit and gets in contact with a team of paranormal investigators. After researching the history of the manor, Ashley Michaels and her paranormal team come to the plantation to rid it of whatever it is that will not let its new owners live in peace. But upon starting their investigation, they soon discover they're dealing with something much more sinister than any of them had realized.

ACKNOWLEDGMENTS

I would like to thank my friends for all their support throughout this project. Once again, I don't need to list them, they know who they are. I would especially, like to thank my beautiful little wife Laura, for all her help creating this book. I have discovered that every good author needs a sounding board, from time to time. Like, "HEY" what do you think about this person, and that situation, or perhaps maybe just to run a new idea by. Well that's what she has been to me and so much more I can't thank her enough for it.

I would like to especially thank her for all her help, encouragement and understanding. Laura, is not only cowriter and editor but she is also my manager, and my soul mate, God has placed us together and has blessed me. She was but only a thought away eager to assist me in whatever I needed and like I have said to give me support. She has a vast knowledge in this field and truly was an asset to me throughout this endeavor. So once again thank you my darling, you truly have made this an enjoyable experience.

My blessing to my readers.

*"**God**" will truly bless all that read this book. And you who understand the difference between good and "**Evil**." For He is truly the Father of us all and like the scriptures say, you need only ask and it shall be given unto you. Like this, for those of you who do not know.*

Wyatt Allen

The Lord's prayer.

Our Father who art in heaven, heavenly and hallowed be thy name, thy kingdom come, thy will be done, on earth as it in heaven. give us this day our daily bread, forgive us our debts, as we forgive our debtors, forgive our trespasses, as we forgive those who trespass against us, forgive us our **"Sins,"** as we forgive those who sin against us. And we do.

"Lord Jesus" I understand you came and died on the cross for my sins. I want to thank you, from the bottom of my heart. I ask you to forgive me of my sins. And to come into my heart, and live. I make you my Lord and Savior.

Lead us not unto temptation, but deliver us from all **"Evil"** for thine is the kingdom, the power and the glory forever and ever.
"Amen"

Printed in the United States
By Bookmasters